"They caught my canoe, and I almost died of fright." — page 139

The Oak Openings

or

The Bee-Hunter

by

James Fenimore Cooper

North Atlantic Books
Berkeley, California

The Oak Openings, or The Bee-Hunter
by James Fenimore Cooper

new material this edition copyright © 1984
Society for the Study of Native Arts and Sciences

ISBN 0-938190-33-4

Publisher's Address:
North Atlantic Books
2320 Blake Street
Berkeley, California 94704

This new edition of *The Oak Openings* is sponsored by the Society for the
Study of Native Arts and Sciences, a nonprofit educational corporation whose
goals are to develop an ecological and crosscultural perspective linking various
scientific, social, and artistic fields; to nurture a holistic view of arts, sciences,
humanities, and healing; and to publish and distribute literature on the relation-
ship of mind, body, and nature.

Library of Congress Cataloging in Publication Data

Cooper, James Fenimore, 1789-1851.
The oak openings, or, The bee-hunter.

Reprint. Originally published: New York: G.P. Putnam's Sons, 1896.
1. Indians of North America—Fiction.   I. Title.
II. Title: Oak openings. III. Title: Bee-hunter.
PS1409.02 1984   813'.2   84-6132
ISBN 0-938190-33-4

PREFACE.

IT ought to be matter of surprise how men live in the midst of marvels without taking heed of their existence. The slightest derangement of their accustomed walks in political or social life shall excite all their wonder, and furnish themes for their discussions for months; while the prodigies that come from above are presented daily to their eyes and are received without surprise, as things of course. In a certain sense, this may be well enough, inasmuch as all which comes directly from the hands of the Creator may be said so far to exceed the power of human comprehension as to be beyond comment; but the truth would show us that the cause of this neglect is rather a propensity to dwell on such interests as those over which we have a fancied control than on those which confessedly transcend our understanding. Thus is it ever with men. The wonders of creation meet them at every turn without awakening reflection, while their minds labor on subjects that are not only ephemeral and illusory, but which never attain an elevation higher than that the most sordid interests can bestow.

For ourselves, we firmly believe that the finger of Providence is pointing the way to all races and colors and nations, along the path that is to lead the East and the West alike to the great goal of human wants. Demons infest that path, and numerous and unhappy are the wanderings of millions who stray from its course: sometimes in reluctance to proceed; sometimes in an indiscreet haste to move faster than their fellows, and always in a forgetfulness of

the great rules of conduct that have been handed down
from above. Nevertheless, the main course is onward ; and
the day, in the sense of time, is not distant, when the whole
earth is to be filled with the knowledge of the Lord, "as
the waters cover the sea."

One of the great stumbling-blocks with a large class of
well-meaning, but narrow-judging moralists, are the seeming wrongs that are permitted by Providence in its control
of human events. Such persons take a one-sided view of
things, and reduce all principles to the level of their own
understandings. If we could comprehend the relations
which the Deity bears to us as well as we can comprehend
the relations we bear to Him, there might be a little seeming
reason in these doubts ; but when one of the parties in this
mighty scheme of action is a profound mystery to the other,
it is worse than idle, it is profane, to attempt to explain those
things which our minds are not yet sufficiently cleared from
the dross of earth to understand. Look at Italy, at this
very moment. The darkness and depression from which
that glorious peninsula is about to emerge are the fruits of
long-continued dissensions and an iron despotism, which is
at length broken by the impulses left behind him by a ruthless conqueror, who, under the appearance and with the
phases of Liberty, contended only for himself. A more concentrated egotism than that of Napoleon probably never existed ; yet has it left behind it seeds of personal rights that
have sprung up by the way-side, and which are likely to
take root with a force that will bid defiance to eradication.
Thus it is ever with the progress of society. Good appears
to arise out of evil, and the inscrutable ways of Providence
are vindicated by general results, rather than by instances
of particular care. We leave the application of these remarks to the intelligence of such of our readers as may have
patience to pursue the work that will be found in the succeeding pages.

We have a few words of explanation to say, in connection with the machinery of our tale. In the first place, we
would remark that the spelling of "burr-oak," as given in
this book, is less our own than an office spelling. We think

it should be "bur-oak," and this for the simple reason that the name is derived from the fact that the acorn borne by this tree is partially covered with a bur. Old Sam Johnson, however, says that "burr" means the lobe, or lap of the ear; and those who can fancy such a resemblance between this and the covering of our acorn are at liberty to use the two final consonants. Having commenced stereotyping with this supernumerary, for the sake of uniformity that mode of spelling, wrong as we think it, has been continued throughout the book.

There is nothing imaginary in the fertility of the West. Personal observation has satisfied us that it much surpasses anything that exists in the Atlantic States, unless in exceptions, through the agency of great care and high manuring, or in instances of peculiar natural soil. In these times men almost fly. We have passed over a thousand miles of territory within the last few days, and have brought the pictures at the two extremes of this journey in close proximity in our mind's eye. Time may lessen that wonderful fertility, and bring the whole country more on a level; but there it now is, a glorious gift from God, which it is devoutly to be wished may be accepted with due gratitude, and with a constant recollection of his unwavering rules of right and wrong, by those who have been selected to enjoy it.

June, 1843.

Preface to the 1984 Edition
of The Oak Openings

"I shall not go to Kalamazoo. It would be of no use. I expect nothing from Michigan, and heartily wish I had never heard of the state. God's will be done."

"Chess. Wife beating [me] terribly at times. Commenced on new part of Openings, and work moderately, but not con amore. This book is not a labour of love, but a labour."

— James Fenimore Cooper, *Letters and Journals,* V, p.383,278.

The Oak Openings, more than many of Cooper's later novels, is a work struggling to find suitable characters and a plot or theme to set those characters in motion. Ben Boden is a rather timid reworking of the sturdy character of Natty Bumppo, and Scalping Peter is a ludicrous attempt to provide Cooper's audience with a born-again Chingachgook. It is difficult to redeem the clumsy mechanisms of this novel with the frontier character types that give vitality to the Leatherstocking Tales. Apart from its adherence to the conventions of the historical novel, *The Oak Openings* has a stagnant quality that reveals the difficulties that Cooper encountered when he attempted to fashion one more meditation on the moral and societal consequences of the idea of PROGRESS.

It is important to look first into the background of Cooper's involvement with the development on Michigan lands. During the first decades of the nineteenth century, Native American cultures were dispossessed and destroyed in the Michigan territory. Once this dispossession was completed, the U.S. government began to sell the lands acquired through treaties or conquest to land speculators who in turn sold Michigan lands to eastern settlers in search of a promised land of plenty.

James Fenimore Cooper's role model in land speculation was his father, William Cooper. William Cooper had acquired a large tract of land (over 40,000 acres) near Cooperstown, New York during the period following the Revolution (1785-86). William Cooper was able to realize sizeable profits from his speculations, and he claimed in his *Guide to the Wilderness* (1810) that:

> I have already settled more acres than any man in America. There are forty thousand souls now holding, directly or indirectly, under me, and I trust that no one amongst so many can justly impute to me any act resembling oppression . . . I must acknowledge that I look back with self complacency upon what I have done, and am proud of having been an instrument in reclaiming such large and fruitful tracts from the waste of creation.

His son, however, did not find that speculation in lands recently obtained from the Indians was as lucrative as it was for his father. In the mid-1830's, James Fenimore Cooper invested in Michigan lands near Kalamazoo with the hope of cashing in on the land boom of that period. The speculative bubble soon burst and Cooper found himself with a bundle of worthless notes. His attempt to redeem these notes forced Cooper to travel to Michigan during the period 1847-1849 in an unsuccessful attempt to recover a portion of his investment through litigation. Cooper had more than a passing interest in the questions of land development and land speculation.

On the one hand, Cooper was suspicious of the individualistic bent in Jacksonian democracy that seemed to promise every able-bodied white male an opportunity to join the westward migrations and own a piece of land:

> It is not, however, that bastard democracy which is coming so much in fashion among ourselves, and which looks into the gutters solely for the "people," forgetting that the landlord has just as much right to protection as the tenant, the master as the servant, the rich as the poor, the gentleman as the blackguard. The Indians know better than all this. (Ch. 8)

Unfortunately, what the Indians "knew" was that the surges of the land speculators led to their extermination or forced removal. It is important to keep in mind that during the 1840's when Cooper so preoccupied himself with questions of land use and tenure, all Native Americans who remained east of the Mississippi river were being forced, sometimes by government troops, to relocate to very barren and alien lands to the west of the Mississippi. The euphemism for this process at the time was Indian "removal" or what was later known as "the trail of tears." This removal was mandated by the U.S. Congress in the Indian removal act of 1830. In many instances, the feverish land speculations of the 1830's were a direct consequence of coerced removal of Indians from their ancestral homelands. Once the Indians were "removed" (for their own benefit since proximity to "civilization" was deemed to be harmful to their survival), land speculation could begin in earnest.

Cooper applauded the opening of western lands to Yankee farmers as a progressive development which conformed to the reigning ideology of eternal progress in all spheres of human endeavor — "the progress of the nation has, by the aid of a beneficent Providence, been onward and onward." (Ch. 12). Progress was celebrated far more as an ideal for Cooper than as an actual change in social structure and development. The redistribution of lands held previously by large landowners such as William Cooper whose holdings resembled feudal estates caused an upheaval in the prevailing social and economic structure. Cooper's inherent conservatism resisted this change in his personal responsibilities as a landholder in Cooperstown and in his extensive invectives against the "people" in his later writings.

While Cooper subscribed reluctantly to the ideology of progress, his tendency in *The Oak Openings* was to reject the progressive implications of western land development and search for a reactionary image of stability in the face of profound change. Ironically, Cooper finds his pillar of stability in the character of Scalping Peter. Fear of the socioeconomic upheaval created by the later developments of Jacksonian democracy causes Cooper to create a "noble savage" who gains nobility only by his conversion to Christianity and his renuciation of tribal culture. Scalping Peter is a repository of traditional Christian values that resist social change at all costs.

Ironically, Native American cultures were subjected to devastating change during this period. The policy and practice of Indian removal often was tantamount to cultural genocide. Christianity was not a viable option for most tribal cultures. Dispossession left the Native Americans without their spiritual and economic center, their ancestral homelands.

The final chapter of *The Oak Openings* brings the novel into a contemporary setting where Cooper's justification of the ways of Divine Providence becomes an advertisement for progress. This chapter of the book has a tacked-on quality that reveals the belabored quality of the novel. Scalping Peter's admonitions have a ludicrously false tone in spite of their overt racist message.

What can a contemporary reader gain from such a laborious task as delving into *The Oak Openings*? Perhaps we need to examine our own immersion in the ideology of progress. We need to sort out when progress is genuine in the service of human liberation, and when progress is only a commodity idea to mask violence and oppression. It is important to remember, when our President Ronald Reagan hawked products under the slogan "progress is our most important product," that the ideology of progress has served to mortgage our survival to the fissionable atom and has served as the rationale for bringing economic slavery and cultural destruction to many Third World cultures. I don't want to make Cooper into a scapegoat for these later developments, but it is crucial to understand that *The Oak Openings* contains the intellectual seeds of the crisis in progressive ideology that we face at the present time.

Randy Byrne, Ph.D
University of California, Berkeley
Island of The Moon Apiaries,
Esparto, California

An Approach to The Oak Openings

I assume you have to read this book. The professor has assigned it, probably because it is the last of Cooper's tales about the Redmen. Or you are the professor. Or the Michigan State Historical Society has commissioned you to prepare an annotated bibliography of texts on the northern front of the War of 1812. Or you are an apiarist whose quaint curiosity has drawn you irresistibly to the subtitle. Or you joined the Peace Corps and have read all the other books in English in the library of your small provincial city in Camaroon. Whatever the reason, here you are with this book and nowhere to go but through it.

That one might seek out *The Oak Openings* for the sheer thrill of reading is, I suppose, possible. But the chances are surely remote. I found my copy in the library of a large university, and when the clerk removed the card glued to the back, we discovered that only one other person had ever withdrawn the book: a certain Waikins, or Walkins, on September 18, 1956 (one hundred and five years and four days after Cooper's death). To the reader who prefers this novel particularly for its entertainment value I can offer little but amazement and the recommendation to get out a bit more, take up a hobby, or travel for a few months. Such things can wonderfully broaden one's views. To those others who, through Heaven knows what strange configuration of circumstance, confront this volume with an obligation to read, I want to suggest an approach.

We must admit at the outset there is no avoiding the work: the drudgery of canoeing across rivers, of creeping near enemy camps in order to overhear long and sometimes tedious harangues, of attending the dialogs between stalwart woodsman, blooming maid, and stern-visag'd savage. There is likewise no avoiding the

author, the fusty old gentleman ensnarled in lawsuits and critical
quarrels, who must interrupt his story every few pages to ser-
monize on his country's political follies or general moral laxity.
And there is no avoiding the style: the elevated, sententious, man-
nered prose of a squire born in the eighteenth century of wealthy
parents in a far province of the English-speaking world.

Such obvious and formidable obstacles to easy reading must be
met head-on. They require a major change of perspective — a kind
of sleight-of-mind, not unlike that which occurs in the development of "camp," when kitsch of past popular culture is resur-
rected and made fashionable. All at once what was garish,
overblown, silly or downright absurd becomes exciting, delightful,
marvelous. These sudden shifts of taste are not entirely arbitrary
and meaningless. Sometimes the resurrection reveals an interesting
quirk of design, or details of craftsmanship once taken for granted,
or a playful quality formerly restrained by the dead hand of the
present. And always the mere action of time brings unavoidable
and legitimate irony and charm, like the patina of rust and garlands
of weeds that come to grace abandoned farm machinery.

In the case of *The Oak Openings*, then — from the properly
skewed point of view — we have a potentially diverting novel.
The garrulous, intrusive narrator, for example. Is Cooper materially
different from modern storytellers like John Fowles (*The French
Lieutenant's Woman*) or E. L. Doctorow (*The Book of Daniel*) or
Nabokov (*Ada*), who cannot resist cranky and lyric asides and justify
them by making their self-consciousness overt? Or another example:
the sudden dodging from one level of diction to another. Cooper,
in the grip of his urge to advance the action, can write terse, vivid
sentences, though his dominant mode is a sort of American
carpenter baroque. In the following short passage he veers abruptly
between two poles, sounding now like Hemingway, now like
Boswell:

> Fire had run over the whole region late that spring, and the
> grass was now as fresh and sweet and short as if the place were
> pastured. The white clover, in particular, abounded, and was then
> just bursting forth into the blossom. Various other flowers had
> also appeared, and around them were buzzing thousands of bees.
> These industrious little animals were hard at work, loading
> themselves with sweets, little foreseeing the robbery contemplated
> by the craft of man.

This sort of switching occurs also in the pages of modern fabulists like Barth and Pynchon, and again is excused by a knowing subtextual wink at the reader. Was Cooper perhaps capable of the rare, ponderous wink? Following a digression on the dialects of the Yankee and Pennsylvanian, he reenters his narrative thusly: "But there was no time for disquisition, the second bee being now ready for a start."

A more serious challenge is the matter of the collapsing plot. After the murder of Parson Amen and Corporal Flint (no worse than Rabbit or Daedalus!), we expect the harum-scarum flight and battle that provide the climax in most of the Leatherstocking Tales. But Cooper betrays us. His villain, Scalping Peter, is shaken by the Parson's prayer for those who are about to slay him, and in the next scene he is so touched by gentle, lovely Blossom's manner that the implacable Indian leader converts abruptly to Christianity. Peter then helps the party of whites to escape his former followers, and after this spiritual rebirth can furnish no more mystery, conflict or subtlety to the story.

It becomes clear immediately that Scalping Peter, in his speeches refuting the Parson's bizarre argument for the Indians' Jewish ancestry, or detailing the dangers of the onrushing white flood, provided all the primary energy and moral complexity of the novel. Without his bitter ferocity and its fine shadow of doubt, evoked convincingly enough by Blossom's influence, the novel has nowhere to go and topples into a smarmy, outrageously pat ending.

Disappointing, indeed. A word hurled often enough at Cooper, and never with more justification than here. Yet the magnitude of that disappointment is also a measure of how far the book has worked us toward experiencing Peter's emotional maelstrom (for it is his story, not the bee-keeper's), and toward hoping that at last, for once, this author will allow his characters to overwhelm his prejudices. He could not, of course. Letting himself go was not a virtue of his generation.

We can, however, be generous and remember that Cooper had lived — like many who came after him — through his success and fame to the bleak, lonely condition of a disregarded and even mocked national monument. His last years were burdened by legal wrangles over property, virulent political disputes, and — the greatest insult — a failing market for his books. We might do well also to remember that famous definition of the novel

(Randall Jarrell's, I believe): "a long prose narrative that has something wrong with it." There are several things wrong with most of Cooper's, it is true, but we can be grateful that this embittered, outdated old patrician could so forget himself as to write the following speech by the Indian charged with torturing Corporal Flint in proper style:

> Squaws are in a hurry; warriors know how to wait. We could kill you at once and hang your scalp on our pole, but it would not be right. We wish to do what is right. . . . It is right to torment so great a brave, and we mean to do it. It is only just to you to do so. An old warrior who has seen so many enemies, and who has so big a heart, ought not to be knocked in the head like a papoose or a squaw. It is his right to be tormented.

We may wish that Cooper could forget himself this way more often, that he could deliver a whole good novel and not three-fifths of one, but such wishes are idle. The best advice, reader, is neither to wish nor to criticize, but to forgive and persevere. There are rewards. Corporal Flint's response, as they bend the saplings to which he will be tied for his ordeal, is not bad. Not bad at all.

Will Baker
Department of English
University of California at Davis

A Note On The Oak Openings

The narrator is most of the time intolerable. It's as if Cooper set out to provide the instance to justify DHL's rule of thumb for classic American literature especially — "Never trust the artist. Trust the tale." In this case it's Cooper's tale versus Cooper the artist. A psychomachy. The result is a novel compromised along its way, afraid of itself. Le Bourdon (not to mention Peter's fate) ends up old General B. who, after years of "growing with the country," now has plenty of land, a respectable dwelling, is out of debt, & "meets his obligations." All of wch are "good traits" Cooper says instructively — the voice of the raffiné 18th c. American gentleman Lawrence saw JFC in large part was. If this voice is attended to the narrative is effete, almost *insists* on its effeteness. You either drop it or tune it in on wave lengths wch circumvent that maladroitness. Like possibly:

— Methodology. (Process. "The dividing line between all that was from Grks . . . to what now is" — Olson.) *Ethos/nomos* continuous with the landscape. An objective idealism; earth pregnant with forms, vs. Socratic immaculate conception. *Sharpness* the value. Le Bourdon's Zen adaptability and pure attention (the few lapses in wch are laid to Margery's effect upon him. After marriage he unloads her in Mass. & back to the wilds like a knight in an old-fashioned book.) How to read the behavior of bees — eyes that can track one a couple hundred yards. How to play the river currents and take advantage of the wild rice cover & the wind. How to fell a tree, at wch Gershom is a master. His drunkenness is wrong because it diminishes his native care and accuracy; thus in putting it down Boden is no Christian prig.

— Myth. "Indians who didn't know who they were anymore,

xv

nor where they came from, and who, when I questioned them, answered me with stories whose mystery and coherence they had garbled." This from Artaud regarding the Tarahumara applies equally to the Whites and Reds at Castle Meal. In this unstoried terrain myth appears as what it radically is, gnosis, the highest form of earth's Knowledge. Parson Amen is a farcical dude who wandered in here out of *Tristram Shandy* bearing an unlikely spiritual kindling — the dry sticks of Protestant literalism. But in the archaic conditions obtaining in the Openings myth takes on an aboriginal potency. The *place* (the whole complexity of immanent circumstance wch is geography) tends to break down & recast story/language (*chienté*: shanty, *Bois Brulé*: Bob Ruly, &c. — Turner wd later address himself to a relatively epiphenomenal expression of same in the nature of frontier, its modification of *institutional* morphology.) Amen's lost tribe theory is only petrifaction. Frontier circumstances drive him deep into his mythology, to its real and efficacious source — Eros, primal creative love. Through his death the dead letter is made flesh again, Peter its witness. New morning. It's an allegory of the American advantage. "Openings" in the Quaker sense.

John Morgan

Cooper and the Middle Border

As we listen to the sounds of speech, we perceive them not simply as sounds but as clues to movements.

— David Abercrombie

Muses/clues to movements.

The muses lead us in

to the source — past, roots, connections, the primal force Hesiod calls Eros —
and out

to whatever prospects — satisfaction of desire, the consciousness which reveals the future to the past, how the story goes.

We are not divided or drawn in any simple way. Uroborus has many heads and tails, and where one hungry mouth strikes a tail (tale), head or tail randomly sprouts from the juncture. Everywhere world splits in two . . . or three. But it comes closer. Everything comes closer.

At the crucial time in the making the fear comes. The sentence is made, the poem, or the monument, the painting, whatever is made and not merely effected, and one finds one's self agoraphobic. I can tell when the crisis is coming to the poem: I need to piss or my throat is suddenly parched; sometimes I am bored by the melodrama of my own theater. It *is* melodrama. Character comes unhinged and nothing remains but action, gross, exaggerated, flirting with the ludicrous. Then the fear comes, rooted deeply in the accidents of any person's life, radically particular, private. There is a necessary will, a beginning, a reconciliation with disequilibrium which can be called *domestic*.

The story of the frontiersman can only be melodrama (to do,

xvii

with music). Exempting himself from human things, human-made things, from civilization and its discontents, from character, he finds in time not perpetual perishing but in Whitehead's fine phrase, "the moving image of eternity."
Because in his success he reconciles the dual impulses he obeys, to move *and* to settle down.

It can also be said, place becomes the local image of, if not the infinite, then, at least, the very large.

> "It seemed to us that we could trace in the dialect of the several members of this family, the gradations and peculiarities that denote the origin and habits of individuals. Thus, the grandmother was not quite as Western in her forms of speech as her matronly daughter, while the grandchildren evidently spoke under the influence of boarding school correction, or like girls who had been often lectured on the subject . . . But these little peculiarities were spots on the sun." (*The Oak Openings*, Ch. XXX)

> Cracks in the crystalline orbs, through
> which to enter a whole, other cosmos. . . .

Cooper is *the* novelist of the northeastern woodlands, as Parkman is the historian. He is truly provincial. The beginnings of the grasslands and the War of 1812 are his limits. West of them, in space and time, the wisdom of the woodlands dissolves into a thousand unanswered questions of fact.

Cooper insists that we be baptized in the woodlands: "Even the ocean with its boundless waste of water, has been found to be rich in its various beauties and marvels; and he who shall *bury himself with us*, once more, in the virgin forests of this widespread land, may possibly discover new subjects of admiration, new causes to adore the being that has brought all into existence, from the universe to its most minute particle." Even for the old salt and naval historian that Cooper was, it is still the woodlands that provide the image of the most general condition he can discover.

And whatever traumahold the sea still has on us, the loss of the inlands as the content of our lives holds fuller sway over our troubled psyches than those more distant losses.

Cooper's prairie in the novel of Natty Bumppo's death fails

as a significant place not because of Cooper's ignorance of it (which was substantial) but because his technique as a maker of plots depends upon the limited field of woodland vision. His prairie is a dispossession. All that passes on it is either absurd, in the genteel love plot, or disintegral — it is the place of Natty's death. "The many feelings, derivatively felt as alien, are" never "transformed into a unity of aesthetic appreciation immediately felt as private" (again, Whitehead). It is not a place inadequately apprehended (felt, fear, caught); it is not a *place* at all.

It is a typical mistake for a forestman to make. It has been estimated that land was cleared for farming in the woodlands at a rate of an acre a month, say, roughly four years to clear forty acres. Trees had to be cut, dragged away, and burned or dressed for use. Depending upon the hardness of the wood, it took another ten to fifteen years for the stumps to rot out. A woodland farmer, with a large family of hard working sons, could put only a small farm fully under cultivation in a life-time.

Cooper misconceived the domestic struggle on the prairie; or more precisely, he didn't conceive it at all. Natty's flight is irresistible because Civilization has never existed for Euroamericans. He is fleeing a specter, an order which does not exist, and so turns destructive.

The East remains Civilization: eastern money (whether in Chicago, Houston, Omaha, or New York), Harvard liberalism, *The Times*, the poetry of personism, the Museum of Modern Art.

And despite the superficial overlay of settlement, the West in Nature: the San Andreas Fault, the deserts, Los Alamos, the Indians replaced by radioactive cities, the wild people of Berkeley, Charles Manson. Manson is Natty Bumppo given a twentieth century incarnation. Richard Nixon is the Noble Savage, and Rotarianism the code of the wilderness.

". . . a people composed of heterogeneous materials, having passed from the task of filling up the vacant spaces of the continent, is now thrown back upon itself, and is seeking equilibrium. The diverse elements are being fused into national unity. The forces of reorganization are turbulent and the nation seems *like a witches' kettle*." Turner's casual metaphor now appears prophetic. The Great

Demo(n)cracy . . . but we are coming to the real issue:

the devil's force is polar, a difference of potential. The sense of the world stays *in* the world; it is uncreative. It remains efficacious only as it remains partial, playing fragment against fragment. When it moves toward completion, as in the last scenes of *Faust*, it is only destructive.

Up to the beginning of the Pisan section, the *Cantos* are demonic in this way: Pound draws his force from the grandest unlocated oppositions. Such is the secret power he tapped in the ideogrammatic method: the ideogram is a neutral ground for any specific content. Only when he takes up residence (which was, need I say, *his* choice, and not the U.S. Army's) in Pisa do the poems begin shaping their own tradition to a fully specific, general condition of life.

Pound is dead. Tonight's news. After the newscast they might have played anything but Mahler. They might have played Vivaldi. But they played Mahler. Then again, no monument seems best. We are not finished with Pound. We still have to determine the legitimate cost of Kulchur.

Likewise Cooper's prairie: the noble trapper, the genteel lovers, good and evil frontiersmen, good and evil savages, all meet on a surface as indifferent as a dice table.

Cooper embodies for us, in one skin, the demonic difference of potential which is the root of American destructiveness. The Leatherstocking tales are evidence to much: coitus interruptus with the she-demon of the continent.

Nothing comes whole in Cooper. All is half realized, or less. He's like America itself. You feel gritty after reading him, the way you do reading a good history of the American Revolution or the Reconstruction, or biographies of American heroes.

He is a father, and so we quarrel with him even over the reality we create for ourselves.

In their westward movement across the continent, the Anglo-Americans met the prairie first in the small occasional openings in the forest — "oak openings" and "barrens."

— James C. Malin

I have been resisting this final section. The ground is prepared; all that remains to be said is that in *The Oak Openings*, at last, three years before his death, Cooper locates a border which need not be crossed. Whether it is in Michigan or Missouri (West Plains, my home town in Missouri, takes its name from an oak opening) or in the middle of the Great Plains, in Kansas or Nebraska, this frontier has no need of some western contr(ar)y. It defines itself against the possibility that someone might *live* there. Any native who notices that fact, that life is possible, is amazed. Carl Sauer wrote several essays trying to convince himself. Dorn's disbelief in "Driving Across the Prairies" is overcome, barely, only by all that he sees. It appears to Ken Irby in the face of a skag death in the Max Douglas poems: such are the alternatives.

If the American inlands are still largely undigested, as Paul Metcalf feels in *Genoa*, it is, wherever it has been blocked, in Cooper's *Openings* that peristalsis begins.

The novel must have cost Cooper immensely. He comes to the limits of his personal order, but it is no surrender to dissolution as his encounter with the prairies had been twenty-one years before. He is beyond Civilization and Nature, those shorthand characters for woodland wisdom.

        I am almost tempted to take the last chapter paragraph by paragraph, to get the beauty of the tone. Some delicate submission speaks in these passages:

> "The vegetation certainly surpassed that of even West New York, the trees alone excepted."

> "There was not a stump on it. . . . "

> "The walk in this wood — which is not an Opening, but an old-fashioned virgin forest — we found delightful of a warm summer's day."

And the page and a half on the combine is as fine as anything Cooper ever wrote. According to the journals he spent his spare time, while he was writing the *Openings*, reading St. Paul. The fear was on him. He is a dangerous man. Every road leads to Damascus. The agon is casualness, which was Cooper's besetting sin (casualness which is egotism, pride, displayed by a gentleman), vs. the blinding light. It's Christian humility, this forestman's attention to the detailed workings of a combine. The dogma is Home Mission Board stuff; the *humilitas* can be credited.

The suave eyes, quiet, not scornful
                              rain also is of the process.
                              (Canto LXXIV)

"Order is not sufficient. What is required, is something more complex. It is order entering upon novelty; so the massiveness of order does not degenerate into mere repetition; and so that the novelty is always reflected upon a back ground of system."
                              (One last time, Whitehead)

The action of *The Oak Openings* is senseless. The literary offences for which Mark Twain scores Cooper become the principle of composition: the Indian nations gather to consider the wisdom of scalping six palefaces; days and weeks pass in preparation for the powwow; the palefaces scramble up and down the Kalamazoo, as if they were on a yo-yo; they build fortresses and confront the Indians with their possible Hebrew origins. Boden's mummery at the Whiskey Spring is embarrassing. That Cooper resorts to the same trick twice in the novel is an insult. Senseless. It *has* to be. We are watching the creation of a morphology which will at least make some action meaningful. But as the process grows, there is nothing. Just covert hostility. The plot is nothing but a mechanism to keep the pressure on, while the pattern of the novel develops:

Chateau au Miel	Whiskey Center
Le Bourdon, the drone, "from the circumstances that he was notorious for laying his hands on the products of others," or Buzzing Ben Boden, and, later, the General. Cooper's heroes are never to be pinned down with a name.	and Blossom
	"Travelling' Centres, and stationary, differs somewhat, I guess; one is always to be found, while t'other must be s'arched a'ter." (Compare Natty Bumppo.)
"How skillfully it builds its cell" (Watts).	"Well, Bourdon, if you prefer that name; though *stranger* is a name I like, it has sich an up and off sound to it. When a man calls all he sees *strangers*,
"It was made of pine logs, in the usual mode, with the addi-	

tional security of possessing a roof of squared timbers, of which the several parts were so nicely fitted together as to shed rain."

"Le Bourdon would not allow a tree of any sort to be felled anywhere near his abode."

"Castle Meal was surrounded by its bristling defences."

Of Pigeonwing: "He might have been said to have assisted Nature, instead of disturbing her."

"She seems to hold her home
*   in view*
and sails as if the path
*   she knew"* (Wilson).

"No sooner was peace made . . . than he returned to his beloved Openings, where he had remained, 'growing with the country,' as it is termed. . . . He has a plenty of land, and that which is good; a respectable dwelling, and is out of debt."

it's a sign he don't let the grass grow in the road for want of movin.' "

"Her brother had fallen back into his old habits; and died ere the war of 1812 ended."

Hestia's image is the hearthfire, the connection between the place as public and the place as private, where all can be turned to hospitality, a welcome to *strangers*, in the place where the story begins.

"This unity and competency," Sauer calls the *oikia* that developed on the middle border.

Domestic, fr L *domus* house, Gk *demein* to build. That the same family of words, by another line of descent, also yields 'timber' indicates how radically the sod hut of the Great Plains departed from the traditions of woodland culture which Cooper knew. To the very roots of the language.

Hestia's image is also, sometimes, the omphallos.

The double pull of the muse — finally it's gravity — pulling down right where we stand, bringing it all home.

Don Byrd
Department of English,
State University of
New York at Albany.

THE OAK
OPENINGS

THE OAK OPENINGS.

CHAPTER I.

" How doth the little busy bee
Improve each shining hour,
And gather honey all the day,
From every opening flower."
WATT'S *Hymns for Children.*

WE have heard of those who fancied that they beheld a signal instance of the hand of the Creator in the celebrated cataract of Niagara. Such instances of the power of sensible and near objects to influence certain minds, only prove how much easier it is to impress the imaginations of the dull with images that are novel, than with those that are less apparent, though of infinitely greater magnitude. Thus, it would seem to be strange, indeed, that any human being should find more to wonder at in any one of the phenomena of the earth than in the earth itself; or, should specially stand astonished at the might of Him who created the world, when each night brings into view a firmament studded with other worlds, each equally the work of his hands !

Nevertheless, there is (at bottom) a motive for adoration, in the study of the lowest fruits of the wisdom and power of God. The leaf is as much beyond our comprehension of remote causes, as much a subject of intelligent admiration, as the tree which bears it : the single tree confounds our knowledge and researches the same as the entire forest ; and though a variety that appears to be endless pervades the world, the same admirable adaptation of means to ends, the same bountiful forethought, and the same benevolent wisdom are to be found in the acorn as in the gnarled branch on which it grew.

The American forest has so often been described as to cause one to hesitate about reviving scenes that may possibly pall, and in retouching pictures that have been so frequently painted as to be familiar to every mind. But God created the woods, and the themes bestowed by his bounty are inexhaustible. Even the ocean, with its boundless waste of water, has been found to be rich in its various beauties and marvels ; and he who shall bury himself with us, once more, in the virgin forests of this widespread land, may possibly discover new subjects of admiration, new causes to adore the Being that has brought all into existence, from the universe to its most minute particle.

The precise period of our legend was in the year 1812, and the season of the year the pleasant month of July, which had now drawn near to its close. The sun was already approaching the western limits of a wooded view, when the actors in its opening scene must appear on a stage that is worthy of a more particular description.

The region was, in one sense, wild, though it offered a picture that was not without some of the strongest and most pleasing features of civilization. The country was what is termed " rolling," from some fancied resemblance to the surface of the ocean when it is just undulating with a long " ground-swell." Although wooded, it was not as the American forest is wont to grow, with tall, straight trees towering towards the light, but with intervals between the low oaks that were scattered profusely over the view, and with much of that air of negligence that one is apt to see in grounds where art is made to assume the character of nature. The trees, with very few exceptions, were what is called the " burr-oak," a small variety of a very extensive genus ; and the spaces between them, always irregular, and often of singular beauty, have obtained the name of " openings " ;

the two terms combined giving their appellation to this
particular species of native forest, under the name of '' Oak
Openings.''

These woods, so peculiar to certain districts of country,
are not altogether without some variety, though possessing
a general character of sameness. The trees were of very
uniform size, being little taller than pear-trees, which they
resemble a good deal in form ; and having trunks that
rarely attain two feet in diameter. The variety is produced
by their distribution. In places they stand with a regularity resembling that of an orchard ; then, again, they are
more scattered and less formal, while wide breadths of the
land are occasionally seen in which they stand in copses,
with vacant spaces, that bear no small affinity to artificial
lawns, being covered with verdure. The grasses are supposed to be owing to the fires lighted periodically by the
Indians in order to clear their hunting-grounds.

Towards one of these grassy glades, which was spread
on an almost imperceptible acclivity, and which might have
contained some fifty or sixty acres of land, the reader is now
requested to turn his eyes. Far in the wilderness as was the
spot, four men were there, and two of them had even some
of the appliances of civilization about them. The woods
around were the then unpeopled forest of Michigan, and
the small winding reach of placid water that was just visible in the distance was an elbow of the Kalamazoo, a beautiful little river that flows westward, emptying its tribute into
the vast expanse of Lake Michigan. Now, this river has
already become known, by its villages and farms, and railroads and mills ; but then, not a dwelling of more pretension
than the wigwam of the Indian, or an occasional shanty of
some white adventurer, had ever been seen on its banks. In
that day the whole of that fine peninsula, with the exception
of a narrow belt of country along the Detroit River, which
was settled by the French as far back as near the close of
the seventeenth century, was literally a wilderness. If a
white man found his way into it, it was as an Indian trader,
a hunter, or an adventurer in some other of the pursuits
connected with border life and the habits of the savages.

Of this last character were two of the men on the open
glade just mentioned, while their companions were of the
race of the aborigines. What is much more remarkable,
the four were absolutely strangers to each other's faces, having met for the first time in their lives only an hour previously to the commencement of our tale. By saying that
they were strangers to each other, we do not mean that the
white men were acquaintances, and the Indians strangers,
but that neither of the four had ever seen either of the party
until they met on that grassy glade, though fame had made
them somewhat acquainted through their reputations. At
the moment when we desire to present this group to the
imagination of the reader, three of its number were grave
and silent observers of the movements of the fourth. The
fourth individual was of middle size, young, active, exceeding well formed, and with a certain open and frank expression
of countenance that rendered him at least well-looking, though
slightly marked with the small-pox. His real name was
Benjamin Boden, though he was extensively known throughout the northwestern territories by the *sobriquet* of Ben Buzz
—extensively as to distances, if not as to people. By the
voyageurs, and other French of that region, he was almost
universally styled *Le Bourdon*, or the "Drone"; not, however, from his idleness or inactivity, but from the circumstance that he was notorious for laying his hands on the
products of labor that proceeded from others. In a word,
Ben Boden was a "bee-hunter," and as he was one of the
first to exercise his craft in that portion of the country,
so was he infinitely the most skilful and prosperous. The
honey of Le Bourdon was not only thought to be purer and
of higher flavor than that of any other trader in the article,
but it was much the most abundant. There were a score of
respectable families on the two banks of the Detroit who
never purchased of any one else, but who patiently waited
for the arrival of the capacious bark canoe of Buzz, in the
autumn, to lay in their supplies of this savory nutriment
for the approaching winter. The whole family of griddle
cakes, including those of buckwheat, Indian, rice, and
wheaten flour, were more or less dependent on the safe

arrival of Le Bourdon for their popularity and welcome. Honey was eaten with all ; and *wild* honey had a reputation rightfully or not obtained, that even rendered it more welcome than that which was formed by the labor and art of the domesticated bee.

The dress of Le Bourdon was well adapted to his pursuits and life. He wore a hunting-shirt and trowsers, made of thin stuff, which was dyed green, and trimmed with yellow fringe. This was the ordinary forest attire of the American rifleman ; being of a character, as it was thought, to conceal the person in the woods, by blending its hues with those of the forest. On his head Ben wore a skin cap, somewhat smartly made, but without the fur ; the weather being warm. His moccasins were a good deal wrought, but seemed to be fading under the exposure of many marches. His arms were excellent ; but all his martial accoutrements, even to a keen, long-bladed knife, were suspended from the rammer of his rifle ; the weapon itself being allowed to lean, in careless confidence, against the trunk of the nearest oak, as if their master felt there was no immediate use for them.

Not so with the other three. Not only was each man well armed, but each man kept his trusty rifle hugged to his person, in a sort of jealous watchfulness ; while the other white man, from time to time, secretly, but with great minuteness, examined the flint and priming of his own piece. This second pale-face was a very different person from him just described. He was still young, tall, sinewy, gaunt, yet springy and strong, stooping and round-shouldered, with a face that carried a very decided top-light in it, like that of the notorious Bardolph. In short, whiskey had dyed the countenance of Gershom Waring with a tell-tale hue, that did not less infallibly betray his destination than his speech denoted his origin, which was clearly from one of the States of New England. But Gershom had been so long at the Northwest as to have lost many of his peculiar habits and opinions, and to have obtained substitutes.

Of the Indians, one, an elderly, wary, experienced warrior, was a Pottawattamie, named Elksfoot, who was well-known at all the trading-houses and "garrisons" of the

Northwestern Territory, including Michigan, as low down as Detroit itself. The other redman was a young Chippewa, or O-jeb-way, as the civilized natives of that nation now tell us the word should be spelled. His ordinary appellation among his own people was that of Pigeonswing; a name obtained from the rapidity and length of his flights. This young man, who was scarcely turned of five-and-twenty, had already obtained a high reputation among the numerous tribes of his nation as a messenger or "runner."

Accident had brought these four persons, each and all strangers to one another, in communication in the glade of the Oak Openings, which has already been mentioned, within half an hour of the scene we are about to present to the reader. Although the rencontre had been accompanied by the usual precautions of those who meet in a wilderness, it had been friendly so far; a circumstance that was in some measure owing to the interest they all took in the occupation of the bee-hunter. The three others, indeed, had come in on different trails, and surprised Le Bourdon in the midst of one of the most exciting exhibitions of his art—an exhibition that awoke so much and so common an interest in the spectators as at once to place its continuance for the moment above all other considerations. After brief salutations, and wary examinations of the spot and its tenants, each individual had, in succession, given his grave attention to what was going on, and all had united in begging Ben Buzz to pursue his occupation, without regard to his visitors. The conversation that took place was partly in English, and partly in one of the Indian dialects, which luckily all the parties appeared to understand. As a matter of course, with a sole view to oblige the reader, we shall render what was said, freely, into the vernacular.

"Let's see, let's see, *stran*ger," cried Gershom, emphasizing the syllable we have put in italics, as if especially to betray his origin, "what you can do with your tools. I've heer'n tell of such doin's, but never see'd a bee lined in all my life, and have a desp'rate fancy for larnin' of all sorts, from 'rithmetic to preachin'."

"That comes from your Puritan blood," answered Le

Bourdon, with a quiet smile, using surprisingly pure English for one in his class of life. "They tell me you Puritans preach by instinct."

"I don't know how that is," answered Gershom, "though I can turn my hand to anything. I heer'n tell, across at Bob Ruly (*Bois Brulé* [1]), of sich doin's, and would give a week's keep at Whiskey Centre to know how 't was done."

"Whiskey Centre" was a sobriquet bestowed by the fresh-water sailors of that region, and the few other white adventurers of Saxon origin who found their way into that trackless region, firstly on Gershom himself, and secondly on his residence. These names were obtained from the intensity of their respective characters in favor of the beverage named. *L'eau de mort* was the place termed by the *voyageurs*, in a sort of pleasant travesty on the *eau de vie* of their distant, but still well-remembered manufactures on the banks of the Garonne. Ben Boden, however, paid but little attention to the drawling remarks of Gershom Waring. This was not the first time he had heard of "Whiskey Centre," though the first time he had ever seen the man himself. His attention was on his own trade, or present occupation; and when it wandered at all, it was principally bestowed on the Indians; more especially on the runner. Of Elk's foot, or Elksfoot, as we prefer to spell it, he had some knowledge by means of rumor; and the little he knew rendered him somewhat more indifferent to his proceedings than he felt towards those of the Pigeonswing. Of this young redskin he had never heard; and while he managed to suppress all exhibition of the feeling, a lively curiosity to learn the Chippewa's business was uppermost in his mind. As for Gershom, he had taken *his* measure at a glance, and had instantly set him down to be what in truth he was, a wandering, drinking, reckless

[1] This unfortunate name, which it may be necessary to tell a portion of our readers means "Burnt Word," seems condemned to all sorts of abuses among the linguists of the West. Among other pronunciations is that of "Bob Ruly"; while an island near Detroit, the proper name of which is "Bois Blanc," is familiarly known to the lake mariners by the name of "Bobolo."

adventurer, who had a multitude of vices and bad qualities, mixed up with a few that, if not absolutely redeeming, served to diminish the disgust in which he might otherwise have been held by all decent people. In the meanwhile, the bee-hunting, in which all the spectators took so much interest, went on. As this is a process with which most of our readers are probably unacquainted, it may be necessary to explain the *modus operandi*, as well as the appliances used.

The tools of Ben Buzz, as Gershom had termed these implements of his trade, were neither very numerous nor very complex. They were all contained in a small, covered wooden pail like those that artisans and laborers are accustomed to carry for the purposes of conveying their food from place to place. Uncovering this, Le Bourdon had brought his implements to view, previously to the moment when he was first seen by the reader. There was a small covered cup of tin; a wooden box; a sort of plate, or platter, made also of wood; and a common tumbler, of a very inferior, greenish glass. In the year 1812 there was not a pane, nor a vessel, of clear, transparent glass made in all America! Now, some of the most beautiful manufactures of that sort known to civilization are abundantly produced among us, in common with a thousand other articles that are used in domestic economy. The tumbler of Ben Buzz, however, was his countryman in more senses than one. It was not only American, but it came from the part of Pennsylvania of which he was himself a native. Blurred, and of a greenish hue, the glass was the best that Pittsburg could then fabricate, and Ben had bought it only the year before, on the very spot where it had been made.

An oak, of more size than usual, had stood a little remote from its fellows, or more within the open ground of the glade than the rest of the "orchard." Lightning had struck this tree that very summer, twisting off its trunk at a height of about four feet from the ground. Several fragments of the body and branches lay near, and on these the spectators now took their seats, watching attentively the movements of the bee-hunter. Of the stump Ben had made a sort of table, first levelling its splinters with an axe, and on it he placed the several implements of his craft, as he had need of each in succession.

The wooden platter was first placed on this rude table. Then Le Bourdon opened his small box, and took out of it a piece of honey-comb that was circular in shape and about an inch and a half in diameter. The little covered tin vessel was next brought into use. Some pure and beautifully clear honey was poured from its spout into the cells of the piece of comb until each of them was about half filled. The tumbler was next taken in hand, carefully wiped, and examined, by holding it up before the eyes of the bee-hunter. Certainly there was little to admire in it, but it was sufficiently transparent to answer his purposes. All he asked was to be able to look through the glass in order to see what was going on in its interior.

Having made these preliminary arrangements, Buzzing Ben—for the *sobriquet* was applied to him in this form quite as often as in the other—next turned his attention to the velvet-like covering of the grassy glade. Fire had run over the whole region late that spring, and the grass was now as fresh and sweet and short as if the place were pastured. The white clover, in particular, abounded, and was then just bursting forth into the blossom. Various other flowers had also appeared, and around them were buzzing thousands of bees. These industrious little animals were hard at work, loading themselves with sweets, little foreseeing the robbery contemplated by the craft of man. As Le Bourdon moved stealthily among the flowers and their humming visitors, the eyes of the two redmen followed his smallest movement, as the cat watches the mouse ; but Gershom was less attentive, thinking the whole curious enough, but preferring whiskey to all the honey on earth.

At length Le Bourbon found a bee to his mind, and watching the moment when the animal was sipping sweets from a head of white clover, he cautiously placed his blurred and green-looking tumbler over it, and made it his prisoner. The moment the bee found itself encircled with the glass, it took wing and attempted to rise. This carried it to the upper part of its prison, when Ben carefully introduced the unoccupied hand beneath the glass, and returned to the stump. Here he sat the tumbler down on the platter in a way to bring the piece of honey-comb within its circle.

So much done successfully, and with very little trouble, Buzzing Ben examined his captive for a moment, to make sure that all was right. Then he took off his cap and placed it over tumbler, platter, honey-comb, and bee. He now waited half a minute, when cautiously raising the cap again, it was seen that the bee, the moment a darkness like that of its hive came over it, had lighted on the comb, and commenced filling itself with the honey. When Ben took away the cap altogether, the head, and half of the body of the bee was in one of the cells, its whole attention being bestowed on this unlooked-for hoard of treasure. As this was just what its captor wished, he considered that part of his work accomplished. It now became apparent why a glass was used to take the bee, instead of a vessel of wood or of bark. Transparency was necessary in order to watch the movements of the captive, as darkness was necessary in order to induce it to cease its efforts to escape, and to settle on the comb.

As the bee was now intently occupied in filling itself, Buzzing Ben, or Le Bourdon, did not hesitate about removing the glass. He even ventured to look around him, and to make another captive, which he placed over the comb, and managed as he had done with the first. In a minute, the second bee was also buried in a cell, and the glass was again removed. Le Bourdon now signed for his companions to draw near.

"There they are, hard at work with the honey," he said, speaking in English and pointing to the bees. "Little do they think, as they undermine that comb, how near they are to the undermining of their own hive! But so it is with us all! When we think we are in the highest prosperity we may be nearest to a fall, and when we are poorest and humblest, we may be about to be exalted. I often think of these things, out here in the wilderness, when I'm alone, and my thoughts are ac*tyve*."

Ben used a very pure English, when his condition in life is remembered ; but, now and then, he encountered a word which pretty plainly proved he was not exactly a scholar. A false emphasis has sometimes an influence on a man's fortune, when one lives in the world ; but it mattered little to one like Buzzing Ben, who seldom saw more than half a dozen human faces in the course of a whole summer's hunting. We remember an Englishman, however, who would never concede talents to Burr, because the latter said, à l'Américaine, Európean, instead of Européan.

"How hive in danger?" demanded Elksfoot, who was very much of a matter-of-fact person. "No see him, no hear him—else get some honey."

"Honey you can have for the asking, for I've plenty of it already in my cabin, though it's somewhat 'arly in the season to begin to break in upon the store. In general, the bee-hunters keep back till August, for they think it better to commence work when the creatures,"—this word Ben pronounced as accurately as if brought up at St. James's, making it neither "creatur'" nor "creatoore"— "to commence work when the creatures have had time to fill up, after their winter's feed. But I like the old stock, and, what is more, I feel satisfied this is not to be a common summer, and so I thought I would make an early start."

As Ben said this, he glanced his eyes at Pigeonswing, who returned the look in a way to prove there was already a secret intelligence between them, though neither had ever seen the other an hour before.

"Waal!" exclaimed Gershom, "this is cur'ous, I'll allow *that* ; yes, it's cur'ous—but we've got an article at Whiskey Centre that'll put the sweetest honey bee ever suck'd altogether out o' countenance!"

"An article of which you suck your share, friend, I'll answer for it, judging by the sign you carry between the windows of your face," returned Ben, laughing ; "but hush, men, hush. That first bee is filled, and begins to think of home. He'll soon be off for *Honey* Centre, and I must keep my eye on him. Now stand a little aside, friends, and give me room for my craft."

The men complied, and Le Bourdon was now all intense attention to his business. The bee first taken had, indeed, filled itself to satiety, and at first seemed to be too heavy to rise on the wing. After a few moments of preparation, however, up it went, circling around the spot, as if uncertain what course to take. The eye of Ben never left it, and when the insect darted off, as it soon did, in an air-line, he saw it for fifty yards after the others had lost sight of it. Ben took the range, and was silent fully a minute while he did so.

"That bee may have lighted in the corner of yonder swamp," he said, pointing, as he spoke, to a bit of low land that sustained a growth of much larger trees than those which grew in the "opening," "or it has crossed the point of the wood, and struck across the prairie beyond, and made for a bit of thick forest that is to be found about three miles farther. In the last case, I shall have my trouble for nothing."

"What t'other do?" demanded Elksfoot, with very obvious curiosity.

"Sure enough; the other gentleman must be nearly ready for a start, and we'll see what road *he* travels. 'T is always an assistance to a bee-hunter to get one creature fairly off, as it helps him to line the next with greater sartainty."

Ben *would* say ac*tyve*, and *sar*tain, though he was above saying creatoore, or creatur'. This is the difference between a Pennsylvanian and a Yankee. We shall not stop, however, to note all these little peculiarities in these individuals, but use the proper or the peculiar dialect, as may happen to be most convenient to ourselves.

But there was no time for disquisition, the second bee being now ready for a start. Like his companion, this insect rose and encircled the stump several times ere it darted away towards its hive, in an air-line. So small was the object, and so rapid its movement, that no one but the bee-hunter saw the animal after it had begun its journey in earnest. To *his* disappointment, instead of flying in the same direction as the bee first taken, this little fellow went buzzing off fairly at a right angle! It was consequently

clear that there were two hives, and that they lay in very
different directions.

Without wasting his time in useless talk, Le Bourdon now
caught another bee, which was subjected to the same process
as those first taken. When this creature had filled itself, it
rose, circled the stump as usual, as if to note the spot for a
second visit, and darted away, directly in a line with the bee
first taken. Ben noted its flight most accurately, and had
his eye on it until it was quite a hundred yards from the
stump. This he was enabled to do by means of a quick
sight and long practice.

"We'll move our quarters, friends," said Buzzing Ben,
good-humoredly, as soon as satisfied with this last observation, and gathering together his traps for a start. "I must
angle for that hive, and I fear it will turn out to be across
the prairie, and quite beyond my reach for to-day."

The prairie alluded to was one of those small, natural
meadows, or pastures, that are to be found in Michigan, and
may have contained four or five thousand acres of open land.
The heavy timber of the swamp mentioned jutted into it,
and the point to be determined was, to ascertain whether the
bees had flown *over* these trees, towards which they had certainly gone in an air-line, or whether they had found their
hive among them. In order to settle this material question,
a new process was necessary.

"I must 'angle' for them chaps," repeated Le Bourdon ;
"and if you will go with me, strangers, you shall soon see
the nicest part of the business of bee-hunting. Many a man
who can 'line' a bee can do nothing at an 'angle.'"

As this was only gibberish to the listeners, no answer was
made, but all prepared to follow Ben, who was soon ready to
change his ground. The bee-hunter took his way across the
open ground to a point fully a hundred rods distant from
his first position, where he found another stump of a fallen
tree, which he converted into a stand. The same process
was gone through with as before, and Le Bourbon was soon
watching two bees that had plunged their heads down into
the cells of the comb. Nothing could exceed the gravity
and attention of the Indians all this time. They had fully

comprehended the business of "lining" the insects towards
their hives, but they could not understand the virtue of the
"angle." The first bore so strong an affinity to their own
pursuit of game as to be very obvious to their senses; but
the last included a species of information to which they were
total strangers. Nor were they much the wiser after Le
Bourbon had taken his "angle"; it requiring a sort of in-
duction to which they were not accustomed, in order to put
the several parts of his proceedings together, and to draw
the inference. As for Gershom, he affected to be familiar
with all that was going on, though he was just as ignorant
as the Indians themselves. This little bit of hypocrisy was
the homage he paid to his white blood; it being very un-
seemly, according to his view of the matter, for a pale-face
not to know more than a redskin.

The bees were some little time in filling themselves. At
length one of them came out of his cell, and was evidently
getting ready for his flight. Ben beckoned to the spectators
to stand farther back, in order to give him a fair chance,
and, just as he had done so, the bee rose. After humming
around the stump for an instant, away the insect flew, taking
a course almost at right angles to that in which Le Bourbon
had expected to see it fly. It required half a minute for him
to recollect that this little creature had gone off in a line
nearly parallel to that which had been taken by the second
of the bees, which he had seen quit his original position.
The line led across the neighboring prairie, and any attempt
to follow these bees was hopeless.

But the second creature was also soon ready, and when it
darted away, Le Bourdon, to his manifest delight, saw that
it held its flight towards the point of the swamp, *into* or
over which two of his first captives had also gone. This
settled the doubtful matter. Had the hive of these bees
been *beyond* that wood, the angle of intersection would not
have been there, but at the hive across the prairie. The
reader will understand that creatures which obey an instinct,
or such a reason as bees possess, would never make a curvature in their flights without some strong motive for it. Thus,
two bees taken from flowers that stood half a mile apart

would be certain not to cross each other's tracks, in returning home, until they met at the common hive : and wherever the intersecting angle in their respective flights might
be, there would that hive be also. As this repository of
sweets was the game Le Bourdon had in view, it is easy to
see how much he was pleased when the direction taken by
the last of his bees gave him the necessary assurance that
its home would certainly be found in that very point of
dense wood.

CHAPTER II.

" How skilfully it builds its cell,
   How neat it spreads the wax,
And labors hard to store it well,
   With the sweet food it makes."
                    WATT's *Hymns for Children.*

THE next thing was to ascertain which was the particular tree in which the bees had found a shelter. Collecting his implements, Le Bourdon was soon ready, and with a light, elastic tread he moved off towards the point of the wood, followed by the whole party. The distance was about half a mile, and men so much accustomed to use their limbs made light of it. In a few moments all were there, and the bee-hunter was busy in looking for his tree. This was the consummation of the whole process, and Ben was not only provided for the necessities of the case, but he was well skilled in all the signs that betokened the abodes of bees.

An uninstructed person might have passed that point of wood a thousand times, without the least consciousness of the presence of a single insect of the sort now searched for. In general, the bees flew too high to be easily perceptible from the ground, though a practised eye can discern them at distances that would almost seem to be marvellous. But Ben had other assistance than his eyes. He knew that the tree he sought must be hollow, and such trees usually give outward signs of the defect that exists within. Then, some species of wood are more frequented by the bees than others, while the instinct of the industrious little creatures generally enables them to select such homes as will not be very likely to destroy all the fruits of their industry by an untimely fall.

In all these particulars, both bees and bee-hunter were well versed, and Ben made his search accordingly.

Among the other implements of his calling, Le Bourdon had a small spy-glass; one scarcely larger than those that are used in theatres, but which was powerful and every way suited to its purposes. Ben was not long in selecting a tree, a half-decayed elm, as the one likely to contain the hive; and by the aid of his glass he soon saw bees flying among its dying branches, at a height of not less than seventy feet from the ground. A little further search directed his attention to a knot-hole, in and out of which the glass enabled him to see bees passing in streams. This decided the point; and putting aside all his implements but the axe, Buzzing Ben now set about the task of felling the tree.

"*Stran*ger," said Gershom, when Le Bourdon had taken out the first chip, "perhaps you'd better let *me* do that part of the job. I shall expect to come in for a share of the honey, and I'm willing to 'arn all I take. I was brought up on axes, and jackknives, and sich sort of food, and can cut, *or* whittle, with the best chopper, or the neatest whittler, in or out of New England."

"You can try your hand if you wish it," said Ben, relinquishing the axe. "I can fell a tree as well as yourself, but have no such love for the business as to wish to keep it all to myself."

"Waal, I can say I *like* it," answered Gershom, first passing his thumb along the edge of the axe, in order to ascertain its state; then swinging the tool with a view to try its "hang."

"I can't say much for your axe, *stran*ger, for this helve has no tarve to 't, to my mind; but sich as it is, down must come this elm, though ten millions of bees should set upon me for my pains."

This was no idle boast of Waring's. Worthless as he was in so many respects, he was remarkably skilful with the axe, as he now proved by the rapid manner in which he severed the trunk of the large elm on which he was at work. He inquired of Ben where he should "lay the tree," and when it came clattering down it fell on the precise spot indi-

2

cated. Great was the confusion among the bees at this sudden downfall of their long-cherished home. The fact was not known to their enemy, but they had inhabited that tree for a long time ; and the prize now obtained was the richest he had ever made in his calling. As for the insects, they filled the air in clouds, and all the invaders deemed it prudent to withdraw to some little distance for a time, lest the irritated and wronged bees should set upon them and take an ample revenge. Had they known their power, this might easily have been done, no ingenuity of man being able to protect him against the assaults of this insignificant-looking animal, when unable to cover himself, and the angry little heroes are in earnest. On the present occasion, however, no harm befell the marauders. So suddenly had the hive tumbled, that its late occupants appeared to be astounded, and they submitted to their fate as men yield to the power of tempests and earthquakes. In half an hour most of them were collected on an adjacent tree, where, doubtless, a consultation on the mode of future proceedings was held, after their fashion.

The Indians were more delighted with Le Bourdon's ingenious mode of discovering the hive than with the richness of the prize ; while Ben, himself, and Gershom, manifested most satisfaction at the amount of the earnings. When the tree was cut in pieces, and split, it was ascertained that years of sweets were contained within its capacious cavities, and Ben estimated the portion that fell to his share at more than three hundred pounds of good honey—comb included—after deducting the portions that were given to the Indians, and which were abstracted by Gershom. The three last, however, could carry but little, as they had no other means of bearing it away than their own backs.

The honey was not collected that night. The day was too far advanced for that ; and Le Bourdon—certainly never was name less merited than this *sobriquet*, as applied to the active young bee-hunter—but Le Bourdon, to give him his quaint appellation, offered the hospitalities of his own cabin to the strangers, promising to put them on their several paths the succeeding day, with a good store of honey in each knapsack.

"They do say there ar' likely to be troublesome times," he continued, with simple earnestness, after having given the invitation to partake of his homely fare ; "and I should like to hear what is going on in the world. From Whiskey Centre I do not expect to learn much, I will own, but I am mistaken if the Pigeonswing here has not a message that will make us all open our ears."

The Indians ejaculated their assent ; but Gershom was a man who could not express anything sententiously. As the bee-hunter led the way towards his cabin, or shanty, he made his comments with his customary freedom. Before recording what he communicated, however, we shall digress for one moment in order to say a word ourselves concerning this term "shanty." It is now in general use throughout the whole of the United States, meaning a cabin that has been constructed in haste, and for temporary purposes. By a licence of speech, it is occasionally applied to more permanent residences, as men are known to apply familiar epithets to familiar objects. The derivation of the word has caused some speculation. The term certainly came from the West,—perhaps from the Northwest,—and the best explanation we have ever heard of its derivation is to suppose "shanty," as we now spell it, a corruption of "*chienté*," which it is thought may have been a word in Canadian French phrase to express a "dog-kennel." "Chenil," we believe, is the true French term for such a thing, and our own word is said to be derived from it— "meute" meaning "a kennel of dogs," or "a pack of hounds," rather than their dwelling. At any rate, "*chienté*" is so plausible a solution of the difficulty that one may hope it is the true one, even though he has no better authority for it than a very vague rumor. Curious discoveries are sometimes made by these rude analogies, however, though they are generally thought not to be very near akin to learning. For ourselves, now, we do not entertain a doubt that the *sobriquet* of "Yankees," which is in every man's mouth, and of which the derivation appears to puzzle all our philologists, is nothing but a slight corruption of the word "Yengeese," the term applied to the "English" by the tribes to whom they first became known. We have no other authority for this derivation than conjecture, and conjectures that are purely our own ; but it is so very plausible as almost to carry conviction of itself.[1]

The "*chienté*," or shanty of Le Bourdon, stood quite near to the banks of the Kalamazoo, and in a most beautiful grove of the burr-oak. Ben had selected the site with much taste, though the proximity of a spring of delicious water had probably its full share in influencing his decision. It was necessary, moreover, that he should be near the river, as his great movements were all made by water, for the convenience of transporting his tools, furniture, etc., as well as his honey. A famous bark canoe lay in a little bay, out of the current of the stream, securely moored, head and stern, in order to prevent her beating against any object harder than herself.

The dwelling had been constructed with some attention to security. This was rendered necessary, in some measure, as Ben had found by experience, on account of two classes of enemies—men and bears. From the first, it is true, the bee-hunter had hitherto apprehended but little. There were few human beings in that region. The northern portions of the noble peninsula of Michigan are somewhat low and swampy, or are too broken and savage to tempt the native hunters from the openings and prairies that then lay, in such rich profusion, farther south and west. With the exception of the shores or coasts, it was seldom that the northern half of the peninsula felt the footstep of man. With the southern half, however, it was very different ; the "openings" and glades and watercourses offering almost as many temptations to the savage as they have since done the civilized man. Nevertheless, the bison, or the buffalo, as the animal is erroneously, but

---

[1] Since writing the above, the author has met with an allusion that has induced him to think he may not have been the first to suggest this derivation of the word "Yankee." With himself, the suggestion is perfectly original, and has long since been published by him ; but nothing is more probable than the fact that a solution so very natural, of this long-disputed question in language, may have suggested itself to various minds.

very generally termed throughout the country, was not often found in the vast herds of which we read, until one reached the great prairies west of the Mississippi. There it was that the redman most loved to congregate ; though always bearing, in numbers, but a trifling proportion to the surface they occupied. In that day, however, near as to the date, but distant as to the events, the Chippewas, Ottawas, and Pottawattamies, kindred tribes, we believe, had still a footing in Michigan proper, and were to be found in considerable numbers in what was called the St. Joseph's country, or along the banks of the stream of that name ; a region that almost merits the lofty appellation of the garden of America. Le Bourdon knew many of their warriors, and was much esteemed among them ; though he had never met with either of those whom chance now had thrown in his way. In general, he suffered little wrong from the redmen, who wondered at his occupation, while they liked his character ; but he had sustained losses, and even ill-treatment, from certain outcasts of the tribes, as well as from vagrant whites, who occasionally found their way to his temporary dwellings. On the present occasion, Le Bourdon felt far more uneasiness from the circumstance of having his abode known to Gershom Waring, a countryman, and fellow-Christian, in one sense, at least, than from its being known to the Chippewa and the Pottawattamie.

The bears were constant and dangerous sources of annoyance to the bee-hunter. It was not often that an armed man —and Le Bourdon seldom moved without his rifle—has much to apprehend from the common brown bear of America. Though a formidable-looking animal, especially when full grown, it is seldom bold enough to attack a human being ; nothing but hunger or care for its young ever inducing it to go so much out of the ordinary track of its habits. But the love of the bear for honey amounts to a passion. Not only will it devise all sorts of bearish expedients to get at the sweet morsels, but it will scent them from afar. On one occasion, a family of Bruins had looked into a shanty of Ben's, that was not constructed with sufficient care, and consummated their burglary by demolishing the last comb.

That disaster almost ruined the adventurer, then quite young in his calling ; and ever since its occurrence he had taken the precaution to build such a citadel as should at least set teeth and paws at defiance. To one who had an axe, with access to young pines, this was not a difficult task, as was proved by the present habitation of our hero.

This was the second season that Le Bourdon had occupied " Castle Meal," as he himself called the shanty. This appellation was a corruption of " *Château au Miel*," a name given to it by a wag of a *voyageur*, who had aided Ben in ascending the Kalamazoo the previous summer, and had remained long enough with him to help him put up his habitation. The building was just twelve feet square, in the interior, and somewhat less than fourteen on its exterior. It was made of pine logs, in the usual mode, with the additional security of possessing a roof of squared timbers, of which the several parts were so nicely fitted together as to shed rain. This unusual precaution was rendered necessary to protect the honey, since the bears would have unroofed the common bark coverings of the shanties with the readiness of human beings, in order to get at stores as ample as those which the bee-hunter had soon collected beneath his roof. There was one window of glass, which Le Bourdon had brought in his canoe ; though it was a single sash of six small lights that opened on hinges ; the exterior being protected by stout bars of riven oak securely let into the logs. The door was made of three thicknesses of oaken plank, pinned well together, and swinging on stout iron hinges so secured as not to be easily removed. Its outside fastening was made by means of two stout staples, a short piece of ox-chain, and an unusually heavy padlock. Nothing short of an iron bar, and that cleverly applied, could force this fastening. On the inside, three bars of oak rendered all secure when the master was at home.

" You set consid'rable store by your honey, I guess, *strang*er," said Gershom, as Le Bourdon unlocked the fastenings and removed the chain, " if a body may judge by the kear (care) you take on't ! Now, down our way, we

an't half so partic'lar ; Dolly and Blossom never so much
as putting up a bar to the door, even when I sleep out,
which is about half the time, now the summer is fairly set
in.''

"And whereabouts is ' down our way,' if one may be so
bold as to ask the question?'' returned Le Bourdon, holding the door half opened, while he turned his face towards
the other, in expectation of the answer.

"Why, down at Whiskey Centre, to be sure, as the
v'y'gerers and other boatmen call the place.''

" And where is Whiskey Centre ? '' demanded Ben, a little
pertinaciously

"Why, I thought everybody would a' known that,'' answered Gershom ; "sin' whiskey is as drawin' as a blister.
Whiskey Centre is just where *I* happen to live ; bein' what
a body may call a travellin' name.   As I 'm now down at
the mouth of the Kalamazoo, why Whiskey Centre 's there,
too.''

" I understand the matter, now,'' answered Le Bourdon,
composing his well-formed mouth in a sort of contemptuous
smile.   " You and whiskey, being sworn friends, are always
to be found in company.   When I came into the river,
which was the last week in April, I saw nothing like
whiskey, nor anything like a Centre at the mouth.''

"If you 'd a' be'n a fortnight later, *stran*ger, you 'd a'
found both.   Travellin' Centres, and stationary, differs somewhat, I guess ; one is always to be found, while t' other
must be s'arched a'ter.''

"And pray who are Dolly and Blossom ; I hope the last
is not a *whiskey* blossom ? ''

"Not she ; she never touches a spoonful, though I tell
her it never hurt mortal !   She tries hard to reason me into
it that it hurts *me ;* but that 's all a mistake, as anybody can
see that jest looks at me.''

Ben *did* look at him ; and, to say truth, came to a somewhat different conclusion.

"Is she so blooming that you call her ' Blossom ' ? '' demanded the bee-hunter, " or is she so young ? ''

" The gal 's a little of both.   Dolly is my wife, and Blossom

is my sister.   The real name of Blossom is Margery Waring,
but everybody calls her Blossom ; and so I gi'n into it, with
the rest on 'em.''

It is probable that Le Bourdon lost a good deal of his
interest in this flower of the wilderness as soon as he
learned she was so nearly related to the Whiskey Centre.
Gershom was so very uninviting an object, and had so
many palpable marks that he had fairly earned the nickname which, as it afterwards appeared, the western adventurers had given *him*, as well as his *abode*, whatever the
last might be, that no one of decently sober habits could
readily fancy anything belonging to him.   At any rate, the
bee-hunter now led the way into his cabin, whither he was
followed without unnecessary ceremony, by all three of his
guests.

The interior of the *chienté*, to use the most poetical,
if not the most accurate word, was singularly clean for an
establishment set up by a bachelor, in so remote a part of
the world.   The honey, in neat, well-constructed kegs,
are carefully piled along one side of the apartment, in a
way to occupy the minimum of room, and to be rather
ornamental than unsightly.   These kegs were made by Le
Bourdon himself, who had acquired as much of the art as
was necessary to that object.   The woods always furnished
the materials ; and a pile of staves that was placed beneath
a neighboring tree sufficiently denoted that he did not yet
deem that portion of his task complete.

In one corner of the hut was a pile of well-dressed bear
skins, three in number, each and all of which had been
taken from the carcasses of fallen foes within the last two
months.   Three more were stretched on saplings, near by,
in the process of curing.   It was a material part of the
bee-hunter's craft to kill this animal, in particular ; and
the trophies of his conflicts with them were proportiona-
bly numerous.   On the pile already prepared he usually
slept.

There was a very rude table, a single board set up on
sticks ; and a bench or two, together with a wooden chest
of some size, completed the furniture.   Tools were sus-

pended from the walls, it is true; and no less than three rifles, in addition to a very neat double-barrelled "shot-gun," or fowling-piece, were standing in a corner. These were arms collected by our hero in his different trips, and retained quite as much from affection as from necessity or caution. Of ammunition there was no very great amount visible; only three or four horns and a couple of pouches being suspended from pegs; but Ben had a secret store, as well as another rifle, carefully secured in a natural magazine and arsenal at a distance sufficiently great from the *chienté*, to remove it from all danger of sharing in the fortunes of his citadel, should disaster befall the last.

The cooking was done altogether out of doors. For this essential comfort Le Bourdon had made very liberal provision. He had a small oven, a sufficiently convenient fire-place, and a store-house, at hand,—all placed near the spring and beneath the shade of a magnificent elm. In the store-house he kept his barrel of flour, his barrel of salt, a stock of smoked or dried meat, and that which the woodsmen, if accustomed in early life to the settlements, prizes most highly, a half-barrel of pickled pork. The bark canoe had sufficed to transport all these stores, merely ballasting handsomely that ticklish craft; and its owner relied on the honey to perform the same office on the return voyage, when trade or consumption should have disposed of the various articles just named.

The reader may smile at the word "trade," and ask where were those to be found who could be parties to the traffic. The vast lakes and innumerable rivers of that region, however, remote as it then was from the ordinary abodes of civilized man, offered facilities for communication that the active spirit of trade would be certain not to neglect. In the first place, there were always the Indians to barter skins and furs against powder, lead, rifles, blankets, and unhappily "fire-water." Then the white men who penetrated to those semi-wilds were always ready to "dicker" and to " swap, and to " trade" rifles and watches, and whatever else they might happen to possess, almost to their wives and children.

But we should be doing injustice to Le Bourdon were we in any manner to confound him with the "dickering" race. He was a bee-hunter quite as much through love of the wilderness and love of adventure as through love of gain. Profitable he had certainly found the employment or he probably would not have pursued it; but there was many a man who—nay, most men, even in his own humble class in life—would have deemed his liberal earnings too hardly obtained when gained at the expense of all intercourse with their own kind. But Buzzing Ben loved the solitude of his situation, its hazards, its quietude, relieved by passing moments of high excitement; and, most of all, the self-reliance that was indispensable equally to his success and his happiness. Woman, as yet, had never exercised her witchery over him, and every day was his passion for dwelling alone, and for enjoying the strange but certainly most alluring pleasures of the woods, increasing and gaining strength in his bosom. It was seldom, now, that he held intercourse even with the Indian tribes that dwelt near his occasional places of hunting; and frequently had he shifted his ground in order to avoid collision, however friendly, with whites who, like himself, were pushing their humble fortunes along the shores of those inland seas, which, as yet, were rarely indeed whitened by a sail. In this respect Boden and Waring were the very antipodes of each other; Gershom being an inveterate gossip, in despite of his attachment to a vagrant and border life.

The duties of hospitality are rarely forgotten among border-men. The inhabitant of a town may lose his natural disposition to receive all who offer at his board, under the pressure of society; but it is only in most extraordinary exceptions that the frontier man is ever known to be inhospitable. He has little to offer, but that little is seldom withheld, either through prudence or niggardliness. Under this feeling, we might call it habit also, Le Bourdon now set himself at work to place on the table such food as he had at command and ready cooked. The meal which he soon pressed his guests to share with him was composed of a good piece of cold boiled pork, which Ben had luckily cooked the day previously, some bear's meat roasted, a fragment of venison steak, both lean and cold, and the remains of a duck that had been shot the day before, in the Kalamazoo, with bread, salt, and what was somewhat unusual in the wilderness, two or three onions, raw. The last dish was highly relished by Gershom, and was slightly honored by Ben; but the Indians passed it over with cold indifference. The dessert consisted of bread and honey, which were liberally partaken of by all at table.

Little was said by either host or guests until the supper was finished, when the whole party left the *chienté* to enjoy their pipes, in the cool evening air, beneath the oaks of the grove in which the dwelling stood. Their conversation began to let the parties know something of each other's movements and characters.

" *You* are a Pottawattamie, and *you* a Chippewa," said Le Bourdon, as he courteously handed to his two red guests pipes of theirs that he had just stuffed with some of his own tobacco, "I believe you are a sort of cousins, though your tribes are called by different names."

"Nation, Ojebway," returned the elder Indian, holding up a finger, by way of enforcing attention.

"Tribe, Pottawattamie," added the runner, in the same sententious manner.

"Baccy, good," put in the senior, by way of showing he was well contented with his comforts.

"Have you nothin' to drink?" demanded Whiskey Centre, who saw no great merit in anything but " fire-water."

"There is the spring," returned Le Bourdon, gravely; " a gourd hangs against the tree."

Gershom made a wry face, but he did not move.

" Is there any news stirring among the tribes? " asked the bee-hunter, waiting, however, a decent interval, lest he might be supposed to betray a womanly curiosity.

Elksfoot puffed away some time, before he saw fit to answer, reserving a salvo in behalf of his own dignity. Then he removed the pipe, shook off the ashes, pressed down the fire a little, gave a reviving draught or two, and quietly replied,—

" Ask my young brother—he runner—he know."

But Pigeonswing seemed to be little more communicative than the Pottawattamie. He smoked on in quiet dignity, while the bee-hunter patiently waited for the moment
when it might suit his younger guest to speak. That moment did not arrive for some time, though it came at last.
Almost five minutes after Elksfoot had made the allusion
mentioned, the Ojebway, or Chippewa, removed his pipe
also, and looking courteously round at his host, he said with
emphasis,—

"Bad summer come soon. Pale-faces call young men
togedder, and dig up hatchet."

"I had heard something of this," answered Le Bourdon,
with a saddened countenance, "and was afraid it might
happen."

"My brother dig up hatchet too, eh?" demanded Pigeonswing.

"Why should I? I am alone here on the Openings, and
it would seem foolish in me to wish to fight."

"Got no tribe—no Ojebway—no Pottawattamie, eh?"

"I have my tribe, as well as another, Chippewa, but can
see no use I can be to it here. If the English and Americans fight, it must be a long way from this wilderness, and
on or near the great salt lake."

"Don't know—nebber know, 'til see. English warrior
plenty in Canada."

"That may be; but American warriors are not plenty
here. This country is a wilderness, and there are no soldiers hereabouts to cut each other's throats."

"What you t'ink him?" asked Pigeonswing, glancing at
Gershom, who, unable to forbear any longer, had gone to
the spring to mix a cup from a small supply that still remained of the liquor with which he had left home. "Got
pretty good scalp?"

"I suppose it is as good as another's; but he and I are
countrymen, and we cannot raise the tomahawk on one
another."

"Don't t'ink so. Plenty Yankee, him!"

Le Bourdon smiled at this proof of Pigeonswing's sagacity, though he felt a good deal of uneasiness at the purport of his discourse.

"You are right enough in *that*," he answered ; "but I'm plenty of Yankee, too."

"No—don't say so," returned the Chippewa ; "no, mustn't say *dat*. English ; no Yankee. *Him* not a bit like you."

"Why, we are unlike each other, in some respects, it is true, though we are countrymen, notwithstanding. My Great Father lives at Washington, as well as his."

The Chippewa appeared to be disappointed ; perhaps he appeared sorry, too ; for Le Bourdon's frank and manly hospitality had disposed him to friendship instead of hostilities, while his admissions would rather put him in an antagonistic position. It was probably with a kind motive that he pursued the discourse in a way to give his host some insight into the true condition of matters in that part of the world.

"Plenty Breetish in woods," he said, with marked deliberation and point. "Yankee no come yet."

"Let me know the truth at once, Chippewa," exclaimed Le Bourdon. "I am but a peaceable bee-hunter, as you see, and wish no man's scalp, or any man's honey, but my own. Is there to be a war between America and Canada, or not ? "

"Some say yes ; some say no ; " returned Pigeonswing, evasively. "My part, don't know. Go, now, to see. But plenty Montreal belt among redskins ; plenty rifle ; plenty powder, too."

"I heard something of this as I came up the lakes," rejoined Ben ; "and fell in with a trader, an old acquaintance, from Canada, and a good friend, too, though he is to be my enemy, accordin' to law, who gave me to understand that the summer would not go over without blows. Still, they all seemed to be asleep at Mackinaw (Michillimackinac) as I passed there ! "

"Wake up pretty soon. Canada warrior take fort."

"If I thought that, Chippewa, I would be off this blessed night to give the alarm."

"No—t'ink better of dat."

"Go, I would, if I died for it the next hour!"

"T'ink better—be no such fool, I tell you."

"And I tell you, Pigeonswing, that go I would, if the whole Ojebway nation was on my trail. I am an American, and mean to stand by my own people, come what will."

"T'ought you only peaceable bee-hunter, just now," retorted the Chippewa, a little sarcastically.

By this time Le Bourdon had somewhat cooled, and he became conscious of his indiscretion. He knew enough of the history of the past to be fully aware that, in all periods of American history, the English, and, for that matter, the French, too, so long as they had possessions on this continent, never scrupled about employing the savages in their conflicts. It is true that these highly polished, and, we may justly add, humane nations (for each is out of all question entitled to that character in the scale of comparative humanity as between communities, and each, if you will take its own account of the matter, stands at the head of civilization in this respect) would, notwithstanding these high claims, carry on their *American* wars by the agency of the tomahawk, the scalping-knife, and the brand. Eulogies, though pronounced by ourselves on ourselves, cannot erase the stains of blood. Even down to the present hour a cloud does not obscure the political atmosphere between England and America that its existence may not be discovered on the prairies by a movement among the Indians. The pulse that is to be felt *there* is a sure indication of the state of the relations between the parties. Every one knows that the savage, in his warfare, slays both sexes and all ages; that the door-post of the frontier cabin is defiled by the blood of the infant whose brains have been dashed against it; and that the smouldering ruins of log-houses, oftener than not, cover the remains of their tenants. But what of all that? Brutus is still "an honorable man," and the American who has not this sin to answer for among his numberless transgressions, is reviled as a semi-barbarian! The time is at hand when the Lion of the West will draw his own picture, too; and fortunate will it be for the character of some who will gather around the easel, if they do not discover traces of their own lineaments among his labors.

The feeling engendered by the character of such a warfare is the secret of the deeply-seated hostility which pervades the breast of the *Western* American against the land of his ancestors. He never sees the *Times*, and cares not a rush for the mystifications of the *Quarterly Review*; but he remembers where his mother was brained, and his father or brother tortured; ay, and by whose instrumentality the foul deeds were mainly done. The man of the world can understand that such atrocities may be committed, and the people of the offending nation remain ignorant of their existence, and, in a measure, innocent of the guilt; but the sufferer, in his provincial practice, makes no such distinction, confounding all alike in his resentments, and including all that bear the hated name in his maledictions. It is a fearful thing to awaken the anger of a nation; to excite in it a desire for revenge; and thrice is that danger magnified when the people thus aroused possess the activity, the resources, the spirit, and the enterprise of the Americans. We have been openly derided, and that recently, because in the fulness of our sense of power and sense of right language that exceeds any direct exhibition of the national strength has escaped the lips of legislators, and, perhaps justly, has exposed them to the imputation of boastfulness. That derision, however, will not soon be repeated. The scenes enacting in Mexico, faint as they are in comparison with what would have been seen had hostilities taken another direction, place a perpetual gag in the mouths of all scoffers. The child is passing from the gristle into the bone, and the next generation will not even laugh, as does the present, at any idle and ill-considered menaces to coerce this republic; strong in the consciousness of its own power, it will treat all such *fanfaronades*, if any future statesman should be so ill-advised as to renew them, with silent indifference.

Now Le Bourdon was fully aware that one of the surest pulses of approaching hostilities between England and America was to be felt in the far West. If the Indians were in movement, some power was probably behind the scenes to set them in motion. Pigeonswing was well known to him by reputation ; and there was that about the man which awakened the most unpleasant apprehensions, and he felt an itching desire to learn all he could from him, without betraying any more of his own feelings, if that were possible.

"I do not think the British will attempt Mackinaw," Ben remarked, after a long pause and a good deal of smoking had enabled him to assume an air of safe indifference.

"Got him, I tell you," answered Pigeonswing, pointedly.

"Got what, Chippewa ? "

"Him—Mac-naw—got fort—got so'gers—got whole island. Know dat, for been dere."

This was astounding news, indeed ! The commanding officer of that ill-starred garrison could not himself have been more astonished when he was unexpectedly summoned to surrender by an enemy who appeared to start out of the earth, than was Le Bourdon at hearing this intelligence. To Western notions, Michillimackinac was another Gibraltar, although really a place of very little strength, and garrisoned by only one small company of regulars. Still, habit has given the fortress a sort of sanctity among the adventurers of that region ; and its fall, even in the settled parts of the country, sounded like the loss of a province. It is now known that, anticipating the movements of the Americans, some three hundred whites, sustained by more than twice that number of Indians, including warriors from nearly every adjacent tribe, had surprised the post on the 17th of July, and compelled the subaltern in command, with some fifty odd men, to surrender. This rapid and highly military measure on the part of the British completely cut off the post of Chicago at the head of Lake Michigan, leaving it isolated on what was then a very remote wilderness. Chicago, Mackinac, and Detroit were the three grand stations of the Americans on the upper lakes, and here were two of them virtually gone at a blow !

CHAPTER III.

"Ho! who's here?
If anything that's civil, speak; if savage,
Take, or lend."

Cymbeline.

NOT another syllable did Le Bourdon utter to the Chippewa, or the Chippewa to him, in that sitting, touching the important event just communicated. Each carefully avoided manifesting any further interest in the subject, but the smoking continued for some time after the sun had set. As the shades of evening began to gather, the Pottawattamie arose, shook the ashes from his pipe, gave a grunt, and uttered a word or two by way of announcing his disposition to retire. On this hint, Ben went into the cabin, spread his skins, and intimated to his guests that their beds were ready for them. Few compliments pass among border-men on such occasions, and one after another dropped off, until all were stretched on the skins but the master of the place. He remained up two hours later, ruminating on the state of things; when, perceiving that the night was wearing on, he also found a nest, and sought his repose.

Nothing occurred to disturb the occupants of "Castle Meal," as Le Bourdon laughingly called his cabin, until the return of day. If there were any bears scenting around the place, as often occurred at night, their instinct must have apprised them that a large reinforcement was present, and caused them to defer their attack to a more favorable opportunity. The first afoot next morning was the bee-hunter himself, who arose and left his cabin just as the earliest streaks of day were appearing in the east.   Although dwelling in a wilderness, the "openings" had not the character of ordinary forests.   The air circulates freely beneath their oaks, the sun penetrates in a thousand places, and grass grows wild but verdant.   There was little of the dampness of the virgin woods ; and the morning air, though cool, as is ever the case, even in midsummer, in regions still covered with trees, was balmy ; and at that particular spot it came to the senses of Le Bourdon loaded with the sweets of many a wide glade of his favorite white clover.   Of course he had placed his cabin near those spots where the insect he sought most abounded ; and a fragrant site it proved to be in favorable conditions of the atmosphere.   Ben had a taste for all the natural advantages of his abode, and was standing in enjoyment of its placid beauties, when some one touched his elbow.   Turning, quick as thought, he perceived the Chippewa at his side.   That young Indian had approached with the noiseless tread of his people, and was now anxious to hold a private communication with him.

"Pottawattamie got long ear—come fudder," said Pigeonswing ; "go cook-house—t'ink we want breakfast."

Ben did as desired ; and the two were soon side by side at the spring, in the outlet of which they made their ablutions, the redskin being totally without paint.   When this agreeable office was performed, each felt in better condition for conference.

"Elksfoot got belt from Canada Fadder," commenced the Chippewa, with a sententious allusion to the British propensity to keep the savages in pay.   "*Know* he got him—*know* he keep him."

"And you, Pigeonswing—by your manner of talking I had set you down for a King's Injin, too."

"*Talk* so—no *feel* bit so.   *My* heart Yankee."

"And have you not had a belt of wampum sent you, as well as the rest of them ? "

"Dat true—got him—don't keep him."

"What ! did you dare to send it back ? "

"An't fool, dough young.   Keep him ; no keep him. Keep him for Canada Fadder ; no keep him for Chippewa brave."

"What have you then done with your belt?"

"Bury him where nobody find him dis war. No—Waubkenewh no hole in heart to let king in."

Pigeonswing, as this young Indian was commonly called in his tribe, in consequence of the rapidity of his movements when employed as a runner, had a much more respectable name, and one that he had fairly earned in some of the forays of his people, but which the commonalty had just the same indisposition to use as the French have to call Marshal Soult the Duc de Dalmatie. The last may be the most honorable title, but it is not that by which he is the best known to his countrymen. Waub-ke-newh was an appellation, notwithstanding, of which the young Chippewa was justly proud; and he often asserted his right to use it, as sternly as the old hero of Toulouse asserted his right to his duchy when the Austrians wished to style him "le Maréchal *Duc* Soult."

"And you are friendly to the Yankees, and an enemy to the red-coats?"

Waubkenewh grasped the hand of Le Bourdon, and squeezed it firmly. Then he said warily,—

"Take care; Elkfoot friend of Blackbird; like to look at Canada belt. Got medal of king, too. Have Yankee scalp bye 'm by. Take care; must speak low when Elkfoot near."

"I begin to understand you, Chippewa: you wish me to believe that *you* are a friend to America, and that the Pottawattamie is not. If this be so, why have you held the speech that you did last night, and seemed to be on a war-path *against* my countrymen?"

"Dat good way, eh? Elkfoot den t'ink me *his* friend, dat very good in war-time."

"But is it true, or false, that Mackinaw is taken by the British?"

"Dat, too true; gone, and warrior all prisoner. Plenty Winnebago, plenty Pottawattamie, plenty Ottawa, plenty redskin, dere."

"And the Chippewas?"

"Some Ojebway, too," answered Pigeonswing after a reluctant pause. "Can't all go on same path, this war. Hatchets, somehow, got two handle—one strike Yankee; one strike King George."

"But what is your business here, and where are you now going, if you are friendly to the Americans? I make no secret of my feelings; I am for my own people, and I wish proof that you are a friend, and not an enemy."

"Too many question, one time," returned the Chippewa, a little distastefully. "No good have so long tongue. Ask one question, answer him; ask anoder, answer *him*, too."

"Well, then, what is your business here?"

"Go to Chicago, for gen'ral."

"Do you mean that you bear a message from some American general to the commandant at Chicago?"

"Just so; dat my business. Guess him, right off; he, he, he."

It is so seldom that an Indian laughs that the bee-hunter was startled.

"Where is the general who has sent you on this errand?" he demanded.

"He at Detroit—got whole army dere—warrior plenty as oak in opening."

All this was news to the bee-hunter, and it caused him to muse a moment, ere he proceeded.

"What is the name of the American general who has sent you on this path?" he then demanded.

"Hell," answered the Ojebway, quietly.

"Hell! You mean to give his Indian title, I suppose, to show that he will prove dangerous to the wicked. But how is he called in our own tongue?"

"Hell—dat he name—good name for so'ger, eh?"

"I believe I understand you, Chippewa; Hull is the name of the governor of the territory, and you must have mistaken the sound; is it not so?"

"Hull—Hell—don't know; just same; one good as t' other."

"Yes, one will do as well as the other, if a body only understands you. So Governor Hull has sent you here?"

"No gubbernor; gen'ral, tell you. Got big army— plenty warrior—eat Breesh up!"

"Now, Chippewa, answer me one thing to my likin', or I shall set you down as a man with a forked tongue, though

you do call yourself a friend of the Yankees. If you have
been sent from Detroit to Chicago, why are you as far north
as this! Why are you here, on the banks of the Kalamazoo, when your path ought to lead you more towards the
St. Joseph's?"

"Been to Mackinaw. Gen'ral say, first go to Mackinaw
and see wid own eye how garrison do; den go to Chicago,
and tell warrior dere what happen, and how he best manage.
Understan' dat, Bourdon?"

"Ay, it all sounds well enough, I will acknowledge.
You have been to Mackinaw to look about you there, and
having seen things with your own eyes, have started for
Chicago to give your knowledge to the commandant at
that place. Now, redskin, have you any proof of what
you say?"

For some reason that the bee-hunter could not yet fathom,
the Chippewa was particularly anxious either to obtain his
confidence or to deceive him. Which he was attempting,
was not yet quite apparent; but that one or other was uppermost in his mind, Ben thought was beyond dispute. As
soon as the question last named was put, however, the
Indian looked cautiously around him, as if to be certain
there were no spectators. Then he carefully opened his
tobacco-pouch, and extricated from the centre of the cut
weed a letter that was rolled into the smallest compass to admit of this mode of concealment, and which was encircled
by a thread. The last removed, the letter was unrolled, and
its superscription exposed. The address was to "Captain
—— Heald, U. S. Army, commanding at Chicago." In one
corner were the words, "On public service, by Pigeonswing."
All this was submitted to the bee-hunter, who read it with
his own eyes.

"Dat good"—asked the Chippewa, pointedly—"dat
tell trut'—b'lieve *him*?"

Le Bourdon grasped the hand of the Indian, and gave it
a hearty squeeze. Then he said frankly, and like a man
who no longer entertained any doubts,—

"I put faith in all you say, Chippewa. That is an officer's letter, and I now see that you are on the right side.

You play'd so deep a game, at first, how'sever, that I did n't know exactly what to make of you. Now, as for the Pottawattamie—do you set him down as friend or foe, in reality?"

"Enemy—take your scalp—take my scalp, in minute—only can't catch him. He got belt from Montreal, and it look handsome in his eye."

"Which way d' ye think he 's travelling? As I understood you, he and you fell into the same path within a mile of this very spot. Was the meeting altogether friendly?"

"Yes; friendly—but ask too many question—too much squaw—ask one question, den stop for answer."

"Very true; I will remember that an Indian likes to do one thing at a time. Which way, then, do you think he 's travelling?"

"Don't know—on'y guess—guess he on path to Blackbird."

"And where is Blackbird, and what is he about?"

"Two question, dat!" returned the Chippewa, smiling, and holding up two of his fingers, at the same time, by way of rebuke. "Blackbird on war-path; when warrior on dat path, he take scalp if can get him."

"But where is his enemy? There are no whites in this part of the country, but here and there a trader, or a trapper, or a bee-hunter, or a *voyageur*."

"Take *his* scalp; all scalp good, in war time. An't partic'lar, down at Montreal. What you call garrison at Chicago?"

"Blackbird, you then think, may be moving upon Chicago. In that case, Chippewa, you should outrun this Pottawattamie, and reach the post in time to let its men know the danger."

"Start, as soon as eat breakfast. Can't go straight, nudder, or Pottawattamie see print of moccasin. Must t'row him off trail."

"Very true; but I'll engage you 're cunning enough to do that twice over, should it be necessary.

Just then Gershom Waring came out of the cabin, gaping like a hound, and stretching his arms, as if fairly wearied with sleep. At the sight of this man the Indian made a gesture of caution, saying, however, in an undertone,—

"How his heart—Yankee or Breesh—love Montreal, eh? Pretty good scalp! Love King George, eh?"

"I rather think not, but am not certain. He is a poor pale-face, however, and it's of no great account how he stands. His scalp would hardly be worth the taking, whether by English or American."

"Sell, down at Montreal—better look out for Pottawattamie. Don't like dat Injin."

"We'll be on our guard against him; and there he comes, looking as if his breakfast would be welcome, and as if he was already thinking of a start."

Le Bourdon had been busy with his pots during the whole time this discourse was going on, and had warmed up a sufficiency of food to supply the wants of all his guests. In a few minutes each was busy quietly eating his morning's meal, Gershom having taken his bitters aside, and, as he fancied, unobserved. This was not so much owing to niggardliness as to a distrust of his having a sufficient supply of the liquor that long indulgence had made, in a measure, necessary to him, to last until he could get back to the barrels that were still to be found in his cabin, down on the shore of the lake.

During the breakfast little was said, conversation forming no material part of the entertainment at the meals of any but the cultivated. When each had risen, however, and by certain preliminary arrangements it was obvious that the two Indians intended to depart, the Pottawattamie advanced to Le Bourdon and thrust out a hand.

"Thankee"—he said, in the brief way in which he clipped his English—"Good supper—good sleep—good breakfast. Now, go. Thankee—when any friend come to Pottawattamie village, good wigwam dere, and no door."

"I thank you, Elksfoot; and should you pass this way ag'in, soon, I hope you'll just step into this *chienté* and help yourself if I should happen to be off on a hunt. Good luck to you, and a happy sight of home."

The Pottawattamie then turned and thrust out a hand

to each of the others, who met his offered leave-taking with apparent friendship. The bee-hunter observed that neither of the Indians said anything to the other touching the path he was about to travel, but that each seemed ready to pursue his own way as if entirely independent, and without the expectation of having a companion.

Elksfoot left the spot the first. After completing his adieus, the Pottawattamie threw his rifle into the hollow of his arm, felt at his belt, as if to settle it into its place, made some little disposition of his light summer covering, and moved off in a southwesterly direction, passing through the open glades, and almost equally unobstructed groves, as steady in his movements as if led by an instinct.

"There he goes, on a bee-line," said Le Bourdon, as the straight form of the old savage disappeared at length behind a thicket of trees. "On a bee-line for the St. Joseph River, where he will shortly be, among friends and neighbors, I do not doubt. What, Chippewa? are you in motion, too?"

"Must go, now," returned Pigeonswing, in a friendly way. "Bye'm by come back and eat more honey—bring sweet news, hope—no Canada here"—placing a finger on his heart—"all Yankee."

"God be with you, Chippewa—God be with you. We shall have a stirring summer of it, and I expect to hear of your name in the wars, as of a chief who knows no fear."

Pigeonswing waved his hand, cast a glance, half friendly, half contemptuously, at Whiskey Centre, and glided away. The two who remained standing near the smouldering fire remarked that the direction taken by the Chippewa was towards the lake, and nearly at right angles to that taken by the Pottawattamie. They also fancied that the movement of the former was about half as fast again as that of the latter. In less than three minutes the young Indian was concealed in the " openings," though he had to cross a glade of considerable width in order to reach them.

The bee-hunter was now alone with the only one of his guests who was of the color and race to which he himself belonged. Of the three, he was the visitor he least respected ; but the dues of hospitality are usually sacred in a wilderness and among savages, so that he could do nothing to get rid of him. As Gershom manifested no intention to quit the place, Le Bourdon set about the business of the hour with as much method and coolness as if the other had not been present. The first thing was to bring home the honey discovered on the previous day ; a task of no light labor ; the distance it was to be transported being so considerable and the quantity so large. But our bee-hunter was not without the means of accomplishing such an object, and he now busied himself in getting ready. As Gershom volunteered his assistance, together they toiled in apparent amity and confidence.

The Kalamazoo is a crooked stream; and it wound from the spot where Le Bourdon had built his cabin to a point within a hundred yards of the fallen tree in which the bees had constructed their hive. As a matter of course, Ben profited by this circumstance to carry his canoe to the latter place, with a view to render it serviceable in transporting the honey. First securing everything in and around the *chienté*, he and Gershom embarked, taking with them no less than four pieces of fire-arms ; one of which was, to use the language of the West, a double-barrelled "shot-gun." Before quitting the place, however, the bee-hunter went to a large kennel made of logs and let out a mastiff of great power and size. Between this dog and himself there existed the best possible intelligence ; the master having paid many visits to the prisoner since his return, feeding and caressing him. Glad, indeed, was this fine animal to be released, bounding back and forth, and leaping about Le Bourdon in a way to manifest his delight. He had been cared for in his kennel, and well cared for, too ; but there is no substitute for liberty, whether in man or beast, individuals or communities.

When all was ready, Le Bourdon and Gershom got into the canoe, whither the former now called his dog, using the name of "Hive," an appellation that was doubtless derived from his own pursuit. As soon as the mastiff leaped into the canoe Ben shoved off, and the light craft was pushed up the stream by himself and Gershom without much difficulty, and with considerable rapidity. But little drift-wood choked the channel ; and, after fifteen minutes of moderate labor, the two men came near to the point of low wooded land in which the bee-tree had stood. As they drew nigh, certain signs of uneasiness in the dog attracted his master's attention, and he pointed them out to Gershom.

"There's game in the wind," answered Whiskey Centre, who had a good knowledge of most of the craft of border life, notwithstanding his ungovernable propensity to drink, and who, by nature, was both shrewd and resolute. "I should n't wonder"—a common expression of his class— "if we found bears prowling about that honey !"

"Such things have happened in my time," answered the bee-hunter ; "and twice in my experience I 've been driven from the field, and forced to let the devils get my 'arnin's.''

"That was when you had no comrade, *stran*ger," returned Gershom, raising a rifle, and carefully examining its flint and its priming. "It will be a large family on 'em that drives *us* from that tree ; for my mind is made up to give Doll and Blossom a taste of the sweets."

If this was said imprudently, as respects ownership in the prize, it was said heartily, so far as spirit and determination were concerned. It proved that Whiskey Centre had points about him which, if not absolutely redeeming, served in some measure to lessen the disgust which one might otherwise have felt for his character. The bee-hunter knew that there was a species of hardihood that belonged to border-men as the fruits of their habits, and apparently he had all necessary confidence in Gershom's disposition to sustain him, should there be occasion for a conflict with his old enemies.

The first measure of the bee-hunter, after landing and securing his boat, was to quiet Hive. The animal being under excellent command, this was soon done ; the mastiff maintaining the position assigned him, in the rear, though evidently impatient to be let loose. Had not Le Bourdon known the precise position of the fallen tree, and through that the probable position of his enemies, he would have placed the mastiff in advance, as a pioneer or scout; but he deemed it necessary, under the actual circumstances, to hold him as a reserve, or a force to be directed whither occasion might require. With this arrangement, then, Le Bourdon and Whiskey Centre advanced side by side, each carrying two pieces, from the margin of the river towards the open land that commanded a view of the tree. On reaching the desired point a halt was called, in order to reconnoitre.

The reader will remember that the bee-elm had stood on the edge of a dense thicket, or swamp, in which the trees grew to a size several times exceeding those of the oaks in the openings; and Le Bourdon had caused it to fall upon the open ground, in order to work at the honey with greater ease to himself. Consequently the fragments lay in full view of the spot where the halt was made. A little to Gershom's surprise, Ben now produced his spy-glass, which he levelled with much earnestness towards the tree. The bee-hunter, however, well knew his business, and was examining into the state of the insects whom he had so violently invaded the night before. The air was filled with them flying above and around the tree; a perfect cloud of the little creatures hovering directly over the hole, as if to guard its treasure.

"Waal," said Gershom, in his drawling way, when Le Bourdon had taken a long look with the glass, "I don't see much use in spy-glassin' in that fashion. Spy-glassin' may do out on the lake, if a body has only the tools to do it with; but here, in the openin's, natur's eyes is about as good as them a body buys in the stores."

"Take a look at them bees, and see what a fret they're in," returned Ben, handing the glass to his companion. "As long as I have been in the business, I've never seen a colony in such a fever. Commonly, a few hours after the bees find that their tree is down, and their plans broken into, they give it up, and swarm; looking for a new hive, and setting about the making more food for the next winter; but here are all the bees yet, buzzing above the hole, as if they meant to hold out for a siege."

"There's an onaccountable grist on 'em"—Gershom was never very particular in his figures of speech, usually terming anything in quantities a "grist"; and meaning in the present instance by "onaccountable," a number not to be counted—"an onaccountable grist on 'em, I can tell you, and if you mean to charge upon sich enemies, you must look out for somebody besides Whiskey Centre for your van-guard. What in natur' has got hold of the critters? They can't expect to set that tree on its legs ag'in!"

"Do you see a flight of them just in the edge of the forest —here, more to the southward?" demanded Le Bourdon.

"Sure enough! There is a lot on 'em there, too, and they seem to be comin' and goin' to the tree, like folks"— Gershom would put his noun of multitude into the plural, *Nova Anglice*—"comin' and goin' like folks carryin' water to a fire. A body would think, by the stir among 'em, them critter's' barrel was empty!"

"The bears are there," coolly returned the bee-hunter. "I've seen such movements before, and know how to account for them. The bears are in the thicket, but don't like to come out in the face of such a colony. I have heard of bears being chased miles by bees, when their anger was up!"

"Mortality! They have a good deal of dander (dandruff) for sich little vipers! But what are *we* to do, Bourdon? for Doll and Blossom *must* taste that honey! Half's mine, you know, and I don't like to give it up."

The bee-hunter smiled at the coolness with which Gershom assigned to himself so large a portion of his property; though he did not think it worth his while, just then, to "demur to his declaration," as the lawyers might have it. There was a sort of border rule, which gave all present equal shares in any forest captures; just as vessels in sight come in for prize-money, taken in time of war by public cruisers. At any rate, the honey of a single tree was not of sufficient value to induce a serious quarrel about it. If there should be any extra trouble or danger in securing the present prize, every craft in view might, fairly enough, come in for its share.

"Doll shall not be forgotten, if we can only house our honey," answered the bee-hunter; "nor Blossom, neither. I've a fancy, already, for that blossom of the wilderness, and shall do all I can to make myself agreeable to her. A man cannot approach a maiden with anything sweeter than honey."

"Some gals like sugar'd words better; but let me tell you one thing, *stran*ger—"

"You have eaten bread and salt with me, Whiskey, and both are scarce articles in a wilderness; and you've slept under my roof: is it not almost time to call me something else than stranger?"

"Well, Bourdon, if you prefer that name; though *stran*ger is a name I like, it has sich an up and off sound to it. When a man calls all he sees *stran*gers, it's a sign he don't let the grass grow in the road for want of movin'; and a movin' man for me, any day, before your stationaries. I was born on the sea-shore, in the Bay State; and here I am, up among the fresh-water lakes, as much nat'ralized as any muskelunge that was ever cotch'd in Huron or about Mackinaw. If I can believe my eyes, Bourdon, there is the muzzle of a bear to be seen, jist under that heavy hemlock— here, where the bees seem thickest!"

"No doubt in the world," answered Le Bourdon, coolly; though he had taken the precaution to look to the priming of each of his pieces, as if he expected there would soon be occasion to use them. "But what was that you were about to say concernin' Blossom? It would not be civil to the young woman to overlook her, on account of a bear or two."

"You take it easy, *stran*ger—Bourdon, I should say— you take it easy! What I was about to say was this: that the whull lake country, and that's a wide stretch to foot it over, I know; but, big as it is, the whull lake country don't contain Blossom's equal. I'm her brother, and perhaps ought to be a little modest in sich matters; but I an't a bit, and let out jist what I think. Blossom's a di'mond, if there be di'monds on 'arth."

"And yonder is a bear, if there be bears on earth!"

exclaimed Le Bourdon, who was not a little amused with Gershom's account of his family, but who saw that the moment was now arrived when it would be necessary to substitute deeds for words. "There they come, in a drove, and they seem in earnest."

This was true enough. No less than eight bears, half of which, however, were quite young, came tumbling over the logs, and bounding up towards the fallen tree, as if charging the citadel of the bees by preconcert. Their appearance was the signal for a general rally of the insects, and by the time the foremost of the clumsy animals had reached the tree, the air above and around him was absolutely darkened by the cloud of bees that was collected to defend their treasures. Bruin trusted too much to the thickness of his hide and to the defences with which he was provided by nature, besides being too much incited by the love of honey, to regard the little heroes, but thrust his nose in at the hole, doubtless hoping to plunge it at once into the midst of a mass of sweets. A growl, a start backwards, and a flourishing of the fore-paws, with sundry bites in the air, at once announced that he had met with greater resistance than he had anticipated. In a minute all the bears were on their hind-legs, beating the air with their fore-paws, and nipping right and left with their jaws, in vigorous combat with their almost invisible foes. Instinct supplies the place of science, and spite of the hides and the long hair that covered them, the bees found the means of darting their stings into unprotected places, until the quadrupeds were fairly driven to rolling about on the grass in order to crush their assailants. This last process had some effect, a great many bees being destroyed by the energetic rollings and tumbling of the bears; but, as in the tide of battle, the place of those who fell were immediately supplied by fresh assailants, until numbers seemed likely to prevail over power, if not over discipline. At this critical instant, when the bears seemed fatigued with their nearly frantic saltations and violent blows upon nothing, Le Bourdon deemed it wise to bring his forces into the combat. Gershom having been apprised of the plan, both fired at the same instant. Each ball took effect ; one killing the largest of all the bears dead on the spot, while the other inflicted a grievous wound on the second. This success was immediately followed by a second discharge, wounding two more of the enemy, while Ben held the second barrel of his "shot-gun" in reserve. While the hurt animals were hobbling off, the men reloaded their pieces ; and by the time the last were ready to advance on the enemy, the ground was cleared of bears and bees alike, only two of the former remaining, of which one was already dead and the other dying. As for the bees, they followed their retreating enemies in a body, making a mistake that sometimes happens to still more intelligent beings : that of attributing to themselves and their own prowess a success that had been gained by others.

The bee-hunter and his friend now set themselves at work to provide a reception for the insects, the return of which might shortly be expected. The former lighted a fire, being always provided with the means, while Gershom brought dry wood. In less than five minutes a bright blaze was gleaming upwards ; and when the bees returned, as most of them soon did, they found this new enemy intrenched, as it might be, behind walls of flame. Thousands of the little creatures perished by means of this new invention of man, and the rest soon after were led away by their chiefs to seek some new deposit for the fruits of their industry.

CHAPTER IV.

" The sad butterfly,
Waving his lacker'd wings, darts quickly on,
And, by his free flight, counsels us to speed
For better lodgings, and a scene more sweet,
Than these dear borders offer us to-night."

SIMMS.

IT was noon before Ben and Gershom dared to commence the process of cutting and splitting the tree, in order to obtain the honey. Until then, the bees lingered around their fallen hive, and it would have been dangerous to venture beyond the smoke and heat in order to accomplish the task. It is true Le Bourdon possessed several secrets, of more or less virtue, to drive off the bees when disposed to assault him, but no one that was as certain as a good fire, backed by a dense column of vapor. Various plants are thought to be so very offensive to the insects that they avoid even their odor; and the bee-hunter had faith in one or two of them; but none of the right sort happened now to be near, and he was obliged to trust, first to powerful heat, and next to the vapor of damp wood.

As there were axes and wedges and a beetle in the canoe, and Gershom was as expert with those implements as a master of fencing is with his foil, to say nothing of the skill of Le Bourdon, the tree was soon laid open, and its ample stores of sweets exposed. In the course of the afternoon the honey was deposited in kegs, the kegs were transferred to the canoe, and the whole deposited in the *chienté*. The day had been one of toil, and when our two border-men sat down near the spring, to take their evening meal, each felt that his work was done.

"I believe this must be the last hive I line, this summer," said Le Bourdon, while eating his supper. "My luck has been good so far, but in troublesome times one had better not be too far from home. I am surprised, Waring, that you have ventured so far from your family, while the tidings are so gloomy."

"That's partly because you don't know *me*, and partly because you don't know *Dolly*. As for leaving hum, with anybody to kear for it, I should like to know who is more to the purpose than Dolly Waring? I have n't no idee that even bees would dare get upon *her*! If they did, they 'd soon get the worst on 't. Her tongue is all-powerful, to say nawthin' of her arm; and if the so'gers can only handle their muskets as she can handle a broom, there is no need of new regiments to carry on this war."

Now nothing could be more false than this character; but a drunkard has little regard to what he says.

"I am glad your garrison is so strong," answered the bee-hunter, thoughtfully; "but mine is too weak to stay any longer, out here in the openings. Whiskey Centre, I intend to break up, and to return to the settlements, before the redskins break loose in earnest. If you will stay, and lend me a hand to embark the honey and stores, and help to carry the canoe down the river, you shall be well paid for your trouble."

"Waal, I 'd about as lief do that as do anything else. Good jobs is scarce, out here in the wilderness, and when a body lights on one he ought to profit by it. I come up here thinkin' to meet you, for I heer'n tell from a voyager that you was a-beeing it, out in the openin's, and there's nawthin' in natur' that Dolly takes to with a greater relish than good wild honey. 'Try whiskey,' I 've told her a thousand times, 'and you 'll soon get to like *that* better than all the rest of creation;' but not a drop could I ever get her, or Blossom, to swallow. It 's true, that leaves so much the more for me; and I 'm a companionable crittur', and don't think I 've drunk as much as I want unless I take it society-like. That's one reason I 've taken so mightily to you, Bourdon; you 're not much at a pull, but you an't downright afeard of a jug, neither."

4

The bee-hunter was glad to hear that all the family had not this man's vice, for he now plainly foresaw that the accidents of his position must bring him and these strangers much in contact, for some weeks, at least. Le Bourdon, though not absolutely "afraid of a jug," as Whiskey Centre had expressed it, was decidedly a temperate man,—drinking but seldom, and never to excess. He too well knew the hazards by which he was surrounded, to indulge in this way, even had he the taste for it; but he had no taste that way, one small jug of brandy forming his supply for a whole season. In these days of exaggeration in all things, exaggeration in politics, in religion, in temperance, in virtue, and even in education, by putting "new wine into old bottles," that one little jug might have sufficed to give him a bad name; but five-and-thirty years ago men had more real independence than they now posess, and were not as much afraid of that *croquemitaine*, public opinion, as they are to-day. To be sure, it was little to Le Bourdon's taste to make a companion of such a person as Whiskey Centre; but there was no choice. The man was an utter stranger to him; and the only means he possessed of making sure that he did not carry off the property that lay so much at his mercy, was by keeping near him. With many men, the bee-hunter would have felt uneasy at being compelled, to remain alone with them in the woods; for cases in which one had murdered another, in order to get possession of the goods in these remote regions, were talked of among the other rumors of the borders; but Gershom had that in his air and manner that rendered Ben confident his delinquencies, at the most, would scarcely reach bloodshed. Pilfer he might; but murder was a crime which he did not appear at all likely to commit.

After supping in company, our two adventurers secured everything, and retiring to the *chienté*, they went to sleep. No material disturbance occurred, but the night passed in tranquillity; the bee-hunter merely experiencing some slight interruption to his slumbers from the unusual circumstance of having a companion. One as long accustomed to be alone as himself would naturally submit to some such sensation, our habits getting so completely the mastery as often to supplant even nature.

The following morning the bee-hunter commenced his preparations for a change of residence. Had he not been discovered, it is probable that the news received from the Chippewa would not have induced him to abandon his present position so early in the season ; but he thought the risk of remaining was too great, under all the circumstances. The Pottawattamie, in particular, was a subject of great distrust to him, and he believed it highly possible some of that old chief's tribe might be after his scalp ere many suns had risen. Gershom acquiesced in these opinions, and as soon as his brain was less under the influence of liquor that was common with him, he appeared to be quite happy in having it in his power to form a species of alliance, offensive and defensive, with a man of his own color and origin. Great harmony now prevailed between the two, Gershom improving vastly in all the better qualities the instant his intellect and feelings got to be a little released from the thralldom of the jug. His own immediate store of whiskey was quite exhausted, and Le Bourdon kept the place in which his own small stock of brandy was secured a profound secret. These glimmerings of returning intellect, and of reviving principles, are by no means unusual with the sot, thus proving that " so long as there is life there is hope," for the moral, as well as for the physical being. What was a little remarkable, Gershom grew less vulgar, even in his dialect, as he grew more sober, showing that in all respects he was becoming a greatly improved person.

The men were several hours in loading the canoe, not only all the stores and ammunition, but all the honey being transferred to it. The bee-hunter had managed to conceal his jug of brandy, reduced by this time to little more than a quart, within a empty powder-keg, into which he had crammed a beaver-skin or two, that he had taken, as it might be incidentally, in the course of his rambles. At length everything was removed and stowed in its proper place on board the capacious canoe, and Gershom expected an announcement on the part of Ben of his readiness to embark. But there still remained one duty to perform. The bee-hunter had killed a buck only the day before the opening of our narrative, and shouldering a quarter, he had left the remainder of the animal suspended from the branches of a tree near the place where it had been shot and cleaned. As venison might be needed before they could reach the mouth of the river, Ben deemed it advisable that he and Gershom should go and bring in the remainder of the carcass. The men started on this undertaking accordingly, leaving the canoe about two in the afternoon.

The distance between the spot where the deer had been killed and the *chienté* was about three miles; which was the reason why the bee-hunter had not brought home the entire animal the day he killed it,—the American woodsman often carrying his game great distances in preference to leaving it any length of time in the forest. In the latter case there is always danger from beasts of prey, which are drawn from afar by the scent of blood. Le Bourdon thought it possible they might now encounter wolves; though he had left the carcass of the deer so suspended as to place it beyond the reach of most of the animals of the wilderness. Each of the men, however, carried a rifle; and Hive was allowed to accompany them, by an act of grace on the part of his master.

For the first half hour nothing occurred out of the usual course of events. The bee-hunter had been conversing freely with his companion, who, he rejoiced to find, manifested far more common sense, not to say good sense, than he had previously shown; and from whom he was deriving information touching the number of vessels, and the other movements on the lakes, that he fancied might be of use to himself when he started for Detroit. While thus engaged, and when distant only a hundred rods from the place where he had left the venison, Le Bourdon was suddenly struck with the movements of the dog. Instead of doubling on his own tracks, and scenting right and left, as was the animal's wont, he was now advancing cautiously, with his head low, seemingly feeling his way with his nose, as if there was a strong taint in the wind.

"Sartain as my name is Gershom," exclaimed Waring, just after he and Ben had come to a halt, in order to look around them—"yonder is an Injin! The crittur' is seated at the foot of the large oak—hereaway, more to the right of the dog, and Hive has struck his scent. The fellow is asleep, with his rifle across his lap, and can't have much dread of wolves or bears!"

"I see him," answered Le Bourdon, "and am as much surprised as grieved to find him there. It is a little remarkable that I should have so many visitors, just at this time, on my hunting-ground, when I never had any at all before yesterday. It gives a body an uncomfortable feeling, Waring, to live so much in a crowd! Well, well—I'm about to move, and it will matter little twenty-four hours hence."

"The chap's a Winnebagoe by his paint," added Gershom; "but let's go up and give him a call."

The bee-hunter assented to this proposal, remarking as they moved forward, that he did not think the stranger of the tribe just named; though he admitted that the use of paint was so general and loose among these warriors as to render it difficult to decide.

"The crittur' sleeps soundly!" exclaimed Gershom, stopping within ten yards of the Indian, to take another look at him.

"He'll never awake," put in the bee-hunter, solemnly; "the man is dead. See; there is blood on the side of his head, and a rifle-bullet has left its hole there."

Even while speaking, the bee-hunter advanced, and raising a sort of shawl, that once had been used as an ornament, and which had last been thrown carelessly over the head of its late owner, he exposed the well-known features of Elksfoot, the Pottawattamie, who had left them little more than twenty-four hours before! The warrior had been shot by a rifle-bullet directly through the temple, and had been scalped. The powder had been taken from his horn, and the bullets from the pouch; but beyond this he had not been plundered. The body was carefully placed against a tree, in a sitting attitude, the rifle was laid across

its legs, and there it had been left, in the centre of the openings, to become food for beasts of prey, and to have its bones
bleached by the snows and rains !

The bee-hunter shuddered as he gazed at this fearful
memorial of the violence against which even a wilderness
could afford no sufficient protection. That Pigeonswing
had slain his late fellow-guest, Le Bourdon had no doubt,
and he sickened at the thought. Although he had himself
dreaded a good deal from the hostility of the Pottawattamie, he could have wished this deed undone. That there
was a jealous distrust of each other between the two Indians had been sufficiently apparent ; but the bee-hunter
could not have imagined that it would so soon lead to results
as terrible as these !

After examining the body, and noting the state of things
around it, the men proceeded, deeply impressed with the
necessity, not only of their speedy removal, but of their
standing by each other in that remote region, now that
violence had so clearly broken out among the tribes. The
bee-hunter had taken a strong liking to the Chippewa, and
he regretted so much the more to think that he had done
this deed. It was true that such a state of things might
exist as to justify an Indian warrior, agreeably to his own
notions, in taking the life of any one of a hostile tribe ;
but Le Bourdon wished it had been otherwise. A man of
gentle and peaceable disposition himself, though of a profoundly enthusiastic temperament in his own peculiar way,
he had ever avoided those scenes of disorder and bloodshed which are of so frequent occurrence in the forest and
on the prairies ; and this was actually the first instance in
which he had ever beheld a human body that had fallen by
human hands. Gershom had seen more of the peculiar
life of the frontiers than his companion, in consequence of
having lived so closely in contact with the " fire-water " ;
but even *he* was greatly shocked with the suddenness and
nature of the Pottawattamie's end.

No attempt was made to bury the remains of Elksfoot,
inasmuch as our adventurers had no tools fit for such a
purpose, and any merely superficial interment would have

been a sort of invitation to the wolves to dig the body up
again.

"Let him lean ag'in the tree," said Waring, as they
moved on towards the spot where the carcass of the deer
was left, "and I'll engage nothin' touches him. There's
that about the face of man, Bourdon, that skears the
beasts; and if a body can only muster courage to stare
them full in the eye, one single human can drive before
him a whull pack of wolves."

"I've heard as much," returned the bee-hunter, "but
should not like to be the 'human' to try the experiment.
That the face of man may have terrors for a beast, I think
likely; but hunger would prove more than a match for such
fear. Yonder is our venison, Waring; safe where I left it."

The carcass of the deer was divided, and each man
shouldering his burden, the two returned to the river, taking care to avoid the path that led by the body of the
dead Indian. As both labored with much earnestness,
everything was soon ready, and the canoe speedily left the
shore. The Kalamazoo is not in general a swift and turbulent stream, though it has a sufficient current to carry
away its waters without any appearance of sluggishness.
Of course, this character is not uniform, reaches occurring
in which the placid water is barely seen to move; and
others, again, are found, in which something like rapids,
and even falls, appear. But on the whole, and more especially in the part of the stream where it was, the canoe
had little to disturb it, as it glided easily down, impelled by
a light stroke of the paddle.

The bee-hunter did not abandon his station without regret. He had chosen a most agreeable site for his *chienté*
consulting air, shade, water, verdure, and groves, as well as
the chances of obtaining honey. In his regular pursuit he
had been unusually fortunate; and the little pile of kegs
in the centre of his canoe was certainly a grateful sight to
his eyes. The honey gathered this season, moreover, had
proved to be of an unusually delicious flavor, affording the
promise of high prices and ready sales. Still, the bee-
hunter left the place with profound regret. He loved his

calling; he loved solitude to a morbid degree, perhaps; and he loved the gentle excitement that naturally attended his "bee-linings," his discoveries, and his gains. Of all the pursuits that are more or less dependent on the chances of the hunt and the field, that of the bee-hunter is one of the most quiet and placid enjoyment. He has the stirring motives of uncertainty and doubt, without the disturbing qualities of bustle and fatigue; and while his exercise is sufficient for health, and for the pleasures of the open air, it is seldom of a nature to weary or unnerve. Then the study of the little animal that is to be watched, and, if the reader will, plundered, is not without a charm for those who delight in looking into the wonderful arcana of nature. So great was the interest that Le Bourdon sometimes felt in his little companions that, on three several occasions that very summer, he had spared hives after having found them, because he had ascertained that they were composed of young bees, and had not yet got sufficiently colonized to render a new swarming more than a passing accident. With all this kindness of feeling towards his victims, Boden had nothing of the transcendental folly that usually accompanies the sentimentalism of the exaggerated, but his feelings and impulses were simple and direct, though so often gentle and humane. He knew that the bee, like all other inferior animals of creation, was placed at the disposition of man, and did not scruple to profit by the power thus beneficently bestowed, though he exercised it gently, and with proper discrimination between its use and its abuse.

Neither of the men toiled much as the canoe floated down the stream. Very slight impulses served to give their buoyant craft a reasonably swift motion, and the current itself was a material assistant. These circumstances gave an opportunity for conversation as the canoe glided onward.

"A'ter all," suddenly exclaimed Waring, who had been examining the pile of kegs for some time in silence—"a'ter all, Bourdon, your trade is an oncommon one! A most extr'ornary and oncommon callin'!"

"More so, think you, Gershom, than swallowing whiskey, morning, noon, and night?" answered the bee-hunter, with a quiet smile.

"Ay, but that's not a rig'lar callin'; only a likin'! Now a man may have a likin' to a hundred things in which he don't deal. I set nothin' down as a business which a man don't live by."

"Perhaps you're right, Waring. More die by whiskey than live by whiskey."

Whiskey Centre seemed struck with this remark, which was introduced so aptly, and was uttered so quietly. He gazed earnestly at his companion for near a minute, ere he attempted to resume the discourse.

"Blossom has often said as much as this," he then slowly rejoined; "and even Dolly has prophesized the same."

The bee-hunter observed that an impression had been made, and he thought it wisest to let the reproof already administered produce its effect, without endeavoring to add to its power. Waring sat with his chin on his breast, in deep thought, while his companion, for the first time since they had met, examined the features and aspect of the man. At first sight, Whiskey Centre certainly offered little that was inviting; but a closer study of his countenance showed that he had the remains of a singularly handsome man. Vulgar as were his forms of speech, coarse and forbidding as his face had become, through the indulgence which was his bane, there were still traces of this truth. His complexion had once been fair almost to effeminacy, his cheeks ruddy with health, and his blue eye bright and full of hope. His hair was light; and all these peculiarities strongly denoted his Saxon origin. It was not so much Anglo-Saxon as Americo-Saxon, that was to be seen in the physical outlines and hues of this nearly self-destroyed being. The heaviness of feature, the ponderousness of limb and movement, had all long disappeared from his race, most probably under the influence of climate, and his nose was prominent and graceful in outline, while his mouth and chin might have passed for having been under the chisel of some distinguished sculptor. It was, in truth, painful to

examine that face, steeped as it was in liquor, and fast
losing the impress left by nature. As yet, the body retained
most of its power, the enemy having insidiously entered the
citadel, rather than having actually subdued it. The bee-
hunter sighed as he gazed at his moody companion, and
wondered whether Blossom had aught of this marvellous
comeliness of countenance, without its revolting accompani-
ments.

All that afternoon, and the whole of the night that succeeded, did the canoe float downward with the current.
Occasionally, some slight obstacle to its progress would present itself; but, on the whole, its advance was steady and
certain. As the river necessarily followed the formation
of the land, it was tortuous and irregular in its course,
though its general direction was towards the northwest or
west a little northerly. The river bottoms being much
more heavily "timbered"—to use a woodsman term—
than the higher grounds, there was little of the park-like
"openings" on its immediate banks, though distant
glimpses were had of many a glade and many a charming
grove.

As the canoe moved towards its point of destination, the
conversation did not lag between the bee-hunter and his
companion. Each gave the other a sort of history of his
life; for, now that the jug was exhausted, Gershom could
talk, not only rationally, but with clearness and force. Vulgar he was, and, as such, uninviting and often repulsive;
still his early education partook of that peculiarity of New
England which, if it does not make her children absolutely
all they are apt to believe themselves to be, seldom leaves
them in the darkness of a besotted ignorance. As usually
happens with this particular race, Gershom had acquired a
good deal for a man of his class in life; and this information, added to native shrewdness, enabled him to maintain
his place in the dialogue with a certain degree of credit.
He had a very lively perception—fancied or real—of all
the advantages of being born in the land of the Puritans,
deeming everything that came of the great "Blarney
Stone" superior to everything else of the same nature else-

where; and, while much disposed to sneer and rail at all other parts of the country, just as much indisposed to "take" as disposed to "give." Ben Boden soon detected this weakness in his companion's character, a weakness so very general as scarce to need being pointed out to any observant man, and which is almost inseparable from half-way intelligence and provincial self-admiration; and Ben was rather inclined to play on it, whenever Gershom laid himself a little more open than common on the subject. On the whole, however, the communications were amicable; and the dangers of the wilderness rendering the parties allies, they went their way with an increasing confidence in each other's support. Gershom, now that he was thoroughly sober, could impart much to Ben that was useful; while Ben knew a great deal that even his companion, coming as he did from the chosen people, was not sorry to learn. As has been already intimated, each communicated to the other, in the course of this long journey on the river, an outline of his past life.

The history of Gershom Waring was one of every-day occurrence. He was born of a family in humble circumstances in Massachusetts, a community in which, however, none are so very humble as to be beneath the paternal watchfulness of the state. The common schools had done their duty by him; while, according to his account of the matter, his only sister had fallen into the hands of a female relative, who was enabled to impart an instruction slightly superior to that which is to be had from the servants of the public. After a time, the death of this relative, and the marriage of Gershom, brought the brother and sister together again, the last still quite young. From this period the migratory life of the family commenced. Previously to the establishment of manufactories within her limits, New England systematically gave forth her increase to the states west and south of her own territories. A portion of this increase still migrates, and will probably long continue so to do; but the tide of young women, which once flowed so steadily from that region, would now seem to have turned, and is setting back in a flood of "factory-girls." But the Warings

lived at too early a day to feel the influence of such a
pass of civilization, and went West, almost as a matter of course. With the commencement of his migratory
life, Gershom began to " dissipate," as it has got to be matter of convention to term " drinking." Fortunately, Mrs.
Waring had no children, thus lessening in a measure the
privations to which those unlucky females were obliged to
submit. When Gershom left his birth-place he had a sum
of money exceeding a thousand dollars in amount, the united
means of himself and sister ; but by the time he had reached
Detroit it was reduced to less than a hundred. Several years,
however, had been consumed by the way, the habits growing worse and the money vanishing, as the family went
farther and farther towards the skirts of society. At length
Gershom attached himself to a sutler, who was going up to
Michillimackinac with a party of troops ; and finally he left
that place to proceed, in a canoe of his own, to the head
of Lake Michigan, where was a post on the present site of
Chicago, which was then known as Fort Dearborn.

In quitting Mackinac for Chicago, Waring had no very
settled plan. His habits had completely put him out of
favor at the former place ; and a certain restlessness urged
him to penetrate still farther into the wilderness. In all his
migrations and wanderings the two devoted females followed
his fortunes ; the one because she was his wife, the other
because she was his sister. When the canoe reached the
mouth of the Kalamazoo, a gale of wind drove it into the
river ; and finding a deserted cabin, ready built, to receive
him, Gershom landed, and had been busy with the rifle for
the last fortnight, the time he had been on shore. Hearing,
from some *voyageurs* who had gone down the lake, that a
bee-hunter was up the river, he had followed the stream in
its windings until he fell in with Le Bourdon.

Such is an outline of the account which Whiskey Centre
gave of himself. It is true, he said very little of his propensity to drink, but this his companion was enabled to conjecture from the context of his narrative, as well as from
what he had seen. It was very evident to the bee-hunter
that the plans of both parties for the summer were about to

be seriously deranged by the impending hostilities, and that some decided movement might be rendered necessary, even for the protection of their lives.

This much he communicated to Gershom, who heard his opinions with interest, and a concern in behalf of his wife and sister that at least did some credit to his heart. For the first time in many months, indeed, Gershom was now *perfectly* sober, a circumstance that was solely owing to his having had no access to liquor for eight-and-forty hours. With the return of a clear head, came juster notions of the dangers and difficulties in which he had involved the two self-devoted women who had accompanied him so far, and who really seemed ready to follow him in making the circuit of the earth.

"It's troublesome times," exclaimed Whiskey Centre, when his companion had just ended one of his strong and lucid statements of the embarrassments that might environ them ere they could get back to the settled portions of the country—"it's troublesome times, truly ! I see all you would say, Bourdon, and wonder I ever got my foot so deep into it, without thinkin' of all, beforehand ! The best on us will make mistakes, hows'ever, and I suppose I've been called on to make mine, as well as another."

"My trade speaks for itself," returned the bee-hunter, "and any man can see why one who looks for bees must come where they're to be found ; but I will own, Gershom, that your speculation lies a little beyond my understanding. Now you tell me you have two full barrels of whiskey—"

"Had, Bourdon—*had*—one of them is pretty nearly half used, I am afeard."

"Well, *had*, until you began to be your own customer. But here you are, squatted at the mouth of the Kalamazoo, with a barrel and a *half* of liquor, and nobody but yourself to drink it ! Where the profits are to come from, exceeds Pennsylvany calculations ; perhaps a Yankee can tell."

"You forget the Injins. I met a man at Mackinaw who only took out in his canoe *one* barrel, and he brought in skins enough to set up a grocery, at Detroit. But I was on the trail of the soldiers, and meant to make a business on 't, at

Fort Dearborn. What between the soldiers and the redskins, a man might sell gallons a day, and at fair prices.''

"It's a sorry business at the best, Whiskey; and now
you're fairly sober, if you'll take my advice you'll remain
so. Why not make up your mind, like a man, and vow
you'll never touch another drop.''

" Maybe I will, when these two barrels is emptied—I've
often thought of doin' some sich matter ; and ag'in and ag'in
has Dolly and Blossom advised me to fall into the plan ; but
it's hard to give up old habits, all at once. If I could only
taper off on a pint a day, for a year or so, I think I might
come round in time. I know as well as you do, Bourdon,
that sobriety is a good thing, and dissipation a bad thing ;
but it's hard to give up all, at once.''

Lest the instructed reader should wonder at a man's using
the term "dissipation" in a wilderness, it may be well to
explain that, in common American parlance, "dissipation"
has got to mean "drunkenness." Perhaps half of the whole
country, if told that a man, or a woman, might be exceedingly dissipated and never swallow anything stronger than
water, would stoutly deny the justice of applying the word
to such a person. This perversion of the meaning of a very
common term has probably arisen from the circumstance
that there is very little dissipation in the country that is not
connected with hard drinking. A dissipated woman is a
person almost unknown in America ; or, when the word is
applied, it means a very different degree of misspending of
time from that which is understood by the use of the same reproach in older and more sophisticated states of society. The
majority rules in this country, and with the majority
excess usually takes this particular aspect ; refinement having very little connection with the dissipation of the masses
anywhere.

The excuses of his companion, however, caused Le
Bourdon to muse, more than might otherwise have been
the case, on Whiskey Centre's condition. Apart from all
considerations connected with the man's own welfare, and
the happiness of his family, there were those which were
inseparable from the common safety, in the present state of

the country. Boden was a man of much decision and firmness of character, and he was clear-headed as to causes and consequences. The practice of living alone had induced in him the habits of reflection ; and the self-reliance produced by his solitary life, a life of which he was fond almost to a passion, caused him to decide warily, but to act promptly. As they descended the river together, therefore, he went over the whole of Gershom Waring's case and prospects with great impartiality and care, and settled in his own mind what ought to be done, as well as the mode of doing it. He kept his own counsel, however, discussing all sorts of subjects that were of interest to men in their situation, as they floated down the stream, avoiding any recurrence to this theme, which was possibly of more importance to them both, just then, than any other that could be presented.

CHAPTER V.

"He was a wight of high renown,
And thou art but of low degree :
'T is pride that pulls the country down—
Then take thine auld cloak about thee."

SHAKESPEARE.

THE canoe did not reach the mouth of the river until near evening of the third day of its navigation. It was not so much the distance, though that was considerable, as it was the obstacles that lay in the way, which brought the travellers to the end of their journey at so late a period. As they drew nearer and nearer to the place where Gershom had left his wife and sister, Le Bourdon detected in his companion signs of an interest in the welfare of the two last, as well as a certain feverish uneasiness lest all might not be well with them, that said something in favor of his heart, whatever might be urged against his prudence and care in leaving them alone in so exposed a situation.

"I 'm afeard a body don't think as much as he ought to do when liquor is in him," said Whiskey Centre, just as the canoe doubled the last point, and the hut came into view ; "else I never *could* have left two women by themselves in so lonesome a place. God be praised ! there is the *chienté* at any rate ; and there's a smoke comin' out of it, if my eyes don't deceive me ! Look, Bourdon, for I can scarcely see, at all."

"There is the house ; and, as you say, there is certainly a smoke rising from it."

"There's comfort in that !" exclaimed the truant husband and brother, with a sigh that seemed to relieve a very

64

loaded breast. "Yes, there's comfort in that! If there's a fire, there must be them that lighted it; and a fire at this season, too, says there's somethin' to eat. I should be sorry, Bourdon, to think I'd left the women folks without food; though, to own the truth, I don't remember whether I did or not."

"The man who drinks, Gershom, has commonly but a very poor memory."

"That's true—yes, I'll own that; and I wish it warn't as true as it is; but reason and strong drink do *not* travel far in company—"

Gershom suddenly ceased speaking; dropping his paddle like one beset by a powerless weakness. The bee-hunter saw that he was overcome by some unexpected occurrence, and that the man's feelings were keenly connected with the cause, whatever that might be. Looking eagerly around in quest of the explanation, Le Bourdon saw a female standing on a point of land that commanded a view of the river and its banks for a considerable distance, unequivocally watching the approach of the canoe.

"There she is," said Gershom, in a subdued tone, "that's Dolly; and there she has been, I'll engage, half the time of my absence, waitin' to get the first glimpse of my miserable body, as it came back to her. Sich is woman, Bourdon; and God forgive me if I have ever forgotten their natur', when I was bound to remember it. But we all have our weak moments, at times, and I trust mine will not be accounted ag'in me more than them of other men."

"This is a beautiful sight, Gershom, and it almost makes me your friend! The man for whom a woman can feel so much concern—that a woman—nay, women; for you tell me your sister is one of the family—but the man whom *decent* women can follow to a place like this, must have some good p'ints about him. That woman is a weepin'; and it must be for joy at your return."

"'T would be just like Dolly to do so—she's done it before, and would be likely to do so agi'n," answered Gershom, nearly choked by the effort he made to speak without betraying his own emotion. "Put the canoe into the p'int,

5

and let me land there. I must go up and say a kind word to poor Dolly; while you can paddle on, and let Blossom know I 'm near at hand.''

The bee-hunter complied in silence, casting curious glances upward at the woman while doing so, in order to ascertain what sort of a female Whiskey Centre could possibly have for a wife. To his surprise, Dorothy Waring was not only decently, but she was neatly clad, appearing as if she had studiously attended to her personal appearance, in the hope of welcoming her wayward and unfortunate husband back to his forest home. This much Le Bourdon saw, by a hasty glance, as his companion landed, for a feeling of delicacy prevented him from taking a longer look at the woman. As Gershom ascended the bank to meet his wife, Le Bourdon paddled on, and landed just below the grove in which was the *chienté*. It might have been his long exclusion from all of the other sex, and most especially from that portion of it which retains its better looks, but the being which now met the bee-hunter appeared to him to belong to another world, rather than to that in which he habitually dwelt. As this was Margery Waring, who was almost uniformly called Blossom by her acquaintances, and who is destined to act an important part in this legend of the "openings," it may be well to give a brief description of her age, attire, and personal appearance at the moment when she was first seen by Le Bourdon.

In complexion, color of the hair, and outline of face, Margery Waring bore a strong family resemblance to her brother. In spite of exposure, and the reflection of the sun's rays from the water of the lake, however, *her* skin was of a clear, transparent white, such as one might look for in a drawing-room, but hardly expect to find in a wilderness; while the tint of her lips, cheeks, and, in a diminished degree, of her chin and ears, were such as one who wielded a pencil might long endeavor to catch without succeeding. Her features had the chiselled outline which was so remarkable in her brother; while in *her* countenance, in addition to the softened expression of her sex and years, there was nothing to denote any physical or moral infirmity, to form a drawback to its witchery and regularity. Her eyes were blue, and her hair as near golden as human tresses well could be. Exercise, a life of change, and of dwelling much in the open air, had given to this unusually charming girl, not only health, but its appearance. Still, she was in no respect coarse, or had anything in the least about her that indicated her being accustomed to toil, with some slight exception in her hands, perhaps, which were those of a girl who did not spare herself when there was an opportunity to be of use. In this particular, the vagrant life of her brother had possibly been of some advantage to her, as it had prevented her being much employed in the ordinary toil of her condition in life. Still, Margery Waring had that happy admixture of delicacy and physical energy which is, perhaps, oftener to be met in the American girl of her class than in the girl of almost any other nation ; and far oftener than in the young American of her sex who is placed above the necessity of labor.

As a stranger approached her, the countenance of this fair creature expressed both surprise and satisfaction ; surprise that any one should have been met by Gershom in such a wilderness, and satisfaction that the stranger proved to be a white man, and seemingly one who did not drink.

"You are Blossom," said the bee-hunter, taking the hand of the half-reluctant girl in a way so respectful and friendly that she could not refuse it, even while she doubted the propriety of thus receiving an utter stranger—" the Blossom of whom Gershom Waring speaks so often, and so affectionately ? "

" You are then my brother's friend," answered Margery, smiling so sweetly that Le Bourdon gazed on her with delight. " We are *so* glad that he has come back ! Five terrible nights have sister and I been here alone, and we have believed every bush was a redman ! "

"That danger is over now, Blossom ; but there is still an enemy near you that must be overcome."

"An enemy ! There is no one here but Dolly and myself. No one has been near us since Gershom went after the bee-hunter, whom we heard was out in the openings. Are you that bee-hunter?"

"I am, beautiful Blossom; and I tell you there is an enemy here, in your cabin, that must be looked to."

"We fear no enemies but the redmen, and we have seen none of them since we reached this river. What is the name of the enemy you so dread, and where is he to be found?"

"His name is Whiskey, and he is kept somewhere in this hut, in casks. Show me the place, that I may destroy him before his friend comes to his assistance."

A gleam of bright intelligence flashed into the face of the beautiful young creature. First she reddened almost to scarlet; then her face became pale as death. Compressing her lips intensely, she stood irresolute—now gazing at the pleasing and seemingly well-disposed stranger before her, now looking earnestly towards the still distant forms of her brother and sister, which were slowly advancing in the direction of the cabin.

"Dare you?" Margery at length asked, pointing towards her brother.

"I dare; he is now quite sober, and may be reasoned with. For the sake of us all, let us profit by this advantage."

"He keeps the liquor in two casks that you will find under the shed, behind the hut."

This said, the girl covered her face with both her hands, and sunk on a stool, as if afraid to be a witness of that which was to follow. As for Le Bourdon, he did not delay a moment, but passed out of the cabin by a second door that opened in its rear. There were the two barrels, and by their side an axe. His first impulse was to dash in the heads of the casks where they stood; but a moment's reflection told him that the odor, so near the cabin, would be unpleasant to every one, and might have a tendency to exasperate the owner of the liquor. He cast about him, therefore, for the means of removing the casks, in order to stave them, at a distance from the dwelling.

Fortunately the cabin of Whiskey Centre stood on the brow of a sharp descent, at the bottom of which ran a brawling brook. At another moment Le Bourdon would have thought of saving the barrels ; but time pressed, and he could not delay. Seizing the barrel next to him, he rolled it without difficulty to the brow of the declivity, and set it off with a powerful shove of his foot. It was the half empty cask, and away it went, the liquor it contained washing about as it rolled over and over, until hitting a rock about half way down the declivity, the hoops gave way, when the staves went over the little precipice, and the water of the stream was tumbling through all that remained of the cask at the next instant. A slight exclamation of delight behind him caused the bee-hunter to look round, and he saw that Margery was watching his movements with an absorbed interest. Her smile was one of joy, not unmingled with terror ; and she rather whispered than said aloud, "The other, the other—*that* is full—be quick ; there is no time to lose." The bee-hunter seized the second cask and rolled it towards the brow of the rocks. It was not quite as easily handled as the other barrel, but his strength sufficed, and it was soon bounding down the declivity after its companion. This second cask hit the same rock as the first, whence it leaped off the precipice, and, aided by its greater momentum, it was literally dashed in pieces at its base.

Not only was this barrel broken into fragments, but its hoops and staves were carried down the torrent, driving before them those of the sister cask, until the whole were swept into the lake, which was some distance from the cabin.

"That job is well done !" exclaimed Le Bourdon, when the last fragment of the wreck was taken out of sight. "No man will ever turn himself into a beast by means of *that* liquor."

"God be praised !" murmured Margery. "He is *so* different, stranger, when he has been drinking, from what he is when he has not ! You have been sent by Providence to do us this good."

"I can easily believe that, for it is so with us all. But you must not call me stranger, sweet Margery ; for, now that you and I have this secret between us, I am a stranger no longer."

The girl smiled and blushed ; then she seemed anxious to ask a question. In the meantime they left the shed, and took seats, in waiting for the arrival of Gershom and his wife. It was not long ere the last entered ; the countenance of the wife beaming with a satisfaction she made no effort to conceal. Dolly was not as beautiful as her sister-in-law ; still, she was a comely woman, though one who had been stricken by sorrow. She was still young, and might have been in the pride of her good looks had it not been for the manner in which she had grieved over the fall of Gershom. The joy that gladdens a woman's heart, however, was now illuminating her countenance, and she welcomed Le Bourdon most cordially, as if aware that he had been of service to her husband. For months she had not seen Gershom quite himself until that evening.

"I have told Dolly all our adventur's, Bourdon," cried Gershom, as soon as the brief greetings were over, "and she tells me all 's right, hereabouts. Three canoe-loads of Injins passed alongshore, goin' up the lake, she tells me, this very a'ternoon ; but they did n't see the smoke, the fire bein' out, and must have thought the hut empty ; if, indeed, they knew anythin' of it, at all."

"The last is the most likely," remarked Margery ; "for I watched them narrowly from the beeches on the shore, and there was no pointing, or looking up, as would have happened had there been any one among them who could show the others a cabin. Houses an't so plenty, in this part of the country, that travellers pass without turning round to look at them. An Injin has curiosity as well as a white man, though he manages so often to conceal it."

"Did n't you say, Blossom, that one of the canoes was much behind the others, and that a warrior in that canoe *did* look up towards this grove, as if searching for the cabin?" asked Dorothy.

"Either it was so, or my fears made it *seem* so. The

two canoes that passed first were well filled with Injins, each having eight in it ; while the one that came last held but four warriors. They were a mile apart, and the last canoe seemed to be trying to overtake the others. I did think that nothing but their haste prevented the men in the last canoe from landing ; but my fears may have made that seem so that was not so.''

As the cheek of the charming girl flushed with excitement, and her face became animated, Margery appeared marvellously handsome ; more so, the bee-hunter fancied, than any other female he had ever before seen. But her words impressed him quite as much as her looks ; for he at once saw the importance of such an event, to persons in their situation. The wind was rising on the lake, and it was ahead for the canoes ; should the savages feel the necessity of making a harbor they might return to the mouth of the Kalamazoo ; a step that would endanger all their lives, in the event of these Indians proving to belong to those whom there was now reason to believe were in British pay. In times of peace, the intercourse between the whites and the redmen was usually amicable, and seldom led to violence, unless through the effects of liquor ; but, a price being placed on scalps, a very different state of things might be anticipated, as a consequence of the hostilities. This was then a matter to be looked to ; and, as evening was approaching, no time was to be lost.

The shores of Michigan are generally low, nor are harbors either numerous or very easy of access. It would be difficult, indeed, to find, in any other part of the world, so great an extent of coast that possesses so little protection for the navigator as that of this very lake. There are a good many rivers, it is true, but usually they have bars, and are not easy of entrance. This is the reason why that very convenient glove, the Constitution, which can be made to fit any hand, has been discovered to have an extra finger in it, which points out a mode by which the Federal Government can create ports wherever nature has forgotten to perform this beneficent office. It is a little extraordinary that the fingers of so many of the great "expounders" turn out to be "thumbs," however; exhibiting clumsiness rather than that adroit lightness which usually characterizes the dexterity of men who are in the habit of rummaging other people's pockets for their own especial purposes. It must be somewhat up-hill work to persuade any disinterested and clearheaded man that a political power to "regulate commerce" goes the length of making harbors,—the one being in a great measure a moral, while the other is exclusively a physical agency,—any more than it goes the length of making warehouses and cranes and carts and all the other physical implements for carrying on trade. Now what renders all this "thumbing" of the Constitution so much the more absurd is the fact that the very generous compact interested does furnish a means by which the poverty of ports on the great lakes may be remedied, without making any more unnecessary rents in the great national glove. Congress clearly possesses the power to create and maintain a navy, which includes the power to create all sorts of necessary physical appliances; and, among others, places of refuge for that navy, should they be actually needed. As a vessel of war requires a harbor, and usually a better harbor than a merchant-vessel, it strikes us the "expounders" would do well to give this thought a moment's attention. Behind it will be found the most unanswerable argument in favor of the light-houses, too.

But to return to the narrative: The Kalamazoo could be entered by canoes, though it offered no very available shelter for a vessel of any size. There was no other shelter for the savages for several miles to the southward; and, should the wind increase, of which there were strong indications, it was not only possible, but highly probable, that the canoes would return. According to the account of the females, they had passed only two hours before, and the breeze had been gradually gathering strength ever since. It was not unlikely, indeed, that the attention paid to the river by the warrior in the last canoe may have had reference to this very state of the weather, and his haste to overtake his companions been connected with a desire to induce them to seek a shelter. All this presented itself to the bee-hunter's mind at once, and it was discussed between the members of the party freely, and not without some grave apprehensions.

There was one elevated point—elevated comparatively if not in a very positive sense—whence the eye could command a considerable distance along the lake shore. Thither Margery now hastened to look after the canoes. Boden accompanied her; and together they proceeded, side by side, with a new-born but lively and increasing confidence, that was all the greater in consequence of their possessing a common secret.

"Brother must be much better than he was," the girl observed, as they hurried on, "for he has not once been into the shed to look at the barrels. Before he went into the openings, he never entered the house without drinking; and sometimes he would raise the cup to his mouth as often as three times in the first half-hour. Now he does not seem even to think of it!"

"It may be well that he can find nothing to put into his cup, should he fall into his old ways. One is never sure of a man of such habits until he is placed entirely out of harm's way."

"Gershom is such a different being when he has not been drinking!" rejoined the sister, in a touching manner. "We love him, and strive to do all we can to keep him up, but it *is* hard."

"I am surprised that *you* should have come into this wilderness with any one of bad habits!"

"Why not? He is my brother, and I have no parents— he is all to me: and what would become of Dorothy if I were to quit her, too? She has lost most of her friends, since Gershom fell into these ways, and it would quite break her heart, did I desert her."

"All this speaks well for you, pretty Margery, but it is not the less surprising—ah, there is my canoe in plain sight of all who enter the river; *that* must be concealed, Injins or no Injins."

"It is only a step farther to the place where we can get a lookout. Just there, beneath the burr oak. Hours and hours have I sat on that spot, with my sewing, while Gershom was gone into the openings.''

"And Dolly—where was she while you were here?''

"Poor Dolly—I do think she passed quite half her time up at the beech-tree, where you first saw her, looking if brother was not coming home. It is a cruel thing to a wife to have a truant husband!''

"Which I hope may never be your case, pretty Margery, and which I think never *can*.''

Margery did not answer: but the speech must have been heard, uttered as it was in a much lower tone of voice than the young man had hitherto used; for the charming maiden looked down and blushed. Fortunately, the two now soon arrived at the tree, and their conversation naturally reverted to the subject which had brought them there. Three canoes were in sight, close in with the land, but so distant as to render it for some time doubtful which way they were moving. At first the bee-hunter said that they were still going slowly to the southward; but he habitually carried his little glass, and, on levelling that, it was quite apparent that the savages were paddling before the wind, and making for the mouth of the river. This was a very grave fact; and as Blossom flew to communicate the fact to her brother and his wife, Le Bourdon moved towards his own canoe, and looked about for a place of concealment.

Several considerations had to be borne in mind, in disposing of the canoes, for that of Gershom was to be secreted as well as that of the bee-hunter. A tall aquatic plant, that is termed wild rice, and which we suppose to be the ordinary rice-plant unimproved by tillage, grows spontaneously about the mouths and on the flats of most of the rivers of the part of Michigan of which we are writing; as, indeed, it is to be found in nearly all the shallow waters of those regions. There was a good deal of this rice at hand; and the bee-hunter, paddling his own canoe and towing the other, entered this vegetable thicket, choosing a channel that had been formed by some accident of nature, and which wound through the herbage in a way soon to conceal all that came within its limits. These channels were not only numerous, but exceedingly winding; and the bee-hunter had no sooner brought his canoes to the firm ground and fastened them there, than he ascended a tree, and studied the windings of these narrow passages, until he had got a general idea of their direction and characters. This precaution taken, he hurried back to the hut.

"Well, Gershom, have you settled on the course to be taken?" were the first words uttered by the bee-hunter when he rejoined the family of Whiskey Centre.

"We have n't," answered the husband. "Sister begs us to quit the *chienté*, for the Indians must soon be here; but wife seems to think that she *must* be safe, now I 'm at home ag'in."

"Then wife is wrong. and sister is right. If you will take my advice, you will hide all your effects in the woods, and quit the cabin as soon as possible. The Injins cannot fail to see this habitation, and will be certain to destroy all they find in it, and that they do not carry off. Besides, the discovery of the least article belonging to a white man will set them on our trail; for scalps will soon bear a price at Montreal. In half an hour all that is here can be removed into the thicket that is luckily so near; and by putting out the fire with care, and using proper caution, we may give the place such a deserted look that the savages will suspect nothing."

"If they enter the river, Bourdon, they will not 'camp out with a wigman so near by; and should they come here, what is to prevent their seein' the foot-prints we shall leave behind us?"

"The night, and that only. Before morning their own footsteps will be so plenty as to deceive them. Luckily we all wear moccasins, which is a great advantage just now. But every moment is precious, and we should be stirring. Let the women take the beds and bedding, while you and I shoulder this chest. Up it goes, and away with it!"

Gersham had got to be so much under his companion's influence that he complied, though his mind suggested various objections to the course taken, to which his tongue gave utterance as they busied themselves in this task. The effects of Whiskey Centre had been gradually diminishing in quantity, as well as in value, for the last three years, and were now of no great amount, in any sense. Still, there were two chests, one large and one small. The last contained all that a generous regard for the growing wants of the family had left to Margery; while the first held the joint wardrobes of the husband and wife, with a few other articles that were considered as valuable. Among other things were half a dozen of very thin silver tea-spoons, which had fallen to Gershom on a division of the family plate. The other six were carefully wrapped up in paper and put in the till of Margery's chest, being her portion of this species of property. The Americans generally have very little plate; though here and there marked exceptions do exist; nor do the humbler classes lay out much of their earnings in jewelry, while they commonly dress far beyond their means in all other ways. In this respect, the European female of the same class in life frequently possesses as much in massive golden personal ornaments as would make an humble little fortune, while her attire is as homely as cumbrous petticoats, coarse cloth, and a vile taste can render it. On the other hand, the American matron that has not a set—one half dozen —of silver tea-spoons must be poor indeed, and can hardly be said to belong to the order of housekeepers at all. By means of a careful mother, both Gershom and his sister had the half dozen mentioned; and they were kept more as sacred memorials of past and better days than as articles of any use. The household goods of Waring would have been limited by his means of transportation, if not by his poverty. Two common low-post maple bedsteads were soon uncorded and carried off, as were the beds and bedding. There was scarcely any crockery, pewter and tin being its substitutes; and as for chairs, there was only one, and that had rockers; a practice of New England that has gradually diffused itself over the whole country, looking down ridicule, the drilling of boarding-schools, the comments of elderly ladies of the old school, the sneers of nurses, and, in a word, all that venerable ideas of decorum could suggest, until this appliance of domestic ease has not only fairly planted itself in nearly every American dwelling, but in a good many of Europe also!

It required about twenty minutes for the party to clear the cabin of every article that might induce an Indian to suspect the presence of white men. The furniture was carried to a sufficient distance to be safe from everything but a search ; and care was had to avoid as much as possible making a trail to lead the savages to the place selected for the temporary store-room. This was merely a close thicket, into which there was a narrow but practicable entrance on the side the least likely to be visited. When all was accomplished the four went to the lookout to ascertain how far the canoes had come. It was soon ascertained that they were within a mile, driving down before a strong breeze and following sea, and impelled by as many paddles as there were living beings in them. Ten minutes would certainly bring them up with the bar, and five more fairly within the river. The question now arose, where the party was to be concealed during the stay of the savages. Dolly, as was perhaps natural to the housewife, wished to remain by her worldly goods, and pretty Margery had a strong feminine leaning to do the same. But neither of the men approved of the plan. It was risking too much in one spot ; and a suggestion that the bee-hunter was not long in making, prevailed.

It will be remembered that Le Bourdon had carried the canoes within the field of wild rice, and bestowed them there with a good deal of attention to security. Now these canoes offered, in many respects, better places of temporary refuge under all the circumstances than any other that could readily be found on shore. They were dry ; and by spreading skins, of which Boden had so many, comfortable beds might be made for the females, which would be easily protected from the night air and dews by throwing a rug over the gunwales. Then, each canoe contained many articles that would probably be wanted ; that of the bee-hunter in particular furnishing food in abundance, as well as divers other things that would be exceedingly useful to persons in their situation. The great advantage of the canoes, however, in the mind of Le Bourdon, was the facilities they offered for flight. He hardly hoped that Indian sagacity would be so far blinded as to prevent the discovery of the many footsteps they must have left in their hurried movements, and he anticipated that with the return of day something would occur to render it necessary for them to seek safety by a stealthy removal from the spot. This might be done, he both hoped and believed, under cover of the rice, should sufficient care be taken to avoid exposure. In placing the canoes, he had used the precaution to leave them where they could not be seen from the cabin or its vicinity, or, indeed, from any spot in the vicinity of the ground that the savages would be likely to visit during their stay. All these reasons Le Bourdon now rapidly laid before his companions, and to the canoes the whole party retired as fast as they could walk.

There was great judgment displayed on the part of the bee-hunter in selecting the wild rice as a place of shelter. At that season it was sufficiently grown to afford a complete screen to everything within it that did not exceed the height of a man, or which was not seen from some adjacent elevation. Most of the land near the mouth of the river was low, and the few spots which formed exceptions had been borne in mind when the canoes were taken into the field. But just as Gershom was on the point of putting a foot into his own canoe, with a view to arrange it for the reception of his wife, he drew back, and exclaimed after the manner of one to whom a most important idea suddenly occurs, —

"Land's sake! I've forgotten all about them barrels! They'll fall into the hands of the savages, and an awful time they'll make with them! Let me pass, Dolly; I must look after the barrels this instant."

While the wife gently detained her eager husband, the bee-hunter quietly asked to what barrels he alluded.

"The whiskey casks," was the answer. "There's two on 'em in the shed behind the hut, and whiskey enough to set a whole tribe in commotion. I wonder I should have overlooked the whiskey ! "

" It is a sign of great improvement, friend Waring, and will lead to no bad consequences," returned Le Bourdon, coolly. " I foresaw the danger, and rolled the casks down the hill, where they were dashed to pieces in the brook, and the liquor has long since been carried into the lake in the shape of grog."

Waring seemed astounded ; but was so completely mystified as not to suspect the truth. That his liquor should be hopelessly lost was bad enough ; but even that was better than to have it drunk by savages without receiving any returns. After groaning and lamenting over the loss for a few minutes, he joined the rest of the party in making some further dispositions which Le Bourdon deemed prudent, if not necessary.

It had occurred to the bee-hunter to divide his own cargo between the two canoes, which was the task that the whole party was now engaged in. The object was to lighten his own canoe in the event of flight, and, by placing his effects in two parcels, give a chance to those in the boat which might escape, of having wherewithal to comfort and console themselves. As soon as this new arrangement was completed, Le Bourdon ran up to a tree that offered the desired facilities, and springing into its branches, was soon high enough to get a view of the bar and the mouth of the river. By the parting light of day he distinctly saw *four* canoes coming up the stream; which was one more than those reported to him by Margery as having passed.

CHAPTER VI.

"And long shall timorous fancy see
The painted chief and pointed spear;
And reason's self shall bow the knee
To shadows and delusions here."

FRENEAU.

A BRIGHT moon reflected on the earth for about an hour the light of the sun, as the latter luminary disappeared. By its aid the bee-hunter, who still continued in the tree, was enabled to watch the movements in the canoes of the Indians, though the persons they contained soon got to be so indistinct as to render it impossible to do more than count their numbers. The last he made out to be five each in three of the canoes, and six of the other, making twenty-one individuals in all. This was too great an odds to think of resisting, in the event of the strangers turning out to be hostile; and the knowledge of this disparity in force admonished all the fugitives of the necessity of being wary and prudent.

The strangers landed just beneath the hut, or at the precise spot where Whiskey Centre was in the habit of keeping his canoe, and whence Boden had removed it only an hour or two before. The savages had probably selected the place on account of its shores being clear of the wild rice, and because the high ground near it promised both a lookout and comfortable lodgings. Several of the party strolled upward, as if searching for an eligible spot to light their fire, and one of them soon discovered the cabin. The warrior announced his success by a whoop, and a dozen of the Indians were shortly collected in and about the *chienté*. All this proved the prudence of the course taken by the fugitives.

Blossom stood beneath the tree, and the bee-hunter told her, as each incident occurred, all that passed among the strangers, when the girl communicated the same to her brother and his wife, who were quite near at hand in one of the canoes. As there was no danger of being over- heard, conversation in an ordinary tone passed between the parties, two of whom at least were now fond of holding this sort of communion.

"Do they seem to suspect the neighborhood of the occu- pants of the cabin?" asked Margery, when the bee-hunter had let her know the manner in which the savages had taken possession of her late dwelling.

"One cannot tell. Savages are always distrustful and cautious when on a war-path; and these seem to be scent- ing about like so many hounds which are nosing for a trail. They are now gathering sticks to light a fire, which is better than burning the *chienté*."

"*That* they will not be likely to do until they have no further need of it. Tell me, Bourdon, do any go near the thicket of alders where we have hidden our goods?"

"Not as yet; though there is a sudden movement and many loud yells among them!"

"Heaven send that it may not be at having discovered anything we have forgotten. The sight of even a lost dip- per or cup would set them bloodhounds on our path, as sure as we are white and they are savages!"

"As I live, they scent the whiskey! There is a rush towards, and a pow-wow in and about the shed—yes, of a certainty they smell the liquor! Some of it has escaped in rolling down the hill, and their noses are too keen to pass over a fragrance that to them equals that of roses. Well, let them *scent* as they may—even an Injin does not get drunk through his *nose*."

"You are quite right, Bourdon: but is not this a most unhappy scent for us, since the smell of whiskey can hardly be there without their seeing it did not grow in the woods of itself, like an oak or a beech?"

"I understand you, Margery, and there is good sense in what you say. They will never think the liquor grew

6

there, like a blackberry or a chestnut, though the place *is* called Whiskey Centre!"

"It is hard enough to know that a family has deserved such a name, without being reminded of it by those that call themselves friends," answered the girl pointedly, after a pause of near a minute, though she spoke in sorrow rather then in anger.

In an instant the bee-hunter was at pretty Margery's side, making his peace by zealous apologies and winning protestations of respect and concern. The mortified girl was soon appeased; and after consulting together for a minute, they went to the canoe to communicate to the husband and wife what they had seen.

"The whiskey after all is likely to prove our worst enemy," said the bee-hunter as he approached. "It would seem that in moving the barrels some of the liquor has escaped, and the nose of an Injin is too quick for the odor it leaves not to scent it."

"Much good may it do them," growled Gershom; "they've lost me that whiskey, and let them long for it without gettin' any as a punishment for the same. My fortun' would have been made could I only have got them two barrels as far as Fort Dearborn before the troops moved!"

"The *barrels* might have been got there, certainly," answered Le Bourdon, so much provoked at the man's regrets for the destroyer which had already come so near to bringing want and ruin on himself and family, as momentarily to forget his recent scene with pretty Margery; "but whether anything would have been *in* them is another question. One of those I rolled to the brow of the hill was half empty as it was."

"Gershom is so troubled with the ague, if he don't take stimulants, in this new country," put in the wife, in the apologetic manner in which woman struggles to conceal the failings of him she loves. "As for the whiskey, I don't grudge *that* in the least; for it's a poor way of getting rich to be selling it to soldiers, who want all the reason liquor has left 'em, and more too. Still Gershom needs bitters, and ought not to have every drop he has taken thrown into his face.''

By this time Le Bourdon was again sensible of his mistake, and he beat a retreat in the best manner he could, secretly resolving not to place himself any more between two fires, in consequence of further blunders on this delicate subject. He now found that it was a very different thing to joke Whiskey Centre himself on the subject of his great failing, from making even the most distant allusion to it in the presence of those who felt for a husband's and a brother's weakness with a liveliness of feeling that brutal indulgence had long since destroyed in the object of their solicitude. He accordingly pointed out the risk there was that the Indians should make the obvious inference, that human beings must have recently been in the hut, to leave the fresh scent of the liquor in question behind them. This truth was so apparent that all felt its force, though to no one else did the danger seem so great as to the bee-hunter. He had greater familiarity with the Indian character than any of his companions, and dreaded the sagacity of the savages in a just proportion to his greater knowledge. He did not fail, therefore, to admonish his new friends of the necessity for vigilance.

'' I will return to the tree and take another look at the movements of the savages,'' Le Bourdon concluded by saying. '' By this time their fire must be lighted ; and by the aid of my glass a better insight may be had into their plans and feelings.''

The bee-hunter now went back to his tree, whither he was slowly followed by Margery ; the girl yielding to a feverish desire to accompany him, at the very time she was half restrained by maiden bashfulness ; though anxiety and the wish to learn the worst as speedily as possible prevailed.

'' They have kindled a blazing fire, and the whole of the inside of the house is as bright as if illuminated,'' said Le Bourdon, who was now carefully bestowed among the branches of his small tree. '' There are lots of the red devils moving about the *chienté*, inside and out ; and they seem to have fish as well as venison to cook. Ay, there goes more dry brush on the fire to brighten up the picture, and daylight is almost eclipsed. As I live, they have a prisoner among 'em!''

"A prisoner!'' exclaimed Margery, in the gentle tones of female pity. "Not a white person, surely?''

"No—he is a redskin like all of them—but—wait a minute till I can get the glass a little more steady. Yes—it is so—I was right at first!''

"What is so, Bourdon—and in what are you right?''

"You may remember, Blossom, that your brother and I spoke of two Injins who visited me in the openings. One was a Pottawattamie and the other a Chippewa. The first we found dead and scalped, after he had left us; and the last is now in yonder hut, bound and a prisoner. He has taken to the lake on his way to Fort Dearborn, and has, with all his craft and resolution, fallen into enemy's hands. Well will it be for him if his captors do not learn what befell the warrior who was slain near my cabin, and left seated against a tree!''

"Do you think these savages mean to revenge the death of their brother on this unfortunate wretch?''

"I know that he is in the pay of our general at Detroit, while the Pottawattamies are in the pay of the English. This of itself would make them enemies, and has no doubt been the cause of his being taken; but I do not well see how Injins on the lake here can know anything of what has happened some fifty miles or so up in the openings.''

"Perhaps the savages in the canoes belong to the same party as the warrior you call Elksfoot, and that they have had the means of learning his death, and by whose hand he fell.''

The bee-hunter was surprised at the quickness of the girl's wit, the suggestion being as discreet as it was ingenious. The manner in which intelligence flies through the wilderness had often surprised him, and certainly it was possible that the party now before him might have heard of the fate of the chief whose body he had found in the openings, short as was the time for the news to have gone so far. The circumstance that the canoes had come from the northward was against the inference, however, and after musing a minute on the facts, Le Bourdon mentioned this objection to his companion.

"Are we certain these are the same canoes as those which I saw pass this afternoon?" asked Margery, who comprehended the difficulty in an instant. "Of those I saw, two passed first, and one followed ; while here are *four* that have landed."

"What you say may be true enough. We are not to suppose that the canoes you saw pass are all that are on the lake. But let the savages be whom they may, prudence tells us to keep clear of them if we can ; and this more so than ever, now I can see that Pigeonswing, who I know to be an American Injin, is treated by them as an enemy."

"How are the savages employed now, Bourdon? Do they prepare to eat, or do they torture their prisoner?"

"No fear of their attempting the last to-night. There is an uneasiness about them, as if they still smelt the liquor ; but some are busy cooking at the fire. I would give all my honey, pretty Margery, to be able to save Pigeonswing ! He is a good fellow for a savage, and is heart and hand with us in this new war, that he tells me has begun between us and the English ! "

"You surely would not risk your own life to save a savage, who kills and scalps at random, as this man has done?"

"In that he has but followed the habits of his color and race. I dare say *we* do things that are quite as bad, according to Injin ways of thinking. I *do* believe, Margery, was that man to see *me* in the hands of the Pottawattamies, as I now see *him*, he would undertake something for my relief."

"But what can you, a single man, do when there are twenty against you?" asked Margery, a little reproachfully as to manner, speaking like one who had more interest in the safety of the young bee-hunter than she chose very openly to express.

"No one can say what he can do till he tries. I do not like the way they are treating that Chippewa, for it looks as if they meant to do him harm. He is neither fed nor suffered to be with his masters ; but there the poor fellow is, bound hand and foot, near the cabin door, and lashed to a tree. They do not even give him the relief of suffering him to sit down.''

The gentle heart of Margery was touched by this account of the manner in which the captive was treated, and she inquired into other particulars concerning his situation, with a more marked interest than she had previously manifested in his state. The bee-hunter answered her questions as they were put ; and the result was to place the girl in possession of a minute detail of the true manner in which Pigeonswing was treated.

Although there was probably no intention on the part of the captors of the Chippewa to torture him before his time, tortured he must have been by the manner in which his limbs and body were confined. Not only were his arms fastened behind his back at the elbows, but the hands were also tightly bound together in front. The legs had ligatures in two places, just above the knees and just below the ankles. Around the body was another fastening, which secured the captive to a beech that stood about thirty feet from the door of the cabin, and so nearly in a line with the fire within and the lookout of Le Bourdon, as to enable the last distinctly to note these particulars, aided as he was by his glass. Relying on the manner in which they had secured their prisoner, the savages took little heed of him ; but each appeared bent on attending to his own comfort, by means of a good supper and by securing a dry lair in which to pass the night. All this Le Bourdon saw and noted too, ere he dropped lightly on his feet by the side of Margery, at the root of the tree.

Without losing time that was precious, the bee-hunter went at once to the canoes and communicated his intention to Waring. The moon had now set, and the night was favorable to the purposes of Le Bourdon. At the first glance it might seem wisest to wait until sleep had fallen upon the savages, ere any attempt were made to approach the hut ; but Boden reasoned differently. A general silence would succeed as soon as the savages disposed of themselves to sleep, which would be much more likely to allow his footsteps to be overheard than when tongues and bodies and teeth were all in active movement. A man who eats after a long march, or a severe paddling, usually concentrates his attention on his food, as Le Bourdon knew by long experience ; and it is a much better moment to steal upon the hungry and weary, to do so when they feed, than to do so when they sleep, provided anything like a watch be kept. That the Pottawattamies would neglect this latter caution Le Bourdon did not believe ; and his mind was made up, not only to attempt the rescue of his Chippewa friend, but to attempt it at once.

After explaining his plan in a few words, and requesting Waring's assistance, Le Bourdon took a solemn leave of the party, and proceeded at once towards the hut. In order to understand the movements of the bee-hunter, it may be well now briefly to explain the position of the *chienté*, and the nature of the ground on which the adventurer was required to act. The hut stood on a low and somewhat abrupt swell, being surrounded on all sides by land so low as to be in many places wet and swampy. There were a good many trees on the knoll, and several thickets of alders and other bushes on the lower ground ; but, on the whole, the swamps were nearly devoid of what is termed "timber." Two sides of the knoll were abrupt ; that on which the casks had been rolled into the lake, and that opposite, which was next to the tree whence Boden had so long been watching the proceedings of the savages. The distance between the hut and this tree was somewhat less than a mile. The intervening ground was low, and most of it was marshy, though it was possible to cross the marsh by following a particular course. Fortunately this course, which was visible to the eye by daylight, and had been taken by the fugitives on quitting the hut, might be dimly traced at night by one who understood the ground, by means of certain trees and bushes, that formed so many finger-posts for the traveller. Unless this particular route were taken, however, a circuit of three or four miles must be made, in order to pass from the *chienté* to the spot where the family had taken refuge. As Le Bourdon had crossed this firm ground by daylight, and had observed it well from his tree, he thought himself enough of a guide to find his way through it in the dark, aided by the marks just mentioned.

The bee-hunter had got as far as the edge of the marsh on his way towards the hut, when pausing an instant to examine the priming of his rifle, he fancied that he heard a light footstep behind him. Turning, quick as thought, he perceived that pretty Margery had followed him thus far. Although time pressed, he could not part from the girl without showing that he appreciated the interest she manifested in his behalf. Taking her hand, therefore, he spoke with a simplicity and truth that imparted to his manner a natural grace that one bred in courts might have envied. What was more, with a delicacy that few in courts would deem necessary under the circumstances, he did not in his language so much impute to concern on his own account this movement of Margery's, as to that she felt for her brother and sister; though in his inmost heart a throbbing hope prevailed that he had his share in it.

"Do not be troubled on account of Gershom and his wife, pretty Margery," said the bee-hunter, "which, as I perceive, is the main reason why you have come here; and as for myself, be certain that I shall not forget who I have left behind, and how much her safety depends on my prudence."

Margery was pleased, though a good deal confused. It was new to her to hear allusions of this sort, but nature supplied the feeling to appreciate them.

"Is it not risking too much, Bourdon?" she said. "Are you sure of being able to find the crossing in the marsh, in a night so very dark? I do not know but looking so long at the bright light in the cabin may blind me, but it *does* seem as if I never saw a darker night!"

"The darkness increases, for the starlight is gone; but I can see where I go, and so long as I can do that there is not much fear of losing my way. I do not like to expose you to danger, but—"

"Never mind me, Bourdon; set me to do anything in which you think I can be of use!" exclaimed the girl, eagerly.

"Well then, Margery, you may do this: Come with me to the large tree in the centre of the marsh, and I will set you on a duty that may possibly save my life. I will tell you my meaning when there."

Margery followed with a light, impatient step; and as neither stopped to speak or to look around, the two soon stood beneath the tree in question. It was a large elm that completely overshadowed a considerable extent of firm ground. Here a full and tolerably near view could be had of the hut, which was still illuminated by the blazing fire within. For a minute both stood silently gazing at the strange scene; then Le Bourdon explained to his companion the manner in which she might assist him.

Once at the elm, it was not so difficult to find the way across the marsh as it was to reach that spot, coming *from* the *chienté*. As there were several elms scattered about in the centre of the marsh, the bee-hunter was fearful that he might not reach the right tree; in which case he would be compelled to retrace his steps, and that at the imminent hazard of being captured. He carried habitually a small dark lantern, and had thought of so disposing of it in the lower branches of this very elm as to form a focus of it, but hesitated about doing that which might prove a guide to his enemies as well as to himself. If Margery would take charge of this lantern, he could hope to reap its advantages without incurring the hazard of having a light suspended in the tree for any length of time. Margery understood the lessons she received, and promised to obey all the injunctions by which they were accompanied.

"Now, God bless you, Margery," added the bee-hunter. "Providence has brought me and your brother's family together in troublesome times; should I get back safe from this adventure, I shall look upon it as a duty to do all I can to help Gershom place his wife and sister beyond the reach of harm."

"God bless you, Bourdon!" half whispered the agitated girl. "I know it is worth some risk to save a human life, even though it be that of an Injin, and I will not try to persuade you from this undertaking; but do not attempt more than is necessary, and rely on my using the lantern just as you have told me to use it."

Those young persons had not yet known each other a single day, yet both felt that confidence which years alone, in the crowds of the world, can ordinarily create in the human mind. The cause of the sympathy which draws heart to heart, which generates friendship and love and passionate attachments, is not obvious to all who choose to talk of it. There is yet a profound mystery in our organization, which has hitherto escaped the researches of both classes of philosophers, and which it probably was the design of the Creator should not be made known to us until we drew nearer to that great end which, sooner or later, is to be accomplished in behalf of our race, when "knowledge will abound," and we shall better understand our being and its objects than is permitted to us in this our day of ignorance. But while we cannot trace the causes of a thousand things, we know and feel their effects. Among the other mysteries of our nature is this of sudden and strong sympathies, which, as between men for men, and women for women, awaken confidence and friendship ; and as between those of different sexes, excite passionate attachments that more or less color their future lives. The great delineator of our common nature, in no one of the many admirable pictures he has drawn of men, manifests a more profound knowledge of his subject than in that in which he portrays the sudden and nearly ungovernable inclination which Romeo and Juliet are made to display for each other ; an inclination that sets reason, habit, prejudice, and family enmities at defiance. That such an attachment is to be commended, we do not say ; that all can feel it, we do not believe ; that connections formed under its influence can always be desirable, we are far from thinking : but that it may exist we believe is just as certain as any of the incomprehensible laws of our wayward and yet admirable nature. We have no Veronese tale to relate here, however, but simply a homely legend, in which human feeling may occasionally be made to bear an humble resemblance to that world-renowned picture which had its scenes in the beautiful capital of Venetian Lombardy.

When Le Bourdon left his companion, now so intensely interested in his success, to pick his way in the darkness across the remainder of the marsh, Margery retired behind the tree, where the first thing she did was to examine her lantern, and to see that its light was ready to perform the very important office which might so speedily be required of it. Satisfied on this point, she turned her eyes anxiously in the direction of the hut. By this time every trace of the bee-hunter was lost, the hillock in his front forming too dark a background to admit of his being seen. But the fire still blazed in the *chienté*, the savages not having yet finished their cooking, though several had satisfied their appetites, and had already sought places where they might stretch themselves for the night. Margery was glad to see that these last individuals bestowed themselves within the influence of the fire, warm as was the night. This was done most probably to escape from the annoyance of the mosquitoes, more or less of which are usually found in the low lands of the new countries, and near the margins of rivers.

Margery could distinctly see the Chippewa, erect and bound to his tree. On him she principally kept her looks riveted, for near his person did she expect first again to find the bee-hunter. Indeed, there was no chance of seeing one who was placed beneath the light of the fire, since the brow of the acclivity formed a complete cover, throwing all below it into deep shade. This circumstance was of the greatest importance to the adventurer, however, enabling him to steal quite near to his friend, favored by a darkness that was getting to be intense. Quitting Margery, we will now rejoin Le Bourdon, who by this time was approaching his goal.

The bee-hunter had some difficulty in finding his way across the marsh ; but floundering through the impediments, and on the whole preserving the main direction, he got out on the firm ground quite as soon as he had expected to do. It was necessary for him to use extreme caution. The Indians, according to their custom, had dogs, two of which had been in sight, lying about half-way between the prisoner and the door of the hut. Boden had seen a savage feeding these dogs; and it appeared to him at the time as if the Indian had been telling them to be watchful of the Chippewa. He well knew the services that the redmen expected of these animals, which are kept rather as sentinels than for any great use they put them to in the hunts. An Indian dog is quick enough to give the alarm, and he will keep on a trail for a long run and with considerable accuracy; but it is seldom that he closes and has his share in the death, unless in the case of very timid and powerless creatures.

Nevertheless, the presence of these dogs exacted extra caution in the movements of the bee-hunter. He had ascended the hill a little out of the stream of light which still issued from the open door of the hut, and was soon high enough to get a good look at the state of things on the bit of level land around the cabin. Fully one half of the savages were yet up and in motion, though the processes of cooking and eating were by this time nearly ended. These men had senses almost as acute as those of their dogs, and it was very necessary to be on his guard against them also. By moving with the utmost caution, Le Bourdon reached the edge of the line of light, where he was within ten yards of the captive. Here he placed his rifle against a small tree, and drew his knife, in readiness to cut the prisoner's thongs. Three several times, while the bee-hunter was making these preparations, did the two dogs raise their heads and scent the air; once, the oldest of the two gave a deep and most ominous growl. Singular as it may seem, this last indication of giving the alarm was of great service to Le Bourdon and the Chippewa. The latter heard the growl, and saw two of the movements of the animals' heads, from all which he inferred that there was some creature or some danger behind him. This naturally enough induced him to bestow a keen attention in that direction, and being unable to turn body, limbs, or head, the sense of hearing was his only means of watchfulness. It was while in this state of profound listening that Pigeonswing fancied he heard his own name, in such a whisper as one raises when he wishes to call from a short distance with the least possible expenditure of voice. Presently the words "Pigeonswing" and "Chippewa" were succeeded by those of "bee-hunter," "Bourdon." This was enough : the quick-witted warrior made a low ejaculation, such as might be mistaken for a half-suppressed murmur that proceeded from pain, but which one keenly on the watch, and who was striving to communicate with him, would be apt to understand as a sign of attention. The whispering then ceased altogether, and the prisoner waited the result with the stoic patience of an American Indian. A minute later the Chippewa felt the thongs giving way, and his arms were released at the elbows. An arm was next passed round his body, and the fastenings at the wrist were cut. At this instant a voice whispered in his ear, "Be of good heart, Chippewa, your friend, Bourdon, is here. Can you stand ?"

"No stand," answered the Indian in a low whisper, "too much tie."

At the next moment the feet of the Chippewa were released, as were also his knees. Of all the fastenings none now remained but that which bound the captive to the tree. In not cutting this, the bee-hunter manifested his coolness and judgment ; for were the stout rope of bark severed, the Indian would have fallen like a log, from total inability to stand. His thongs had impeded the circulation of the blood, and the usual temporary paralysis had been the consequence. Pigeonswing understood the reason of his friend's forbearance, and managed to rub his hands and wrists together, while the bee-hunter himself applied friction to his feet, by passing his own arms around the bottom of the tree. The reader may imagine the intense anxiety of Margery the while, for she witnessed the arrival of Le Bourdon at the tree, and could not account for the long delay which succeeded.

All this time the dogs were far from being quiet or satisfied. Their masters, accustomed to being surrounded at night by wolves and foxes, or other beasts, took little heed, however, of the discontent of these creatures, which were in the habit of growling in their lairs. The bee-hunter, as he kept rubbing at his friend's legs, felt now but little apprehension of the dogs, though a new source of alarm presented itself by the time the Chippewa was barely able to sustain his weight on his feet, and long before he could use them with anything like his former agility. The manner in which the savages came together in the hut, and the gestures made by their chief, announced pretty plainly that a watch was about to be set for the night. As it was probable that the sentinel would take his station near the prisoner, the bee-hunter was at a loss to decide whether it were better to commence the flight before or after the rest of the savages were in their lairs. Placing his mouth as close to the ear of Pigeonswing as could be done without bringing his head into the light, the following dialogue passed between Le Bourdon and the captive.

"Do you see, Chippewa," the bee-hunter commenced, "the chief is telling one of his young men to come and keep guard near you?"

"See him, well 'nough. Make too many sign no to see."

"What think you—shall we wait till the warriors are asleep, or try to be off before the sentinel comes?"

"Bess wait, if one t'ing. You got rifle—got tomahawk—got knife, eh?"

"I have them all, though my rifle is a short distance behind me, and a little down the hill."

"Dat bad—nebber let go rifle on war-path. Well, *you* tomahawk him—*I* scalp him—dat 'll do."

"I shall kill no man, Chippewa, unless there is great occasion for it. If there is no other mode of getting you off, I shall choose to cut this last thong, and leave you to take care of yourself."

"Give him tomahawk, den—give him knife, too."

"Not for such a purpose. I do not like to shed blood without a good reason for it."

"No call war good reason, eh? Bess reason in world.

Pottawattamie dig up hatchet ag'in Great Fadder at Wash'-
ton ; dat no good reason why take his scalp, eh ? ''

In whispering these last words the Chippewa used so
much energy that the dogs again raised their heads from
between their fore paws and growled. Almost at that
instant the chief and his few remaining wakeful companions
laid themselves down to sleep, and the young warrior designated as the sentinel left the hut and came slowly towards
the prisoner. The circumstances admitted of no delay ;
Le Bourdon pressed the keen edge of his knife across the
withe that bound the Indian to the tree, first giving him
notice, in order that he might be prepared to sustain his own
weight. This done, the bee-hunter dropped on the ground,
crawling away out of the light, though the brow of the
hill almost immediately formed a screen to conceal his person from all near the hut. In another instant he had regained his rifle, and was descending swiftly towards the
crossing at the marsh.

CHAPTER VII.

"We call them savage—Oh, be just!
  Their outraged feelings scan;
A voice comes forth, 't is from the dust—
  The savage was a man!"

SPRAGUE.

AS soon as Le Bourdon reached the commencement of that which might be called his path across the marsh, he stopped and looked backward. He was now sufficiently removed from the low acclivity to see objects on its summit, and had no difficulty in discerning all that the waning fire illuminated. There stood the Chippewa erect against the tree as if still bound with thongs, while the sentinel was slowly approaching him. The dogs were on their feet, and gave two or three sharp barks, which had the effect to cause five or six of the savages to lift their heads in their lairs. One arose, even, and threw an armful of dried branches on the fire, producing a bright blaze, that brought everything around the hut, and which the light could touch, into full view.

The bee-hunter was astonished at the immovable calmness with which Pigeonswing still stood to his tree, awaiting the approach of the sentinel. In a few moments the latter was at his side. At first the Pottawattamie did not perceive that the prisoner was unbound. He threw him into shadow by his own person, and it required a close look to note the circumstance. Boden was too far from the spot to see all the minor movements of the parties, but there was soon a struggle that could not be mistaken. As the Pottawattamie was examining the prisoner, an exclamation that escaped him betrayed the sudden conscious-

ness that the Chippewa was unbound. The sound was no
sooner uttered than Pigeonswing made a grasp at the sentinel's knife, which, however, he did not obtain, when the
two closed and fell, rolling down the declivity into the darkness. When the Pottawattamie seized the Chippewa, he
uttered a yell, which instantly brought every man of his
party to his feet. As the savages now united in the whoops,
and the dogs began to bark wildly, an infernal clamor was
made.

At first Le Bourdon did not know how to act. He greatly
feared the dogs, and could not but think of Margery, and
the probable consequences should those sagacious animals
follow him across the marsh. But he did not like the idea
of abandoning Pigeonswing, when a single blow of his
arm, or a kick of his foot, might be the cause of his escape.
While deliberating in painful uncertainty, the sounds of the
struggle ceased, and he saw the sentinel rising again into
the light, limping like one who had suffered by a fall.
Presently he heard a footstep near him, and calling in a
low voice, he was immediately joined by Pigeonswing. Before the bee-hunter was aware of his intention, the Chippewa seized his rifle, and levelling it at the sentinel, who
still stood on the brow of the hill, drawn in all his savage
outlines distinctly in the light of the flames, he fired. The
cry, the leap into the air, and the fall announced the unerring character of the aim. In coming to the earth, the
wounded man fell over the brow of the sharp declivity, and
was heard rolling towards its base.

Le Bourdon felt the importance of now improving the
precious moments, and was in the act of urging his companion to follow, when the latter passed an arm around his
body, whipped his knife from the girdle and sheath, and
dropping the rifle into his friend's arms, bounded away
in the darkness, taking the direction of his fallen enemy.
There was no mistaking all this; the Chippewa, led by his
own peculiar sense of honor, risking everything to obtain
the usual trophy of victory. By this time, a dozen of the
savages stood on the brow of the hill, seemingly at a loss
to understand what had become of the combatants. Per-

2

ceiving this, the bee-hunter profited by the delay and reloaded his rifle. As everything passed almost as swiftly as the electric spark is known to travel, it was but a moment after the Pottawattamie fell ere his conqueror was through with his bloody task. Just as Le Bourdon threw his rifle up into the hollow of his arm, he was rejoined by his red friend, who bore the reeking scalp of the sentinel at his belt; though fortunately the bee-hunter did not see it on account of the obscurity, else might he not have been so willing to continue to act with so ruthless an ally.

Further stay was out of the question; for the Indians were now collected in a body on the brow of the hill, where the chief was rapidly issuing his orders. In a minute the band dispersed, every man bounding into the darkness, as if aware of the danger of remaining within the influence of the bright light thrown from the fire. Then came such a clamor from the dogs as left no doubt in the mind of the bee-hunter that they had scented and found the remains of the fallen man. A fierce yell came from the same spot, the proof that some of the savages had already discovered the body; and Le Bourdon told his companion to follow, taking his way across the marsh as fast as he could overcome the difficulties of the path.

It has already been intimated that it was not easy, if indeed it were possible, to cross that piece of low wet land in a direct line. There was tolerably firm ground on it, but it lay in an irregular form, its presence being generally to be noted by the growth of trees. Le Bourdon had been very careful in taking his land-marks, foreseeing the probability of a hasty retreat, and he had no difficulty for some time in keeping in the right direction. But the dogs soon left the dead body, and came bounding across the marsh, disregarding its difficulties, though their plunges and yells, soon made it apparent that even they did not escape altogether with dry feet. As for the savages, they poured down the declivity in a stream, taking the dogs as their guides; and safe ones they might well be accounted, so far as the *scent* was concerned, though they did not happen to be particularly well acquainted with all the difficulties of the path.

At length Le Bourdon paused, causing his companion to stop also. In the hurry and confusion of the flight, the former had lost his land-marks, finding himself amidst a copse of small trees, or large bushes, but not in the particular copse he sought. Every effort to get out of this thicket, except by the way he had entered it, proved abortive, and the dogs were barking at no great distance in his rear. It is true that these animals no longer approached ; for they were floundering in the mud and water ; but their throats answered every purpose to lead the pursuers on, and the low calls that passed from mouth to mouth let the pursued understand that the Pottawattamies were at their heels, if not absolutely on their trail.

The crisis demanded both discretion and decision ; qualities in which the bee-hunter, with his forest training, was not likely to be deficient. He looked out for the path by which he had reached the unfortunate thicket, and, having found it, commenced a retreat by the way he had come. Nerve was needed to move almost in a line towards the dogs and their masters ; but the nerve was forthcoming, and the two advanced like veterans expecting the fire of some concealed but well-armed battery. Presently Le Bourdon stopped and examined the ground on which he stood.

"*Here* we must turn, Chippewa," he said, in a guarded voice. "This is the spot where I must have missed my way."

"Good place to turn 'bout," answered the Indian ; "dog too near."

"We must shoot the dogs if they press us too hard," returned the bee-hunter, leading off rapidly, now secure in the right direction. "They seem to be in trouble just at this time ; but animals like them will soon find their way across this marsh."

"Bess shoot Pottawattamie," coolly returned Pigeons-wing. "Pottawattamie got capital scalp—dog's ears no good for nuttin', any more."

"Yonder, I believe, is the tree I am in search of !" exclaimed Le Bourdon. "If we can reach that tree I think all will go well with us."

The tree was reached, and the bee-hunter proceeded to make sure of his course from that point. Removing from his pouch a small piece of moistened powder that he had prepared ere he liberated the Chippewa, he stuck it on a low branch of the tree he was under, and on the side next the spot where he had stationed Margery. When this was done, he made his companion stand aside, and lighting some spunk with his flint and steel, he fired his powder. Of course this little preparation burned like the fire-works of a boy, making sufficient light, however, to be seen in a dark night for a mile or more. No sooner was the wetted powder hissing and throwing off its sparks than the bee-hunter gazed intently into the now seemingly tangible obscurity of the marsh. A bright light appeared and vanished. It was enough; the bee-hunter threw down his own signal and extinguished it with his foot; and, as he wished, the lantern of Margery appeared no more. Assured now of the accuracy of his position, as well as of the course he was to pursue, Le Bourdon bade his companion follow, and pressed anew across the marsh. A tree was soon visible, and towards that particular object the fugitives steadily pressed, until it was reached. At the next instant Margery was joined; and the bee-hunter could not refrain from kissing her, in the excess of his pleasure.

"There is a dreadful howling of dogs," said Margery, feeling no offence at the liberty taken, in a moment like that, "and it seems to me that a whole tribe is following at their heels. For Heaven's sake, Bourdon, let us hasten to the canoes; brother and sister must think us lost!"

The circumstances pressed, and the bee-hunter took Margery's arm, passing it through one of his own, with a decided and protecting manner, that caused the girl's heart to beat with emotions not in the least connected with fear, leaving an impression of pleasure even at that perilous moment. As the distance was not great, the three were soon on the beach and near to the canoes. Here they met Dorothy, alone, and pacing to and fro like a person distressed. She had doubtless heard the clamor, and was aware that the savages were out looking for their party.

As Margery met her sister, she saw that something more than common had gone wrong, and in the eagerness of her apprehensions she did not scruple about putting her questions.

"What has become of brother? Where is Gershom?" demanded the sensitive girl, at once.

The answer was given in a low voice, and in that sort of manner with which woman struggles to the last to conceal the delinquencies of him she loves.

"Gershom is not himself, just now," half whispered the wife; "he has fallen into one of his old ways, ag'in."

"Old ways," slowly repeated the sister, dropping her own voice to tones similar to those in which the unpleasant news had just been communicated. "How is that possible, now that all the whiskey is emptied?"

"It seems that Bourdon had a jug of brandy among his stores, and Gershom found it out. I blame no one; for Bourdon, who never abuses the gifts of Providence, had a right to his comforts at least; but it *is* a pity that there was anything of the sort in the canoes!"

The bee-hunter was greatly concerned at this unwelcome intelligence, feeling all its importance far more vividly than either of his companions. They regretted as women; but he foresaw the danger, as a man accustomed to exertion in trying scenes. If Whiskey Centre had really fallen into his old ways, so as to render himself an incumbrance, instead of being an assistant at such a moment, the fact was to be deplored, but it could only be remedied by time. Luckily they had the Indian with them, and he could manage one of the canoes, while he himself took charge of the other. As no time was to be lost, the barking of the dogs and the cries of the savages too plainly letting it be known that the enemy was getting through the marsh by some means or other, he hurried the party down to the canoes, entering that of Whiskey Centre at once.

Le Bourdon found Gershom asleep, but with the heavy slumbers of the drunkard. Dolly had removed the jug and concealed it, as soon as the state of her husband enabled her to do so without incurring his violence. Else might the unfortunate man have destroyed himself, by indulging in a liquor so much more palatable than that he was accustomed to use, after so long and compelled an abstinence. The jug was now produced, however, and Le Bourdon emptied it in the river, to the great joy of the two females, though not without a sharp remonstrance from the Chippewa. The bee-hunter was steady, and the last drop of the liquor of Gascony was soon mingling with the waters of the Kalamazoo. This done, the bee-hunter desired the women to embark, and called to the Chippewa to do the same. By quitting the spot in the canoes, it was evident their pursuers would be balked, temporarily at least, since they must recross the marsh in order to get into their own boats, without which further pursuit would be fruitless.

It might have been by means of a secret sympathy, or it was possibly the result of accident, but certain it is that the Chippewa was placed in the stern of Gershom's canoe, while Margery found a place in that of Le Bourdon. As for Whiskey Centre, he lay like a log in the bottom of his own light bark, cared for only by his affectionate wife, who had made a pillow for his head ; but, fortunately, if no assistance just then, not any material hindrance to the movements of his friends. By the time Le Bourdon and the Chippewa had got their stations, and the canoes were free at the bottom, it was evident by the sounds that not only the dogs, but divers of their masters, had floundered through the swamp and were already on the firm ground east of it. As the dogs ran by scent, little doubt remained of their soon leading the savages down to the place of embarkation. Aware of this, the bee-hunter directed the Chippewa to follow, and urged his own canoe away from the shore, following one of three of the natural channels that united just at that point.

The clamor now sensibly increased, and the approach of the pursuers was much faster than it had previously been, in consequence of there no longer being wet land beneath their feet. At the distance of fifty yards from the shore, however, the channel, or open avenue among the rice plants, that the canoes had taken, made a short turn to the northward; for all the events we have just been recording occurred on the northern or leeward side of the river. Once around this bend in the channel, the canoes would have been effectually concealed from those on the beach, had it even been broad daylight, and of course were so much more hidden from view under the obscurity of a very dark night. Perceiving this, and fearful that the dip of the paddles might be heard, Le Bourdon ceased to urge his canoe through the water, telling the Chippewa to imitate his example, and let the boats drift. In consequence of this precaution the fugitives were still quite near the shore when first the dogs, and then a party of their masters, came rushing down to the very spot whence the canoes had departed scarcely two minutes before. As no precautions were taken to conceal the advance of the pursuers, the pursued, or the individuals among them who alone understood the common language of the Great Ojebway Nation well, had an opportunity of hearing and understanding all that was said. Le Bourdon had brought the two canoes together; and the Chippewa, at his request, now translated such parts of the discourse of their enemies as he deemed worthy of communicating to the females.

"Say, now, nobody dere!" commenced the Indian, coolly. "T'ink he no great way off—mean to look for him—t'ink dog uneasy—won'er why dog so uneasy."

"Them dogs are very likely to scent us here in the canoes, we are so near them," whispered Le Bourdon.

"S'pose he do, can't catch us," coolly answered the Chippewa; "beside, shoot him, don't take care; bad for dog to chase warrior too much."

"There is one speaking now who seems to have authority."

"Yes—he chief—know he voice—hear him too often—he mean to put Pigeonswing to torture. Well, let him catch Pigeonswing fust—swift bird do dat, eh?"

"But what says he? It may be of importance to learn what the chief says, just now."

"Who care what he *say*—can't *do* nuttin'—if get good chance, take *his* scalp, too."

"Ay, that I dare say—but he is speaking earnestly, and

in a low voice; listen, and let us know what he says. I do not well understand at this distance.''

The Chippewa complied, and maintained an attentive silence until the chief ceased to speak. Then he rendered what had been said into such English as he could command, accompanying the translation by the explanations that naturally suggested themselves to one like himself.

'' Chief talk to young men,'' said the Chippewa; '' all chief talk to young men; tell him dat Pigeonswing muss get off in canoe—don't see canoe, nudder—but muss be canoe, else he swim. T'ink more dan one Injin here—don't know, dough—maybe, maybe not—can't tell till see trail, morrow mornin'—''

'' Well, well; but what does he tell his young men to *do*?'' demanded the bee-hunter, impatiently.

'' Don't be squaw, Bourdon—tell all by'em by. Tell young men s'pose he get canoe, den he may get *our* canoe, and carry 'em off—s'pose he swim; dat Chippewa devil swim down stream and get *our* canoe dat fashion—bess go back, some of you, and see arter *our* canoe—dat what he tell young men most.''

'' That is a lucky thought!'' exclaimed Le Bourdon; '' let us paddle down at once, and seize all their canoes before they can get there. The distance by water, owing to this bend in the river, is not half as great as that by land, and the marsh will double the distance to them.''

'' Dat good council!'' said Pigeonswing; '' you go—I follow.''

This was no sooner said than the canoes were again got in motion. The darkness might now have been a sufficient protection had there been no rice, but the plant would have concealed the movement even at noon-day. The fire in the hut served as a beacon, and enabled Le Bourdon to find the canoes. When he reached the landing, he could still hear the dogs barking on the marsh, and the voices of those with them, calling in loud tones to two of the savages who had remained at the *chienté*, as a sort of camp-guard.

'' What do them chaps say?'' asked Le Bourdon of the Chippewa. '' They yell as if striving to make the two men at the door of the hut hear them. Can you make out what they are bawling so loud?"

"Tell two warrior to come down and take care of canoe—dat all—let 'em come—find two here take care of *dem*—got good scalp, dem two rascal Pottawattamie!"

"No, no, Pigeonswing; we must have no more of that work to-night, but must set about towing these four canoes off the shore as fast as we can. Have you got hitches on your two?"

"Fast 'nough—so fast, he follow," answered the Indian, who, notwithstanding his preparations to help to remove the canoes, was manifestly reluctant to depart without striking another blow at his enemies. "Now good time for dem rascal to lose scalp!"

"Them rascals, as you call them, begin to understand their friends in the marsh, and are looking to the priming of their rifles. We must be moving, or they may see us, and give us a shot. Shove off, Chippewa, and paddle at once for the middle of the bay."

As Le Bourdon was much in earnest, Pigeonswing was fain to comply. Had the last possessed a rifle of his own, or even a knife, it is highly probable he would have leaped ashore, and found the means of stealing on some one of his enemies unawares, and thus secured another trophy. But the bee-hunter was determined, and the Chippewa, however reluctant, was compelled to obey; for not only had Le Bourdon kept his rifle at his side, but he had used the precaution of securing his knife and tomahawk, both of which he carried habitually, the same as a redman.

The canoes had now a somewhat difficult task. The wind still blew fresh, and it was necessary for one of these light craft, pretty well loaded with its proper freight, and paddled by only a single person, to tow two other craft of equal size dead to windward. The weight in the towing craft, and the lightness of those that were towed, rendered this task, however, easier than it might otherwise have proved. In the course of a couple of minutes all the canoes were far enough from the shore to be out of sight of the two Indians, who by that time had got down to the beach to look after their own craft. The yell these savages raised on finding themselves too late not only announced their disappointment, but communicated the extent of the disaster to their friends, who were still floundering through the marsh.

The great advantage that the party of the bee-hunter had now obtained must be very apparent to all. In possession of *all* the canoes, their enemies were, or would be for some time at least, confined to the northern side of the river, which was so wide near its mouth as to present an effectual barrier between them and those who occupied the opposite bank. The canoes, also, enabled the weaker party to change their position at will, carrying with them as many of their effects as were on board, and which included the whole of the property of Le Bourdon; while their loss deprived their enemies of all extra means of motion, and would be very likely to induce them to proceed on their expedition by land. The objects of that expedition could only be conjectured by the bee-hunter, until he had questioned the Chippewa; a thing he did not fail to do as soon as he believed the party quite safe, under the south shore. Here the fugitives landed, proceeding up a natural channel in the wild rice in order to do so, and selecting a bit of dry beach for their purpose. Margery set about lighting a fire, in order to keep the mosquitoes at a distance, selecting a spot to kindle it, behind a swell of the land, that concealed the light from all on the other shore. In the morning, it would be necessary to extinguish that fire, lest its smoke should betray their position. It was while these things were in progress, and after Le Bourdon had himself procured the fuel necessary to feed pretty Margery's fire, that he questioned the Chippewa touching his captivity.

"Yes, tell all 'bout him," answered the Indian, as soon as interrogated; "no good to hide trail from friend. 'Member when say good-bye up in openin' to Bourdon?"

"Certainly; I remember the very instant when you left me. The Pottawattamie went on one path, and you went on another. I was glad of that, as you seemed to think he was not your friend."

"Yes; good not to travel on same path as inimy, 'cause

he quarrel sometime," coolly returned the Indian. "Dis
time, path come togedder, somehow; and Pottawattamie
lose he scalp."

"I am aware of all that, Pigeonswing, and I wish it had
not been so. I found the body of Elksfoot sitting up against
a tree soon after you left me, and knew by whose hands he
had fallen."

"Did n't find scalp, eh?"

"No, the scalp had been taken; though I accounted that
but for little, since the man's life was gone. There is little
gained by carrying on war in this manner, making the
woods and the openings and the prairies alike unsafe. You
see, now, to what distress this family is reduced by your
Injin manner of making war."

"How you make him, den—want to hear. Go kiss, and
give venison to inimy, or go get his scalp, eh? Which bess
fashion to make him afeard, and own you master?"

"All that may be done without killing single travellers,
or murdering women and children. The peace will be made
none the sooner between England and America because you
have got the scalp of Elksfoot."

"No habe n't got him any longer; wish had. Pottawattamie take him away, and say he bury him. Well, let him
hide him in a hole deep as white man's well, can't hide
Pigeonswing honor dere, too. Dat is safe as notch cut on
stick can make him!"

This notch on a stick was the Indian mode of gazetting
a warrior; and a certain number of these notches was
pretty certain to procure for him a sort of savage brevet,
which answered his purpose quite as well as the modern
mode of brevetting at Washington answers our purpose.
Neither brings any pay, we believe, nor any command,
except in such cases as rarely occur, and then only to the
advantage of government. There are varieties in honor, as
in any other human interest; so are there many moral degrees in warfare. Thus, the very individual who admires
the occupation of Algiers, or that of Tahiti, or the attack
on Canton, together with the long train of Indian events
which have dyed the peninsulas of the East in the blood of

their people, sees an alarming enormity in the knocking
down of the walls of Vera Cruz, though the breach opened
a direct road into San Juan de Ulloa. In the eyes of the
same profound moralists, the *garitas* of Mexico ought to
have been respected, as so many doors opening into the
boudoirs of the beautiful dames of that fine capital ; it being
a monstrous thing to fire a shot into the streets of a town,
no matter how many came out of them. We are happy,
therefore, to have it in our power to add these touches of
philosophy that came from Pigeonswing to those of the
sages of the Old World, by way of completing a code of
international morals on this interesting subject, in which
the student shall be at a loss to say which he most admires—
that which comes from the schools, or that which comes
direct from the wilderness.

"So best," answered the bee-hunter. "I wish I could
persuade you to throw away that disgusting thing at your
belt. Remember, Chippewa, you are now among Christians, and ought to do as Christians wish."

"What Christians *do*, eh?" returned the Indian, with a
sneer. "Get drunk like Whiskey Centre, dere? Cheat
poor redman ; den get down on knee and look up at Manitou? *Dat* what Christian do, eh?"

"They who do such things are Christians but in name ;
you must think better of such as are Christians in fact."

"Ebberybody call himself Christian, tell you—all pale-
face Christian, dey say. Now, listen to Chippewa. Once
talk long talk wit' missionary—tell all about Christian—
what Christian do—what Christian say—how he eat, how
he sleep, *how* he drink !—all good—wish Pigeonwing Christian—den 'member so'ger at garrison—no eat, no sleep, no
drink Christian fashion—do ebberyt'ing so'ger fashion—
swear, fight, cheat, get drunk—wuss dan Injin—dat Christian, eh?"

"No, that is not acting like a Christian ; and I fear very
few of us who call ourselves by that name act as if we were
Christians, in truth," said Le Bourdon, conscious of the
justice of the Chippewa's accusation.

"Just dat—now I get him—ask missionary, one day,

where all Christian go to, so that Injin can't find him—
none in woods—none on prairie—none in garrison—none
at Mack'naw—none at Detroit—where all go to, den, so
Injin can't find him, on'y in missionary talk?''

"I am curious to know what answer your missionary
made to that question.''

"Well, tell you : say, on'y one in ten t'ousant *raal*
Christian 'mong pale-face, dough all call himself Christian !
Dat what Injin t'ink queer, eh ? ''

"It is not easy to make a redman understand all the ways
of the pale-faces, Pigeonswing ; but we will talk of these
things another time, when we are more at our ease. Just
now, I wish to learn all I can of the manner in which you
fell into the hands of the Pottawattamies.''

"Dat plain 'nough—wish Christian talk half as plain.
You see, Bourdon, dat Elkfoot on scout when we meet in
openin', up river. I know'd his ar'nd, and so took scalp.
Dem Pottawattamie his friend ; when dey come to meet
ole chief, no find him ; but find Pigeonwing ; got me when
tired and 'sleep ; got Elkfoot scalp wid me—sorry for dat
—know scalp by scalp-lock, which had gray hair and some
mark. So put me in canoe, and meant to take Chippewa to
Chicago to torture him—but too much wind. So, when
meet friend in t'odder canoe, come back here to wait little
while.''

This was the simple explanation of the manner in which
Pigeonswing had fallen into the hands of his enemies. It
would seem that Elksfoot had come in a canoe from the
mouth of the St. Joseph's to a point about half way between
that river and the mouth of the Kalamazoo, and there
landed. What the object of the party was does not exactly
appear, though it is far from being certain that it was not to
seize the bee-hunter and confiscate his effects. Although
Le Bourdon was personally a stranger to Elkfoot, news
flies through the wilderness in an extraordinary manner ;
and it was not at all unlikely that the fact of a white American's being in the openings should soon spread, along with
the tidings that the hatchet was dug up, and that a party
should go out in quest of his scalp and the plunder. It

would seem that the savage tact of the Chippewa detected that in the manner of the Pottawattamie chief which assured him the intentions of the old warrior were not amicable ; and that he took the very summary process which has been related, not only to secure *his* scalp, but effectually to put it out of his power to do any mischief to one who was an ally, and, by means of recent confidence, now a friend. All this the Indian explained to his companion, in his usual clipped English, but with a clearness sufficient to make it perfectly intelligible to his listener. The bee-hunter listened with the most profound attention, for he was fully aware of the importance of comprehending all the hazards of his own situation.

While this dialogue was going on, Margery had succeeded in lighting her fire, and was busy in preparing some warm compound, which she knew would be required by her unhappy brother after his debauch. Dorothy passed often between the fire and the canoe, feeling a wife's anxiety in the fate of her husband. As for the Chippewa, intoxication was a very venial offence in his eyes ; though he had a contempt for a man who would thus indulge while on a warpath. The American Indian does possess this merit of adapting his deportment to his circumstances. When engaged in war, he usually prepares himself in the coolest and wisest manner to meet its struggles, indulging only in moments of leisure and of comparative security. It is true that the march of what is called civilization is fast changing the redman's character, and he is very apt now to do that which he sees done by the " Christians " around him.

Le Bourdon, when his dialogue with the Chippewa was over, and after a few words of explanation with Margery, took his own canoe, and paddled through the rice plants into the open water of the river, to reconnoitre. The breadth of the stream induced him to float down before the wind until he reached a point where he could again command a view of the hut. What he there saw, and what he next did, must be reserved for a succeeding chapter.

CHAPTER VIII.

"The elfin cast a glance around,
    As he lighted down from his courser toad,
Then round his breast his wings he wound,
    And close to the river's brink he strode ;
He sprang on a rock, he breathed a prayer,
    Above his head his arms he threw,
Then tossed a tiny curve in air,
    And headlong plunged in the water blue."

DRAKE.

AN hour had intervened between the time when Le Bourdon had removed the canoes of the Pottawattamies and the time when he returned alone to the northern side of the river. In the course of that hour the chief of the savages had time to ascertain all the leading circumstances that had just been related, and to collect his people in and around the hut for a passing council. The moment was one of action, and not of ceremonies. No pipe was smoked, nor any of the observances of the great councils of the tribe attended to ; the object was merely to glean facts and to collect opinions. In all the tribes of this part of North America, something very like a principle of democracy is the predominant feature of their politics. It is not, however, that bastard democracy which is coming so much in fashion among ourselves, and which looks into the gutters solely for the "people," forgetting that the landlord has just as much right to protection as the tenant, the master as the servant, the rich as the poor, the gentleman as the blackguard. The Indians know better than all this. They understand, fully, that the chiefs are entitled to more respect than the loafers in their villages, and listen to the former, while their ears are shut to the latter. They appear to have a common sense which teaches them to avoid equally the exaggerations of those who believe in blood, and of those who believe in blackguardism. With them the doctrines of "new men" would sound as an absurdity, for they never submit to change for change's sake. On the contrary, while there is no positive hereditary rank, there is much hereditary consideration; and we doubt if a redman could be found in all America who is so much of a simpleton as to cite among the qualifications of any man for a situation of trust and responsibility, that he had never been *taught* how to perform its duties. They are not guilty of the contradiction of elevating men *because* they are self-taught, while they expend millions on schools. Doubtless they have, after a fashion of their own, demagogues and Cæsars, but they are usually kept within moderate limits; and in rare instances, indeed, do either ever seriously trespass on the rights of the tribe. As human nature is everywhere the same, it is not to be supposed that pure justice prevails even among savages; but one thing would seem to be certain, that, all over the world, man in his simplest and wildest state is more apt to respect his own ordinances than when living in what is deemed a condition of high civilization.

When Le Bourdon reached the point whence he could get a good view of the door of the hut, which was still illuminated by the fire within, he ceased using the paddle beyond the slight effort necessary to keep the canoe nearly stationary. He was quite within the range of a rifle, but trusted to the darkness of the night for his protection. That scouts were out, watching the approaches to the hut, he felt satisfied; and he did not doubt that some were prowling along the margin of the Kalamazoo, either looking for the lost boats or for those who had taken them away. This made him cautious, and he took good care not to place his canoe in a position of danger.

It was very apparent that the savages were in great uncertainty as to the number of their enemies. Had not the rifle been fired, and their warrior killed and scalped, they might have supposed that their prisoner had found the means of releasing his limbs himself, and thus effected his escape; but they knew that the Chippewa had neither gun nor knife, and as all their own arms, even to those of the dead man, were still in their own possession, it was clear that he had been succored from without. Now the Pottawattamies had heard of both the bee-hunter and Whiskey Centre, and it was natural enough for them to ascribe some of these unlooked-for feats to one or the other of these agents. It is true, the hut was known to have been built three or four years earlier, by an Indian trader, and no one of the party had ever actually seen Gershom and his family in possession; but the conjectures on this head were as near the fact as if the savages had passed and repassed daily. There was only one point on which these close calculators of events were at fault. So thoroughly had everything been removed from the *chienté*, and so carefully the traces of its recent occupation concealed, that no one among them suspected that the family had left the place only an hour before their own arrival. The bee-hunter, moreover, was well assured that the savages had not blundered on the hiding-place of the furniture. Had this been discovered, its contents would have been dragged to light, and seen around the fire; for there is usually little self-restraint among the redmen when they make a prize of this sort.

Nevertheless, there was one point about which even those keen-scented children of the forest were much puzzled, and which the bee-hunter perfectly comprehended, notwithstanding the distance at which he was compelled to keep himself. The odor of the whiskey was so strong, in and about the *chienté*, that the Pottawattamies did not know what to make of it. That there should be the remains of this peculiar smell—one so fragrant and tempting to those who are accustomed to indulge in the liquor—in the hut itself was natural enough; but the savages were perplexed at finding it so strong on the declivity down which the barrels had been rolled. On this subject were they conversing when Le Bourdon first got near enough to observe their proceedings. After discussing the matter for some time,

8

torches were lighted, and most of the party followed a grim old warrior, who had an exceedingly true nose for the scent of whiskey, and who led them to the very spot where the half-barrel had been first stove, by rolling off a rock, and where its contents had been mainly spilled. Here the earth was yet wet, in places, and the scent was so strong as to leave no doubt of the recent nature of the accident which had wasted so much of a liquor that was very precious in Pottawattamie eyes; for accident they thought it must be, since no sane man could think of destroying the liquor intentionally.

All the movements, gestures, and genuflections of the savages were plainly seen by the bee-hunter. We say the genuflections, for nearly all of the Indians got on their knees and applied their noses to the earth, in order to scent the fragrance of the beloved whiskey; some out of curiosity, but more because they loved even this tantalizing indulgence, when no better could be had. But Le Bourdon was right in his conjectures that the matter was not to end here. Although most of the Indians scented the remains of the whiskey out of love for the liquor, a few of their number reasoned on the whole transaction with quite as much acuteness as could have been done by the shrewdest natural philosopher living. To them it was very apparent that no great length of time, a few hours at most, could have elapsed since that whiskey was spilled; and human hands must have brought it there, in the first place, and poured it on the ground, in the second. There must have been a strong reason for such an act, and that reason presented itself to their minds with unerring accuracy. Their own approach must have been seen, and the liquor was destroyed because it could not be removed in time to prevent its falling into their hands. Even the precise manner in which the whiskey had been disposed of was pretty nearly conjectured by a few of the chiefs, acute and practised as they were, who, accustomed to this species of exercise of their wits, had some such dexterity in examining facts of this nature, and in arriving at just results, as the men of the schools manifest in the inquiries that more especially belonged to their habits and training. But their conclusions were confined to themselves ; and they were also sufficiently enveloped in doubts to leave those who made them ready enough to receive new impressions on the same subject.

All this, moreover, Le Bourdon both saw and understood ; or, if not absolutely all, so much of it as to let him comprehend the main conclusions of the savages, as well as the process by which they were reached. To obtain light, the Indians made a fire near the charmed spot, which brought themselves and their movements into plain view from the canoe of the bee-hunter. Curiosity now became strongly awakened in the latter, and he ventured in nearer to the shore, in order to get the best possible view of what was going on. In a manner, he was solving an enigma ; and he experienced the sort of pleasure we all feel at exercising our wits on difficulties of that nature. The interest he felt rendered the young man careless as respected the possession of his canoe, which drifted down before the strong breeze, until Le Bourdon found himself in the very edge of the wild rice, which at this point formed but a very narrow belt along the beach. It was this plant, indeed, that contributed to make the young man so regardless of his drift, for he looked upon the belt of rice as a species of land-mark to warn him when to turn. But at no other spot along that whole shore, where the plant was to be found at all, was its belt so narrow as at this, immediately opposite to the new fire of the savages, and almost within the influence of its rays. To Le Bourdon's surprise, and somewhat to his consternation, just as his little craft touched the rice, the forms of two stout warriors passed along the beach, between him and the light, their feet almost dipping in the water. So near were these two warriors to him that, on listening intently, he heard not only their voices, as they communicated their thoughts to each other in low tones, but the tread of their moccasined feet on the ground. Retreat, under the circumstances, would not be safe, for it must have been made under the muzzles of the rifles ; and but one resource presented itself. By grasping in his hand two or three stalks of the rice-plant, and holding them firmly, the drift of the canoe was arrested.

After a moment's reflection, Le Bourdon was better satisfied with this new station than he had been on first gaining it. To have ventured on such a near approach to his enemies he would have regarded as madness ; but now he was there, well concealed among the rice, he enjoyed the advantages of observation it gave him, and looked upon the chance that brought him there as lucky. He found a thong of buckskin, and fastened his canoe to the stalks of the plant, thus anchoring or mooring his little bark, and leaving himself at liberty to move about in it. The rice was high enough to conceal him, even when erect, and he had some difficulty in finding places favorable to making his observations through it. When the bee-hunter made his way into the bow of his canoe, however, which he did with a moccasined and noiseless foot, he was startled at perceiving how small was his cover. In point of fact, he was now within three feet of the inner edge of the rice-plants, which grew within ten feet of the shore, where the two warriors already mentioned were still standing, in close communication with each other. Their faces were turned towards the fire, the bright light from which, at times, streamed over the canoe itself, in a way to illumine all it contained. The first impulse of Le Bourdon, on ascertaining how closely he had drifted to the shore, was to seize a paddle and make off, but a second thought again told him it would be far safer to remain where he was. Taking his seat, therefore, on a bit of board laid athwart, from gunwale to gunwale, if such a craft can be said to have gunwales at all, he patiently awaited the course of events.

By this time, all or nearly all of the Pottawattamies had collected at this spot, on the side of the hill. The hut was deserted, its fire got to be low, and darkness reigned around the place. On the other hand, the Indians kept piling brush on their new fire, until the whole of that hill-side, the stream at its foot, and the ravine through which the latter ran, were fairly illuminated. Of course, all within the influence of this light was to be distinctly seen, and the bee-hunter was soon absorbed in gazing at the movements of savage enemies under circumstances so peculiar.

The savages seemed to be entranced by the singular and to most of them unaccountable circumstance of the earth's giving forth the scent of fresh whiskey, in a place so retired and unknown. While two or three of the number had certain inklings of the truth, as has been stated, to much the greater portion of their body it appeared to be a profound mystery; and one that, in some inexplicable manner, was connected with the recent digging up of the hatchet. Ignorance and superstition ever go hand in hand, and it was natural that many, perhaps that most, of these uninstructed beings should thus consider so unusual a fragrance on such a spot. Whiskey has unfortunately obtained a power over the redmen of this continent that it would require many Fathers Matthew to suppress, and which can only be likened to that which is supposed to belong to the influence of witchcraft. The Indian is quite as sensible as the white man of the mischief that the "fire-water" produces; but, like the white man, he finds how hard it is to get rid of a master passion, when we have once submitted ourselves to its sway. The portion of the band that could not account for the fact of the scent of their beloved beverage's being found in such a place, and it was all but three of their whole party, were quite animated in their discussions on the subject, and many and crude were the suggestions that fell from their lips. The two warriors on the beach were more deeply impressed than any of their companions with the notion that some "medicine charm" was connected with this extraordinary affair.

The reader will not be surprised to hear that Le Bourdon gazed on the scene before him with the most profound attention. So near did he seem to be, and so near was he, in fact, to the savages who were grouped around the fire, that he fancied he could comprehend what they were saying, by the expressions of their grim and swarthy countenances. His conjectures were in part just, and occasionally the bee-hunter was absolutely accurate in his notions of what was said. The frequency with which different individuals knelt on the ground, to scent an odor that is always so pleasant to the redman, would of itself have given a clew to the general character of the discourse ; but the significant and expressive gestures, the rapid enunciation, and the manner in which the eyes of the speakers glanced from the faces near themselves to the spot consecrated by the whiskey, pretty plainly told the story. It was while thus intently occupied in endeavoring to read the singular impression made on the minds of most of those wild beings, by an incident so much out of the usual track of their experience, that Le Bourdon suddenly found the bow of his canoe thrusting itself beyond the inner margin of the rice, and issuing into open water, within ten feet of the very spot where the two nearest of the savages were still confering together, apart. The buckskin thong which served as a fastening had got loosened, and the light craft was again drifting down before the strong southerly wind, which still continued to blow a little gale.

Had there been an opportunity for such a thing, the bee-hunter would have made an effort to escape. But so sudden and unexpected was this exposure, that he found himself almost within reach of a rifle, before he was aware of his approaching the two warriors on the shore at all. His paddle was in the stern of the canoe, and had he used the utmost activity, the boat would have grounded on the beach ere he could have obtained it. In this situation, therefore, he was absolutely without any other means than his hands, of stopping the canoe, had there even been time.

Le Bourdon understood his real situation without stopping to reflect ; and, though his heart made one violent leap as soon as he perceived he was out of cover, he immediately bethought him of the course he ought to pursue. It would have been fatal to betray alarm or to attempt flight. As accident had thus brought him, as it might be on a visit, to the spot, he at once determined to give his arrival the character of a friendly call, and the better to support the pretension, to blend with it, if possible, a little of the oracular or " medicine " manner, in order to impose on the imaginations of the superstitious beings into whose power he had so unwittingly fallen.

The instant the canoe touched the shore, and it was only a moment after it broke through the cover, Le Bourdon arose, and, extending his hand to the nearest Indian, saluted him with the mongrel term of "Sago." A slight exclamation from this warrior communicated to his companion an arrival that was quite as much a matter of surprise to the Indians as to their guest, and through this second warrior to the whole party on the hill-side. A little clamor succeeded, and presently the bee-hunter was surrounded with savages.

The meeting was marked by the self-command and dignified quiet that are so apt to distinguish the deportment of Indian warriors when they are on the war-path and alive to the duties of manhood. The bee-hunter shook hands with several, who received his salutations with perfect calmness, if not with absolute confidence and amity. This little ceremony gave our hero an opportunity to observe the swarthy countenances by which he was surrounded, most of which were fierce in their paint, as well as to reflect a little on his own course. By a fortunate inspiration he now determined to assume the character of a "medicine-man," and to connect his prophecies and juggleries with this lucky accident of the whiskey. Accordingly, he inquired if any one spoke English, not wishing to trust his explanations to his own imperfect knowledge of the Ojebway tongue, which is spoken by all the numerous tribes of that widely-extended nation. Several could render themselves intelligible in English, and one was so expert as to render communication with him easy, if not very agreeable. As the savages, however, soon insisted on examing the canoe, and taking a look at its contents, previously to listening to their visitor's explanations, Le Bourdon was fain to submit, and to let the young men satisfy their curiosity.

The bee-hunter had come on his hazardous expedition in his own canoe. Previously to quitting the south shore, however, he had lightened the little craft by landing everything that was not essential to his present purpose. As nearly half of his effects were in the canoe of Whiskey Centre, the task was soon performed, and lucky it was for our hero that he

had bethought him of the prudence of the measure. His
sole object had been to render the canoe swifter and lighter,
in the event of a chase ; but, as things turned out, he saved
no small portion of his property by using the precaution.
The Indians found nothing in the canoe but one rifle, with
a horn and pouch, a few light articles belonging to the bee-
hunter's domestic economy, and which he had not thought
it necessary to remove, and the paddles. All the honey, and
the skins and stores and spare powder and lead, and, in short,
everything else that belonged to Le Bourdon, was still safe,
on the other side of the river. The greatest advantage
gained by the Pottawattamies was in the possession of the
canoe itself, by means of which they would now be enabled
to cross the Kalamazoo, or make any other similar expedition
by water.

But as yet not a sign of hostility was betrayed by either
party. The bee-hunter seemed to pay no attention to his
rifle and ammunition, or even to his canoe, while the savages, after having warily examined the last, together with
its contents, returned to their visitor, to re-examine him,
with a curiosity as lively as it was full of distrust. At this
stage in the proceeding, something like a connected and
intelligible conversation commenced between the chief who
spoke English, and who was known in most of the northwestern garrisons of the Americans by the name of Thunder-
cloud, or Cloud, by way of abbreviation, on account of his
sinister looks, though the man actually sustained a tolerably
fair reputation for one of those who, having been wronged,
was so certain to be calumniated. No man was ever yet
injured, that he has not been slandered.

"Who kill and scalp my young man ?" asked Cloud, a
little abruptly.

"Has my brother lost a warrior?" was the calm reply.
"Yes, I see that he has. A medicine-man can see that,
though it is dark."

"Who kill him, if can see ? Who scalp him, too ?"

"An enemy did both," answered Le Bourdon, oracularly.
"Yes, 't was an enemy that killed him ; and an enemy
that took his scalp."

"Why do it, eh? Why come here to take Pottawattamie scalp, when no war-path open, eh?"

"Pottawattamie, the truth must always be said to a medicine-man. There is no use in trying to hide the truth from *him*. There *is* a war-path open; and a long and a tangled path it is. My Great Father at Washington has dug up the hatchet against my Great Father at Quebec. Enemies always take scalps when they can get them."

"Dat true—dat right, too—nobody grumble at *dat*—but who enemy? pale-face or redskin?"

"This time it was redskin—a Chippewa—one of your own nation, though not of your own tribe. A warrior called Pigeonswing, whom you had in thongs, intending to torture him in the morning. He cut his thongs, and shot your young man—after which he took his scalp."

"How know dat?" demanded Cloud, a little fiercely. "You 'long, and help kill Pottawattamie, eh?"

"I know it," answered Le Bourdon, coolly, "because medicine-men know most of what happens. Do not be so hasty, chief, for this is a medicine spot—whiskey *grows* here."

A common exclamation escaped all of the redmen who comprehended the clear, distinct, and oracular-like language and manner of the bee-hunter. He intended to make an impression on his listeners, and he succeeded admirably; perhaps as much by means of manner as of matter. As has been said, all who understood his words—some four or five of the party—grunted forth their surprise at this evidence of their guest's acquaintance with the secrets of the place, in which they were joined by the rest of their companions as soon as the words of the pale-face had been translated. Even the experienced and wary old chiefs, who had more than half conjectured the truth in connection with this mysterious odor of whiskey, were much unsettled in their opinions concerning the wonder, and got to be in that condition of mind when a man does not know what to think of any particular event. The bee-hunter, quick-witted, and managing for his life, was not slow to perceive the advantage he had gained, and he proceeded at

once to clinch the nail he had so skilfully driven. Turning from Cloud to the head chief of the party, a warrior
whom he had no difficulty in recognizing, after having so
long watched his movements in the earlier part of the night,
he pushed the same subject a little further.

"Yes; this place is called by the whites Whiskey
Centre," he added; "which means that it is the centre of
all the whiskey of the country round about."

"Dat true," said Cloud, quickly; "I hear so'ger at Fort
Dearborn call him Whiskey Centre!"

This little circumstance greatly complicated the mystery,
and Le Bourdon perceived that he had hit on a lucky explanation.

"Soldiers far and near—soldiers drunk or sober—soldiers with scalps and soldiers without scalps—all know
the place by that name. But you need not believe with
your eyes shut and noses stopped, chief, since you have
the means of learning for yourselves the truth of what I tell
you. Come with me, and I will tell you where to dig in
the morning for a whiskey spring."

This communication excited a tremendous feeling among
the savages when its purport came to be explained to the
whole party. Apart from the extraordinary, miraculous
nature of such a spring, which in itself was sufficient to
keep alive expectation and gratify curiosity, it was so comfortable to have an inexhaustible supply of the liquor
running out of the bowels of the earth, that it is no wonder
the news spread infinite delight among the listeners. Even
the two or three of the chiefs who had so shrewdly divined
the manner in which the liquor had been spilled were
staggered by the solemnity and steadiness of the bee-
hunter's manner, and perhaps a little carried away by sympathy with those around them. This yielding of the human
mind to the influence of numbers is so common an occurrence as scarcely to require explanation, and is the source
of half the evils that popular associations inflict on themselves. It is not that men capable of *seeing* the truth are
ever wanting, but men capable of *maintaining* it, in the
face of clamor and collected power.

It will be readily conceived that a medicine-man, who is supposed to possess the means of discovering a spring that should overflow with pure whiskey, would not be left without urgent demands for a speedy exercise of his art. This was now the case with Le Bourdon, who was called on from all sides to point out the precise spot where the young men were to commence digging in order to open on the treasure. Our hero knew that his only hope of escape was connected with his steadily maintaining his assumed character; or, of maintaining this assumed character, with his going on at once to do something that might have the effect, temporarily at least, of satisfying the impatience of his now attentive listeners. Accordingly, when the demand was made on him to give some evidence of his power, he set about the task, not only with composure, but with a good deal of ingenuity.

Le Bourdon, it will be remembered, had, with his own hands, rolled the two barrels of whiskey down the declivity. Feeling the great importance of effectually destroying them, he had watched their descent from the top to the bottom of the hill, and the final disappearance of the staves, etc., in the torrent which brawled at its foot. It had so happened that the half-filled cask broke and let out its liquor at a point much more remote from the stream than the filled cask. The latter had held together until it went over the low rocky precipice already mentioned, and was stove at its base, within two yards of the torrent, which received all its fragments and swept them away, including most of the liquor itself; but not until the last had been spilled. Now the odorous spot which had attracted the noses of the savages, and near which they had built their fire, was that where the smallest quantity of the whiskey had fallen. Le Bourdon reasoned on these circumstances in this wise : If half a barrel of the liquor can produce so strong a scent, a barrel filled ought to produce one still stronger ; and I will manifest my medicine-character by disregarding for the present moment the spot on the hill-side, and proceed at once to that at the foot of the rocks. To this latter point, therefore, did he direct all the ceremony, as well as his own footsteps, when he yielded to the solicitations of the Pottawattamies, and undertook to point out the position of the whiskey spring.

The bee-hunter understood the Indian character too well to forget to embellish his work with a proper amount of jugglery and acting. Luckily, he had left in the canoe a sort of frock of mottled colors, that he had made himself, to wear in the woods in the autumn as a hunting dress, under the notion that such a covering would conceal his approach from his game, by blending its hues with those of the autumn leaf. This dress he now assumed, extorting a good deal of half-suppressed admiration from the younger warriors by the gay appearance he made. Then he drew out his spy-glass to its greatest length, making various mysterious signs and gestures as he did so. This glass proved to be a great auxiliary, and possibly alone kept the doubters in awe. Le Bourdon saw at once that it was entirely new, even to the oldest chief, and he felt how much it might be made to assist him. Beckoning to Cloud, and adjusting the focus, he directed the small end of his glass to the fire, and placed the large end to that Indian's eye. A solitary savage, who loved the scent of whiskey too much to tear himself away from the spot, was lingering within the influence of the rays, and of course was seen by the chief, with his person diminished to that of a dwarf, and his form thrown to a seeming distance.

An eloquent exclamation followed this exhibition of the medicine-man's power ; and each of the chiefs, and most of the other warriors, were gratified with looks through the glass.

"What dat mean?" demanded Cloud, earnestly. "See Wolfeye well 'nough—why he so little?—why he so far off, eh?"

"That is to show you what a medicine-man of the pale-faces can do, when he is so minded. That Indian is named Wolfseye, and he loves whiskey too well. That I know as well as I know his name."

Each of these exhibitions of intelligence extorted exclamations of wonder. It is true that one or two of the higher chiefs understood that the name might possibly have been obtained from Cloud ; but how was the medicine-man to know that Wolfseye was a drunkard? This last had not been said in terms; but enough had been said to let those who were aware of the propensity feel that more was meant than had been expressed. Before there was time, however, to deliberate on, or to dissect this specimen of mysterious knowledge, Le Bourdon reversed the glass, and applied the small end to the eye of Cloud, after having given it its former direction. The Indian fairly yelled, partly with dread and partly with delight, when he saw Wolfseye, large as life, brought so near himself that he fancied he might be touched with his own hand.

"What dat mean!" exclaimed Cloud, as soon as surprise and awe enabled him to find his voice. "Fuss he little, den he big—fuss he great way, den he close by—what dat mean, eh?"

"It means that I am a medicine-man, and this is a medicine-glass, and that I can see with it into the earth, deeper than the wells, or higher than the mountains!"

These words were translated and explained to all there. They extorted many ejaculations of wonder, and divers grunts of admiration and contentment. Cloud conferred a moment with the two principal chiefs; then he turned eagerly to the bee-hunter, saying,—

"All good, but want to hear more—want to l'arn more —want to *see* more."

"Name your wants freely, Pottawattamie," answered Le Bourdon, with dignity ; "they shall be satisfied."

"Want to see—want to *taste* whiskey spring—see won't do—want to *taste*."

"Good—you shall smell first ; then you shall see ; after that you shall taste. Give me room, and be silent ; a great medicine is near."

Thus delivering himself, Le Bourdon proceeded with his necromancy.

CHAPTER IX.

" He turn'd him round, and fled amain
  With hurry and dash to the beach again ;
  He twisted over from side to side,
  And laid his cheek to the cleaving tide ;
  The strokes of his plunging arms are fleet,
  And with all his might he flings his feet,
  But the water-sprites are round him still,
  To cross his path and work him ill."

The Culprit Fay.

THE first step in the conjuration of the bee-hunter
was to produce an impression on the minds of his
untutored observers, by resorting to a proper
amount of mummery and mystical action. This
he was enabled to do with some effect, in consequence of
having practised, as a lad, in similar mimicry by way of
pastime. The Germans, and the descendants of Germans
in America, are not of a very high class as respects education,
taken as a body, and they retain many of the most inveterate
superstitions of their Teutonic ancestors. Although the
bee-hunter himself was of purely English descent, he came
from a State that was in part peopled by these Germans and
their descendants ; and by intercourse with them he had
acquired a certain knowledge of their notions on the subject
of necromancy, that he now found was of use. So far as
gravity of mien, solemn grimaces, and unintelligible mutter-
ings were concerned, Le Bourdon played his part to admiration ; and by the time he had led the party half the distance
he intended to go, our necromancer, or "medicine-man,"
had complete possession of the imaginations of all the
savages, the two or three chiefs already mentioned alone

excepted. At this stage of the proceedings occurred a little incident which goes to prove the disposition of the common mind to contribute in deceiving itself, and which was of considerable assistance to Le Bourdon in maintaining his assumed character.

It will be remembered that the place where the Indians had found their strongest scent was on the hill-side, or at the spot where the half-filled barrel had let out most of its contents. Near this spot their new fire was still brightly blazing, and there Wolfseye remained, regaling one of his senses, at least, with an odor that he found so agreeable. But the bee-hunter knew that he should greatly increase the wonder of the savages by leading them to a *new* scent-spot, one to which there was no visible clew, and where the odor was probably much stronger than on the hill-side. Accordingly he did not approach the fire, but kept around the base of the hill, just enough within the influence of the light to pick his way readily, and yet so distant from it as to render his countenance indistinct and mysterious. No sooner, however, had he got abreast of the scent-spot known to the savages, than the crowd endeavored to lead him towards it by gestures and hints, and finally by direct intimations that he was going astray. All this our "medicine-man" disregarded ; he held his way steadily and solemnly toward that place at the foot of the hill where he knew that the filled barrel had let out its contents, and where he reasonably enough expected to find sufficient traces of the whiskey to answer his purposes. At first, this pertinacity provoked the crowd, which believed he was going wrong ; but a few words from Crowsfeather, the principal chief, caused the commotion to cease. In a few more minutes Le Bourdon stopped, near the place of his destination. As a fresh scent of whiskey was very perceptible here, a murmur of admiration, not unmixed with delight, passed among the attendants.

"Now let the young men build a fire for *me*," said the bee-hunter, solemnly ; "not such a fire as that which is burning on the hill, but a medicine-fire. I *smell* the whiskey spring, and want a medicine-light to *see* it."

A dozen young men began to collect the brush; in a minute a pile of some size had been accumulated on a flat rock, within twenty feet of the spot where Le Bourdon knew that the cask had been dashed to pieces. When he thought the pile sufficiently large, he told Crowsfeather that it might be lighted by bringing a brand from the other fire.

"This will not be a medicine-light, for that can come only from 'medicine-matches,' " he added; "but I want a fire to see the shape of the ground. Put in the brand, brothers; let us have a flame."

The desire of the bee-hunter was gratified, and the whole of the base of the hill, around the spot where the filled cask had broken, was illuminated.

"Now let all the Pottawattamies stand back," added Le Bourdon, earnestly. "It might cost a warrior his life to come forward too soon; or, if not his life, it might give a rheumatism that can never be cured, which is worse. When it is time for my red brothers to advance, they will be called."

As the bee-hunter accompanied this announcement by suitable gestures, he succeeded in ranging all of the silent but excited savages on three sides of his fire, leaving that next his mysterious spring to himself alone. When all was arranged, Le Bourdon moved slowly, but unaccompanied, to the precise spot where the cask had broken. Here he found the odor of the whiskey so strong as to convince him that some of the liquor must yet remain. On examining more closely, he ascertained that several shallow cavities of the flat rock on which the cask had been dashed still contained a good deal of the liquor; enough to prove of great assistance to his medicine character.

All this while the bee-hunter kept one portion of his faculties on the alert, in order to effect his escape. That he might deceive for a time, aided as he was by so many favorable circumstances, he did not doubt; but he dreaded the morning and the results of a night of reflection and rest. Crowsfeather, in particular, troubled him; and he foresaw that his fate would be terrible, did the savages once get an inkling of the deception he was practising. As he stood there, bending over the little pools of whiskey, he glanced his eyes towards the gloom which pervaded the northern side of the hill, and calculated the chances of escape by trusting to his speed. All of the Pottawattamies were on the opposite side, and there was a thicket, favorably placed for a cover, so near that the rifle would scarce have time to perform its fatal office, ere he might hope to bury himself within its leaves. So tempting did the occasion appear that for a single instant Le Bourdon forgot his caution and his mummeries, and had actually advanced a step or two in the direction towards which he contemplated flight, when, on glancing an uneasy look behind him, he perceived Crows-feather and his two intimate counsellors stealthily preparing their rifles, as if they distrusted his intentions. This at once induced a change of plan, and brought the bee-hunter back to a sense of his critical position, and of the indispensable necessity of caution to a man in his situation.

Le Bourdon now seemingly gave all his attention to the rocks where he stood, and out of which the much-coveted liquor was expected to flow; though his thoughts were still busily employed in considering the means of escape the whole time. While stooping over the different pools, and laying his plans for continuing his medicine-charms, the bee-hunter saw how near he had been to committing a great mistake. It was almost as indispensable to carry off the canoe as it was to carry off himself; since, with the canoe, not only would all his own property, but pretty Margery, and Gershom and his wife, be at the mercy of the Pottawattamies; whereas by securing the boat, the wide Kalamazoo would serve as a nearly impassable barrier, until time was given to the whites to escape. His whole plan was changed by this suggestion, and he no longer thought of the thicket and of flight inland. At the same time that the bee-hunter was laying up in his mind ideas so important to his future movements, he did not neglect the necessary examination of the means that might be required to extend and prolong his influence over the minds of the superstitious children of the forest, on whom

9

he was required to practise his arts. His thoughts reverted
to the canoe, and he concocted a plan by which he believed
it possible to get possession of his little craft again. Once
on board it, by one vigorous shove, he fancied, he might
push it within the cover of the rice-plant, where he would
be in reasonable safety against the bullets of the savages.
Could he only get the canoe on the outer side of the narrow
belt of the plant, he should deem himself safe !

Having arranged his course in his own mind, Le Bourdon now beckoned to Crowsfeather to draw near, at the
same time inviting the whole party to approach within a
few feet of the spot where he himself stood. The bee-
hunter had brought with him from the boat a fragment of
the larger end of a cane fishing-rod, which he used as a
sort of wand. Its size was respectable, and its length about
eight feet. With this wand he pointed out the different
objects he named, and it answered the very important purpose of enabling him to make certain small changes in the
formation of the ground, that were of the greatest service
to him, without permitting curious eyes to come so near as
to detect his artifices.

"Now open your ears, Crowsfeather ; and you, Cloud ;
and all of you, young braves," commenced the bee-hunter,
solemnly, and with a steadiness that was admirable ; "yes,
open wide your ears. The Great Spirit has given the redman a nose that he might smell ; does the Cloud smell more
than common ?"

"Sartain—smell whiskey—this Whiskey Centre dey say
—nat'ral dat such smell be here."

"Do all the chiefs and warriors of the Pottawattamies who
are present also smell the same ? "

"S'pose so—why he don't, eh? Got nose—can smell
whiskey good way, tell you."

"It is right they should smell the liquor here, for out of
this rock a whiskey spring will soon begin to run. It will
begin with a very small stream, but soon will there be
enough to satisfy everybody. The Great Manitou knows
that his red children are dry ; he has sent a 'medicine-
man' of the pale-faces to find a spring for them. Now,

look at this piece of rock; it is dry; not even the dew has yet moistened it. See! it is made like a wooden bowl, that it may hold the liquor of the spring. Let Crows-feather smell it—smell it, Cloud—let all my young men smell it, too, that they may be certain that there is nothing there.''

On this invitation, accompanied as it was by divers flourishes of the wand, and uttered in a deep solemn tone of voice, the whole party of the Indians gathered around the small hollow basin-like cavity pointed out by the bee-hunter, in order both to see and smell. Most knelt, and each and all applied their noses to the rock, as near the bowl as they could thrust them. Even the dignified and distrustful Crowsfeather could not refrain from bending in the crowd. This was the moment for which Le Bourdon wished, and he instantly prepared to carry out his design.

Previously, however, to completing the project origin-ally conceived, a momentary impulse prevailed which urged him to adopt a new mode of effecting his escape. Now that most of the savages were on their hands and knees, struggling to get their noses as near as possible to the bowl, and all were intent on the same subject, it occurred to the bee-hunter, who was almost as active as the panther of the American forest, that he might dash on towards the canoe, and make his escape without further mummery. Had it been only a question of human speed, perhaps such would have been the wisest thing he could do; but a mo-ment's reflection told him how much swifter than any foot of man was the bullet of a rifle. The distance exceeded a hundred yards, and it was altogether in bright light, by means of the two fires, Wolfseye continuing to pile brush on that near which he still maintained his post, as if afraid the precious liquor would start out of the scent-spot and be wasted should he abandon his ward. Happily, there-fore, Le Bourdon relinquished this dangerous project almost as soon as it was entertained, turning his attention imme-diately to the completion of the plan originally laid.

It has been said that the bee-hunter made sundry flour-ishes with his wand. While the savages were most eager in endeavoring to smell the rock, he lightly touched the earth that confined the whiskey in the largest pool, and opened a passage by which the liquor could trickle down the side of the rock, selecting a path for itself, until it actually came into the bowl, by a sinuous but certain channel!

Here was a wonder! Liquor could not only be smelled, but it could be actually seen! As for Cloud, not satisfied with gratifying the two senses connected with the discoveries named, he began to lap with his tongue, like a dog, to try the effect of taste.

"The Manitou does not hide his face from the Pottawattamies!" exclaimed this savage, rising to his feet in astonishment; "this is fire-water, and such as the pale-faces bring us for skins!"

Others imitated his example, and the exclamations of wonder and delight flew from mouth to mouth, in a torrent of vehement assertions and ejaculations. So great a "medicine" charm had never before been witnessed in that tribe, or in that region, and a hundred more might succeed, before another should equal this in its welcome character. There was whiskey, of a certainty, not much in quantity, to be sure, but of excellent quality, as several affirmed, and coming in a current that was slowly increasing! This last sign was owing to the circumstance that Le Bourdon had deepened the outlet of the pool, permitting a larger quantity to flow down the little channel.

The moment had now come for a decisive step. The bee-hunter knew that this precious rivulet would soon cease to run, and that he must carry out his design under the first impressions of his charm, or that he probably would not be permitted to carry it out at all. At this moment even Crowsfeather appeared to be awed by what he had seen; but a chief so sagacious might detect the truth, and disappointment would then be certain to increase the penalties he would incur.

Making many sweeps of his wand, and touching various points of the rock, both to occupy the attention of the savages, and to divert it from his pool, the bee-hunter next felt in his pocket and drew out a small piece of resin that he knew was there ; the remains of a store with which he resined the bow of his fiddle ; for our hero had a violin among his effects, and often used it in his solitary abodes in the openings. Breaking this resin on a coal, he made it flash and blaze ; but the quantity was too small to produce the '' medicine-fire '' he wanted.

"I have more in my canoe," he said, addressing himself to the interpreter ; '' while I go for it, the redmen must not stir, lest they destroy a pale-face's doings. Least of all must they go near the spring. It would be better for the chiefs to lead away their young men, and make them stand under that oak, where nothing can be done to hurt the ' medicine charm.' ''

The bee-hunter pointed to a tree that stood in the direction of the canoe, in order to prevent distrust, though he had taken care to select a spot, whence the little craft could not be seen, on account of an intervening swell in the land. Crowsfeather led his warriors to the indicated place, where they took their stations, in silent and grave attention.

In the meanwhile Le Bourdon continued his incantations aloud ; walking towards his canoe, waving his wand, and uttering a great deal of gibberish as he slowly proceeded. In passing the tree, our hero, though he did not turn his head, was sensible that he was followed by the chiefs, a movement against which he did not dare to remonstrate, though it sadly disappointed him. Neither hastening nor retarding his steps, however, in consequence of this unpleasant circumstance, the young man continued on ; once or twice sweeping the wand behind him, in order to ascertain if he could reach his followers. But Crowsfeather and his companions stopped when they reached the swell of land which concealed the canoe, suffering the '' medicine-man '' to move on, alone. Of this fact Le Bourdon became aware by turning three times in a circle, and pointing upwards at the heavens with his wand as he did so.

It was a nervous moment when the bee-hunter reached the canoe. He did not like to look behind him again, lest the chiefs should suspect his motive, and, in shoving off from the shore, he might do so within a few yards of the

muzzle of a hostile rifle. There was no time to lose, however, for any protracted delay on his part would certainly
cause the savages to approach, through curiosity, if not
through distrust of his motives. He stepped into his light
craft, therefore, without any delay, still flourishing his wand,
and muttering his incantations. The first thing was to
walk to the stern of the canoe, that his weight might raise
the bow from the shore, and also that he might have an
excuse for turning round, and thus get another look at the
Indians. So critical was his situation, and so nervous did
it make our young hero, that he took no heed of the state
of matters in the canoe until the last moment. When he
had turned, however, he ascertained that the two principal
chiefs had drawn so near as to be within twenty yards of
him, though neither held his rifle at "ready," but each
leaned on it in a careless manner, as if in no anticipation
of any necessity to make a speedy use of the weapon. This
state of things could not last, and Le Bourdon braced his
nerves for the final trial. On looking for his paddle, however, he found that of three, which the canoe had contained
when he left it, not one was to be seen. These wily savages
had, out of all question, taken their opportunity to remove
and secrete these simple but almost indispensable means
of motion.

At the instant when first apprised of the loss just mentioned, the bee-hunter's heart sunk within him, and he fell
into the seat in the stern of the canoe, nearly with the
weight of so much lead. Then a species of desperation
came over him, and putting an end of his cane wand upon
the bottom, with a vigorous shove, he forced the canoe
swiftly astern and to windward. Sudden as was this attempt, and rapid as was the movement, the jealous eyes
and ready hands of the chiefs seemed to anticipate it. Two
shots were fired within a few seconds after the canoe had
quitted the shore. The reports of the rifles were a declaration of hostilities, and a general yell, accompanied by a
common rush towards the river, announced that the whole
band now understood that some deception had been practised
at their expense.

Although the two chiefs in advance had been so very prompt, they were not quick enough for the rapid movement of the canoe. The distance between the stern of the boat and the rice-plants was so small, that the single desperate shove given by the bee-hunter sufficed to bury his person in the cover before the leaden messengers reached him. Anticipating this very attempt, and knowing that the savages might get their range from the part of the canoe that was still in sight, Le Bourdon bent his body far over the gunwale, grasping the rice-plants at the same time, and hauling his little craft through them, in the way that sailors call "hand over hand." This expedient most probably saved his life. While bending over the gunwale, he heard the crack of the rifles, and the whizzing of two bullets that appeared to pass just behind him. By this time the whole of the canoe was within the cover.

In a moment like that we are describing, incidents pass so rapidly as almost to defy description. It was not twenty seconds from the instant when Le Bourdon first put his wand down to push the canoe from the land, ere he found his person emerging from the cover on its weather side. Here he was effectually concealed from his enemies, not only on account of the cover made by the rice-plants, but by reason of the darkness; the light not extending far enough from the fire to illumine objects on the river. Nevertheless, new difficulties presented themselves. When clear of the rice, the wind, which still blew strong, pressed upon his canoe to such a degree as not only to stop its further movement from the shore, but so as to turn it broadside to, to its power. Trying with his wand, the bee-hunter ascertained that it would no longer reach the bottom. Then he attempted to use the cane as a paddle, but soon found it had not sufficient hold of the water to answer for such an implement. The most he could effect with it in that way was to keep the canoe for a short distance along the outer edge of the rice, until it reached a spot where the plant extended a considerable distance farther towards the middle of the river. Once within this little forest of the wild rice, he was enabled to drag the canoe farther and farther from the north shore, though his progress was both slow and laborious, on account of the resistance met.

All this time the savages were not idle.   Until the canoe got within its new cover, it was at no instant fifty yards from the beach, and the yells, and orders, and whoopings sounded as if uttered directly in Le Bourdon's ear.   A splashing in the water soon announced that our fugitive was pursued by swimmers.   As the savages knew that the bee-hunter was without a paddle, and that the wind blew fresh, the expecta- tion of overtaking their late captive, in this manner, was by no means chimerical.   Half a dozen active young men would prove very formidable to one in such a situation, more espe- cially while entangled in the mazes of the rice-plant.   The bee-hunter was so well convinced of this circumstance, that no sooner did he hear the plashes of the swimmers than he redoubled his exertions to pull his canoe farther from the spot.   But his progress was slow, and he was soon convinced that his impunity was more owing to the fact that his pur- suers did not know where to find him, than to the rapidity of his flight.

Notwithstanding his exertions, and the start obtained, Le Bourdon soon felt assured that the swimmers were within a hundred feet of him, their voices coming from the outer margin of the cover in which he now lay stationary. He had ceased dragging the canoe ahead, from an appre- hension of being heard, though the rushing of the wind and the rustling of the rice might have assured him that the slight noises made by his own movements would not be very likely to rise above those sounds.   The splashing of the swimmers, and their voices, gradually drew nearer, until the bee-hunter took up his rifle, determined to sac- rifice the first savage who approached ; hoping thereby to intimidate the others.   For the first time, it now occurred to him that the breech of his rifle might be used as a paddle, and he was resolved to apply it to that service, could he once succeed in extricating himself from the enemies by whom he was nearly environed, and from the rice.   c

Just as Le Bourdon fancied that the crisis had arrived, and that he should soon be called on to kill his man, a shout was given by a savage at some distance in the river, and presently calls passed from mouth to mouth, among the swimmers. Our hero now listened to a degree that kept his faculty of hearing at a point of painful attention. The voices and plashes on the water receded, and, what was startling, a sound was heard resembling that which is produced by a paddle when struck incautiously against the side of a canoe. Was it then possible that the Chippewa was out, or had the Pottawattamies one boat that had escaped his attention? The last was not very probable, as he had several times counted their little fleet, and was pretty sure of having taken it all to the other side of the river. The sound of the paddle was repeated, however; then it occurred to the bee-hunter that Pigeonswing might be on the scent for another scalp.

Although the conjecture just mentioned was exceedingly unpleasant to Le Bourdon, the chase of the strange canoe gave him an opportunity to drag his own light craft ahead, penetrating deeper and deeper among the wild rice, which now spread itself to a considerable distance from the shore, and grew so thick as to make it impossible to get through the waving mass. At length, wearied with his exertions, and a little uncertain as to his actual position, our hero paused, listening intently, in order to catch any sounds that might direct his future movements.

By this time the savages had ceased to call to each other; most probably conscious of the advantage it gave the fugitive. The bee-hunter perfectly understood that his pursuers must be aware of its being entirely out of his power to get to windward, and that they would keep along the shore of the river, as he did himself, expecting to see his canoe, sooner or later, driven by the wind on the beach. This had made him anxious to drag his boat as much towards the outer edge of the rice as he could get it, and, by the puffs of wind that he occasionally felt, he hoped he had, in a great measure, effected his purpose. Still he had his apprehensions of the savages; as some would be very apt

to swim quite out into the stream, not only to look for him,
but to avoid being entangled among the plants.   It was
only in the natural channels of the rice, of which there were
a good many, that a swimmer could very readily make his
way, or be in much safety.   By waiting long enough, moreover, the bee-hunter was sure he should tire out his pursuers, and thus get rid of them.

Just as Le Bourdon began to think this last mentioned
purpose had been accomplished, he heard low voices directly
to windward, and the plashing of water, as if more than one
man was coming down upon him, forcing the stalks of the
plants aside.   He grasped the rifle and let the canoe drift,
which it did slowly, under the power of the wind, notwithstanding the protection of the cover.   The swimmers forced
their way through the stalks ; but it was evident, just then,
that they were more occupied by their present pursuit than
in looking for him.   Presently, a canoe came brushing
through the rice, forced by the wind, and dragged by two
savages, one of whom swam on each bow.   The last did
not see the bee-hunter, or his canoe, the one nearest having his face turned in the opposite direction ; but they were
distinctly seen by the former.   Surprised that a seizure
should be made with so little fracas, Le Bourdon bent forward to look the better, and, as the stern of the strange
canoe came almost under his eyes, he saw the form of
Margery lying in its bottom.   His blood curdled at this
sight ; for his first impression was that the charming young
creature had been killed and scalped ; but there being no
time to lose, he sprang lightly from one canoe to the other,
carrying the rifle in his hand.   As he struck in the bottom
of the boat of Gershom, he heard his name uttered in a
sweet female voice, and knew that Margery was living.
Without stopping, however, to inquire more, he moved to
the head of the canoe, and, with a sharp blow on the fingers,
made each of the savages release his grasp.   Then, seizing
the rice-plants, he dragged the little craft swiftly to windward
again.   All this was done, as it might be, in an instant ; the
savages and the canoe being separated some twenty feet in
much less time than is required to relate the occurrence.

"Bourdon, are you injured?" asked Margery, her voice trembling with anxiety.

"Not in the least, dear Margery—and you, my excellent girl?"

"They caught my canoe, and I almost died of fright; but they have only dragged it towards the shore."

"God be praised! Is there any paddle in the canoe?"

"There are several; one is at your feet, Bourdon—and here, I have another."

"Then let us search for my canoe, and get out of the rice. If we can but find my canoe, we shall be safe enough, for the savages have nothing in which to cross the river. Keep your eyes about you, Margery, and look among the rice for the other boat."

The search was not long, but it was intently anxious. At length Margery saw the lost canoe just as it was drifting past them, and it was secured immediately. In a few minutes Le Bourdon succeeded in forcing the two craft into open water, when it was easy for him to paddle both to windward. The reader can readily imagine that our hero did not permit many minutes to elapse ere he questioned his companion on the subject of her adventures. Nor was Margery reluctant to tell them. She had become alarmed at Le Bourdon's protracted absence, and taking advantage of Pigeonswing lying down, she unloaded her brother's canoe, and went out into the river to look for the absent one. As a matter of course—though so feminine and far removed from all appearance of coarseness, a true American girl in this respect—Margery knew perfectly well how to manage a bark canoe. The habits of her life for the last few years made her acquainted with this simple art; and strength being much less needed than skill, she had no difficulty in going whither she wished. The fires served as beacons, and Margery had been a distant witness of the bee-hunter's necromancy as well as of his escape. The instant the latter was effected, she endeavored to join him; and it was while incautiously paddling along the outer edge of the rice, with this intention, that her canoe was seized by two of the swimmers. As soon as these last ascertained that they had captured a "squaw," they did not give themselves the trouble to get into the canoe—a very difficult operation with one made of bark, and which is not loaded—but they set about towing the captured craft to the shore, swimming each with a single hand, and holding on by the other.

"I shall not soon forget this kindness of yours, Margery," said Le Bourdon, with warmth, when the girl had ended her simple tale, which had been related in the most artless and ingenuous manner. "No man could forget so generous a risk on the part of a young woman in his behalf."

"I hope you do not think it wrong, Bourdon; I should be sorry to have you think ill of me!"

"Wrong, dear Margery!—but no matter. Let us get ourselves out of present difficulties, and into a place of safety; then I will tell you honestly what I think of it, and of you, too. Was your brother awake, dear Margery, when you left the family?"

"I believe not; he sleeps long and heavily after drinking. But he can now drink no more until he reaches the settlements."

"Not unless he find the Whiskey Spring," returned the bee-hunter, laughing.

The young man then related to his wondering companion the history of the mummery and incantations of which she had been a distant spectator. Le Bourdon's heart was light, after his hazards and escape, and his spirits rose as his narrative proceeded. Nor was pretty Margery in a mood to balk his humor. As the bee-hunter recounted his contrivances to elude the savages, and most especially when he gave the particulars of the manner in which he managed to draw whiskey out of the living rock, the girl joined in his merriment, and filled the boat with that melody of the laugh of her years and sex which is so beautifully described by Halleck.

CHAPTER X.

"The things that once she loved are still the same
Yet now there needs another name
To give the feeling which they claim,
  While she the feeling gives;
She cannot call it gladness or delight;
And yet there seems a richer, lovelier light
  On e'en the humblest thing that lives."

WASHINGTON ALSTON.

THE history given by Le Bourdon lasted until the canoes reached the south shore. Glad enough was Dorothy to see them both safe back, for neither of her companions had yet awoke. It was then midnight, and all now retired to seek the rest which might be so needful to prepare them for the exertions of the next day. The bee-hunter slept in his canoe, while Margery shared the buffalo-skin of her sister.

As perfect security, for the moment at least, was felt by the sleepers, their slumbers were sound, and reached into the morning. Then Le Bourdon arose, and withdrawing to a proper distance, he threw off his clothes and plunged into the stream, in conformity with a daily practice of his at that genial season of the year. After bathing, the young man ascended a hill, whence he might get a good view of the opposite shore, and possibly obtain some notion of what the Pottawattamies were about. In all his movements, however, the bee-hunter had an eye to the concealment of his person, it being of the last importance that the savages should not learn his position. With the intention of concealment, the fire had been suffered to go down, a smoke being a sign that no Indian would be likely to overlook.

As for the canoes and the bivouac of the party, the wild rice, and an intermediate hill, formed a perfect cover, so long as nothing was shown above them.

From the height to which he ascended, the bee-hunter, aided by his glass, got a very clear view of Whiskey Centre and the parts adjacent. The savages were already stirring, and were busy in the various avocations of the redman on a war-path. One party was disposing of the body of their dead companion. Several were cooking, or cleaning the wild fowl shot in the bay, while a group was collected near the spot of the wished-for spring, reluctant to abandon the hopes to which it had given birth, at the very moment they were plotting to obtain the scalp of the "medicine-man." The beloved "fire-water," that seduces so many to their destruction who have enjoyed the advantages of moral teaching, and which has been a withering curse on the red-man of this continent, still had its influence; and the craving appetites of several of the drunkards of the party brought them to the spot as soon as their eyes opened on the new day. The bee-hunter could see some of this cluster kneeling on the rocks, lapping like hounds at the scattered little pools of the liquor, while others scented around, in the hope of yet discovering the bird that laid the golden egg. Le Bourdon had now little expectation that his assumed character could be maintained among these savages any longer, did accident again throw him in their way. The chiefs, he saw, had distrusted him all along, but had given him an opportunity to prove what he could do, in order to satisfy the more vulgar curiosity of their young men. He wisely determined, therefore, to keep out of the hands of his enemies.

Although Le Bourdon could hold a conversation in the tongue of the Ojebways, he was not fond of so doing. He comprehended without difficulty nearly all of what was said by them, and had observed the previous night that the warriors made many allusions to a chief, whom they styled Onoah, but whom he himself knew was usually called Scalping Peter among the whites of that frontier. This savage had a fearful reputation at all the garrisons, though he never showed himself in them; and he was now spoken of by the Pottawattamies present, as if they expected to meet him soon, and to be governed by his commands or his advice. The bee-hunter had paid great attention whenever this dreaded name was mentioned, for he was fully aware of the importance of keeping clear of an enemy who bore so bad a reputation that it was not considered prudent for a white man to remain long in his company, even in a time of peace. His English *sobriquet* had been obtained from the circumstance of its being reputed that this chief, who seemed to belong to no tribe in particular, while he had great influence with all, had on divers occasions murdered the pale-faces who fell in his way, and then scalped them. It was added, that he had already forty notches on his pole, to note that number of scalps taken from the hated whites. In short, this Indian, a sort of chief by birth, though of what tribe no one exactly knew, appeared to live only to revenge the wrongs done his color by the intruders, who had come from towards the rising sun to drive his people into the great salt lake on the other side of the Rocky Mountains. Of course there was a good deal that was questionable in these reports; a rumor in the "openings" and on the prairies, having this general resemblance to those that circulate in towns, and in drawing-rooms, and at feasts, that no one of them all can be relied on as rigidly exact. But Le Bourdon was still young, and had yet to learn how little of that which we all hear is true, and how very much is false. Nevertheless, as an Indian tradition is usually more accurate than a white man's written history, so is a rumor of the forest generally entitled to more respect than the ceaseless gossipings, of the beings who would be affronted were they not accounted civilized.

The bee-hunter was still on the elevated bit of ground, making his observations, when he was joined by Margery. The girl appeared fresh and handsome, after a night of sleep, and coming from her dressing-room in a thicket, and over a stream of sweet, running water; but she was sad and thoughtful. No sooner had Le Bourdon shaken her hand, and repeated his thanks for the succor of the past night, than the full heart of Margery poured out its feelings, as the swollen stream overflows its banks, and began to weep.

"Brother is awake," she said, so soon as her sobs were quieted by a powerful effort; "but, as is usual with him after hard drinking, *so* stupid that Dolly cannot make him understand our danger. He tells her he has seen too many Injins to be afraid of these, and that they will never harm a family that has brought so much liquor into their country."

"His senses must be at a low ebb, truly, if he counts on Injin friendship because he has sold fire-water to the young men!" answered Le Bourdon, with a nice understanding of not only Indian nature, but of human nature. "We may like the sin, Margery, while we detest the tempter. I have never yet met with the man, pale-face or redskin, who did not curse, in his sober moments, the hand that fed his appetite while intoxicated."

"I dare say that may be very true," returned the girl, in a low voice; "but one has need of his reason to understand it. What will become of us now, it is hard to say!"

"Why *now*, Margery, more than yesterday, or the day before?"

"Yesterday there were no savages near us, and Gershom had all along told us he intended to start for the garrison, at the head of the lake, as soon as he got back from his visit to the openings. He *is* back; but not in a state to protect his wife and sister from the redmen, who will be looking for us as soon as they can build a canoe, or anything that will do to cross the river with."

"Had they even a canoe," returned Le Bourdon, coolly, "they would not know where to look for us. Thank Heaven! *that* will be a job that would take some time; nor is a bark canoe built in a minute. But, Margery, if your brother be a little dull and heavy after his debauch, *I* am sober, and as much awake as ever I was in my life."

"Oh! you have no weakness like that of poor brother's, to make you otherwise; but, Bourdon, you will naturally wish to take care of yourself and your property and will quit us the first good opportunity. I 'm sure that we have

no right to expect you will stay a minute longer than it is
your interest to do so, and I do not know that I wish it.''

'' Not wish it ! Margery,'' exclaimed the bee-hunter, in
the manner of a disappointed man. '' I had supposed you
would have wished my company. But, now I know the
contrary, I shall not much care how soon I go, or into whose
hands I fall.''

It is strange how apt are those who ought to understand
one another so readily, to misinterpret each other's thoughts.
Margery had never seen the bee-hunter twenty-four hours
before, though she had often heard of him, and of his success in his art ; for the fame of a man of good reputation
and active qualities spreads far on a frontier. The very
individual whose existence would be nearly overlooked in
a crowded region, shall be spoken of, and known by his
qualities, a hundred leagues from his place of residence,
when settlements are few and far apart. In this way, Margery had heard of Boden, or of ''Bourdon,'' as she called
him, in common with hundreds who, confounding his real
name with his *sobriquet*, made the mistake of using the
last, under the impression that it was the true appellation.
Margery had no other knowledge of French than the few
words gleaned in her slow progress along a frontier on
which, it is true, more of that language than of any other
was heard, but heard under circumstances that were not
particularly favorable to the acquisition of a foreign tongue.
Had she understood the real meaning of ''Bourdon,'' she
would have bitten off her tongue before she would have
once called Boden by such an appellation ; though the
bee-hunter himself was so accustomed to his Canadian
nickname as to care nothing at all about it. But Margery
did not like to give pain to any one ; and, least of all,
would she desire to inflict it on the bee-hunter, though he
were only an acquaintance of a day. Still Margery could
not muster sufficient courage to tell her new friend how
much he was mistaken, and that of all the youths she had
ever met, she would most prefer to keep him near her
brother and sister in their distress ; while the young man,
inspired by a pure and infant passion, was just in the frame

10

of mind to believe the worst of himself, and of his claims to the attention of her who had begun to occupy so many of his thoughts.

No explanation occurring, our young people descended from the hill, misconceiving each other's meaning and wishes, and unhappy under the influence of an ideal source of misery, when actual circumstances created so many that were substantial and real. Gershom was found awake, but, as his sister had described him, stupid and lethargic. The bee-hunter at once saw that, in his present condition, Whiskey Centre would still be an incumbrance rather than of any service, in the event of an occasion for extraordinary exertion. Margery had hinted that it usually took twenty-four hours to bring her brother entirely round, after one of his serious debauches; and within that time it was more than probable that the fate of the family would be decided.

Le Bourdon thought intently, during breakfast, of the condition of his party, and of the best mode of proceeding, while the pallid and anxious young creature at his side believed he was deliberating solely on the best means of extricating himself and his store of honey from the savages on the other shore. Had the acquaintance between these young people been of longer date than it actually was, Margery could not have entertained a notion so injurious to the bee-hunter for a single moment; but there was nothing either violent or depreciating in supposing that one so near being a total stranger would think first of himself and his own interests, in the situation in which this young man was now placed.

Little was said during the meal. Dorothy was habitually silent; the result of grief and care. As for her husband, he was too stupid to talk, though usually somewhat garrulous; while the Indian seldom did two things at the same time. This was the hour for acting; when that for talking should arrive, he would be found equal to its duties. Pigeonswing could either abstain from food, or could indulge in it without measure, just as occasion offered. He had often gone for days without tasting a mouthful, with the exception of a few berries, perhaps; and he had lain about the camp-fire a week at a time, gorging himself with venison, like an anaconda. It is perhaps fortunate for the American Indian that this particular quality of food is so very easy of digestion, since his excesses on it are notorious, and so common to his habits as almost to belong to his nature. Death might otherwise often be the consequence.

When the breakfast was ended it was time to consult about the future course. As yet the Pottawattamies had made no new discovery; but the sagacity of the redman was ever to be feared, when it came to be merely a question of finding his foe in a forest.

"We have obtained one advantage over the enemy," said Le Bourdon, "by crossing the river. Water leaves no trail; even had Crowsfeather a canoe, he might not know where to go in it, in order to find us."

"Dat not so," put in the Chippewa, a little dogmatically; "know we hab canoe—know cross river in him."

"*Why* should they know this, Pigeonswing? We may have gone out upon the lake, or we may have gone up into the oak openings again, for anything the Pottawattamies can know to the contrary."

"Tell you, not so. Know don't go on lake, cause wind blow. Know don't go up river, cause dat hard work: know come here, cause dat easy. Injin like to do what easy, and pale-face do just what Injin do. Crowsfeather make raft, pretty soon; *den* he come look arter scalp."

"Yes," said Margery, gently; "you had better load your canoe at once, and go on the lake, while the savages cannot reach you. The wind is fair for them that are to go north; and I have heard you say that you are bound to Mackinaw."

"I shall load my canoe, and I shall load *yours*, too, Margery; but I shall not go away from this family so long as any in it stand in need of my services."

"Brother will be able to help us by afternoon. He manages a canoe well, when himself; so go, Bourdon, while you can. I dare say you have a mother at home; or a sister—perhaps a wife— "

"Neither," interrupted the bee-hunter, with emphasis. "No one expects me; no one has a *right* to expect me."

The color stole into pretty Margery's cheeks as she heard these words, and a ray of comfort gleamed on an imagination that, for the last hour, had been portraying the worst. Still, her generous temper did not like the idea of the bee-hunter's sacrificing himself for those who had so few claims on him, and she could not but again admonish him of the necessity of losing no time.

"You will think better of this, Bourdon," the girl resumed. "We are going south, and cannot quit the river with this wind; but you could not have a better time to go north, unless the wind blows harder than I think it does."

"The lake is a bad water for a canoe, when there is much wind," put in Gershom, yawning after he had spoken, as if the effort fatigued him. "I wonder what we're all doin' over on this side of the river! Whiskey Centre is a good enough country for me; I'm going back to look arter my casks, now I've breakfasted. Come, Doll; let's load up, and be off."

"You are not yourself yet, Gershom," returned the sorrowful wife, "or you would not talk in this way. You had better listen to the advice of Bourdon, who has done so much for us already, and who will tell you the way to keep out of Injin clutches. We owe our lives to Bourdon, Gershom, and you should thank him for it."

Whiskey Centre muttered a few half-intelligible words of thanks, and relapsed into his state of drowsy indifference. The bee-hunter saw, however, that the effects of the brandy were leaving him, and he managed to get him on one side, where he persuaded the fellow to strip and go into the water. The bath did wonders for the poor creature, who soon got to be so far himself again as to be of use instead of being an incumbrance. When sober, and more especially when sober for several consecutive days, Gershom was a man of sufficient energy, possessing originally great personal strength and activity, which had been essentially lessened, however, by his excesses in liquor. It has already been stated what a different being he became, in a moral point of view, after having been sober for any length of time.

On his return from the bathing Le Bourdon again joined the females. Margery had been weeping ; but she smiled in a friendly way, on meeting his eye, and appeared less anxious for his departure than she had been an hour before. As the day advanced, and no signs of the savages were seen, a sense of greater security began to steal over the females, and Margery saw less necessity for the departure of their new friend. It was true, he was losing a wind ; but the lake was rough, and after all it might be better to wait. In short, now that no immediate danger was apparent, Margery began to reason in conformity with her wishes, as is so apt to be the case with the young and inexperienced. The bee-hunter perceived this change in the deportment of his fair friend, and was well enough disposed to hope it would admit of a favorable construction.

All this time the Chippewa had taken little visible interest in the state of the party to which he had now attached himself. The previous evening had been fertile in excitement and in gratification, and he had since slept and ate to his entire content. He was ready to meet events as they might arise, and began to plot the means of obtaining more Pottawattamie scalps. Let not the refined reader feel disgust at this exhibition of the propensities of an American savage. Civilized life has had, and still has very many customs little less excusable than that of scalping. Without dragging into the account the thousand and one sins that disgrace and deform society, it will be sufficient to look into the single interest of civilized warfare, in order to make out our case. In the first place, the noblest strategy of the art is, to put the greatest possible force on the least of the enemy, and to slay the weaker party by the mere power of numbers. Then, every engine that ingenuity can invent is drawn into the conflict ; and rockets, revolvers, shells, and all other infernal devices are resorted to in order to get the better of an enemy who is not provided with such available means of destruction. And after the battle is over, each side commonly claims the victory : sometimes, because a partial success has been obtained in a small portion of the field ; sometimes, because half a dozen horses have run away with a gun, carrying it into the hostile ranks ; and again, because a bit of rag has fallen from the hands of a dead man, and been picked up by one of the opposing side.   How often has it happened that a belligerent, well practised in his art, has kept his own colors out of the affair, and boasted that they were not lost !   Now an Indian practises no such shameless expedients.   His point of honor is not a bit of rag, but a bit of his skin.   He shaves his head because the hair incumbers him ; but he chivalrously leaves a scalp-lock, by the aid of which his conqueror can the more easily carry away the coveted trophy.   The thought of cheating in such a matter never occurs to his unsophisticated mind ; and as for leaving his "colors" in barracks, while he goes into the field himself, he would disdain it—nay, cannot practise it, for the obvious reason that his head would have to be left with them.

Thus was it with Pigeonswing.   He had made his toilet for the war-path, and was fierce in his paint, but honest and fair-dealing in other particulars.   If he could terrify his enemies by looking like a skeleton, or a demon, it was well ; his enemy would terrify him, if possible, by similar means.   But neither would dream, or did dream, of curtailing, by a single hair, that which might be termed the flag-staff of his scalp.   If the enemy could seize it, he was welcome to the prize ; but if he could seize that of the enemy, no scruples on the score of refinement or delicacy would be apt to interfere with his movements.   It was in this spirit, then, that Pigeonswing came to the canoe, where Le Bourdon was holding a little private discourse with Margery, and gave utterance to what was passing in his mind.

"Good time, now, get more scalp, Bourdon," said the Chippewa, in his clipping, sententious English.

"It is a good time, too, to keep our own, Chippewa," was the answer.   "Your scalp-lock is too long to be put before Pottawattamie eyes without good looking after it."

"Nebber mind him—if go, go ; if stay, stay.   Always good for warrior to bring home scalp."

"Yes ; I know your customs in this respect, Pigeonswing; but ours are different. We are satisfied if we can keep out of harm's way, when we have our squaws and pappooses with us.''

'' No pappoose here,'' returned the Indian, looking around him—'' dat your squaw, eh ? ''

The reader can readily imagine that this abrupt question brought blushes into the cheeks of pretty Margery, making her appear ten times more handsome than before; while even Le Bourdon did not take the interrogatory wholly undisturbed. Still the latter answered manfully, as became his sex.

'' I am not so fortunate as to have a squaw, and least of all to have *this*,'' said Le Bourdon.

'' Why no hab her—she good squaw,'' returned the literal-minded Indian—'' han'some 'nough for chief. *You* ask ; *she* hab—know squaw well—always like warrior to ask him fuss ; den say, yes.''

'' Ay, that may do with your redskin squaws,'' Le Bourdon hastily replied ; for he saw that Margery was not only distressed, but a little displeased—'' but not with the young women of the pale-faces. I never saw Margery before last evening ; and it takes time for a pale-face girl to know a youth.''

'' Just so wid redskin—sometime don't know, till too late ! See plenty dat, in wigwam.''

'' Then it is very much in the wigwams as it is in the houses. I have heard this before.''

'' Why not same?—skin make no difference—pale-face spile squaw, too—make too much of her.''

'' That can *never* be ! '' exclaimed Le Bourdon, earnestly. '' When a pretty, modest, warm-hearted young woman accepts a youth for a husband, he can never make *enough* of her ! ''

On hearing sentiments so agreeable to a woman's ears, Margery looked down, but she looked pleased. Pigeons-wing viewed the matter very differently ; and being somewhat of a partisan in matters relating to domestic economy, he had no thought of leaving a point of so much importance in so bad a way. Accordingly, it is not surprising that, in pursuing the subject, he expressed opinions in several essentials diametrically the reverse of those of the bee-hunter.

"Easy 'nough spile squaw," rejoined the Chippewa. "What she good for, don't make her work? Can't go on war-path—can't take scalp—can't shoot deer—can't hunt—can't kill warrior—so *muss* work. Dat what squaw good for."

"That may do among redmen, but we pale-faces find squaws good for something else—we love them and take care of them—keep them from the cold in winter, and from the heat in summer; and try to make them as comfortable and happy as we can."

"Dat good talk for young squaw's ear," returned the Chippewa, a little contemptuously as to manner; though his real respect for the bee-hunter, of whose prowess he had so lately been a witness, kept him a little within bounds— "but it bess not take nobody in. What Injin say to squaw, he do—what pale-face say, he no do."

"Is that true, Bourdon?" demanded Margery, laughing at the Indian's earnestness.

"I shall be honest, and own that there may be some truth in it—for the Injin promises nothing, or next to nothing, and it is easy to square accounts, in such cases. That white men undertake more than they always perform, is quite likely to be the fact. The Injin gets his advantage in this matter, by not even thinking of treating his wife as a woman should be treated."

"How should treat woman?" put in Pigeonswing with warmth. "When warrior eat venison, gib her rest, eh? Dat no good—what you call good, den? If good hunter husband, she get 'nough—if ain't good hunter, she don't get 'nough. Just so wid Injin—sometime hungry, sometime full. Dat way to live!"

"Ay, that may be your redman's ways, but it is not the manner in which we wish to treat our wives. Ask pretty Margery, here, if she would be satisfied to wait until her husband had eaten his dinner, and then come for the scraps. No—no—Pigeonswing: we feed our women and children *first*, and come in last, ourselves."

" Dat good for pappoose—he little ; want vension—squaw tough ; use to wait. Do her good."

Margery now laughed outright at these specimens of Indian gallantry, which only too well embody the code of the redman's habits. Doubtless the heart has its influence among even the most savage people, for nature has not put into our breasts feelings and passions to be discarded by one's own expedients or wants. But no advocate of the American Indian has ever yet been able to maintain that woman fills her proper place in his estimate of claims. As for Margery, though so long subject to the whims, passions, and waywardness of a drunkard, she had reaped many of the advantages of having been born in that woman's paradise, New England. We are no great admirers of the legacy left by the Puritan to his descendant, taken as an inheritance in morals, manners, and customs, and as a whole ; though there are parts, in the way of codicils, that there is no portion of the Christian world which might not desire to emulate. In particular do we allude to the estimate put upon and the treatment received by their women. Our allusion is not to the refinement and gracefulness of polished intercourse ; for of *them*, the Blarney Rock of Plymouth has transmitted but a meagre account in the inventory, and perhaps the less that is said about this portion of the family property the better ; but, dropping a few degrees in the social scale, and coming down to the level where we are accustomed to regard people merely as men and women, we greatly question if any other portion of the world can furnish a parallel to the manly, considerate, rational, and wisely discriminating care that the New England husband, as a rule, bestows on his wife ; the father on his daughter ; or the brother on his sister. Gershom was a living, and, all things considered, a remarkable instance of these creditable traits. When sober, he was uniformly kind to Dorothy, and for Margery he would at any time risk his life. The latter, indeed, had more power over him than his own wife possessed, and it was her will and her remonstrances that most frequently led him back from the verge of that precipice over which he was so often disposed to cast himself. By some secret link she bound him closest to the family dwelling, and served most to recall the days of youth and comparative innocence, when they dwelt together beneath the paternal roof, and were equally the objects of the affection and solicitude of the same kind mother. His attachment to Dorothy was sincere, and, for one so often brutalized by drink, steady; but Dorothy could not carry him as far back, in recollections, as the one only sister who had passed the morning of life with him, in the same homely but comfortable abode.

We have no disposition to exaggerate the character of those whom it is the fashion to term the American yeomen, though why such an appellation should be applied to any in a state of society to which legal distinctions are unknown is what we could never understand. There are no more of esquires and yeomen in this country than there are of knights and nobles, though the quiet manner in which the transition from the old to the new state of things has been made, has not rendered the public mind very sensible to the changes. But recurring to the class, which is a positive thing and consequently ought to have a name of some sort or other, we do not belong to those that can sound its praises without some large reservations on the score of both principles and manners. Least of all, are we disposed to set up these yeomen as a privileged class, like certain of the titular statesmen of the country, and fall down and worship a calf—not a golden one by the way—of our own setting up. We can see citizens in these yeomen, but not princes, who are to be especially favored by laws made to take from others to bestow on them. But, making allowances for human infirmities, the American freeholder belongs to a class that may justly hold up its head among the tillers of the earth. He improves daily, under the influence of beneficent laws, and if he don't get spoiled, of which there is some danger, in the eagerness of factions to secure his favor, and through that favor his *vote* —if he escape this danger, he will ere long make a reasonably near approach to that being which the tongue of the flatterer would long since have persuaded him he had already more than got to be.

To one accustomed to be treated kindly, as was the case with Margery, the Chippewa's theory for the management of squaws contained much to excite her mirth, as well as her resentment, as she now made apparent by her remarks.

"You don't deserve to *have* a wife, Pigeonswing," she cried, half-laughing, yet evidently alive to the feelings of her sex—"can have no gratitude of a wife's tenderness and care. I wonder that a Chippewa girl can be found to have you!"

"Don't want him," coolly returned the Indian, making his preparations to light his pipe—"got Winnebagoe squaw, already; good 'nough for me. Shoot her t'other husband and take his scalp—den she come into my wigwam."

"The wretch!" exclaimed Margery.

But this was a word the savage did not understand, and he continued to puff at the newly lighted tobacco with all of a smoker's zeal. When the fire was secured he found time to continue the subject.

"Yes, dat good war-path—got rifle; got wife; got *two* scalp! Don't do so well ebbery day."

"And that woman hoes your corn and cooks your venison?" demanded the bee-hunter.

"Sartain—capital good to hoe—no good to cook—make deer meat too dry. Want to be made to mind business. Bye'm by teach him. No l'arn all at once, like pale-face pappoose in school."

"Pigeonswing, have you never observed the manner in which the white man treats his squaw?"

"Sartain—see him make much of her—put her in warm corner—wrap blanket round her—give her venison 'fore he eat himself—see all dat, often—what den? *Dat* don't make it right."

"I give you up, Chippewa, and agree with Margery in thinking you ought not to have a squaw at all."

"T'ink alike den—why no get marry?" asked the Indian, without circumlocution.

Margery's face became red as fire; then her cheeks settled into the color of roses, and she looked down, embarrassed. The bee-hunter's admiration was very apparent to the Indian, though the girl did not dare to raise her eyes from the ground, and so did not take heed of it.   But this gossiping was suddenly brought to an end by a most unexpected cause of interruption; the manner and form of which it shall be our office to relate in the succeeding chapter.

CHAPTER XI.

"So should it be—for no heart beats
  Within his cold and silent breast;
To him no gentle voice repeats
  The soothing words that make us blest."

PEABODY.

THE interruption came from Dorothy, who, on ascending the little height, had discovered a canoe coming into the mouth of the river, and who was running, breathless with haste, to announce the circumstance to the bee-hunter. The latter immediately repaired to the eminence, and saw for himself the object that so justly had alarmed the woman.

The canoe was coming in from the lake, after running before the wind, which now began to abate a little in its strength, and it evidently had been endeavoring to proceed to the northward. The reason for its entering the river was probably connected with the cookery or food of the party, since the lake was each minute getting to be safer, and more navigable for so light a craft. To Le Bourdon's great apprehension, he saw the savages on the north shore making signals to this strange canoe by means of smoke, and he foresaw the probability of his enemies obtaining the means of crossing the stream, should the strangers proceed in the desired direction. To counteract this design, he ran down to a spot on the beach where there was no rice-plant, and showing himself to the strangers, invited them to land on the south side, which was much the nearest, and in other visible respects quite as convenient as the opposite bank of the river. One of the strangers soon made a gesture with an arm, implying assent, and the bows of this strange canoe were immediately turned toward the spot where the bee-hunter stood.

As the canoe drew near, the whole party, including Pigeonswing, came to the margin of the water to receive the strangers. Of the last there were three; one paddling at each end of the light bark, and a third seated in its centre, doing nothing. As the bee-hunter had his glass, with which he examined these visitors, he was soon questioned by his companions concerning their character and apparent purposes.

"Who are they, Bourdon?" demanded the impatient Margery,—"and why do they come here?"

"The last is a question they must answer for themselves, but the person paddling in the bows of the canoe seems to be a white man, and a soldier—or a half-soldier, if one may judge from his dress. The man in the middle of the canoe is white, also. This last fellow seems to be a parson—yes, he *is* a clergyman, though pretty well used up in the wilderness, as to dress. The third man is a redskin, beyond all doubt."

"A clergyman!" repeated Margery, in surprise. "What should a clergyman be doing here?"

"There are missionaries scattered about among the savages, I suppose you know, and this is probably one of them. A body can tell one of these parsons by his outside, as far as he can see him. The poor man has heard of the war, most likely, and is trying to get back into the settlements, while his scalp is safe on his head."

"Don't hurt *him*," put in the Chippewa, pointedly. "Know *mean* well—talk about Great Spirit—Injin don't scalp sich medicine-men—if don't mind what he say, no good to take his scalp."

"I'm glad to hear this, Pigeonswing, for I had begun to think *no* man's scalp was safe under *your* fingers. But what can the so'ger be doing down this away? A body would think there was business enough for all the so'gers up at the garrison, at the head of the lake. By the way, Pigeonswing, what has become of your letter to the captain at Fort Dearborn, to let him know of the war?"

" Chaw him up, like so much 'baccy,'' answered the Chip-pewa—" yes, chaw him up, lest Pottawattamie get hold on him, and ask one of King George's men to read him. No good to hab letter in sich times.''

" The general who employed you to carry that letter will scarce thank you for your care."

" Yes he do—t'ank all same—pay all same—letter no use, now."

" How can you know that? The letter might be the means of preventing the garrison from falling into the enemy's hands."

" Got dere, already. Garrison all kill, scalp, or pris'ner. Pottawattamie talk tell me *dat*."

" Is this possible ! Mackinaw and Chicago both gone, already ! John Bull must have been at work among the sav-ages a long time, to get them into this state of readiness ! ''

" Sartain—work long as can 'member. *Alway* somebody talkin' for Great Montreal Fadder among redmen."

" It must be as you say, Chippewa ; but here are our visitors—let us see what we can make of *them*.''

By this time the canoe was so near as to render it easy to distinguish countenances and dress without the aid of the glass—so near, indeed, that a swift-moving boat, like the canoe, might be expected soon to reach the shore. The truth of the observation of the bee-hunter was confirmed as the strangers approached. The individual in the bows of the canoe was clearly a soldier, in a fatigue dress, and the musket between his legs was one of those pieces that govern-ment furnishes to the troops of the line. The man in the middle of the boat could no more be mistaken than he in its bows. Each might be said to be in uniform ;—the well-worn, nay, almost thread-bare black coat of the " minister,'' as much denoting him to be a man of peace as the fatigue-jacket and cap on the person of his hard-featured and weather-beaten companion indicated that the last was a man of war. As for the redman, Pigeonswing declared that he could not yet tell his tribe, though there was that about his air, attire, and carriage, that proclaimed him a chief—and, as the Chip-pewa fancied, a chief of note. In another minute the bows of the light craft grated gently on the shingle of the beach.

"Sago, sago," said the soldier, rising to step ashore; "sago all, friends, and I hope we come to a welcome camp."

"You are welcome," returned the bee-hunter. "Welcome as strangers met in the wilderness; but more welcome, as I see by your dress that you are a veteran of one of Uncle Sam's regiments."

"Quite true, Mr. Bee-hunter; for such I see is *your* callin', by the honey vessel and glass you carry, and by the other signs about you. We are travelling towards Mackinaw, and hope to fare as friends while we stay in your good company."

"In going to Mackinaw, do you expect to meet with an *American*, or an *English* garrison?"

"One of our own, to be sure," returned the soldier, looking up from his work, like one struck by the question.

"Mackinaw has fallen, and is now an English post, as well as Chicago."

"This, then, must alter our plans, Mr. Amen!" exclaimed the soldier, addressing the minister. "If the enemy has Mackinaw, it will not do for us to trust ourselves on the island."

"Amen" was not the real name of the missionary; but it was a *sobriquet* bestowed by the soldiers, on account of the unction with which this particular word was ordinarily pronounced, and quite likely, too, because it was the word of all others most pleasant to their ears after a sermon or a prayer. It had, by long use, got to be so familiar that the men did not scruple to use it to the good man's face. This missionary was a Methodist; a sect that possessed, in that day, very few clergymen of education, most of its divines coming of a class in life that did not predispose them to take offence at light invasions on their dignity, and whose zeal and habitual self-denial had schooled them into a submission to far more positive personal privations than any connected with the mere tongue. That there are "wolves in sheep's clothing" among the Methodists, as well as among the other religious sects of the country, our daily experience shows; but the mind must be sadly in-

clined to believe evil of others which does not see, in the
humble and untiring efforts of this particular sect of Christians, more than mere fanaticism or hypocrisy can produce.

"You are right, corporal," returned the missionary.
"Since this is the case, I see no better course for us to
pursue than to put ourselves altogether in the hands of
Onoah. He has counselled us well, hitherto, and will do
better by us than any other guide to be found out in this
wilderness."

Le Bourdon could scarce trust his sense of hearing.
Onoah was the Indian appellation of the terrible and much
dreaded savage who, in English, went by the name of
Scalping Peter, or "Scalping Pete," among all the white
dwellers on that frontier, and at all the garrisons of the
Americans, far and near. The Indian name, indeed, was
said to mean "scalp," in several of the dialects of the
Iroquois. Perhaps it may be well also to explain here,
that the term "garrison" did not imply, in the language of
that region, the troops only who garrisoned a post, but it
was even oftener applied to the post itself than to those
who held it. Thus old, empty, and deserted forts, those
that have actually been abandoned, and are devoted to de-
cay, are almost universally styled the "garrisons," even
though a soldier had not put foot in them for a quarter of
a century. This is one of the proofs of the convertible
nature of our language, of which the country affords so
many, and which has changed the smaller sized "rivers"
into "creeks," "lakes" into "ponds," "squares" into
"parks," public promenades on the water into "batteries";
to all of which innovations, bad as they may be, and useless
and uncalled for, and wanton as they are, we are much
more willing to submit, than to the new-fangled and lub-
berly abomination of saying "*on* a steamboat," or "*on* a
ship."

While Le Bourdon was so much astounded at hearing
the terrible name of Onoah, which was familiar enough to
him, neither of his white companions betrayed any emotion.
Had the Indian been termed "Scalping Peter," it is prob-

11

able that both Dorothy and Margery would have screamed, if not actually fled; but they knew nothing of the appellation that was given to this mysterious chief in the language of the redmen. To this circumstance, therefore, was it owing that the utterance of his name did not produce a general commotion. The bee-hunter observed, nevertheless, a great change in the demeanor of the Chippewa the instant the missionary had uttered the ominous word, though he did not seem to be alarmed. On the contrary, Boden fancied that his friend, Pigeonswing, was pleased, rather than terrified, at ascertaining the character of their visitor, though he no longer put himself forward, as had been the case previously; and from that moment the young warrior appeared to carry himself in a more subdued and less confident manner than was his wont. This unexpected demeanor on the part of his friend somewhat confounded Le Bourdon, though it in a degree relieved his apprehensions of any immediate danger. All this time the conversation between the missionary and the corporal went on in as quiet and composed a manner as if each saw no ground for any other uneasiness than that connected with the fall of Mackinaw.

"Yes, sir," returned the soldier, "Onoah is a good guide, and a great hand at a council-fire; but these is war-times, and we must stand to our arms, each accordin' to his edication and temper—you, sir, with preachin' and prayin', and I with gun and baggonet."

"Ah! corporal, the preaching and praying would be of quite as much account with you men of war as your arms and ammunition, if you could only be made to think so. Look at Fort Dearborn! It was defended by human means, having its armed band, and its guns and swords, and captains and corporals; yet you have seen their pride lowered, their means of defence destroyed, and a large part of your comrades massacred. All this has been done to armed men, while the Lord has brought *me*, an unarmed and humble teacher of his word, safely out of the hands of the Philistines, and placed me here in safety, on the shores of the Kalamazoo."

" For that matter, Mr. Amen, the Lord has done the same by *me*, with a musket on my shoulder and a baggonet by my side," returned the literal corporal. " Preachin' may be good on some marches ; but arms and ammunition answers well enough on others. Hearken to the Hebrew, who knows all the ways of the wilderness, and see if he don't give you the same opinion."

"The Hebrew is one of the discarded of the Lord, as he is one chosen of the Lord !" returned the missionary. " I agree with you, however, that he is as safe an adviser, for a human adviser, as can be easily found ; therefore will I consult him. Child of the seed of Abraham," he added, turning to Onoah, "thou hast heard the tidings from Mackinaw ; we cannot think, any longer, of pursuing our journey in that direction ; whither, then, wouldst thou advise that we shall direct our steps ? I ask this question of *thee* first, as an experienced and sagacious dweller in the wilderness ; at a more fitting time, I intend to turn to the Lord, and seek divine aid for the direction of our footsteps."

" Ay," observed the corporal, who entertained a good deal of respect for the zealous but slightly fanatical missionary, though he believed an Indian was always safe to consult in matters of this sort ; " try *both*—if one staff should fail, it may be well to have another to lean on. A good soldier always keeps a part of his troops for a resarve. I remember when Mad Anthony gave the command to charge the inemy, at the Mawmee, we was all for going forward like so many furious devils, but the old man said, ' No ; keep them men in resarve,' he said, ' for no one knows when his flank may be turned, or he may catch a volley from his rear.' Well, what does Onoah tell you, Mr. Amen ? "

By this time the strange Indian had landed, thus giving Le Bourdon an opportunity of examining his person and attire more closely than he had hitherto done. This renowned savage—renowned, as fame is regarded on a frontier, where the posts of the whites were then a hundred leagues asunder—was in the summer-dress of the woods, and any one acquainted with the customs of the North

American Indian could at once perceive that he bore on his person the symbols of authority and rank. The insignia of the Golden Fleece, or of the Saint Esprit, are not more infallible evidences of high personal degree among the nobles of Europe, than were the emblems borne by this savage, of his consideration among the people of his color and origin, along the shores of those wild and inland seas of fresh water, which then were seldom plowed by a keel ; which have since got to be familiar with the steamer, the propeller, brig, ship, and schooner ; and which, ere the close of the present century, will, in all probability, be whitened, like the Mediterranean, with the canvas of the thousand craft that will be required for the navigation of their borders.[1] Around his neck Onoah wore what might be termed a gorget of tubes, made of the red pipe-stone of the West, and which were carved and wrought with care, if not with much skill. Above this he had a rude representation of a rattlesnake drawn on his breast with yellow paint. This was understood to be the " totem," or "arms," of his tribe ; though what that tribe was, where it dwelt, or whence it came, it was commonly believed among both the redskins and pale-faces of the region, no one but himself knew. On a small silver medal that was suspended above the gorget was stamped the image of that cross on which the Son of God, in his human character, suffered death for the redemption of men. It would seem that this savage, keen, sharp-witted, and observant as he was, though not a believer in the doctrines inculcated by the Bible, had none of that holy horror of this sacred emblem that so singularly besets the imaginations of many who profess to place all their hopes of salvation on the sacrifice that was made on its great original. He wore an ancient medal of the Jesuits, one that had passed through generations of his

[1] In crossing Lake Erie, within the last few months, the writer, in a run of twenty-four hours, counted no less than sixty-three vessels, met, overtaken, and seen. He remembers that water, in the first ten years of the present century, when a single sail was an object of interest and curiosity. The change must have been witnessed to be appreciated.

family, as a political rather than as a religious symbol,
though perfectly aware of the spirit in which it had been
first bestowed. He probably saw that the cross was re-
vered by one class of missionaries, while another scarce
endeavored to conceal their distaste for it, a circumstance
that might have confounded a neophyte of less acuteness
than himself.[1]

Beneath the rattlesnake, or "totem" of his tribe, Onoah
had rudely drawn an expanded hand, in that attitude which
denotes caution, or "beware." This might be termed the
motto of his coat of arms ; the "*gare à qui la touche*," or
"noli me tangere," of his device.

The head was shaved, as is usual with a warrior, carrying
only the chivalrous scalp-lock, but the chief was not in
his paint. The outline of this celebrated savage's features
was bold and eagle-like ; a comparison that his steady, calm,
piercing eye well sustained. The chin was full and expanded,
the lips compressed and firm, the teeth were short, but even
and sound, his smile courteous, and, at times, winning.

[1] In the times of the crusades, the cross was adopted as an emblem of
general use. All the castles and churches were adorned with this touching memorial of the origin of the Christian faith, in beautiful commem-
oration of the price paid for human salvation. Apertures were made
for the windows, and a stone cross was erected in each, whence the
French term of "*croissée.*" The same thing was done for the doors,
which, by removing the panels, would be found to contain so many
crosses. This last custom became general, and a cross, or crosses,
are to be found at this very hour in nearly every old panelled door in
the country, even to the humblest dwellings of the descendants of the
Puritans and Quakers. Ignorance preserved the emblems at the very
moment these pious and critical saints were throwing aside gowns and
cassocks, church music and kneeling, along with everything else that
by the perversity of human ingenuity could be made to appear connected in the remotest degree with the simplicity of human faith.
There is something amusing in finding these quiet little material
emblems of the crucifixion intrenching themselves in the very bed-
rooms and "cupboards" (to use the vernacular) of "the saints," *par
excellence*, at the precise period when not only their voices but their
hands were raised to dislodge them from that most appropriate of all
positions, the summit of the church-spire—that "silent finger pointing to the skies"—in order to put (still in honor of the vernacular) a
"rooster" in its stead !

In the way of attire, Onoah was simply dressed, consulting the season and his journey. He had a single eagle's feather attached to the scalp-lock, and wore a belt of wampum of more than usual value, beneath which he had thrust his knife and tomahawk ; a light, figured, and fringed hunting-shirt of cotton covered his body, while leggings of deer-skin, with a plain moccasin of similar material, rose to his knee. The latter, with the lower part of a stout, sinewy thigh, was bare. He also carried a horn and pouch, and a rifle of the American rather than of the military fashion— that is, one long, true, and sighted to the deviation of a hair.

On landing, Peter (for so he was generally called by the whites, when in courtesy they omitted the prefix of "scalping") courteously saluted the party assembled around the bow of the canoe. This he did with a grave countenance, like a true American, but in simple sincerity, so far as human eye could penetrate his secret feelings. To each man he offered his hand, glancing merely at the two females, though it may be questioned if he ever before had looked upon so perfect a picture of female loveliness as Margery at that precise instant presented, with her face flushed with excitement, her spirited blue eye wandering with curiosity, and her beautiful mouth slightly parted in admiration.

"Sago, sago !" said Peter, in his deep, guttural enunciation, speaking reasonably good English. "Sago, sago all, ole and young, friend come to see you, and eat in your wigwam—which head-chief, eh ?"

"We have neither wigwam nor chief here," answered Le Bourdon, though he almost shrunk from taking the hand of one of whom he had heard the tales of which this savage had been the hero ; "we are common people, and have no one among us who holds the States' commission. I live by taking honey, of which you are welcome to all you can want, and this man is a helper of the sutlers, at the garrisons. He was travelling south to join the troops at the head of the lake, and I was going north to Mackinaw, on my way in, towards the settlements."

"Why is my brother in such haste?" demanded Peter, mildly. "Bees get tired of making honey ?"

"The times are troubled, and the redmen have dug up the hatchet; a pale-face cannot tell when his wigwam is safe."

"Where my brodder wigwam?" asked Peter, looking warily around him. "See he an't here; where is he?"

"Over in the openings, far up the Kalamazoo. We left it last week, and had got to the hut on the other shore, when a party of Pottawattamies came in from the lake, and drove us over here for safety."

On hearing this, Peter turned slowly to the missionary, raising a finger as one makes a gesture to give emphasis to his words.

"Tole you so," said the Indian. "Know dere was Pottawattamie dere. Can tell 'em great way off."

"We fear them, having women in our party," added the bee-hunter, "and think they might fancy our scalps."

"Dat like enough; all Injin love scalp in war-time. You Yankee, dey, Br'ish; can't travel on same path now, and not quarrel. Muss not let Pottawattamie catch you."

"How are we to help it, now you have come in. We had all the canoes on this side of the river, and were pretty safe, but should you cross and place your canoe in their hands, there is nothing to prevent them from doing what they please with us. If you will promise not to cross the river till we can get out well on the lake, we may shift our ground, however, and leave no trail."

"Muss cross over—yes, muss cross over, else Pottawattamie t'ink it strange—yes, muss cross over. Shan't touch canoe, dough."

"How can you help it, if they be so minded? You are but a single man, and they are twenty?"

On hearing this, Corporal Flint pricked up his ears, and stood if possible more erect than ever, for he considered himself a part of a man at least, and one moreover who had served in all the wars of the West, from the great battle of St. Clair to that of Mad Anthony. He was spared the necessity of a reply, however, for Peter made a significant gesture which as much as told him that he would take that office on himself.

"No need be afeard," said Peter, quietly.   "Know Pot-tawattamie—know all chief.   Nobody touch canoe of Onoah when he say don't touch him."

"Yet they are Injins of the British, and I see you here in company with a soldier of Uncle Sam."

"No matter; Onoah go just where he please. Some-time to Pottawattamie; sometime to Iroquois. All Ojeb-ways know Onoah. All Six Nation know him well. All Injin know him. Even Cherokee know him now, and open ears when he speak. Muss cross river, and shake hand with Crowsfeather."

There was nothing boastful or vaunting in Peter's man-ner while he thus announced his immunity or power, but he alluded to it in a quiet, natural way, like one accus-tomed to being considered a personage of consequence. Mankind in general make few allowances for the influence of habit; the sensibilities of the vainglorious themselves being quite as often wounded by the most natural and direct allusions of those who enjoy advantages superior to their own, as by those that are intended to provoke comparisons. In the present instance, however, no such feeling could exist, the Indian asserting no more than his extended repu-tion would fully maintain.

When Peter had thus expressed himself, the missionary thought it meet to add a few words in explanation. This he did, however, aside, walking a little apart with the bee-hunter, in order so to do. As for Gershom, no one seemed to think him of sufficient importance to throw away any interest or care on him.

"You can trust to Peter, friend bee-hunter," the mis-sionary observed, "for what he promises he will perform. I know him well, and have put myself altogether in his hands. If he says that the Pottawattamies are not to have his canoe, the Pottawattamies will not get it. He is a man to be depended on."

"Is not this, then, Scalping Peter, who bears so terrible a name on all this frontier?" demanded Le Bourdon.

"The same; but do not disturb yourself with *names*: they hurt no one, and will soon be forgotten. A descendant of Abraham, and of Isaac, and of Jacob, is not placed in this wilderness by the hand of divine power for no purpose; since he is here, rely on it, it is for good."

"A descendant of Abraham, and Isaac, and Jacob! Is not Peter, then, a redskin and an Injin?"

"Certainly; though no one knows his *tribe* but myself. I know it, friend bee-hunter, and shortly shall proclaim it throughout the length and breadth of the land. Yes, it has been given to *me* to make this important discovery, though I sometimes think that Peter himself is really as ignorant as all around him of the tribe to which he properly belongs."

"Do you wish to keep it a secret from me, too? I own that, in my eyes, the tribe of a redskin goes a good way in making up my opinion of the man. Is he a Winnebagoe?"

"No, my friend, the Winnebagoes have no claims on him at all."

"Nor a Pottawattamie, Ottawa, or Ojebway of any sort?"

"He is none of these. Peter cometh of a nobler tribe than any that beareth such names."

"Perhaps he is an Injin of the Six Nations? They tell me that many such have found their way hither since the War of the Revolution."

"All that may be true, but Peter cometh not of Pottawattamie, Ottawa, nor Ojebway."

"He can hardly be of the Sacs or the Foxes; he has not the appearance of an Injin from a region so far West."

"Neither, neither, neither," answered Parson Amen, now so full of his secret as fairly to let it overflow. "Peter is a son of Israel; one of the lost children of the land of Judea, in common with many of his red brethren,—mind, I do not say *all*, but with *many* of his red brethren,—though he may not know exactly of what tribe himself. This last point has exercised me greatly, and days and nights have I pondered over the facts. Turn to Genesis xlix. and 14th, and there will you find all the authorities recorded. 'Zebulon shall dwell at the haven of the sea.' That refers to some other

red brother, nearer to the coast, most clearly. ' Issachar
is a strong ass, crouching down between two burdens;'
'and bowed his shoulder to bear, and became a servant unto tribute.' That refers, most manifestly, to the
black man of the southern states, and cannot mean Peter.
' Dan shall be a serpent by the way, an adder in the path.'
There is the redman for you, drawn with the pencil of
truth ! ' Gad, a troop shall overcome him.' Here, corporal, come this way and tell our new friend how Mad Anthony with his *troopers* finally routed the redskins. You
were there, and know all about it. No language can be
plainer : until the ' long-knives and leather-stockings ' came
into the woods, the redman had his way. Against *them*,
he *could* not prevail."

"Yes," returned Corporal Flint, who delighted in talking of the wars, "it was very much as Parson Amen says.
The savages, by their nimbleness and artifices, would first
ambush us, and then break away from our charges, until
the gin'ral bethought him of bringing cavalry into the wilderness. Nobody ever thought of such a plan, until old
Anthony invented it. As soon as we got the fire of the
savages, at the Mawmee, we charged with the baggonet,
and put 'em up ; and no sooner was they up, than away
went the horse into them, flourishing the ' long knife,' and
pressing the heel of the ' leather-stocking ' into the flanks
of their beasts. Mr. Amen has found a varse in Scriptur's
that does come near to the p'int, and almost foretells our
victory, and that, too, as plain as it stood in dispatches,
arterward, from head-quarters."

" ' Gad, a *troop* shall overcome him,' " put in the missionary, triumphantly.

" That 's it—that 's it ; there was just one troop on 'em,
and not a man more ! Mad Anthony said a troop would
answer, arter we had put the redskins up out of their ambushes, or any other bushes ; and so it did. I must acknowledge that I think more of the Scriptur's than ever,
since Parson Amen read to me that varse."

"Hearken unto this, friend bee-hunter," added the missionary, who by this time had fairly mounted his hobby

and fancied he saw a true Israelite in every other Indian of the west, "and tell me if words were ever more prophetic—'Benjamin shall ravin as a wolf; in the morning he shall devour his prey, and at night he shall divide the spoil.' The art of man could not draw a more faithful picture of these Indians."

Boden was not much skilled in sacred lore, and scarce knew what to make of all this. The idea that the American Indians were the descendants of the lost tribes of Israel was entirely new to him; nor did he know anything to boast of, touching those tribes, even in their palmiest days, and while in possession of the promised land; still he had some confused recollection of that which he had read when a child—what American has not?—and was enabled to put a question or two, in return for the information now received.

"What, do you take the savages of America for Jews?" he asked, understanding the general drift of the missionary's meaning.

"As sure as you are there, friend bee-hunter, though you are not to suppose that I think Peter Onoah of the tribe of Benjamin. No, I turn to the 21st verse for the tribe of Peter. Naphthali—Naphthalis, the root of his stock. 'Naphthali is a hind, let loose: he giveth goodly words.' Now, what can be plainer than this? A hind let loose is a deer running at large, and, by a metaphor, that deer includes the man that hunts him. Now, Peter has been—nay, is still—a renowned hunter, and is intended to be enumerated among the hinds let loose: 'he giveth goodly words,' would set that point at rest, if anything were wanting to put it beyond controversy, for Onoah is the most eloquent speaker ear ever listened to! No one, that has ever heard him speak, can doubt that he is the one who 'giveth goodly words.'"

To what other circumstance the well-intentioned missionary would next have alluded, in the course of this demonstration of a theory that had got to be a favorite with him, is more than can now be related, since the Indian himself drew near, and put an end to the conversation. Peter had made up his mind to cross the river at once;

and came to say as much to his companions, both of whom he intended to leave behind him. Le Bourdon could not arrest this movement, short of an appeal to force; and force he did not like to use, doubting equally its justice and its prudence.

CHAPTER XII.

" There is no other land like thee,
        No dearer shore ;
    Thou art the shelter of the free ;
    The home, the port of liberty
    Thou hast been, and shalt ever be
        'Till time is o'er.
    Ere I forget to think upon
    My land, shall mother curse the son
        She bore."

PERCIVAL.

THE independent, not to say controlling, manner of Peter, would seem to put all remonstrances and arguments at defiance. Le Bourdon soon had occasion to see that both the missionary and the corporal submitted to his wishes, and that there was no use in gainsaying anything he proposed. In all matters he did as he pleased ; his two companions submitting to his will as completely as if one of them had seen in this supposed child of Israel, Joshua the son of Nun, and the other even Aaron the high priest, himself.

Peter's preparations were soon made. Everything belonging to the missionary and the corporal was removed from the canoe, which then contained only the extra clothing and the special property of the Indian himself. As soon as ready, the latter quietly and fearlessly paddled away, his canoe going easily and swiftly down before the wind. He had no sooner got clear of the rice, than the bee-hunter and Margery ran away to the eminence, to watch his movements, and to note his reception among the Pottawattamies. Leaving them there, we shall accompany the canoe, in its progress towards the northern shore.

At first Peter paddled quietly on, as if he had no other object before him than the passage of the river. When quite clear of the rice, however, he ceased, and undid his bundle of clothes, which were carefully put away in the knapsack of a soldier. From this repository of his effects the chief carefully drew forth a small bundle, on opening which, no less than seven fresh human scalps appeared. These he arranged in order on a wand-like pole, when, satisfied with the arrangement, he resumed the paddle. It was apparent, from the first, that the Pottawattamies on the north shore had seen the strange canoe when it entered the river, and they now collected in a group, at the ordinary landing beneath the *chienté*, to await its approach. Peter ceased his own exertions as soon as he had got within a hundred yards of the beach, took the scalp-pole in his hand, arose, and permitted the canoe to drift down before the wind, certain it would take the desired direction, from the circumstances of his having placed it precisely to windward of the landing. Once or twice he slowly waved the pole in a way to draw attention to the scalps, which were suspended from its end, each obvious and distinct from its companions.

Napoleon, when he returned from the campaign of Austerlitz ; or Wellington, when he entered the House of Commons to receive the thanks of its speaker, on his return from Spain ; or the chief of all the battles of the Rio Bravo del Norte ; or him of the valley of Mexico, whose exploits fairly rival those of Cortes himself, could scarcely be a subject of greater interest to a body of spectators, assembled to do him honor, than was this well-known Indian, as he drew near to the Pottawattamies, waving his scalps, in significant triumph ! Glory, as the homage paid by man to military renown is termed, was the common impulse with them all. It is true, that, measured by the standards of reason and right, the wise and just might find motives for appreciating the victories of those named differently from the manner in which they are usually regarded through the atmosphere of success ; but in the common mind it was all glory, alike.   The name of " Onoah " passed in murmurs of admiration, from mouth to mouth for, as it appeared, the person of this renowned Indian was recognized by many on the shore some time ere he reached it himself.

Crowsfeather, and the other chiefs, advanced to meet the visitor ; the young men standing in the background, in respectful admiration.   Peter now stepped from the canoe, and greeted each of the principal men with the courteous gravity of a savage.   He shook hands with each, calling one or two by name, a proof of the parties having met before ; then the following dialogue occurred.   All spoke in the tongue of the Pottawattamies, but, as we have had occasion to remark on previous occasions, it is to be presumed that the reader would scarcely be able to understand what was said, were we to record it word for word in the language in which it was uttered.   In consequence of this difficulty, and for other reasons to which it may not be necessary to allude, we shall endeavor to translate that which passed, as closely as the English idioms will permit us so to do.

" My father is very welcome ! " exclaimed Crowsfeather, who, by many degrees, exceeded all his companions in consideration and rank.   " I see he has taken many scalps, as is his practice, and that the pale-faces are daily getting to be fewer.   Will the sun ever rise on that day when their wigwams will look like the branches of the oak in winter ? Can my father give us any hope of seeing that hour ? "

" It is a long path from the salt-lake out of which the sun rises, to that other salt-lake in which it hides itself at night.   The sun sleeps each night beneath water, but it is so hot that it is soon dried when it comes out of its bed in the morning.   This is the Great Spirit's doings, and not ours.   The sun is *his* sun ; the Indians can warm themselves by it, but they cannot shorten its journey a single tomahawk-handle's length.   The same is true of time ; it belongs to the Manitou, who will lengthen or shorten it as he may see fit.   We are his children, and it is our duty to submit. He has not forgotten us. He made us with his own hand, and will no more turn us out of the land than a father will turn his child from the wigwam.

"We hope this is so; but it does not *seem* thus to our poor weak eyes, Onoah. We count the pale-faces, and every summer they grow fast as the grass on the prairies. We can see more when the leaf falls than when the tree is in bud; and then more when the leaf is in bud than when it falls. A few moons will put a town where the pine stood, and wigwams drive the wolves from their homes. In a few years we shall have nothing but dogs to eat, if the pale-face dogs do not eat us."

"Squaws are impatient, but men know how to wait. This land was given to the redman by the Great Spirit, as I have often told you, my children; if he has let in the pale-faces for a few winters, it is to punish us for having done wrong. Now that we are sorry for what we have done, he will help us to drive away the strangers, and give us the woods again to hunt in by ourselves. Have not messengers from our Great Father in Montreal been among the Pottawattamies to strengthen their hearts?"

"They are always whispering in the ears of our tribes. I cannot remember the time when whisperers from Montreal have not been among us. Their blankets are warm, their fire-water is strong, their powder is good, and their rifles shoot well; but all this does not stop the children of Uncle Sam from being more at night than they were in the morning. The redmen get tired of counting them. They have become plentier than the pigeons in the spring. My father has taken many of their scalps, but the hair must grow after his knife, their scalps are still so many."

"See!" rejoined Peter, lowering his pole so that all might examine his revolting trophies, "these come from the soldiers at the head of the lake. Blackbird was there with his young men; no one of them all got as many scalps! This is the way to stop the white pigeons from flying over us in such flocks as to hide and darken the sun."

Another murmur of admiration passed through the crowd,

as each young warrior bent forward to count the number of
the scalps, and to note, by signs familiar to themselves, the
ages, sex, and condition of the different victims.   Here was
another, among a hundred others of which they had heard,
of the prowess of the mysterious Onoah, as well as of his
inextinguishable hatred of the race that was slowly, but un-
erringly, supplanting the ancient stock, causing the places
that once knew the people of their tribes "to know them
no more."   As soon as this little burst of feeling had sub-
sided, the conversation went on.

"We have had a pale-face medicine-man among us,
Onoah," continued Crowsfeather, " and he has so far
blinded us that we know not what to think."

The chief then recounted the leading events of the visit
of the bee-hunter to the place, stating each occurrence
fairly, as he understood it, and as fairly confessing that
even the chiefs were at a loss to know what to make of the
affair.   In addition to this account, he gave the mysterious
Onoah the history of the prisoner they had taken, the death
of Elksfoot, their intention to torture that very morning the
Chippewa they had captured, and his flight, together with
the loss of their young man, and the subsequent escape of
their unknown enemies, who had taken away all of their
own canoes.   How far the medicine-man had anything to
do with the other events of his narrative, Crowsfeather
very candidly admitted he could not even conjecture.   He
was still at a loss whether to set down the conjurer for a
pretender, or as a real oracle.   Peter, however, was less
credulous even than the chiefs.   He had his superstitious
notions, like all uneducated men, but a clear head and
quick intellect placed him far above the weaknesses of the
redman in general.   On receiving a description of the
person of the unknown " medicine-man," he at once recognized the bee-hunter.   With an Indian to describe, and
an Indian to interpret or apply, escape from discovery was
next to impossible.

Although Onoah, or the " Tribeless," as he was also frequently called by the redmen, from the circumstance of
no one's knowing to what particular section of the great

12

Indian family he belonged, perfectly understood that the bee-hunter he had seen on the other shore was the individual who had been playing the part of a conjurer among these Pottawattamies, he was very careful not to reveal the fact to Crowsfeather. He had his own policy, and was fully aware of all the virtue there is in mystery and reserve. With an Indian these qualities go further even than with a white man ; and we of the Circassian race are not entirely exempt from the folly of being deceived by appearances. On the present occasion Peter kept his knowledge to himself, still leaving his red brethren in doubt and uncertainty ; but he took care to be right in his own opinions by putting as many questions as were necessary for that purpose. Once assured of his fact, he turned to other subjects of even greater interest to himself and his companions.

The conference which now took place between the "Tribeless" and Crowsfeather was held apart, both being chiefs of too much importance to be intruded on at a moment like that. The two chiefs exhibited a very characteristic picture while engaged in this conference. They seated themselves on a bank, and drawing their legs partially under them, sat face to face, with their heads less than two feet asunder, occasionally gesticulating with dignity, but each speaking in his turn with studied decorum. Crowsfeather was highly painted, and looked fierce and warlike, but Onoah had nothing extraordinary about him, with the exception of the decorations and dress already described, unless it might be his remarkable countenance. The face of this Indian ordinarily wore a thoughtful cast, an expression which it is not unusual to meet with in a savage ; though at times it lighted up, as it might be with the heat of inward fires, like the crater giving out its occasional flames beneath the hues of a saddened atmosphere. One accustomed to study the human face, and to analyze its expressions, would possibly have discovered in that countenance lines of deep artifice, together with the traces of a profound and constitutional enthusiasm. He was bent, at that very moment, on a scheme worthy of the loftiest spirit living ; the regeneration and union of the people of his race, with a view to recover the possessions they had yielded to the pale-faces; but it was a project blended with the ferocity and revenge of a savage—noble while ferocious.

Not idly had the whites, scattered along that frontier, given the *sobriquet* of "Scalping" to Peter. As his pole now showed, it had been earned in a hundred scenes of bloody vengeance; and so great had been his success, that the warrior, prophet, and councillor, for all these characters were united in his single person, began to think the attainment of his wishes possible. As a matter of course, much ignorance of the power of the Anglo-Saxon race on this continent was blended with these opinions and hopes; but it was scarcely an ignorance exceeding that of certain persons of far higher pretensions in knowledge, who live in another hemisphere, and who often set themselves up as infallible judges of all things connected with man, and his attributes. Peter, the "Tribeless," was not more in fault, than those who fancied they saw the power of this great Republic in the gallant little band collected at Corpus Christi, under its indomitable chief, and who, march by march, nay, foot by foot, as it might be, have perseveringly predicted the halt, the defeat, the disasters, and final discomfiture, which it has not yet pleased Divine Providence to inflict on this slight effort of the young Hercules, as he merely moves in his cradle. Alas! the enemy that most menaces the overthrow of this new and otherwise invincible exhibition of human force is within; seated in the citadel itself; and must be narrowly watched, or he will act his malignant purpose, and destroy the fairest hopes that ever yet dawned on the fortunes of the human race!

The conference between the chiefs lasted fully an hour. Crowsfeather possessed much of the confidence of Peter, and, as for Onoah, neither Tecumthe, nor his brother the Prophet, commanded as much of the respect of Crowsfeather as he did himself. Some even whispered that the "Tribeless" was the individual who lay behind all, and that the others named merely acted as he suggested or advised. The reader will obtain all the insight into the fut-

ure that it is necessary now to give him, by getting a few
of the remarks made by the two colloquists, just before they
joined the rest of the party.

" My father, then, intends to lead his pale-faces on a
crooked path, and take their scalps when he has done with
them," said Crowsfeather, who had been gravely listening
to Peter's plans of future proceeding ; " but who is to get
the scalp of the Chippewa ?"

" One of my Pottawattamie young men ; but not until I
have made use of him. I have a medicine-priest of the
pale-faces and a warrior with me, but shall not put their
scalps on my pole until they have paddled me farther.
The council is to be first held in the Oak Openings,"—
we translate this term freely, that used by Peter meaning
rather "the open woods of the prairies,"—"and I wish to
show my prisoners to the chiefs, that they may see how
easy it is to cut off all the Yankees. I have now four men
of that people, and two squaws, in my power ; let every
redman destroy as many, and the land will soon be clear
of them all ! "

This was uttered with gleamings of ferocity in the
speaker's face that rendered his countenance terrible.
Even Crowsfeather quailed a little before that fierce aspect ; but the whole passed away almost as soon as betrayed, and was succeeded by a friendly and deceptive smile
that was characteristic of the wily Asiatic rather than of
the aboriginal American.

" They cannot be counted," returned the Pottawattamie
chief, as soon as his restraint was a little removed by this
less terrific aspect of his companion ; " if all I hear is true,
Blackbird says that even the squaws of the pale-faces are
numerous enough to overcome all the redmen that remain."

" There will be two less, when I fasten to my pole the
scalps of those on the other side of the river," answered
Peter, with another of his transient but startling gleams
of intense revenge. " But no matter, now : my brother
knows all I wish him to do. Not a hair of the head of
any of these pale-faces must be touched by any hand but
mine. When the time comes, the knife of Onoah is sure.

The Pottawattamies shall have their canoes, and can follow us up the river. They will find us in the Openings, and near the Prairie Round. They know the spot; for the redmen love to hunt the deer in that region. Now, go and tell this to your young men; and tell them that corn will not grow, nor the deer wait to be killed by any of your people, if they forget to do as I have said. Vengeance shall come when it is time."

Crowsfeather communicated all this to his warriors, who received it as the ancients received the words of their oracles. Each member of the party endeavored to get an accurate notion of his duty, in order that he might comply to the very letter with the injunctions received. So profound was the impression made among all the redmen of the Northwest by the previous labors of the "Tribeless" to awaken a national spirit, and so great was their dread of the consequences of disobedience, that every warrior present felt as if his life were the threatened penalty of neglect or disinclination to obey.

No sooner, however, had Crowsfeather got through with his communication, than a general request was made that the problem of the whiskey-spring might be preferred to Onoah for solution. The young men had strong hopes, notwithstanding all that had passed, that this spring might yet turn out to be a reality. The scent was still there, strong and fragrant, and they could not get rid of the notion that " fire-water " grew on that spot. It is true, their faith had been somewhat disturbed by the manner in which the medicine-man had left them, and by his failure to draw forth the gushing stream which he had impliedly promised, and in a small degree performed; nevertheless, little pools of whiskey had been found on the rock, and several had tasted and satisfied themselves of the quality of the liquor. As is usual, that taste had created a desire for more, a desire that seldom slumbered on an Indian palate when strong drinks were connected with its gratification.

Peter heard the request with gravity, and consented to look into the matter with a due regard to his popularity and influence.   He had his own superstitious views, but among them there did not happen to be one which admitted the possibility of whiskey's running in a stream from the living rock.   Still he was willing to examine the charmed spot, scent the fragrant odor, and make up his own estimate of the artifices by which the bee-hunter had been practising on the untutored beings into whose hands chance had thrown him.

While the young men eagerly pointed out the precise spots where the scent was the strongest, Peter maintained the most unmoved gravity.   He did not kneel to smell the rocks like the other chiefs, for this an innate sense of propriety told him would be undignified ; but he made his observations closely, and with a keen Indian-like attention to every little circumstance that might aid him in arriving at the truth.   All this time, great was the awe and deep the admiration of the lookers-on.   Onoah had succeeded in creating a moral power for himself among the Indians of the Northwest which much exceeded that of any other redman of that region.   The whites scarcely heard of him, knew but little of his career, and less of his true character, for both were shrouded in mystery.   There is nothing remarkable in this ignorance of the pale-faces of the time.   They did not understand their own leaders ; much less the leaders of the children of the openings, the prairies, and the forest.   At this hour, what is really known by the mass of the American people of the true characters of their public men ?   No nation that has any claim to civilization and publicity knows less, and for several very obvious reasons.   The want of a capital in which the intelligence of the nation periodically assembles, and whence a corrected public opinion on all such matters ought constantly to flow as truth emanates from the collisions of minds, is one of these reasons.   The extent of the country, which separates men by distances that no fact can travel over without incurring the dangers of being perverted on the road, is another.   But the most fatal of all the influences that tend to mislead the judgment of the American citizen is to be found in the abuse of a machinery that was intended to produce an exactly contrary effect. If the tongue was given to man to communicate ideas to his fellows, so has philosophy described it as "a gift to conceal his thoughts." If the press was devised to circulate truth, so it has been changed into a means of circulating lies. One is easily, nay, more easily, sent abroad on the four winds of the heavens than the other. Truth requires candor, impartiality, honesty, research, and industry; but a falsehood, whether designed or not, stands in need of neither. Of that which is the most easily produced, the country gets the most; and it were idle to imagine that a people who blindly and unresistingly submit to be put, as it might be, under the feet of falsehood, as respects all their own public men, can ever get very accurate notions of those of other nations.

Thus was it with Onoah. His name was unknown to the whites, except as a terrible and much dreaded avenger of the wrongs of his race. With the redmen it was very different. They had no "forked tongues" to make falsehood take the place of truth; or if such existed, they were not believed. The Pottawattamies now present knew all about Tecumseh,[1] of whom the whites had also various and ample accounts. This Shawanee chief had long been active among them, and his influence was extended far and near. He was a bold, restless, and ingenious warrior; one, perhaps, who better understood the art of war, as it was practised among redmen, than any Indian then living. They knew the name and person, also, of his brother Elkswatawa,[2] or the Prophet, whose name has also become incorporated with the histories of the times. These two chiefs were very powerful, though scarce dwelling regularly in any tribe; but their origin, their careers, and their characters were known to all, as were those of their common father, Pukeesheno,[3] and their mother, Meethetaske.[4] But with Onoah it was very different. With him the past was as much of a mystery as the future. No Indian could say even of what tribe he was born. The to-

[1] "A tiger stooping for his prey."
[2] "A door opened."
[3] "I light from flying."
[4] "A turtle laying her eggs in the sand."

tem that he bore on his person belonged to no people then
existing on the continent, and all connected with him, his
history, nation, and family, was conjecture and fancy.

It is said that the Indians have traditions which are communicated only to a favored few, and which by them have
been transmitted from generation to generation.   An enlightened and educated redman has quite recently told us in
person, that *he* had been made a repository of some of these
traditions, and that he had thus obtained enough of the history of his race to be satisfied that they were *not* derived from
the lost tribes of Israel, though he declined communicating
any more.   It is so natural to resort to secrecy in order to
extend influence, that we can have no difficulty in believing
the existence of the practice ; there probably being no other
reason why Free Masonry or Odd Fellowship should have
recourse to such an expedient, but to rule through the imagination in preference to the judgment.   Now Peter enjoyed all the advantages of mystery.   It was said that even
his real name was unknown, that of Onoah having been
given in token of the many scalps he took, and that of Wa-
wa-nosh, which he also sometimes bore, having been bestowed upon him by adoption in consequence of an act of
favor extended to him from an Ojebway of some note, while
that of Peter was clearly derived from the whites.   Some
of his greatest admirers whispered that when the true name
of the "Tribeless" should get to be known, his origin, early
career, and all relating to him would at once become familiar
to every redman.   At present the Indians must rest content
with what they saw and understood.   The wisdom of Wa-
wa-nosh made itself felt in the councils ; his eloquence no
speaker has equalled for ages ; as for his vengeance on the
enemies of his race, *that* was to be estimated by the scalps
he had taken.   More than this, no Indian was to be permitted
to know, until the mission of this oracle and chief was
completed.

Had one enlightened by the education of a civilized man
been there, to watch the movements and countenance of
Peter as he scented the whiskey, and looked in vain for the
cause of the odor, and for a clue to the mystery which so

much perplexed the Pottawattamies, he would probably have discovered some reason to distrust the sincerity of this remarkable savage's doubts. If ever Peter was an actor, it was on this occasion. He did not in the least fall into any of the errors of his companions ; but the scent a good deal confounded him at first. At length he came to the natural conclusion, that this unusual odor was in some way connected with the family he had left on the other shore ; and from that moment his mind was at ease.

It did not suit the views of Peter, however, to explain to the Pottawattamies that which was now getting to be so obvious to himself. On the contrary, he rather threw dust into the eyelids of the chiefs, with a view to bring them also under the influence of superstition. After making his observations with unmoved gravity, he promised a solution of the whole affair when they should again meet in the openings, and proposed to re-cross the river. Before quitting the shore, Peter and Crowsfeather had a clear understanding on the subject of their respective movements ; and, as soon as the former began to paddle up against the wind, the latter called his young men together, made a short address, and led them into the woods, as if about to proceed on a march of length. The party, notwithstanding, did not proceed more than a mile and a half, when it came to a halt, and lighted a fire in order to cook some venison taken on the way.

When Peter reached the south shore, he found the whole group assembled to receive him. His tale was soon told. He had talked with the Pottawattamies, and they were gone. The canoes, however, must be carried to the other shore and left there, in order that their owners might recover their property when they returned. This much had Peter promised, and his pale-face friends must help him to keep his word. Then he pointed to the openings as to their place of present safety. There they would be removed from all immediate danger, and he would accompany them and give them the countenance and protection of his name and presence. As for going south on the lake, that was impossible so long as the wind lasted, and it was useless even could it be done. The troops had all left Chicago, and the fort was destroyed.

Parson Amen and Corporal Flint, both of whom were completely deluded by Peter, fancying him a secret friend of the whites, in consequence of his own protestations to that effect and the service he had already rendered them, in appearance at least, instantly acquiesced in this wily savage's proposal. It was the best, the wisest, nay, the only thing that now could be done. Mackinaw was gone as well as Chicago, and Detroit must be reached by crossing the Peninsula instead of taking the easier but far more circuitous route of the lakes. Gershom was easily enough persuaded into the belief of the feasibility, as well as of the necessity, of this deviation from his original road, and he soon agreed to accompany the party.

With Le Bourdon the case was different. He understood himself and the wilderness. For him the wind was fair, and there was no necessity for his touching at Mackinaw at all. It is true, he usually passed several days on that pleasant and salubrious island, and frequently disposed of lots of honey there; but he could dispense with the visit and the sales. There was certainly danger now to be apprehended from the Ottawas, who would be very apt to be out on the lake after this maritime excursion against the fort; but it was possible even to elude their vigilance. In a word, the bee-hunter did not believe in the prudence of returning to the openings, but thought it by far the wisest for the whole party to make the best of its way by water to the settlements. All this he urged warmly on his white companions, taking them aside for that purpose, and leaving Peter and Pigeonswing together while he did so.

But Parson Amen would as soon have believed that his old congregation in Connecticut was composed of Philistines, as not to believe that the redmen were the lost tribes, and that Peter, in particular, was not especially and elaborately described in the Old Testament. He had become so thoroughly possessed by this crotchet as to pervert everything that he saw, read, or heard into evidence, of some sort or other, of the truth of his notions. In this respect there was nothing peculiar in the good missionary's weakness, it being a failing common to partisans of a theory to discover proofs of its truth in a thousand things in which indifferent persons can find even no connection with the subject at all. In this frame of mind the missionary would as soon think of letting go his hold on the Bible itself, as think of separating from an Indian who might turn out any day to be a direct representative of Abraham, and Isaac, and Jacob. Not to speak irreverently, but to use language that must be familiar to all, the well-meaning missionary wished to be in at the death.

Corporal Flint, too, had great faith in Peter. It was a part of the scheme of the savage to make this straight-forward soldier an instrument in placing many scalps in his power; and though he had designed from the first to execute his bloody office on the corporal himself, he did not intend to do so until he had made the most of him as a stool-pigeon. Here were four more pale-faces thrown in his power, principally by means of the confidence he had awakened in the minds of the missionary and the soldier; and that same confidence might be made instrumental in adding still more to the number. Peter was a sagacious, even a far-seeing savage, but he labored under the curse of ignorance. Had his information been of a more extended nature, he would have seen the utter fallacy of his project to destroy the pale-faces altogether, and most probably would have abandoned it.

It is a singular fact that, while such men as Tecumthe, his brother the Prophet, and Peter, were looking forward to the downfall of the republic on the side of the forest, so many, who ought to have been better informed on such a subject, were anxiously expecting, nay confidently *predicting* it, from beyond the Atlantic. Notwithstanding these sinister soothsayers, the progress of the nation has, by the aid of a beneficent Providence, been onward and onward, until it is scarcely presumptuous to suppose that even England has abandoned the expectation of classing this country again among her dependencies. The fortunes of America, under God, depend only on herself. America *may* destroy America; of that there *is* danger; but it is pretty certain that Europe united could make no serious impression on her. Favored by position, and filled with a population that we have ever maintained was one of the most military in existence, a truth that recent events are hourly proving to be true, it much exceeds the power of all the enemies of her institutions to make any serious impression on her. There is an enemy who may prove too much for her; it exists in her bosom; and God alone can keep him in subjection, and repress his desolation.

These were facts, however, of which Wa-wa-nosh, or Onoah, was as ignorant as if he were an English or French minister of State, and had got his notions of the country from English or French travellers, who *wished* for what they *predicted*. He had heard of the towns and population of the Republic; but one gets a very imperfect notion of any fact of this sort by report, unless previous experience has prepared the mind to make the necessary comparisons, and fitted it to receive the images intended to be conveyed. No wonder, then, that Peter fell into a mistake common to those who had so many better opportunities of forming just opinions, and of arriving at truths that were sufficiently obvious to all who did not wilfully shut their eyes to their existence.

CHAPTER XIII.

"Hearest thou voices on the shore
That our ears perceive no more,
Deafened by the cataract's roar?

Bear, through sorrow, wrong and ruth,
In thy heart the dew of youth,
On thy lips the smile of truth."

LONGFELLOW.

FROM all that has been stated, the reader will probably be prepared to learn that Boden did not succeed in his effort to persuade Gershom, and the other *Christians*, to accompany him on his voyage round by Lake Huron. Corporal Flint was obdurate, and Parson Amen confiding. As for Gershom, he did not like the thought of retracing his steps so soon, and the females were obliged to remain with the husband and brother.

"You had better get out of the river while all the canoes are on this side," said Margery, as she and Le Bourdon walked towards the boats in company, the council having ended, and everything beginning to assume the appearance of action. "Remember, you will be quite alone, and have a long, long road to travel!"

"I do remember all this, Margery, and see the necessity for all of us getting back to the settlements as fast as we can. I don't half like this Peter; his name is a bad one in the garrisons, and it makes me miserable to think that you may be in his power."

"The missionary and the corporal, as well as my brother, seem willing to trust him—what can two females do, when their male protector has made up his mind in such a matter?"

"One who would very gladly be *your* protector, pretty Margery, has not made up his mind to the prudence of trusting Peter, at all. Put yourself under my care, and my life shall be lost, or I will carry you safe to your friends in Detroit."

This might be deemed tolerably explicit; yet was it not sufficiently so to satisfy female scruples or female rights. Margery blushed, and she looked down, while she did not look absolutely displeased. But her answer was given firmly, and with a promptitude that showed she was quite in earnest.

"I cannot quit Dorothy, placed as she is—and it is my duty to die with brother," she said.

"Have you thought enough of this, Margery? may not reflection change your mind?"

"This is a duty on which a girl is not called to reflect; she must *feel*, in a matter of conscience."

The bee-hunter fairly sighed, and from a very resolute he became a very irresolute sort of person. As was natural to one in his situation, he let out the secret current his thoughts had taken in the remarks which followed.

"I do not like the manner in which Peter and Pigeons-wing are now talking together," he said. "When an Injin is so earnest, there is generally mischief brewing. Do you see Peter's manner?"

"He seems to be telling the young warrior something that makes both forget themselves. I never saw two men who seem so completely to forget all the rest of the world as them two savages! What can be the meaning, Bourdon, of so much fierce earnestness?"

"I would give the world to know—possibly the Chippewa may tell me. We understand each other tolerably well, and, just as you spoke, he gave me a secret sign that I have a right to think means confidence and friendship. That savage is either a fast friend or a thorough villain."

"Is it safe to trust any of them, Bourdon? No—no— your best way will be to go down the lakes, and get back to Detroit as soon as you can. Not only your property, but your *life*, is at risk."

" Go, and leave you here, Margery—here, with a brother whose failing you know as well as I do, and who may, at any moment, fall back into his old ways ! I should not be a man to do it ! "

" But brother can get no liquor now, for it is all emptied. When himself for a few days, Gershom is a good protector, as well as a good provider. You must not judge brother too harshly, from what you have seen of him, Bourdon."

" I do not wish to judge him at all, Margery. We all have our failin's, and whiskey is his. I dare say mine are quite as bad, in some other way. It's enough for me, Margery, that Gershom is *your* brother, to cause me to try to think well of him. We must not trust to there being no more liquor among us ; for, if that so'ger is altogether without his rations, he's the first so'ger I ever met who was ! "

" But this corporal is a friend of the minister, and ministers ought not to drink ! "

" Ministers are like other men, as them that live much among 'em will soon find out. Hows'ever, if you *will* stay, Margery, there is no more to be said. I must *cache*[1] my honey, and get the canoe ready to go up stream again. Where you go, Margery, I go too, unless you tell me that you do not wish my company."

This was said quietly, but in the manner of one whose mind was made up. Margery scarce knew how to take it. That she was secretly delighted cannot be denied ; while, at the same time, that she felt a generous and lively concern for the fortunes of Le Bourdon is quite as certain. As Gershom just then called to her to lend her assistance in preparing to embark, she had no leisure for expostulation, nor do we know that she now seriously wished to divert the bee-hunter from his purpose.

It was soon understood by every one that the river was to be crossed, in order that Gershom might get his household effects previously to ascending the Kalamazoo. This set all at work but the Chippewa, who appeared to Le

---

[1] A western term, obviously derived from *cacher*, to conceal. *Cache* is much used by the western adventurers.

Bourdon to be watchful and full of distrust. As the latter had a job before him that would be likely to consume a couple of hours, the others were ready for a start long before he had his hole dug. It was therefore arranged that the bee-hunter should complete his task, while the others crossed the stream, and went in quest of Gershom's scanty stock of household goods. Pigeonswing, however, was not to be found when the canoes were ready, and Peter proceeded without him. Nor did Le Bourdon see anything of his friend until the adventurers were fairly on the north shore, when he rejoined Le Bourdon, sitting on a log, a curious spectator of the latter's devices to conceal his property, but not offering to aid him in a single movement. The bee-hunter too well understood an Indian warrior's aversion to labor of all sorts, unless it be connected with his military achievements, to be surprised at his companion's indifference to his own toil. As the work went on, a friendly dialogue was kept up between the parties.

"I didn't know, Pigeonswing, but you had started for the openings before us," observed Le Bourdon. "That tribeless old Injin made something of a fuss about your being out of the way; I dare say he wanted you to help back the furniture down to the canoes."

"Got squaw—what he want better to do dat?"

"So you would put that pretty piece of work on such persons as Margery and Dolly!"

"Why not, no? Bot' squaw—bot' know how. Dere business to work for warrior."

"Did you keep out of the way, then, lest old Peter should get you at a job that is onsuitable to your manhood?"

"Keep out of the way of Pottawattamie," returned the Chippewa; "no want to lose scalp—radder take his'n."

"But Peter says the Pottawattamies are all gone, and that we have no longer any reason to fear them; and this medicine-priest tells us that what Peter says we can depend on for truth."

"Dat good medicine-man, eh? T'ink he know a great great deal, eh?"

"That is more than I can tell you, Pigeonswing; for though I've been a medicine-man myself so lately, it is in a different line altogether from that of Parson Amen's."

As the bee-hunter uttered this answer, he was putting the last of his honey-kegs into the *cache*, and as he rose from completing the operation, he laughed heartily like one who saw images in the occurrences of the past night that tended to divert himself, if they had not the same effect on the other spectators.

"If you medicine-man, can tell who Peter be? Winnebagoe, Sioux, Fox, Ojebway, Six Nation, all say don't know him. Medicine-man ought to know—who he be, eh?"

"I am not enough of a medicine-man to answer your question, Pigeonswing. Set me at finding a Whiskey Spring, or any little job of that sort, and I'll turn my back to no other Whiskey Spring finder on the whole frontier; but as for Peter, he goes beyond my calculations, quite. Why is he called *Scalping* Peter in the garrisons, if he be so good an Injin, Chippewa?"

"You ask question—you answer. Don't know, 'less he take a good many scalp. Hear he do take all he can find,—den hear he don't."

"But you take all you can find, Pigeonswing; and that which is good in you cannot be so bad in Peter."

"Don't take scalp from friend. When you hear Pigeonswing scalp *friend*, eh?"

"I never did hear it; and hope I never shall. But when did you hear that Peter is so wicked?"

"S'pose he don't, 'cause he got no friend among paleface. Bes' take care of dat man!"

"I'm of your way of thinking, myself, Chippewa; though the corporal and the priest think him all in all. When I asked Parson Amen how he came to be the associate of one who went by a scalping name, even, he told me it was all *name*; that Peter hadn't touched a hair of a human head, in the way of scalping, since his youth, and that most of his notions and ways were quite Jewish. The parson has almost as much faith in Peter as he has in his religion; I'm not quite sure he has not even more."

13

"No matter. Bes' always for pale-face to trust pale-face, and Injin to trust Injin. Dat most likely to be right."

"Nevertheless, I trust *you*, Pigeonswing; and, hitherto, you have not deceived me."

The Chippewa cast a glance of so much meaning on the bee-hunter that the last was troubled by it. For many a day did Le Bourdon remember that look; and painful were the apprehensions to which it gave birth. Until that morning, the intercourse between the two had been of the most confidential character; but something like a fierce hatred was blended in that look. Could it be that the feelings of the Chippewa were changed? and was it possible that Peter was in any way connected with this alteration in looks and sentiments? All these suspicions passed through Le Bourdon's mind as he finished his *cache*; and sufficiently disagreeable did he find it to entertain them. The circumstances, however, did not admit of any change of plan; and in a few minutes the two were in the canoe, and on their way to join their companions.

Peter had dealt fairly enough with those who accompanied him. The Pottawattamies were nowhere to be seen, and Gershom led the corporal to the place where his household goods had been secreted in so much confidence that both the men left their arms behind them. Such was the state of things when Le Bourdon reached the north shore. The young man was startled when his eyes first fell on the rifles; but, on looking around, there did not really appear to be any sufficient reason why they might not be laid aside for a few minutes.

The bee-hunter, having disposed of all his honey, had now a nearly empty canoe; accordingly he received a portion of Gershom's effects, all of which were safely transported from their place of concealment to the water side. Their owner was slowly recovering the use of his body and mind, though still a little dull from his recent debauch. The females supplied his place, however, in many respects; and two hours after the party had landed, it was ready again to proceed on its journey into the interior. The last article was stowed in one of the canoes, and Gershom announced his willingness to depart.

At this moment Peter led the bee-hunter aside, telling his friends that he would speedily rejoin them. Our hero followed his savage leader along the foot of the declivity in the rear of the hut, until the former stopped at the place where the first and principal fire of the past night had been lighted. Here Peter made a sweeping gesture of his hand, as if to invite his companion to survey the different objects around. As this characteristic gesture was made, the Indian spoke.

"My brother is a medicine-man," he said. "He knows where whiskey grows; let him tell Peter where to find the spring."

The recollection of the scene of the previous night came so fresh and vividly over the imagination of the bee-hunter, that, instead of answering the question of the chief, he burst into a hearty fit of laughter. Then, fearful of giving offence, he was about to apologize for a mirth so ill-timed, when the Indian smiled, with a gleam of intelligence on his swarthy face, that seemed to say, "I understand it all," and continued,—

"Good—the chief with three eyes"—in allusion to the spy-glass that Le Bourdon always carried suspended from his neck—"is a very great medicine-man; he knows when to laugh, and when to look sad. The Pottawattamies were dry, and he wanted to find them some whiskey to drink, but could not—our brother in the canoe had drunk it all. Good."

Again the bee-hunter laughed; and though Peter did not join in his mirth, it was quite plain that he understood its cause. With this good-natured sort of intelligence between them, the two returned to the canoes; the bee-hunter always supposing that the Indian had obtained his object, in receiving his indirect admission that the scene of the previous night had been merely a piece of ingenious jugglery. So much of a courtier, however, was Peter, and so entire his self-command, that on no occasion afterwards did he ever make any further allusion to the subject.

The ascent of the river was now commenced. It was not a difficult matter for Le Bourdon to persuade Margery that her brother's canoe would be too heavily loaded for such a passage, unless she consented to quit it for his own. Pigeonswing took the girl's place, and was of material assistance in forcing the light, but steady craft, up stream. The three others continued in the canoe in which they had entered the river. With this arrangement, therefore, our adventurers commenced this new journey.

Every reader will easily understand, that ascending such a stream as the Kalamazoo was a very different thing from descending it. The progress was slow, and at many points laborious. At several of the ''rifts'' it became necessary to ''track'' the canoes up; and places occurred at which the only safe way of proceeding was to unload them altogether, and transport boats, cargoes and all, on the shoulders of the men, across what are called, in the language of the country, ''portages,'' or ''carrying-places.'' In such toil as this, the corporal was found to be very serviceable; but neither of the Indians inclined to lend their assistance in work of this manly character. By this time, moreover, Gershom had come round, and was an able-bodied, vigorous assistant once more. If the corporal was the master of any alcohol, he judiciously kept it a secret; for not a drop passed any one's lips during the whole of that toilsome journey.

Although the difficult places in the river were sufficiently numerous, most of the reaches were places having steady, but not swift currents towards the lake. In these reaches the paddles, and those not very vigorously applied, enabled the travellers to advance as fast as was desirable; and such tranquil waters were a sort of resting-places to those who managed the canoes. It was while ascending these easy channels that conversation most occurred; each speaker yielding, as was natural, to the impulses of the thoughts uppermost in his mind. The missionary talked much of the Jews; and, as the canoes came near each other, he entered at large, with their different occupants, into the reasons he had for believing that the redmen of America

were the lost tribes of Israel. "The very use of the word
'tribes,'" would this simple-minded, and not very profound
expounder of the word of God, say, "is one proof of the
truth of what I tell you. Now, no one thinks of dividing
the white men of America into 'tribes.' Who ever heard
of the 'tribe' of New England, or of the 'tribe' of Vir-
ginia, or of the 'tribe' of the Middle States?[1] Even among
the blacks there are no tribes. There is a very remarkable
passage in the sixty-eighth Psalm, that has greatly struck
me since my mind has turned to this subject : 'God shall
wound the *head* of his enemies,' saith the Psalmist, 'and
the *hairy scalp* of such a one as goeth on still in his wickedness.' Here is a very obvious allusion to a well-known,
and, what we think, a barbarous practice of the redmen ;
but rely on it, friends, nothing that is permitted on earth
is permitted in vain. The attentive reader of the inspired
book, by gleaning here and there, can collect together much
authority for this new opinion about the lost tribes ; and
the day will come, I do not doubt, when men will marvel
that the truth hath been so long hidden from them. I can
scarcely open a chapter in the Old Testament, that some
passage does not strike me as going to prove this identity
between the redmen and the Hebrews ; and, were they all
collected together and published in a book, mankind would
be astonished at their lucidity and weight. As for scalping,
it is a horrid thing in our eyes, but it is honorable with the
redmen ; and I have quoted to you the words of the Psalm-

[1] The reader is not to infer any exaggeration in this picture.
There is no end to the ignorance and folly of sects and parties,
when religious or political zeal runs high. The writer well remembers to have heard a Universalist, of more zeal than learning, adduce
as an argument in favor of his doctrine the twenty-fifth chapter and
forty-sixth verse of St. Matthew, where we are told that the wicked
"shall go away into *everlasting* punishment ; but the righteous into
life *eternal* ;" by drawing a distinction between the adjectives ; and
this so much more, because the Old Testament speaks of " *everlasting* hills," and "*everlasting* valleys" ; thus proving, from the
Bible, a substantial difference between "everlasting" and "eternal."
Now, every sophomore knows that the word used in Matthew is the
same in both cases, being " αἰώνιον," or "existing forever."

ist, in order to show the manner in which divine wisdom
inflicts penalties on sin.   Here is plain justification of the
practice, provided always that the sufferer be in the bond-
age of transgression and obnoxious to divine censure.   Let
no man, therefore, in the pride of his learning, and, perhaps, of his prosperity, disdain to believe things that are so
manifestly taught and foretold ; but let us all bow in humble
submission to the will of a Being who to our finite understanding is so perfectly incomprehensible.''

We trust that no one of our readers will be disposed to
deride Parson Amen's speculations on this interesting subject, although this may happen to be the first occasion on
which he has ever heard the practice of taking scalps justified by Scripture.   Viewed in a proper spirit, they ought
merely to convey a lesson of humility, by rendering apparent the wisdom, nay the necessity, of men's keeping themselves within the limits of the sphere of knowledge they
were designed to fill, and convey, when rightly considered,
as much of a lesson to the Puseyite, with abstractions that
are quite as unintelligible to himself as they are to others ;
to the high-wrought and dogmatical Calvinist, who, in the
midst of his fiery zeal, forgets that love is the very essence
of the relation between God and man ; to the Quaker, who
seems to think the cut of a coat essential to salvation ; to
the descendants of the Puritan, who, whether he be Socinian,
Calvinist, Universalist, or any other "ist," appears to believe that the "rock " on which Christ declared he would
found his church was the " Rock of Plymouth " ; and to the
unbeliever, who, in deriding all creeds, does not know
where to turn to find one to substitute in their stead.   Humility, in matters of this sort, is the great lesson that all
should teach and learn ; for it opens the way to charity,
and eventually to faith, and through both of these to hope ;
finally, through all of these, to heaven.

The journey up the Kalamazoo lasted many days, the
ascent being often so painful, and no one seeming in a
hurry.   Peter waited for the time set for his council to
approach, and was as well content to remain in his canoe
as to "camp out" in the openings.   Gershom never was in

haste, while the bee-hunter would have been satisfied to pass the summer in so pleasant a manner, Margery being seated most of the time in his canoe. In his ordinary excursions Le Bourdon carried the mastiff as a companion ; but, now that his place was so much better filled, Hive was suffered to roam the woods that lined most of the river-banks, joining his master from time to time at the portages or landings.

As for the missionary and the corporal, impatience formed no part of their present disposition. The first had been led, by the artful Peter, to expect great results to his theory from the assembly of chiefs which was to meet in the "openings " ; and the credulous parson was, in one sense, going as blindly on the path of destruction as any sinner it had ever been his duty to warn of his fate was proceeding in the same direction in another. The corporal, too, was the dupe of Peter's artifices. This man had heard so many stories to the Indian's prejudice at the different posts where he had been stationed, as at first to render him exceedingly averse to making the present journey in his company. The necessity of the case, as connected with the preservation of his own life after the massacre of Fort Dearborn, and the influence of the missionary, had induced him to over-look his ancient prejudices, and to forget opinions that, it now occurred to him, had been founded in error. Once fairly within the influence of Peter's wiles, a simple-minded soldier, like the corporal, was soon completely made the Indian's dupe. By the time the canoe reached the mouth of the Kalamazoo, as has been related, each of these men placed the most implicit reliance on the good faith, and friendly feelings of the very being whose entire life, both sleeping and waking thoughts, were devoted, not only to his destruction, but to that of the whole white race on the American continent. So bland was the manner of this terrible savage, when it comported with his views to conceal his ruthless designs, that persons more practised and observant than either of his two companions might have been its dupes not to say its victims. While the missionary was completely mystified by his own headlong desire to establish a theory, and to announce to the religious world where the lost tribes were to be found, the corporal had aided in deceiving himself also by another process. With *him* Peter had privately conversed of war, and had insinuated that he was secretly laboring in behalf of his great father at Washington, and against the other great father down at Montreal. As between the two, Peter professed to lean to the interests of the first ; though, had he laid bare his inmost soul, a fiery hatred of each would have been found to be its predominate feeling. But Corporal Flint fondly fancied he was making a concealed march with an ally, while he thus accompanied one of the fiercest enemies of his race.

Peter is not to be judged too harshly. It is always respectable to defend the fireside and the land of one's nativity, although the cause connected with it may be sometimes wrong. This Indian knew nothing of the principles of colonization, and had no conception that any other than its original owners—original so far as his traditions reached—could have a right to his own hunting-grounds. Of the slow but certain steps by which an overruling Providence is extending a knowledge of the true God, and of the great atonement through the death of his blessed Son, Peter had no conception ; nor would it probably have seemed right to his contracted mind, had he even seen and understood this general tendency of things. To him, the pale-face appeared only as a rapacious invader, and not a creature obeying the great law of his destiny, the end of which is doubtless to help knowledge to abound, until it shall "cover the whole earth as the waters cover the sea." Hatred, inextinguishable and active hatred, appeared to be the law of this man's being ; and he devoted all the means, aided by all the intelligence he possessed, to the furtherance of his narrow and short-sighted means of vengeance and redress. In all this, he acted in common with Tecumthe and his brother, though his consummate art kept him behind a veil, while the others were known and recognized as open and active foes. No publication speaks of this Peter, nor does any orator enumerate his qualities, while the other two chiefs have been the subjects of every specie of descriptive talent, from that of the poet to that of the painter.

As day passed after day, the feeling of distrust in the bosom of the bee-hunter grew weaker and weaker, and Peter succeeded in gradually worming himself into his confidence also. This was done, moreover, without any apparent effort. The Indian made no professions of friendship, laid himself out for no particular attention, nor ever seemed to care how his companions regarded his deportment. His secret purposes he kept carefully smothered in his own breast, it is true; but, beyond that, no other sign of duplicity could have been discovered, even by one who knew his objects and schemes. So profound was his art that it had the aspect of nature. Pigeonswing alone was alive to the danger of this man's company; and he knew it only by means of certain semi-confidential communications received in his character of a redman. It was no part of Peter's true policy to become an ally to either of the great belligerents of the day. On the contrary, his ardent wish was to see them destroy each other, and it was the sudden occurrence of the present war that had given a new impulse to his hopes and a new stimulus to his efforts, as a time most propitious to his purposes. He was perfectly aware of the state of the Chippewa's feelings, and he knew that this man was hostile to the Pottawattamies as well as to most of the tribes of Michigan; but this made no difference with *him*. If Pigeonswing took the scalp of a white man, he cared not whether it grew on an English or an American head; in either case, it was the destruction of *his* enemy. With such a policy constantly in view, it cannot be matter of surprise that Peter continued on just as good terms with Pigeonswing as with Crowsfeather. But one precaution was observed in his intercourse with the first. To Crowsfeather, then on the war-path in quest of Yankee scalps, he had freely communicated his designs on his own white companions, while he did not dare to confide to the Chippewa this particular secret, since that Indian's relations with the bee-hunter were so amicable as to be visible to every observer. Peter felt the necessity of especial caution in his communication with this savage, therefore ; and this was the reason why the Chippewa was in so much painful uncertainty as to the other's intentions. He had learned enough to be distrustful, but not enough to act with decision.

Once, and once only, during their slow passage up the Kalamazoo, did the bee-hunter observe something about Peter to awaken his original apprehensions. The fourth day after leaving the mouth of the river, and when the whole party were resting after the toil of passing a "carrying-place," our hero had observed the eyes of that tribeless savage roaming from one white face to another, with an expression in them so very fiendish as actually to cause his heart to beat quicker than common. The look was such an one as Le Bourdon could not remember to have ever before beheld in a human countenance. In point of fact, he had seen Peter in one of those moments when the pent fires of the volcano that ceaselessly raged within his bosom were becoming difficult to suppress ; and when memory was busiest in recalling to his imagination scenes of oppression and wrong, that the white man is only too apt to forget amid the ease of his civilization and the security of his power. But the look, and the impression produced by it on Le Bourdon, soon passed away, and were forgotten by him to whom it might otherwise have proved to be a most useful warning.

It was a little remarkable that Margery actually grew to be attached to Peter, often manifesting towards the chief attentions and feelings such as a daughter is apt to exhibit towards a father. This arose from the high and courteous bearing of this extraordinary savage. At all times an Indian warrior is apt to maintain the dignified and courteous bearing that has so often been remarked in the race, but it is very seldom that he goes out of his way to manifest attention to the squaws. Doubtless these men have the feelings of humanity, and love their wives and offspring like others ; but it is so essential a part of their training to suppress the exhibition of such emotions, that it is seldom

the mere looker-on has occasion to note them. Peter, however, had neither wife nor child ; or if they existed, no one
knew where either was to be found. The same mystery
shrouded this part of his history as veiled all the rest. In
his hunts, various opportunities occurred for exhibiting to
the females manly attentions, by offering to them the choicest pieces of his game, and pointing out the most approved
Indian modes of cooking the meats so as to preserve their
savory properties. This he did sparingly at first, and as a
part of a system of profound deception ; but day by day, and
hour after hour, most especially with Margery, did his manner become sensibly less distant, and more natural. The
artlessness, the gentle qualities, blended with feminine spirit
as they were, and the innocent gayety of the girl, appeared to
win on this nearly remorseless savage, in spite of his efforts
to resist her influence. Perhaps the beauty of Margery contributed its share in exciting these novel emotions in the
breast of one so stern. We do not mean that Peter yielded
to feelings akin to love ; of this he was in a manner incapa-
ble ; but a man can submit to a gentle regard for woman
that shall be totally free from passion. This sort of regard
Peter certainly began to entertain for Margery ; and like be-
getting like, as money produces money, it is not surprising
that the confidence of the girl herself, as well as her sympathies, should continue to increase in the favor of this terrible Indian.

But the changes of feeling, and the various little incidents
to which we have alluded, did not occur in a single moment
of time. Day passed after day, and still the canoes were
working their way up the winding channels of the Kalamazoo, placing at each setting sun longer and longer reaches
of its sinuous stream between the travellers and the broad
sheet of Michigan. As Le Bourdon had been up and down
the river often in his various excursions, he acted as the
pilot of the navigation ; though all worked, even to the missionary and the Chippewa. On such an expedition toil was
not deemed to be discreditable to a warrior, and Pigeonswing
used the paddle and the pole as willingly and with as much
dexterity as any of the party.

It was only on the eleventh day after quitting the mouth of the river that the canoes came-to in the little bay where Le Bourdon was in the habit of securing his light bark, when in the openings. Castle Meal was in full view, standing peacefully in its sweet solitude ; and Hive, who, as he came within the range of his old hunts, had started off and got to the spot the previous evening, now stood on the bank of the river to welcome his master and his friends to the *chienté*. It wanted a few minutes of sunset as the travellers landed, and the parting rays of the great luminary of our system were glancing through the various glades of the openings, imparting a mellow softness to the herbage and flowers. So far as the bee-hunter could perceive, not even a bear had visited the place in his absence. On ascending to his abode and examining the fastenings, and on entering the hut, storehouse, etc., Le Bourdon became satisfied that all the property he had left behind was safe, and that the foot of man—he almost thought of beast too—had not visited the spot at all during the last fortnight.

CHAPTER XIV.

"Hope in your mountains, and hope in your streams,
Bow down in their worship, and loudly pray ;
Trust in your strength, and believe in your dreams,
But the wind shall carry them all away."

BRAINARD.

THE week which succeeded the arrival of our party
at Chateau au Miel, or Castle Meal, as Le Bourdon used to call his abode, was one of very active
labor. It was necessary to house the adventurers,
and the little habitation already built was quite insufficient
for such a purpose. It was given to the females, who used it
as a private apartment for themselves, while the cooking,
eating, and even sleeping, so far as the males were concerned,
were all done beneath the trees of the openings. But a new
chienté was soon constructed, which, though wanting in the
completeness and strength of Castle Meal, was sufficient for
the wants of those sojourners in a wilderness. It is surprising with how little of those comforts which civilization
induces us to regard as necessaries we can get along when
cast into the midst of the western wilds. The female whose
foot has trodden, from infancy upward, on nothing harder
than a good carpet,—who has been reared amid all the appliances of abundance and art,—seems at once to change
her nature along with her habits, and often proves a heroine
and an active assistant, when there was so much reason to
apprehend she might turn out to be merely an incumbrance.
In the course of a life that is now getting to be well stored
with experience of this sort, as well as of many other varieties, we can recall a hundred cases of women, who were
born and nurtured in all affluence and abundance, who have

cheerfully quitted the scenes of youth, their silks and satins, their china and plate, their mahogany and Brussels, to follow husbands and fathers into the wilderness, there to compete with the savage often for food, and always for the final possession of the soil !

But, in the case of Dorothy and Blossom, the change had never been of this very broad character, and habit had long been preparing them for scenes even more savage than that into which they were now cast.   Both were accustomed to work, as, blessed be God ! the American woman usually works ; that is to say, within doors, and to render home neat, comfortable, and welcome.   As housewives, they were expert and willing, considering the meagreness of their means ; and Le Bourdon told the half-delighted, half-blushing Margery, ere the latter had been twenty-four hours in his *chienté*, that nothing but the presence of such an one as herself was wanting to render it an abode fit for a prince ! Then, the cooking was so much improved !   Apart from cleanliness, the venison was found to be more savory ; the cakes were lighter ; and the pork less greasy.   On this subject of grease, however, we could wish that a sense of right would enable us to announce its utter extinction in the American kitchen ; or, if not absolutely its extinction, such a subjection of the unctuous properties as to bring them within the limits of a reasonably accurate and healthful taste.   To be frank, Dorothy carried a somewhat heavy hand in this respect ; but pretty Margery was much her superior. How this difference in domestic discipline occurred is more than we can say ; but of its existence there can be no doubt. There are two very respectable sections of the civilized world to which we should imagine no rational being would ever think of resorting, in order to acquire the art of cookery, and these are Germany and the Land of the Pilgrims.   One hears, and reads in those elegant specimens of the polite literature of the day, the letters from Washington, and from various travellers who go up and down this river in steamboats, or along that railway, *gratis*, much in honor of the good things left behind the several writers in the " Region of the Rock " ; but, woe betide the wight who is silly enough to believe in all this political imagery, and who travels in that direction in the expectation of finding a good table! It is extraordinary that such a marked difference does exist, on an interest of this magnitude, among such near neighbors; but of the fact we should think no intelligent and experienced man can doubt. Believing as we do that no small portion of the elements of national character can be and are formed in the kitchen, the circumstance may appear to us of more moment than to some of our readers. The vacuum left in cookery, between Boston and Baltimore, for instance, is something like that which exists between Le Verrier's new planet and the sun.

But Margery could even fry pork without causing it to swim in grease, and at preparing a venison steak a professed cook was not her superior. She also understood various little mysteries in the way of converting the berries and fruits of the wilderness into pleasant dishes; and Corporal Flint soon affirmed that it was a thousand pities she did not live in a *garrison*, which, agreeably to his view of things, was something like placing her at the *comptoir* of the Café de Paris, or of marrying her to some second Vatel.

With the eating and drinking, the building advanced *pari passu*. Pigeonswing brought in his venison, his ducks, his pigeons, and his game of different varieties, daily, keeping the larder quite as well supplied as comported with the warmth of the weather; while the others worked on the new *chienté*. In order to obtain materials for this building, one so much larger than his old abode, Ben went up the Kalamazoo about half a mile, where he felled a sufficient number of young pines, with trunks of about a foot in diameter, cutting them into lengths of twenty and thirty feet respectively. These lengths, or trunks, were rolled into the river, down which they slowly floated, until they arrived abreast of Castle Meal, where they were met by Peter, in a canoe, who towed each stick, as it arrived, to the place of landing. In this way, at the end of two days' work, a sufficient quantity of materials was collected to commence directly on the building itself.

Log-houses are of so common occurrence as to require

no particular description of the one now put up from us. It was rather less than thirty feet in length, and one third narrower than it was long. The logs were notched, and the interstices were filled by pieces of the pine, split to a convenient size. The roof was of bark, and of the simplest construction, while there was neither door nor window; though one aperture was left for the first, and two for the last. Corporal Flint, however, was resolved that not only a door should be made, as well as shutters for the windows, but that the house should, in time, be picketed. When Le Bourdon remonstrated with him on the folly of taking so much unnecessary pains, it led to a discussion, in which the missionary even felt constrained to join.

"What's the use—what's the use?" exclaimed Le Bourdon, a little impatiently, when he found the corporal getting to be in earnest in his proposal. "Here have I lived, safely, two seasons in Castle Meal, without any pickets or palisades; and yet you want to turn this new house into a reg'lar garrison!"

"Ay, Bourdon, that was in *peaceable* times; but these is *war* times. I've seen the fall of Fort Dearborn, and I don't want to see the fall of another post this war. The Pottawattamies is hostile, even Peter owns; and the Pottawattamies has been here once, as you say yourself, and may come ag'in."

"The only Pottawattamie who has ever been at this spot, to my knowledge, is dead, and his bones are bleaching up yonder in the openings. No fear of him, then."

"His body is gone," answered the corporal; "and what is more, the rifle is gone with it. I heard that his rifle had been forgotten, and went to collect the arms left on the field of battle, but found nothing. No doubt his friends have burned or buried the chief, and they will be apt to take another look in this quarter of the country, having l'arnt the road."

Boden was struck with this intelligence, as well as with the reasoning, and after a moment's pause, he answered in a way that showed a wavering purpose.

"It will take a week's work to picket or palisade the

house," he answered, "and I wish to be busy among the bees once more."

"Go to your bees, Bourdon, and leave me to fortify and garrison, as becomes *my* trade. Parson Amen, here, will tell you that the children of Israel are often bloody-minded, and are not to be forgotten."

"The corporal is right," put in the missionary; "the corporal is quite right. The whole history of the ancient Jews gives us this character of them; and even Saul of Tarsus was bent on persecution and slaughter, until his hand was stayed by the direct manifestation of the power of God. I can see glimmerings of this spirit in Peter, and this at a moment when he is almost ready to admit that he's a descendant of Israel."

"Is Peter ready to allow that?" asked the bee-hunter, with more interest in the answer than he would have been willing to allow.

"As good as that—yes, quite as good as that. I can see plainly that Peter has some heavy mystery on his mind; sooner or later we shall learn it. When it *does* come out, the world may be prepared to learn the whole history of the Ten Tribes!"

"In my judgment," observed the corporal, "that chief could give the history of twenty, if he was so minded."

"There were but ten of them, brother Flint—but *ten*; and of those ten he could give us a full and highly interesting account. One of these days we shall hear it all; in the meantime, it may be well enough to turn one of these houses into some sort of a garrison."

"Let it then be Castle Meal," said Le Bourdon; "surely, if any one is to be defended and fortified in this way, it ought to be the women. You may easily palisade that hut, which is so much stronger than this, and so much smaller."

With this compromise the work went on. The corporal dug a trench four feet deep, encircling the "castle," as happy as a lord the whole time; for this was not the first time he had been at such work, which he considered to be altogether in character and suitable to his profession. No youthful engineer, fresh from the Point, that seat of mili-

14

tary learning to which the Republic is even more indebted
for its signal successes in Mexico than to the high military
character of its population,—no young aspirant for glory,
fresh from this useful school, could have greater delight
in laying out his first bastion, or counter-scarp, or glacis,
than Corporal Flint enjoyed in fortifying Castle Meal.
It will be remembered that this was the first occasion he
was ever actually at the head of the engineering department. Hitherto it had been his fortune to follow; but
now it had become his duty to lead. As no one else of
that party had ever been employed in such a work on any
previous occasion, the corporal did not affect to conceal
the superior knowledge with which he was overflowing.
Gershom he found a ready and active assistant; for, by
this time, the whiskey was well out of him, and he toiled
with the greater willingness as he felt that the palisades
would add to the security of his wife and sister. Neither
did Parson Amen disdain to use the pick and shovel; for,
while the missionary had the fullest reliance in the fact
that the redmen of that region were the descendants of
the Children of Israel, he regarded them as a portion of
the chosen people who were living under the ban of the
divine displeasure, and as more than usually influenced by
those evil spirits whom St. Paul mentions as the powers
of the air. In a word, while the good missionary had all
faith in the final conversion and restoration of these children of the forests, he did not overlook the facts of their
present barbarity and great propensity to scalp. He was
not quite as efficient as Gershom at this novel employment, but a certain inborn zeal rendered him both active
and useful. As for the Indians, neither of them deigned
to touch a tool. Pigeonswing had little opportunity for so
doing, indeed, being usually, from the rising to the setting
sun, out hunting for the support of the party; while
Peter passed most of his time in ruminations and solitary
walks. This last paid little attention to the work about
the castle, either knowing it would at any moment, by
an act of treachery, be in his power to render all these
precautions of no avail; or, relying on the amount of

savage force that he knew was about to collect in the openings. Whenever he cast a glance on the progress of the work it was with an eye of great indifference ; once he even carried his duplicity so far as to make a suggestion to the corporal, by means of which, as he himself expressed it, in his imperfect English—" Injin no get inside, to use knife and tomahawk." This seeming indifference on the part of Peter did not escape the observation of the bee-hunter, who became still less distrustful of that mysterious savage, as he noted his conduct in connection with the dispositions making for defence.

Le Bourdon would not allow a tree of any sort to be felled anywhere near his abode. While the corporal and his associates were busy in digging the trench, he had gone to a considerable distance, quite out of sight from Castle Meal, and near his great highway, the river, where he cut and trimmed the necessary number of burr-oaks for the palisades. Boden labored the more cheerfully at this work for two especial reasons. One was the fact that the defences might be useful to himself hereafter, as much against bears as against Indians ; and the other, because Margery daily brought her sewing or knitting and sat on the fallen trees, laughing and chatting as the axe performed its duties. On three several occasions Peter was present also, accompanying Blossom, with a kindness of manner, and an attention to her pretty little tastes in culling flowers, that would have done credit to a man of a higher school of civilization.

The reader is not to suppose, however, because the Indian pays but little outward attention to the squaws that he is without natural feeling or manliness of character. In some respects his chivalrous devotion to the sex is, perhaps, in no degree inferior to that of the class which makes a parade of such sentiments, and this quite as much from convention and ostentation as from any other motive. The redman is still a savage beyond all question ; but he is a savage with so many of the nobler and more manly qualities, when uncorrupted by communion with the worst class of whites and not degraded by extreme poverty, as justly to render him a subject of our admiration in self-respect, in dignity, and in simplicity of deportment. The Indian chief is usually a gentleman ; and this though he may have never heard of Revelation, and has not the smallest notion of the Atonement, and of the deep obligations it has laid on the human race.

Amid the numberless exaggerations of the day, one of particular capacity has arisen connected with the supposed character of a gentleman. Those who regard all things through the medium of religious feeling are apt to insist that he who is a Christian is necessarily a gentleman ; while he can be no thorough gentleman who has not most of the qualities of the Christian character. This confusion in thought and language can lead to no really useful result, while it embarrasses the minds of many, and renders the expression of our ideas less exact and comprehensive than they would otherwise be.

We conceive that a man may be very much of a Christian and very little of a gentleman ; or very much of a gentleman and very little of a Christian. There is, in short, not much in common between the two characters, though it is possible for them to become united in the same individual. That the finished courtesies of polished life may wear some of the aspects of that benevolence which causes the Christian " to love his neighbor as himself " is certainly true, though the motives of the parties are so very different as to destroy all real identity between them. While the moving principle of a gentleman is self-respect, that of a Christian is humility. The first is ready to lay down his life in order to wipe away an imaginary dishonor, or to take the life of another ; the last is taught to turn the other cheek when smitten. In a word, the first keeps the world, its opinions, and its estimation ever uppermost in his thoughts ; the last lives only to reverence God and to conform to his will, in obedience to his revealed mandates. Certainly, there is that which is both grateful and useful in the refined deportment of one whose mind and manners have been polished even in the schools of the world ; but it is degrading to the profoundly beautiful submission of the truly Christian temper to imagine that anything like a moral parallel can justly be run between them.

Of course, Peter had none of the qualities of him who sees and feels his own defects, and relies only on the merits of the Atonement for his place among the children of light, while he had so many of those qualities which depend on the estimate which man is so apt to place on his own merits. In this last sense this Indian had a great many of the essentials of a gentleman ; a lofty courtesy presiding over all his intercourse with others, when passion or policy did not thrust in new and sudden principles of action. Even the missionary was so much struck with the gentleness of this mysterious savage's deportment in connection with Margery, as at first to impute it to a growing desire to make a wife of that flower of the wilderness. But closer observation induced greater justice to the Indian in this respect. Nothing like the uneasiness, impatience, or distrust of passion could be discerned in his demeanor ; and when Parson Amen perceived that the bee-hunter's marked devotion to the beautiful Blossom rather excited a benevolent and kind interest in the feelings of Peter, so far at least as one could judge of the heart by external appearances, than anything that bore the fierce and uneasy impulses of jealousy, he was satisfied that his original impression was a mistake.

As Le Bourdon flourished his axe, and Margery plied her needles, making a wholesome provision for the coming winter, the mysterious Indian would stand a quarter of an hour at a time, immovable as a statue, his eyes riveted first on one and then on the other. What passed at such moments in that stern breast it exceeds the penetration of man to say ; but that the emotion thus pent within barriers that none could pass or destroy were not always ferocious and revengeful, a carefully observant spectator might possibly have suspected, had such a person been there to note all the signs of what was uppermost in the chief's thoughts. Still, gleamings of sudden but intense ferocity did occasionally occur ; and, at such instants, the countenance of this extraordinary being was truly terrific. Fortunately, such bursts of uncontrollable feeling were transient, being of rare occurrence and of very short duration.

By the time the corporal had his trenches dug, Le Bourdon was prepared with his palisades, which were just one hundred in number, being intended to inclose a space of forty feet square. The men all united in the transportation of the timber, which was floated down the river on a raft of white pine, the burr oak being of a specific gravity that fresh water would not sustain. A couple of days, however, sufficed for the transportation by water, and as many more for that by land, between the place of landing and Castle Meal. This much accomplished, the whole party rested from their labors, the day which succeeded being the Sabbath.

Those who dwell habitually amid the haunts of men alone thoroughly realize the vast importance that ought to be attached to the great day of rest. Men on the ocean and men in the forest are only too apt to overlook the returns of this Sabbath; thus slowly, but inevitably, alienating themselves more and more from the dread Being who established the festival, as much in his own honor as for the good of man. When we are told that the Almighty is jealous of his rights and desires to be worshipped, we are not to estimate this wish by any known human standard, but are ever to bear in mind that it is exactly in proportion as we do reverence the Creator and Ruler of heaven and earth that we are nearest or farthest from the condition of the blessed. It is probably for his own good that the adoration of man is pleasing in the eyes of God.

The missionary, though a visionary and an enthusiast, as respected the children of Israel, was a zealous observer of his duties. On Sundays he never neglected to set up his tabernacle, even though it were in a howling wilderness, and went regularly through the worship of God, according to the form of the sect to which he belonged. His influence on the present occasion was sufficient to cause a suspension of all labor, though not without some remonstrances on the part of the corporal. The latter contended that, in military affairs, there was no Sunday known, unless it might be in peaceable times; and that he had never heard of entrenchments "resting from their labors," on the part of either the besieger or the besieged. Work of that sort, he thought, ought to go on day and night, by means of reliefs; and, instead of pausing to hold church, he had actually contemplated detailing fatigue parties to labor through, not only that day, but the whole of the succeeding night.

As for Peter, he never offered the slightest objection to any of Parson Amen's sermons or prayers. He listened to both with unmoved gravity, though no apparent impression was ever made on his feelings. The Chippewa hunted on the Sabbaths as much as on any other day; and it was in reference to this fact that the following little conversation took place between Margery and the missionary, as the party sat beneath the oaks passing a tranquil eventide at midsummer.

"How happens it, Mr. Amen," said Margery, who had insensibly adopted the missionary's *sobriquet*, "that no redman keeps the Sabbath-day, if they are all descended from the Jews? This is one of the most respected of all the commandments, and it does not seem natural"—Margery's use of terms was necessarily influenced by association and education—"that any of that people should wholly forget the day of rest."

"Perhaps you are not aware, Margery, that the Jews, even in civilized countries, do not keep the same Sabbath as the Christians," returned the missionary. "They have public worship on a Saturday, as we do on a Sunday. Now, I did think I saw some signs of Peter's privately worshipping yesterday, while *we* were all so busy at our garrison. You may have observed how thoughtful and silent the chief was in the middle of the afternoon."

"I *did* observe it," said the bee-hunter, "but must own I did not suspect him of holding meeting for any purposes within himself. That was one of the times when I like the manners and behavior of this Injin the least."

"We do not know—we do not know—perhaps his spirit struggled with the temptations of the Evil One. To me he appeared to be worshipping, and I set the fact down as a proof that the redmen keep the Jewish Sabbath."

"I did not know that the Jews keep a Sabbath different

from our own, else I might have thought the same. But I never saw a Jew, to my knowledge. Did you, Margery?"

"Not to know him for one," answered the girl; and true enough was the remark of each. Five and thirty years ago, America was singularly not only a Christian but a Protestant nation. Jews certainly did exist in the towns, but they were so blended with the rest of the population, and were so few in number, as scarcely to attract attention to them as a sect. As for the Romanists, they too had their churches and their dioceses; but what untravelled American had then ever seen a nun? From monks, Heaven be praised, we are yet spared; and this is said without any prejudice against the denomination to which they usually belong. He who has lived much in countries where that sect prevails, if a man of a particle of liberality, soon learns that piety and reverence for God, and a deep sense of all the Christian obligations, can just as well, nay better, exist in a state of society where a profound submission to well-established dogmas is to be found, than in a state of society where there is so much political freedom as to induce the veriest pretenders to learning to imagine that each man is a church and a hierarchy in his own person! All this is rapidly changing. Romanists abound, and spots that, half a century since, appeared to be the most improbable places in the world to admit of the rites of the priests of Rome, now hear the chants and prayers of the mass-books. All this shows a tendency towards that great commingling of believers, which is doubtless to precede the final fusion of sects, and the predicted end.

On the Monday that succeeded the Sabbath mentioned, the corporal had all his men at work early, pinning together his palisades, making them up into manageable bents, and then setting them up on their legs. As the materials were all there, and quite ready to be put together, the work advanced rapidly; and by the time the sun drew near the western horizon once more, Castle Meal was surrounded by its bristling defences. The whole was erect and stay-lathed, waiting only for the earth to be shovelled back into the trench, and to be pounded well down.   As it was, the palisades offered a great increase of security to those in the *chienté*, and both the females expressed their obligations to their friends for having taken this important step towards protecting them from the enemy. When they retired for the night, everything was arranged so that the different members of the party might know where to assemble within the works.   Among the effects of Gershom were a conch and a horn ; the latter being one of those common instruments of tin which are so much used in and about American farm-houses to call the laborers from the field.   The conch was given to the men, that, in case of need, they might sound the alarm from without, while the horn, or trumpet of tin, was suspended by the door of the *chienté*, in order that the females might have recourse to it at need.

About midnight, long after the whole party had retired to rest, and when the stillness of the hours of deepest repose reigned over the openings, the bee-hunter was awoke from his sleep by an unwonted call.   At first, he could scarce believe his senses, so plaintive, and yet so wild, was the blast. But there could be no mistake ; it was the horn from the *chienté*, and, in a moment, he was on his feet.   By this time the corporal was afoot, and presently all the men were in motion.   On this occasion, Gershom manifested a readiness and spirit that spoke equally well for his heart and his courage.   He was foremost in rushing to the assistance of his wife and sister, though Le Bourdon was very close on his heels.

On reaching the gate of the palisade, it was found closed and barred within ; nor did any one appear until Dorothy was summoned by repeated calls, in the well-known voice of her husband.   When the two females came out of the *chienté*, great was their wonder and alarm ! No horn had been blown by either of them, and there the instrument itself hung on its peg, as quiet and mute as if a blast had never blown into it. The bee-hunter, on learning this extraordinary fact, looked around him anxiously, in order to ascertain who might be absent.   Every man was present, and each person stood by his arms, no one betraying the slightest consciousness of

knowing whence the unaccountable summons had proceeded !

" This has been done by you, corporal, in order to bring
us together under arms, by way of practice," Le Bourdon at
length exclaimed.

" False alarms is useful if not overdone, especially among
raw troops," answered Flint, coolly ; " but I have given
none to-night. I will own I did intend to have you all out
in a day or two, by way of practice, but I have thought it
useless to attempt too much at once. When the garrison is
finished, it will be time enough to drill the men to the alarm-
posts."

" What is your opinion, Peter ? " continued Le Bourdon.
" You understand the wilderness and its ways. To what is
this extr'or'nary call owing? Why have we been brought
here at this hour ? "

" Somebody blow horn, most likely," answered Peter, in
his unmoved, philosophical manner. " 'Spose don't know ;
den can't tell. Warrior often hear 'larm on war-path."

" This is an onaccountable thing ! If I ever heard a
horn, I heard one to-night ; yet this is the only horn we
have, and no one has touched it ! It was not the conch I
heard ; there is no mistaking the difference in sound between a shell and a horn ; and there is the conch hanging
at Gershom's neck, just where it has been the whole night."

" No one has touched the conch. I will answer for *that*,"
returned Gershom, laying a hand on the shell as if to make
certain all was right.

" This is most extr'or'nary ! I heard the horn, if ears of
mine ever heard such an instrument ! "

Each of the white men added as much, for every one of
them had distinctly heard the blast. Still neither could suggest any probable clue to the mystery. The Indians said
nothing ; but it was so much in conformity with their habits
for redmen to maintain silence, whenever any unusual events
awakened feelings in others, that no one thought their deportment out of rule. As for Peter, a statue of stone could
scarcely have been colder in aspect than was this chief, who
seemed to be altogether raised above every exhibition of hu-

man feeling. Even the corporal gaped, though much excited, for he had been suddenly aroused from a deep sleep; but Peter was as much superior to physical as to moral impressions on this occasion. He made no suggestion, manifested no concern, exhibited no curiosity; and when the men withdrew again to their proper habitation, he walked back with them, in the same silence and calm, as those with which he had advanced. Gershom, however, entered within the palisade, and passed the remainder of the night with his family.

The bee-hunter and the Chippewa accidentally came together, as the men moved slowly towards their own hut, when the following short dialogue occurred between them.

"Is that you, Pigeonswing?" exclaimed Le Bourdon, when he found his friend touching an elbow, as if by chance.

"Yes, dis me—want better friend, eh?"

"No; I'm well satisfied to have you near me, in an alarm, Chippewa. We've stood by each other once, in troublesome times; and I think we can do as much, ag'in."

"Yes; stand by friend—dat honor. Nebber turn back on friend; dat my way."

"Chippewa, who blew the blast on the horn? Can you tell me *that*?"

"Why you don't ask Peter? He wise chief—know ebberyt'ing. Young Injin ask ole Injin when don't know —why not young pale-face ask ole man, too, eh?"

"Pigeonswing, if truth was said, I believe it would be found that you suspect Peter of having a hand in this business!"

This speech was rather too idiomatic for the comprehension of the Indian, who answered according to his own particular view of the matter.

"Don't blow horn wid hand," he said; "Injin blow wid mout', just like pale-face."

The bee-hunter did not reply; but his companion's remark had a tendency to revive in his breast certain unpleasant and distrustful feelings towards the mysterious savage, which the incidents and communications of the last two weeks had had a strong tendency to put to sleep.

CHAPTER XV.

"None knows his lineage, age, or name :
His looks are like the snows of Caucasus ; his eyes
Beam with the wisdom of collected ages.
In green, unbroken years he sees, 't is said,
The generations pass like autumn fruits,
Garner'd, consumed, and springing fresh to life,
Again to perish."

HILLHOUSE.

NO further disturbance took place that night, and the men set about filling up the trenches in the morning steadily as if nothing had happened. They talked a little of the extraordinary occurrence, but more was *thought* than *said*. Le Bourdon observed, however, that Pigeonswing went earlier than usual to the hunt, and that he made his preparations as if he expected to be absent more than the customary time.

As there were just one hundred feet of ditch to fill with dirt, the task was completed, and that quite thoroughly, long ere the close of the day. The pounding down of the earth consumed more time and was much more laborious than the mere tumbling of the earth back into its former bed ; but even this portion of the work was sufficiently attended to. When all was done, the corporal himself, a very critical sort of person in what he called " garrisons," was fain to allow that it was as " pretty a piece of palisading " as he had ever laid eyes on. The " garrison " wanted only one thing, now, to render it a formidable post—and that was water. No spring or well existing within its narrow limits, however, he procured two or three empty barrels, portions of Le Bourdon's effects, placed them within the works, and had them filled with sweet water. By emptying this water two or three times a week, and refilling the barrels, it was thought that a sufficient provision of that great necessary would be made and kept up. Luckily the corporal's "garrison" did not drink, and the want was so much the more easily supplied for the moment.

In truth, the *chienté* was now converted into a place of some strength, when it is considered that artillery had never yet penetrated to those wilds. More than half the savages of the west fought with arrows and spears in that day, as most still do when the great prairies are reached. A rifleman so posted as to have his body in a great measure covered by the trunk of a burr-oak tree, would be reasonably secure against the missives of an Indian, and, using his own fatal instrument of death under a sense of personal security, he would become a formidable opponent to dislodge. Nor was the smallness of the work any objection to its security. A single well-armed man might suffice to defend twenty-five feet of palisades, when he would have been insufficient to make good his position with twice the extent. Then Le Bourdon had cut loops on three sides of the hut itself, in order to fire at the bears, and sometimes at the deer, which had often approached the building in its days of solitude and quiet, using the window on the fourth side for the same purpose. In a word, a sense of increased security was felt by the whole party when this work was completed, though one arrangement was still wanting to render it perfect. By separating the real garrison from the nominal garrison during the night, there always existed the danger of surprise ; and the corporal, now that his fortifications were finished, soon devised a plan to obviate this last-named difficulty. His expedient was very simple, and had somewhat of barrack-life about it.

Corporal Flint raised a low platform along one side of the *chienté*, by placing there logs of pine that were squared on one of their sides. Above, at the height of a man's head, a roof of bark was reared on poles, and prairie grass, aided by skins, formed very comfortable barrack-beds beneath. As the men were expected to lie with their heads to the wall of the hut, and their feet outwards, there was ample space for twice their number. Thither, then, were all the homely provisions for the night transported; and, when Margery closed the door of the *chienté*, after returning the bee-hunter's cordial good-night, it was with no further apprehension for the winding of the mysterious horn.

The first night that succeeded the new arrangement passed without any disturbance. Pigeonswing did not return, as usual, at sunset, and a little uneasiness was felt on his account; but as he made his appearance quite early in the morning, this source of concern ceased. Nor did the Chippewa come in empty-handed; he had killed not only a buck, but he had knocked over a bear in his rambles, besides taking a mess of famously fine trout from a brawling stream at no great distance. The fish were eaten for breakfast, and immediately after that meal was ended, a party started to bring in the venison and bear's meat, under the lead of the Chippewa. This party consisted of the corporal, Gershom, the bee-hunter, and Pigeonswing himself. When it left the garrison, the females were spinning beneath the shade of the oaks, and the missionary was discoursing with Peter on the subject of the customs of the latter's people, in the hope of deriving facts to illustrate his theory of the ten lost tribes.

The buck was found, suspended from a tree, as usual, at the distance of only a mile from the "garrison," as the corporal now uniformly called "Castle Meal." Here the party divided; Flint and Gershom shouldering the venison, and Pigeonswing leading the bee-hunter still farther from home in quest of Bruin. As the two last moved through the park-like trees and glades of the openings, a dialogue occurred that it may help along the incidents of our legend to record.

"You made a long hunt of it yesterday, Pigeonswing," observed Le Bourdon, as soon as he found himself alone with his old ally. "Why did n't you come in at night accordin' to custom?"

"Too much *see*—too much *do*. Dat good reason, eh?" was the answer.

"Your *do* was to kill one buck and one bear, no such great matter after all ; and your *see* could not much alter the case, since seeing a whole regiment of the creatures could n't frighten a man like you."

" No said frighten," returned the Chippewa, sharply. "Squaw frighten, not warrior."

" I ask your pardon, Pigeonswing, for supposing such a thing *possible*; though you will remember I did not think it very likely to be the fact with *you*. I will give you one piece of advice, however, Chippewa, which is this—do not be ready to jump down every man's throat who may happen to think it possible that you might be a little skeary when enemies are plenty. It is the man who feels himself strongest in such matters that is the least likely to take offence at any loose remark of this nature. Your fiery devils go off sometimes at half-cock, because they have a secret whisperer within that tells 'em the charge is true. That 's all I 've to say just now, Chippewa."

" Don't know—don't hear (understand) what you say. No frighten, tell you—dat 'nuff."

" No need of being like a steel-trap, Injin—I understand, if you don't. Now, I own I *am* skeary when there is reason for it, and all I can say in my own favor is, that I don't begin to run before the danger is in sight." Here the bee-hunter paused, and walked some distance in silence. When he did resume the discourse, it was to add, —"Though I must confess a man may *hear* danger as well as *see* it. That horn has troubled me more than I should like to own to Dorothy and pretty Blossom."

" Bess alway let squaw know most den, sometime she help as well as warrior. Bourdon, you right—*ought* to feel afeard of dat horn."

" Ha ! Do you then know anything about it, Pigeonswing, that you give this opinion?"

" Hear him juss like rest. Got ear, why not hear, eh ?"

" Ay, but your manner of speaking just now said more than this. Perhaps you blew the horn yourself, Chippewa?"

" Did n't touch him," returned the Indian, coldly. " Want to sleep—don't want to blow trumpet."

" Whom do you then suspect ?   Is it Peter ?''

" No—don't touch him nudder. Lay down by me dere when horn blow.''

" I 'm glad to hear this from you, Pigeonswing, for, to own the truth, I 've had my misgivings about that onac- countable Injin, and I did think he might have been up, and have got hold of the horn.''

" No touch him at all.   Fast 'sleep when horn blow. What made Peter come in openin', eh?   You know ?''

" I know no more than he has himself told me.   By his account there is to be a great council of redmen on the prairie, a few miles from this spot; he is waiting for the appointed day to come, in order to go and make one of the chiefs that will be there.   Is not this true, Chippewa ?''

" Yes, dat true—what dat council smoke round fire for, eh?   You know ?''

" No, I do not, and would be right glad to have you tell me, Pigeonswing.   Perhaps the tribes mean to have a meetin' to determine in their own minds which side they ought to take in this war.''

" Not dat nudder.   Know well 'nough which side take. Got message and wampum from Canada fadder, and most all Injin up thisaway look for Yankee scalp.   Not dat nudder.''

"Then I have no notion what is at the bottom of this council.   Peter seems to expect great things from it ; that I can see by his way of talking and looking whenever he speaks of it.''

" Peter want to see him very much.   Smoke at great many sich council fire.''

" Do you intend to be present at this council on Prairie Round ?'' asked the bee-hunter, innocently enough.   Pig- eonswing turned to look at his companion, in a way that seemed to inquire how far he was really the dupe of the mysterious Indian's wiles.   Then, suddenly aware of the importance of not betraying all he himself knew until the proper moment had arrived, he bent his eyes forward again, continuing onward and answering somewhat eva- sively.

"Don't know," he replied. "Hunter nebber tell. Chief want venison, and he must hunt. Just like squaw in the pale-face wigwam—work, work—sweep, sweep—cook, cook —never know when work done. So hunter hunt—hunt— hunt."

"And for that matter, Chippewa, just like squaw in the redman's village, too. Hoe, hoe—dig, dig—carry, carry —so that she never knows when she may sit down to rest."

"Yes," returned Pigeonswing, coolly nodding his assent as he moved steadily forward. "Dat do right way wid squaw—juss what he good for—juss what he *made* for —work for warrior and cook his dinner. Pale-face make too much of squaw."

"Not accordin' to your account of their manner of getting along, Injin. If the work of our squaws is never done, we can hardly make too much of them. Where does Peter keep *his* squaw?"

"Don't know," answered the Chippewa. "Nobody know. Don't know where his tribe even."

"This is very extr'or'nary, considering the influence the man seems to enjoy. How is it that he has so completely got the ears of all the redmen, far and near?"

To this question Pigeonswing gave no answer. His own mind was so far under Peter's control that he did not choose to tell more than might be prudent. He was fully aware of the mysterious chief's principal design, that of destroying the white race altogether, and of restoring the redmen to their ancient rights, but several reasons prevented his entering into the plot heart and hand. In the first place, he was friendly to the "Yankees," from whom he, personally, had received many favors and no wrongs; then, the tribe or half-tribe to which he belonged had been employed, more or less, by the agents of the American government as runners, and in other capacities, ever since the peace of 1783; and, lastly, he himself had been left much in different garrisons, where he had not only acquired his English, but a habit of thinking of the Americans as his friends. It might also be added that Pigeonswing,

15

though far less gifted by nature than the mysterious Peter,
had formed a truer estimate of the power of the "Yankees,"
and did not believe they were to be annihilated so easily.
How it happened that this Indian had come to a conclusion
so much safer than that of Peter's, a man of twice his capacity, is more than we can explain; though it was probably owing to the accidental circumstances of his more
intimate associations with the whites.

The bee-hunter was by nature a man of observation, a
faculty that his habits had both increased and stimulated.
Had it not been for the manner in which he was submitting to the influence of Margery, he would long before have
seen that in the deportment of the Chippewa which would
have awakened his distrust; not that Margery in any way
endeavored to blind him to what was passing before his
face, but that he was fast getting to have eyes only for her.
By this time she filled not only his waking, but many of
his sleeping thoughts; and when she was not actually before him, charming him with her beauty, enlivening him
with her artless gayety, and inspiring him with her innocent humor, he fancied she was there, imagination, perhaps,
heightening all those advantages which we have enumerated. When a man is thoroughly in love, he is quite apt
to be fit for very little else but to urge his suit. Such, in
a certain way, proved to be the case with Le Bourdon, who
allowed things to pass unheeded directly before his eyes
that, previously to his acquaintance with Margery, would
not only have been observed, but which would have most
probably led to some practical results. The conduct of Pigeonswing was among the circumstances that were thus overlooked by our hero. In point of fact, Peter was slowly
but surely working on the mind of the Chippewa, changing
all his opinions radically, and teaching him to regard every
pale-face as an enemy. The task, in this instance, was not
easy; for Pigeonswing, in addition to his general propensities in favor of the "Yankees," the result of mere accident, had conceived a real personal regard for Le Bourdon,
and was very slow to admit any views that tended to his
injury. The struggle in the mind of the young warrior

was severe; and twenty times was he on the point of warning his friend of the danger which impended over the whole party, when a sense of good faith towards Peter, who held his word to the contrary, prevented his so doing. This conflict of feeling was now constantly active in the breast of the young savage.

Pigeonswing had another source of uneasiness, to which his companions were entirely strangers. While hunting his keen eyes had detected the presence of warriors in the openings. It is true he had not seen even one, but he knew that the signs he had discovered could not deceive him. Not only were warriors at hand, but warriors in considerable numbers. He had found one deserted lair, from which its late occupants could not have departed many hours when it came under his own notice. By means of that attentive sagacity which forms no small portion of the education of an American Indian, Pigeonswing was enabled to ascertain that this party, of itself, numbered seventeen, all of whom were men and warriors. The first fact was easily enough to be seen, perhaps, there being just seventeen different impressions left in the grass; but that all these persons were armed men was learned by Pigeonswing through evidence that would have been overlooked by most persons. By the length of the lairs he was satisfied none but men of full stature had been there; and he even examined sufficiently close to make out the proofs that all but four of these men carried fire-arms. Strange as it may seem to those who do not know how keen the senses become when whetted by the apprehensions and wants of savage life, Pigeonswing was enabled to discover signs which showed that the excepted were provided with bows and arrows and spears.

When the bee-hunter and his companion came in sight of the carcase of the bear, which they did shortly after the last remark which we have given in the dialogue recorded, the former exclaimed with a little surprise,—

"How 's this, Chippewa! You have killed this beast with your bow! Did you not hunt with the rifle yesterday?"

"Bad fire rifle off nowadays," answered Pigeonswing, sententiously. "Make noise—noise no good."

"Noise!" repeated the perfectly unsuspecting bee-hunter. "Little good or little harm can noise do in these openings, where there is neither mountains to give back an echo or ear to be startled. The crack of my rifle has rung through these groves a hundred times and no harm come of it."

"Forget war-time now. Bess nebber fire, less can't help him. Pottawattamie hear great way off."

"Oh! That's it, is it? You're afraid our old friends the Pottawattamies may find us out, and come to thank us for all that happened down at the river's mouth. Well," continued Le Bourdon, laughing, "if they wish another whiskey-spring, I have a small jug left, safely hid against a wet day; a very few drops will answer to make a tolerable spring. You redskins don't know everything, Pigeonswing, though you are so keen and quick-witted on a trail."

"Bess not tell Pottawattamie any more 'bout spring," answered the Chippewa, gravely; for by this time he regarded the state of things in the openings to be so serious as to feel little disposition to mirth. "Why you don't go home, eh? Why don't med'cine-man go home, too? Bess for pale-face to be wid pale-face when redman go on war-path. Color bess keep wid color."

"I see you want to be rid of us, Pigeonswing; but the parson has no thought of quitting this part of the world until he has convinced all the redskins that they are Jews."

"What *he* mean, eh?" demanded the Chippewa, with more curiosity than it was usual for an Indian warrior to betray. "What sort of man Jew, eh? Why call redman Jew?"

"I know very little more about it than you do yourself, Pigeonswing; but such as my poor knowledge is, you're welcome to it. You've heard of the Bible, I dare say?"

"Sartain—med'cine-man read him Sunday. Good book to read, some t'ink."

"Yes, it's all that, and a great companion have I found

my Bible, when I've been alone with the bees out here in
the openings. It tells us of our God, Chippewa; and
teaches us how we are to please him, and how we may
offend. It's a great loss to you, redskins, not to have such
a book among you."

"Med'cine-man bring him—don't do much good, yet;
some day, p'r'aps, do better. How dat make redman
Jew?"

"Why, this is a new idea to me, though Parson Amen
seems fully possessed with it. I suppose you know what
a Jew is?"

"Don't know anyt'ing 'bout him. Sort o' nigger, eh?"

"No, no, Pigeonswing, you're wide of the mark this
time. But, that we may understand each other, we'll
begin at the beginning like, which will let you into the
whole history of the pale-face religion. As we've had a
smart walk, however, and here is the bear's meat safe and
sound, just as you left it, let us sit down a bit on this
trunk of a tree, while I give you our tradition from beginning to end, as it might be. In the first place, Chippewa,
the earth was made without creatures of any sort to live on
it—not so much as a squirrel or a woodchuck."

"Poor country to hunt in, dat," observed the Chippewa,
quietly, while Le Bourdon was wiping his forehead after
removing his cap. "Ojebways stay in it very little time."

"This, according to our belief, was before any Ojebway
lived. At length, God made a man, out of clay, and fashioned him, as we see men fashioned, and living all around
us."

"Yes," answered the Chippewa, nodding his head in
assent. "Den Manitou put plenty blood in him—*dat*
make *red* warrior. Bible good book, if tell dat tradition."

"The Bible says nothing about any colors; but we suppose the man first made to have been a pale-face. At any
rate, the pale-faces have got possession of the best parts of
the earth, as it might be, and I think they mean to keep
them. First come, first served, you know. The pale-faces
are many, and are strong."

"Stop!" exclaimed Pigeonswing, in a way that was

very unusual for an Indian to interrupt another when
speaking; "want to ask question.   How many pale-face
you t'ink is dere?   Ebber count him?"

"Count them!   Why, Chippewa, you might as well
count the bees as they buzz around a fallen tree.   You
saw me cut down the tree I last discovered, and saw the
movement of the little animals, and may judge what success tongue, or eye, would have in counting *them*; now,
just as true would it be to suppose that any man could
count the pale-faces on this earth."

"Don't want count *all*," answered Pigeonswing.   "Want
to know how many dis side of great salt lake."

"That's another matter, and more easily come at.   I
understand you, now, Chippewa; you wish to know how
many of us there are in the country we call America?"

"Juss so," returned Pigeonswing, nodding in assent.
"Dat juss it—juss what Injin want to know."

"Well, we do have a count of our own people, from
time to time, and I suppose come about as near to the
truth as men can come in such a matter.   There must
be about eight millions of us altogether; that is, old and
young, big and little, male and female."

"How many warrior you got?—don't want to hear about
squaw and pappoose."

"No, I see you're warlike this morning, and want to
see how we are likely to come out of this struggle with
your Great Canada Father.   Counting all round, I think
we might muster hard on upon a million of fighting-men
—good, bad, and indifferent; that is to say, there must be
a million of us of proper age to go into the wars."

Pigeonswing made no answer for near a minute.   Both
he and the bee-hunter had come to a halt alongside of the
bear's meat, and the latter was beginning to prepare his
own portion of the load for transportation, while his companion stood thus motionless, lost in thought.   Suddenly,
Pigeonswing recovered his recollection, and resumed the
conversation, by saying—

"What million mean, Bourdon?   How many time so'ger
at Detroit, and so'ger on lakes?"

"A million is more than the leaves on all the trees in these openings"—Le Bourdon's notions were a little exaggerated, perhaps, but this was what he *said*; "yes, more than the leaves on all these oaks, far and near. A million is a countless number, and I suppose would make a row of men as long as from this spot to the shores of the great salt lake, if not farther."

It is probable that the bee-hunter himself had no very clear notion of the distance of which he spoke, or of the number of men it would actually require to fill the space he mentioned; but his answer sufficed deeply to impress the imagination of the Indian, who now helped Le Bourdon to secure his load to his back, in silence, receiving the same service in return. When the meat of the bear was securely bestowed each resumed his rifle, and the friends commenced their march in towards the *chienté*, conversing, as they went, on the matter which still occupied their minds. When the bee-hunter again took up the history of the creation it was to speak of our common mother.

"You will remember, Chippewa," he said, "that I told you nothing on the subject of any woman. What I have told you, as yet, consarned only the first *man*, who was made out of clay, into whom God breathed the breath of life."

"Dat good—make warrior fuss. Juss right. When breat' in him, fit to take scalp, eh?"

"Why, as to that, it is not easy to see whom he was to scalp, seeing that he was quite alone in the world, until it pleased his Creator to give him a woman for a companion."

"Tell 'bout dat," returned Pigeonswing, with interest— "tell how he got squaw."

"Accordin' to the Bible, God caused this man to fall into a deep sleep, when he took one of his ribs, and out of that he made a squaw for him. Then he put them both to live together in a most beautiful garden, in which all things excellent and pleasant was to be found—some such place as these openings, I reckon."

"Any bee dere?" asked the Indian, quite innocently. "Plenty honey, eh?"

"That will I answer for! It could hardly be otherwise, when it was the intention to make the first man and first woman perfectly happy. I dare say, Chippewa, if the truth was known, it would be found that bees was a sipping at every flower in that most delightful garden!"

"Why pale-face quit dat garden, eh? Why come here to drive poor Injin 'way from game? Tell me dat, Bourdon, if he can? Why pale-face ever leave *dat* garden when he so han'some, eh?"

"God turned him out of it, Chippewa—yes, he was turned *out* of it, with shame on his face, for having disobeyed the commandments of his Creator. Having left the garden, his children have scattered over the face of the earth."

"So come here to drive off Injin! Well, dat 'e way wid pale-face! Did ever hear of redman comin' to drive off pale-face?"

"I have heard of your red warriors often coming to take our scalps, Chippewa. More or less of this has been done every year since our people have landed in America. More than that they have not done, for we are too many to be driven very far in by a few scattering tribes of Injins."

"T'ink, den, more pale-face dan Injin, eh?" asked the Chippewa, with an interest so manifest that he actually stopped in his semi-trot in order to put the question— "More pale-face warrior dan redmen?"

"More! Ay, a thousand times more, Chippewa. Where you could show one warrior, we could show a thousand!"

Now, this was not strictly true, perhaps, but it answered the purpose of deeply impressing the Chippewa with the uselessness of Peter's plans, and, sustained as it was by his early predilections, it served to keep him on the right side in the crisis which was approaching. The discourse continued, much in the same strain, until the men got in with their bear's meat, having been preceded some time by the others with the venison.

It is a little singular that neither the questions nor the manner of Pigeonswing awakened any distrust in the bee-hunter. So far from this, the latter regarded all that had passed as perfectly natural, and as likely to arise in conversation, in the way of pure speculation, as in any other manner. Pigeonswing intended to be guarded in what he said and did, for as yet he had not made up his mind which side he would really espouse, in the event of the great project coming to a head. He had the desire, natural to a redman, to avenge the wrongs committed against his race; but this desire existed in a form a good deal mitigated by his intercourse with the "Yankees," and his regard for individuals. It had, nevertheless, strangely occurred to the savage reasoning of this young warrior that, possibly, some arrangement might be effected, by means of which he should take scalps from the Canadians, while Peter and his other followers were working their will on the Americans. In this confused condition was the mind of the Chippewa when he and his companion threw down their loads near the place where the provision of game was usually kept. This was beneath the tree, near the spring and the cook house, in order that no inconvenience should arise from its proximity to the place where the party dwelt and slept. For a siege, should there be occasion to shut themselves up within the "garrison," the men depended on the pickled pork and a quantity of dried meat, of the latter of which the missionary had brought a considerable supply in his own canoe. Among these stores were a few dozen of buffaloes', or bisons', tongues, a delicacy that would honor the best table in the civilized world, though then so common, among the western hunters as scarce to be deemed food as good as the common salted pork and beef of the settlements.

The evening that followed proved to be one of singular softness and sweetness. The sun went down in a cloudless sky, and gentle airs from the southwest fanned the warm cheeks of Margery, as she sat, resting from the labors of the day, with Le Bourdon at her side, speaking of the pleasures of a residence in such a spot. The youth was eloquent, for he felt all that he said, and the maiden was pleased. The young man could expatiate on bees in a way to arrest any one's attention; and Margery delighted to hear him relate his adventures with these little creatures, his successes, losses, and journeys.

" But are you not often lonely, Bourdon, living here in the openings, whole summers at a time, without a living soul to speak to ? " demanded Margery, coloring to the eyes the instant the question was asked, lest it should subject her to an imputation against which her modesty reverted, that of wishing to draw the discourse to a discussion on the means of preventing this solitude in future.

" I have not been, hitherto," answered Le Bourdon, so frankly as at once to quiet his companion's sensitiveness, "though I will not answer for the future. Now that I have so many with me, we may make some of them necessary. Mind—I say *some*, not all of my present guests. If I could have my pick, pretty Margery, the present company would give me *all* I can desire, and more too. I should not think of going to Detroit for that companion, since she is to be found so much nearer."

Margery blushed and looked down—then she raised her eyes, smiled, and seemed grateful as well as pleased. By this time she had become accustomed to such remarks, and she had no difficulty in discovering her lover's wishes, though he had never been more explicit. The reflections natural to her situation threw a shade of gentle seriousness over her countenance, rendering her more charming than ever, and causing the youth to plunge deeper and deeper into the meshes that female influence had cast around him. In all this, however, one of the parties was governed by a manly sincerity, and the other by girlish alertness. Diffidence, one of the most certain attendants of a pure passion, alone kept Le Bourdon from asking Margery to become his wife ; while Margery herself sometimes doubted whether it were possible that any reputable man could wish to connect himself and his fortunes with a family that had sunk as low as persons could well sink, in this country, and not lose their characters altogether. With these doubts and distrusts, so naturally affecting the mind of each, these young people were rapidly becoming more and more enamored ; the bee-hunter betraying his passion in the close, absorbed at-

tentions that more properly belong to his sex, while that of
Margery was to be seen in sudden blushes, the thoughtful
brow, the timid glance, and a cast of tenderness that came
over her whole manner, and, as it might be, her whole being.

While our young folk were thus employed, now conversing cheerfully, now appearing abstracted and lost in thought,
though seated side by side, Le Bourdon happened to look
behind him, and saw that Peter was regarding them with
one of those intense but mysterious expressions of the
countenance that had now, more than once, attracted his
attention; giving reason, each time, for a feeling in which
doubt, curiosity, and apprehension were singularly mingled,
even in himself.

At the customary hour, which was always early in that
party of simple habits, the whole family sought its rest; the
females withdrew within the *chienté*, while the males arranged their skins without. Ever since the erection of the
palisades, Le Bourdon had been in the habit of calling Hive
within the defences, leaving him at liberty to roam about
inside at pleasure. Previously to this new arrangement, the
dog had been shut up in his kennel, in order to prevent his
getting on the track of a deer, or in close combat with some
bear, when his master was not present to profit by his efforts.
As the palisades were too high for his leap, this putting him
at liberty within them answered the double purpose of giving the mastiff room for healthful exercise, and of possessing a most vigilant sentinel against dangers of all sorts. On
the present occasion, however, the dog was missing, and
after calling and whistling for him some time, the bee-
hunter was fain to bar the gate and leave him on the outside. This done, he sought his skin and was soon asleep.

It was midnight when the bee-hunter felt a hand laid on
his own arm. It was the corporal, making this movement
in order to awake him. In an instant the young man was
on his feet, with his rifle in his hand.

"Did you not hear it, Bourdon?" demanded the corporal,
in a tone so low as scarce to exceed a whisper.

"Hear what? I've been sleeping, sound as a bee in
winter."

"The horn! The horn has been blown twice, and, I think, we shall soon hear it again."

"The horn was hanging at the door of the *chienté*, and the conch too. It will be easy to see if they are in their places."

It was only necessary to walk around the walls of the hut to its opposite side, in order to ascertain this fact. Le Bourdon did so, accompanied by the corporal, and just as each laid a hand on the instruments, which were suspended in their proper places, a heavy rush was made against the gate, as if to try its fastenings. These pushes were repeated several times, with a violence that menaced the bars. Of course the two men stepped to the spot, a distance of only a few paces, the gateway of the palisades and the door of the *chienté* being contiguous to each other, and immediately ascertained that it was the mastiff, endeavoring to force his way in. The bee-hunter admitted the dog, which had been trained to suppress his bark, though this animal was too brave and large to throw away his breath when he had better rely on his force. Powerful animals of this race are seldom noisy, it being the province of the cur, both among dogs and men, to be blustering and spitting out their venom at all hours and seasons. Hive, however, in addition to his natural disposition, had been taught, from the time he was a pup, not to betray his presence unnecessarily by a bark ; and it was seldom that his deep throat opened beneath the arches of the oaks. When it did, it told like the roaring of the lion in the desert.

Hive was no sooner admitted to the "garrison" than he manifested just as strong a desire to get out as, a moment before, he had manifested to get in. This, Le Bourdon well knew, indicated the presence of some thing or creature that did not properly belong to the vicinity. After consulting with the corporal, Pigeonswing was called ; and leaving him as a sentinel at the gate, the two others made a sortie. The corporal was as brave as a lion, and loved all such movements, though he fully anticipated encountering savages, while his companion expected an interview with bears.

As this movement was made at the invitation of the dog,

it was judiciously determined to let him act as a pioneer on the advance. Previously to quitting the defences, however, the two adventurers looked closely to their arms. Each examined the priming, saw that his horn and pouch were accessible, and loosened his knife in its sheath. The corporal, moreover, fixed his "baggonet," as he called the formidable, glittering instrument that usually embellished the end of his musket,—a *musket* being the weapon he chose to carry,—while the bee-hunter himself was armed with a long western *rifle*.

CHAPTER XVI.

" The raptures of a conqueror's mood
    Rush'd burning through his frame ;
The depths of that green solitude
    Its torrents could not tame,
Though stillness lay, with eve's last smile,
Round those far fountains of the Nile."

MRS. HEMANS.

WHEN the bee-hunter and Corporal Flint thus
went forth at midnight from the "garrison"
of Castle Meal (Château au Miel), as the latter would have expressed it, it was with no
great apprehension of meeting any other than a four-footed
enemy, notwithstanding the blast of the horn the worthy
corporal supposed he had heard. The movements of the
dog seemed to announce such a result rather than any other,
for Hive was taken along as a sort of guide. Le Bourdon,
however, did not permit his mastiff to run off wide, but,
having the animal at perfect command, it was kept close to
his own person.

The two men first moved toward the grove of the Kitchen,
much to Hive's discontent. The dog several times halted,
and he whined and growled and otherwise manifested his
great dislike to proceed in that direction. At length so
decided did his resistance become that his master said to
his companion,—

"It seems to me best, corporal, to let the mastiff lead us.
I have never yet seen him so set on not going in one way,
and on going in another. Hive has a capital nose, and we
may trust him."

"Forward," returned the corporal, wheeling short in

238

the direction of the dog; "one thing should be understood, however, Bourdon, which is this: you must act as light troops in this sortie, and I as the main body. If we come on the inimy, it will be your duty to skrimmage in front as long as you can, and then fall back on your resarves. I shall depend chiefly on the baggonet, which is the best tool to put an Injin up with; and as he falls back before my charge, we must keep him under as warm a fire as possible. Having no cavalry, the dog might be made useful in movements to the front and on our flanks."

"Pooh, pooh, corporal, you're almost as much set in the notions of your trade as Parson Amen is set in his idees about the lost tribes. In my opinion there'll be more tribes *found* in these openings before the summer is over than we shall wish to meet. Let us follow the dog, and see what will turn up."

Hive *was* followed, and he took a direction that led to a distant point in the openings, where not only the trees were much thicker than common, but where a small tributary of the Kalamazoo ran through a ravine, from the higher lands adjacent into the main artery of all the neighboring watercourses. The bee-hunter knew the spot well, having often drank at the rivulet, and cooled his brow in the close shades of the ravine, when heated by exertions in the more open grounds. In short, the spot was one of the most eligible for concealment, coolness, and pure water, within several miles of Castle Meal. The trees formed a spacious grove around it, and by means of the banks their summits and leaves answered the purpose of a perfect screen to those who might descend into the ravine, or, it would be better to say, to the bottom. Le Bourdon was no sooner satisfied that his mastiff was proceeding towards the great spring which formed the rivulet, at the head of the ravine mentioned, than he suspected Indians might be there. He had seen signs about the spot, which wore an appearance of its having been used as a place of encampment,—or for " camping out," as it is termed in the language of the West,—and, coupling the sound of the horn with the dog's movements, his quick apprehension seized on the facts as affording reasonable grounds of distrust. Consequently he resorted to great caution, as he and the corporal entered the wood which surrounded the spring and the small oval bit of bottom that lay spread before it, like a little lawn. Hive was kept close at his master's side, though he manifested a marked impatience to advance. " Now, corporal," said the bee-hunter in a low tone, " I think we have lined some savages to their holes. We will go round the basin and descend to the bottom, in a close wood which grows there. Did you see that?"

" I suppose I did," answered the corporal, who was as firm as a rock. "You meant to ask me if I saw fire?"

" I did. The redmen have lighted their council fire in this spot, and have met to talk around it. Well, let 'em hearken to each other's thoughts, if they will ; we shall be neither the better nor the worse for it."

" I don't know that. When the commander-in-chief calls together his principal officers, something usually comes of it. Who knows but this very council is called in order to take opinions on the subject of besieging or of storming our new garrison? Prudent soldiers should always be ready for the worst."

" I have no fear so long as Peter is with us. That chief is listened to by every redskin ; and while we have him among us there will be little to care for. But we are getting near to the bottom, and must work our way through these bushes with as little noise as possible. I will keep the dog quiet."

The manner in which that sagacious animal now behaved was truly wonderful. Hive appeared to be quite as much aware of the necessity of extreme caution as either of the men, and did not once attempt to precede his master his own length. On one or two occasions he actually discovered the best passages, and led his companions through them with something like the intelligence of a human being. Neither growl nor bark escaped him ; on the contrary, even the hacking breathing of an impatient dog was suppressed, precisely as if the animal knew how near he was getting to the most watchful ears in the world.

After using the greatest care, the bee-hunter and the corporal got just such a station as they desired. It was within a very few feet of the edge of the cover, but perfectly concealed, while small openings enabled them to see all that was passing in their front. A fallen tree, a relic of somewhat rare occurrence in the Openings of Michigan, even furnished them with a seat, while it rendered their position less exposed. Hive placed himself at his master's side, apparently trusting to other senses than that of sight for his information, since he could see nothing of what was going on in front.

As soon as the two men had taken their stations, and began to look about them, a feeling of awe mingled with their curiosity. Truly, the scene was one so very remarkable and imposing that it might have filled more intellectual and better fortified minds with some such sensation. The fire was by no means large, nor was it particularly bright; but sufficient to cast a dim light on the objects within reach of its rays. It was in the precise centre of a bit of bottom land of about half an acre in extent, which was so formed and surrounded as to have something of the appearance of the arena of a large amphitheatre. There was one break in the encircling rise of ground, it is true, and that was at a spot directly opposite the station of Le Bourdon and his companion, where the rill which flowed from the spring found a passage out toward the more open ground. Branches shaded most of the mound, but the arena itself was totally free from all vegetation but that which covered the dense and beautiful sward with which it was carpeted. Such is a brief description of the natural accessories of this remarkable scene.

But it was from the human actors, and their aspects, occupations, movements, dress, and appearance generally, that the awe which came over both the bee-hunter and the corporal had its origin. Of these, near fifty were present, offering a startling force by their numbers alone. Each man was a warrior, and each warrior was in his paint. These were facts that the familiarity of the two white men with Indian customs rendered only too certain. What

16

was still more striking was the fact that all present appeared to be chiefs, a circumstance which went to show that an imposing body of redmen was most likely somewhere in the Openings, and that too at no great distance. It was while observing and reflecting on all these things, a suspicion first crossed the mind of Le Bourdon that the great council was about to be held, at the midnight hour, and so near his own abode, for the purpose of accommodating Peter, whose appearance in the dark crowd from that instant he began to expect.

The Indians already present were not seated. They stood in groups, conversing, or stalked across the arena, resembling so many dark and stately spectres. No sound was heard among them, a circumstance that added largely to the wild and supernatural aspect of the scene. If any spoke, it was in a tone so low and gentle as to carry the sound no farther than to the ears that were listening ; two never spoke at the same time and in the same group, while the moccasin permitted no foot-fall to be audible. Nothing could have been more unearthly than the picture presented in that little, wood-circled arena of velvet-like grass and rural beauty. The erect, stalking forms, half naked, if not even more ; the swarthy skins ; the faces fierce in the savage conceits which were intended to strike terror into the bosoms of enemies, and the glittering eyes that fairly sparkled in their midst, all contributed to the character of the scene, which Le Bourdon rightly enough imagined was altogether much the most remarkable of any he had ever been in the way of witnessing.

Our two spectators might have been seated on the fallen tree half an hour, all of which time they had been gazing at what was passing before their eyes, with positively not a human sound to relieve the unearthly nature of the picture. No one spoke, coughed, laughed, or exclaimed, in all that period. Suddenly every chief stood still, and all the faces turned in the same direction. It was towards the little gate-way of the rill, which, being the side of the arena most remote from the bee-hunter and the corporal, lay nearly in darkness as respected them. With the redmen it must have been different, for *they* all appeared to be in intent expectation of some one from that quarter. Nor did they have to wait long, for in half a minute two forms came out of the obscurity, advancing with a dignified and deliberate tread to the centre of the arena. As these new-comers got more within the influence of the flickering light, Le Bourdon saw that they were Peter and Parson Amen. The first led, with a slow, imposing manner, while the other followed, not a little bewildered with what he saw. It may be as well to explain here that the Indian was coming alone to this place of meeting, when he encountered the missionary wandering among the oaks, looking for Le Bourdon and the corporal, and, instead of endeavoring to throw off this unexpected companion, he quietly invited him to be of his own party.

It was evident to Le Bourdon, at a glance, that Peter was expected, though it was not quite so clear that such was the fact as regarded his companion. Still, respect for the great chief prevented any manifestations of surprise or discontent, and the medicine-man of the pale-faces was received with as grave a courtesy as if he had been an invited guest. Just as the two had entered the dark circle that formed around them, a young chief threw some dry sticks on the fire, which, blazing upward, cast a stronger light on a row of as terrifically looking countenances as ever gleamed on human forms. This sudden illumination, with its accompanying accessories, had the effect to startle all the white spectators, though Peter looked on the whole with a calm like that of the leafless tree when the cold is at its height, and the currents of the wintry air are death-like still. Nothing appeared to move *him*, whether expected or not ; though use had probably accustomed his eye to all the aspects in which savage ingenuity could offer savage forms. He even smiled, as he made a gesture of recognition, which seemed to salute the whole group. It was just then, when the fire burned brightest, and when the chiefs pressed most within its influence, that Le Bourdon perceived that his old acquaintances, the head men of the Pottawattamies, were present among the other chiefs so strangely and portentously assembled in these grounds which he had so long possessed almost entirely to himself.

A few of the oldest of the chiefs now approached Peter, and a low conversation took place between them. What was said did not reach Le Bourdon, of course; for it was not even heard in the dark circle of savages who surrounded the fire. The effect of this secret dialogue, however, was to cause all the chiefs to be seated, each taking his place on the grass, the whole preserving the original circle around the fire. Fortunately for the wishes of Le Bourdon, Peter and his companions took their stations directly opposite to his own seat, thus enabling him to watch every lineament of that remarkable chief's still more remarkable countenance. Unlike each and all of the redmen around him, the face of Peter was not painted, except by the tint imparted by nature, which in his case was that of copper a little tarnished, or rendered dull by the action of the atmosphere. The bee-hunter could distinctly trace every lineament; nor was the dark, roving eye beyond the reach of his own vision. Some attention was given to the fire, too, one of the younger chiefs occasionally throwing on it a few dried sticks, more to keep alive the flame, and to renew the light, than from any need of warmth. One other purpose, however, this fire *did* answer: that of enabling the young chiefs to light the pipes that were now prepared; it seldom occurring that the chiefs thus assembled without *smoking* around their council fire.

As this smoking was just then more a matter of ceremony than for any other purpose, a whiff or two sufficed for each chief, the smoker passing the pipe to his neighbor as soon as he had inhaled a few puffs. The Indians are models of propriety in their happiest moods, and every one in that dark and menacing circle was permitted to have his turn with the pipe, before any other step was taken. There were but two pipes lighted, and mouths being numerous, some time was necessary in order to complete this ceremony. Still, no sign of impatience was seen, the lowest chief having as much respect paid to his feelings, as related to this attention, as the highest. At length the pipes completed their circuit, even Parson Amen getting, and using, his turn, when a dead pause succeeded. The silence resembled that of a Quaker meeting, and was broken only by the rising of one of the principal chiefs, evidently about to speak. The language of the great Ojebway nation was used on this occasion, most of the chiefs present belonging to some one of the tribes of that stock, though several spoke other tongues, English and French included. Of the three whites present, Parson Amen alone fully comprehended all that was said, he having qualified himself in this respect to preach to the tribes of that people ; though Le Bourdon understood nearly all, and even the corporal comprehended a good deal. The name of the chief who first spoke at this secret meeting, which was afterwards known among the Ojebways by the name of the "Council of the Bottom Land, near to the spring of gushing water," was Bear's Meat, an appellation that might denote a distinguished hunter, rather than an orator of much renown.

"Brothers of the many tribes of the Ojebways," commenced this personage, "the Great Spirit has permitted us to meet in council. The Manitou of our fathers is now among these oaks, listening to our words and looking in at our hearts. Wise Indians will be careful what they say in such a presence, and careful of what they think. All should be said and thought for the best. We are a scattered nation, and the time is come when we must stop in our tracks, or travel beyond the sound of each other's cries. If we travel beyond the hearing of our people, soon will our children learn tongues that Ojebway ears cannot understand. The mother talks to her child, and the child learns her words. But no child can hear across a great lake. Once we lived near the rising sun. Where are we now? Some of our young men say they have seen the sun go down in the lakes of sweet water. There can be no hunting-grounds beyond *that* spot ; and if we would live, we must stand still in our tracks. How to do this, we have met to consider.

"Brothers, many wise chiefs and braves are seated at this council fire. It is pleasant to my eyes to look upon them.

Ottaways, Chippeways, Pottawattamies, Menominees, Hurons, and all. Our father at Quebec has dug up the hatchet against the Yankees. The war-path is open between Detroit and all the villages of the redmen. The prophets are speaking to our people, and we listen. One is here; he is about to speak. The council will have but a single sense, which will be that of hearing."

Thus concluding, Bear's Meat took his seat, in the same composed and dignified manner as that in which he had risen, and deep silence succeeded. So profound was the stillness that, taken in connection with the dark lineaments, the lustrous eye-balls that threw back the light of the fire, the terrific paint and the armed hands of every warrior present, the picture might be described as imposing to a degree that is seldom seen in the assemblies of the civilized. In the midst of this general but portentous calm, Peter arose. The breathing of the circle grew deeper, so much so as to be audible, the only manner in which the intensity of the common expectation betrayed itself. Peter was an experienced orator, and knew how to turn every minutia of his art to good account. His every movement was deliberate, his attitude highly dignified—even his eye seemed eloquent.

Oratory! what a power art thou, wielded, as is so often the case, as much for evil as for good. The very reasoning that might appear to be obtuse, or which would be overlooked entirely when written and published, issuing from the mouth, aided by the feelings of sympathy and the impulses of the masses, seems to partake of the wisdom of divinity. Thus is it, also, with the passions, the sense of wrong, the appeals to vengeance, and all the other avenues of human emotion. Let them be addressed to the cold eye of reason and judgment, in the form of written statements, and the mind pauses to weigh the force of arguments, the justice of the appeals, the truth of facts; but let them come upon the ear aided by thy art, with a power concentrated by sympathy, and the torrent is often less destructive in its course than that of the whirlwind that thou canst awaken!

"Chiefs of the great Ojebway nation, I wish you well," said Peter, stretching out his arms towards the circle, as if desirous of embracing all present. "The Manitou has been good to me. He has cleared a path to this spring and to this council fire. I see around it the faces of many friends. Why should we not all be friendly? Why should a redman ever strike a blow against a redman? The Great Spirit made us of the same color, and placed us on the same hunting-grounds. He meant that we should hunt in company, not take each other's scalps. How many warriors have fallen in our family wars? Who has counted them? Who can say? Perhaps enough, had they not been killed, to drive the pale-faces into the sea!"

Here Peter, who as yet had spoken only in a low and barely audible voice, suddenly paused, in order to allow the idea he had just thrown out to work on the minds of his listeners. That it was producing its effect was apparent by the manner in which one stern face turned towards another, and eye seemed to search in eye some response to a query that the mind suggested, though no utterance was given to it with the tongue. As soon, however, as the orator thought time sufficient to impress that thought on the memories of the listeners had elapsed, he resumed, suffering his voice gradually to increase in volume, as he warmed with his subject.

"Yes," he continued, "the Manitou has been very kind. Who is the Manitou? Has any Indian ever seen him? Every Indian has seen him. No one can look on the hunting-grounds, on the lakes, on the prairies, on the trees, on the game, without seeing his hand. His face is to be seen in the sun at noon-day, his eyes in the stars at night. Has any Indian ever heard the Manitou? When it thunders, he speaks. When the crash is loudest, then he scolds. Some Indian has done wrong. Perhaps one redman has taken another redman's scalp!"

Another pause succeeded, briefer and less imposing than the first, but one that sufficed to impress on the listeners anew the great evil of an Indian's raising his hand against an Indian.

"Yes, there is no one so deaf as not to hear the voice of the Great Spirit when he is angry," resumed Peter. "Ten thousands of buffalo bulls, roaring together, do not make as much noise as his whisper. Spread the prairies, and the openings, and the lakes, before him, and he can be heard in all, and on all, at the same time.

"Here is a medicine-priest of the pale-faces; he tells me that the voice of the Manitou reaches into the largest villages of his people, beneath the rising sun, when it is heard by the redman across the great lakes, and near the rocks of the setting sun. It is a loud voice; woe to him who does not remember it. It speaks to all colors, and to every people and tribe and nation.

"Brothers, that is a lying tradition which says there is one Manitou for a Sac and another for the Ojebway— one Manitou for the redman and another for the pale-face. In this we are alike. One Great Spirit made all, governs all, rewards all, punishes all. He may keep the Happy Hunting-grounds of an Indian separate from the white man's Heaven, for he knows that their customs are different, and what would please a warrior would displease a trader; and what would please a trader would displease a warrior. He has thought of these things, and has made several places for the spirits of the good, let their colors be what they may. Is it the same with the places of the spirits of the bad? I think not. To me it would seem best to let *them* go together, that they may torment one another. A wicked Indian and a wicked pale-face would make a bad neighborhood. I think the Manitou will let *them* go together.

"Brothers, if the Manitou keeps the good Indian and the good pale-face apart in another world, what has brought them together in this? If he brings the bad spirits of all colors together in another world, why should they come together here, before their time? A place for wicked spirits should not be found on earth. This is wrong; it must be looked into.

"Brothers, I have now done; this pale-face wishes to speak, and I have said that you would hear his words. When he has spoken his mind, I may have more to tell you. Now, listen to the stranger. He is a medicine-priest of the white men, and says he has a great secret to tell our people ; when he has told it, I have another for their ears, too. Mine must be spoken when there is no one near but the children of red clay.''

Having thus opened the way for the missionary, Peter courteously took his seat, producing a little disappointment among his own admirers, though he awakened a lively curiosity to know what this medicine-priest might have to say on an occasion so portentous. The Indians in the regions of the great lakes had long been accustomed to missionaries, and it is probable that even some of their own traditions, so far as they related to religious topics, had been insensibly colored by, if not absolutely derived from, men of this character ; for the first whites who are known to have penetrated into that portion of the continent were Jesuits, who carried the cross as their standard and emblem of peace. Blessed emblem ! that any should so confound their own names and denunciatory practices with the revealed truth as to imagine that a standard so appropriate should ever be out of season and place, when it is proper for man to use aught at all, that is addressed to his senses, in the way of symbols, rites, and ceremonies ! To the Jesuits succeeded the less ceremonious and less imposing priesthood of America, as America peculiarly was in the first years that followed the Revolution. There is reason to believe that the Spirit of God, in a greater or less degree, accompanied all ; for all were self-denying and zealous, though the fruits of near two centuries of labor have as yet amounted to little more than the promise of the harvest at some distant day. Enough, however, was known of the missionaries and their views in general to prepare the council in some small degree for the forthcoming exhibition.

Parson Amen had caught some of the habits of the Indians, in the course of years of communication and intercourse. Like them he had learned to be deliberate, calm, and dignified in his exterior, and like them he had acquired a sententious mode of speaking.

'' My children,'' he said, for he deemed it best to assume

the parental character, in a scene of so great moment. "as Peter has told you, the Spirit of God is among you. Christians know that such has he promised to be always with his people, and I see faces in this circle that I am ready to claim as belonging to those who have prayed with me, in days that are long past. If your souls are not touched by divine love, it does not kill the hope I entertain of your yet taking up the cross, and calling upon the Redeemer's name. But not for this have I come with Peter this night. I am now here to lay before you an all-important fact, that Providence has revealed to me as the fruit of long labor in the vineyard of study and biblical inquiry. It is a tradition—and redmen love traditions. It is a tradition that touches your own history, and which it will gladden your hearts to hear, for it will teach you how much your nation and tribes have been the subject of the especial care and love of the Great Spirit. When my children say speak, I shall be ready to speak."

Here the missionary took his seat, wisely awaiting a demonstration on the part of the council, ere he ventured to proceed any further. This was the first occasion on which he had ever attempted to broach, in a direct form, his favorite theory of the "lost tribes." Let a man get once fairly possessed of any peculiar notion, whether it be on religion, political economy, morals, politics, arts, or anything else, and he sees little beside his beloved principle, which he is at all times ready to advance, defend, demonstrate, or expatiate on. Nothing can be simpler than the two great dogmas of Christianity, which are so plain that all can both comprehend them and feel their truth. They teach us to love God, the surest way to obey him, and to love our neighbor as ourselves. Any one can understand this ; all can see how just it is, and how much of moral sublimity it contains. It is godlike, and brings us near the very essence of the Divinity, which is love, mercy, and truth. Yet how few are content to accept the teachings of the Saviour in this respect, without embarrassing them with theories that have so much of their origin in human fancies. We do not mean by this, however, that Parson

Amen was so very wrong in bestowing a part of his attention on that wonderful people who, so early set apart by
the Creator as the creatures of his own especial ends, have
already played so great a part in the history of nations,
and who are designed, so far as we can penetrate revelation, yet to enact their share in the sublime drama of human events.

As for the council, its members were moved by more
than ordinary curiosity to hear what further the missionary
might have to say, though all present succeeded admirably
in suppressing the exhibition of any interest that might
seem weak and womanly. After a decent delay, therefore,
Bear's Meat intimated to the parson that it would be
agreeable to the chiefs present to listen to him further.

" My children, I have a great tradition to tell you," the
missionary resumed, as soon as on his feet again ; "a very
great and divine tradition ; not a tradition of man's, but
one that came direct from the Manitou himself. Peter has
spoken truth ; there is but one Great Spirit ; he is the
Great Spirit of all colors and tribes and nations. He made
all men of the same clay." Here a slight sensation was
perceptible among the audience, most of whom were very
decidedly of a different opinion on this point of natural
history. But the missionary was now so far warmed with
his subject as to disregard any slight interruption, and
proceeded as if his listeners had betrayed no feeling.
"And he divided them afterwards into nations and tribes.
It was then that he caused the color of his creatures to
change. Some he kept white, as he had made them. Some
he put behind a dark cloud, and they became altogether
black. Our wise men think that this was done in punishment for their sins. Some he painted red, like the nations
on this continent." Here Peter raised a finger, in sign
that he would ask a question ; for, without permission
granted, no Indian would interrupt the speaker. Indeed,
no one of less claims than Peter would hardly have presumed to take the step he now did, and that because he
saw a burning curiosity gleaming in the bright eyes of so
many in the dark circle.

" Say on, Peter," answered the missionary to this sign ;
" I will reply."

" Let my brother say *why* the Great Spirit turned the
Indian to a red color. Was he angry with him? or did
he paint him so out of love ? "

" That is more than I can tell you, friends. There are
many colors among men, in different parts of the world,
and many shades among people of the same color. There
are pale-faces fair as the lily, and there are pale-faces so
dark as scarcely to be distinguished from blacks. The sun
does much of this ; but no sun, nor want of sun, will ever
make a pale-face a redskin, or a redskin a pale-face."

" Good—that is what we Indians say. The Manitou
has made us different ; he did not mean that we should live
on the same hunting-grounds," rejoined Peter, who rarely
failed to improve every opportunity in order to impress on
the minds of his followers the necessity of now crushing
the serpent in its shell.

" No man can say that," answered Parson Amen. " Unless my people had come to this continent, the word of
God could not have been preached by me along the shores
of these lakes. But I will now speak of our great tradition. The Great Spirit divided mankind into nations
and tribes. When this was done, he picked out one for
his chosen people. The pale-faces call that favorite, and
for a long time much favored people, Jews. The Manitou
led them through a wilderness, and even through a salt
lake, until they reached a promised land, where he permitted
them to live for many hundred winters. A great triumph
was to come out of that people—the triumph of truth and
of the law over sin and death. In the course of time—"

Here a young chief rose, made a sign of caution, and
crossing the circle rapidly, disappeared by the passage
through which the rill flowed. In about a minute he returned, showing the way into the centre of the council to
one whom all present immediately recognized as a runner,
by his dress and equipments. Important news was at
hand ; yet not a man of all that crowd either rose or spoke,
in impatience to learn what it was !

CHAPTER XVII.

"Who will believe that with a smile whose blessing
    Would, like the patriarch's, soothe a dying hour;
With voice as low, as gentle and caressing,
    As e'er won maiden's lips in moonlit bower;

"With look like patient Job's, eschewing evil;
    With motions graceful as the birds in air;
Thou art, in sober truth, the veriest devil
    That e'er clinched fingers in a captive's hair?"
                  HALLECK'S *Red-Jacket.*

ALTHOUGH the arrival of the runner was so totally unexpected, it scarcely disturbed the quiet of that grave assembly. His approaching step had been heard, and he was introduced in the manner mentioned, when the young chief resumed his seat, leaving the messenger standing near the centre of the circle, and altogether within the influence of the light. He was an Ottawa, and had evidently travelled far and fast. At length he spoke, no one having put a single question to him or betrayed the least sign of impatient curiosity.

"I come to tell the chiefs what has happened," said the runner. "Our Great Father from Quebec has sent his young men against the Yankees. Red warriors, too, were there in hundreds"—here a murmur of interest was slightly apparent among the chiefs—"their path led them to Detroit; it is taken."

A low murmur, expressive of satisfaction, passed round the circle, for Detroit was then the most important of all the posts held by the Americans, along the whole line of the great lakes. Eye met eye in surprise and admiration;

253

then one of the older chiefs yielded to his interest in the subject, and inquired,—

"Have our young men taken many pale-face scalps?"

"So few that they are not worth counting. I did not see one pole that was such as an Indian loves to look on."

"Did our young men keep back, and let the warriors from Quebec do all the fighting?"

"No one fought. The Yankees asked to be made prisoners, without using their rifles. Never before have so many captives been led into the villages with so little to make their enemies look on them with friendly eyes."

A gleam of fierce delight passed athwart the dark features of Peter. It is probable that he fell into the same error, on hearing these tidings, as that which so generally prevailed for a short time among the natives of the Old World, at the commencement of both of the two last wars of the republic, when the disasters with which they opened induced so many to fall into the fatal error of regarding Jonathan as merely a "shopkeeper." A shopkeeper, in a certain sense, he may well be accounted; but among his wares are arms, that he has the head, the heart, and the hands to use as man has very rarely been known to use them before. Even at this very instant, the brilliant success which has rendered the armed citizens of this country the wonder of Europe is re-acting on the masses of the Old World, teaching them their power, and inciting them to stand up to the regularly armed bands of their rulers with a spirit and confidence that, hitherto, has been little known in their histories. Happy, thrice happy will it be, if the conquerors use their success in moderation, and settle down into the ways of practical reason, instead of suffering their minds to be led astray in quest of the political jack-o'-lanterns that are certain to conduct their followers into the quagmires of impracticable and visionary theories. To abolish abuses, to set in motion the car of state on the track of justice and economy, and to distinguish between that which is really essential to human happiness and human rights and that which is merely the result of some wild and bootless proposition in political economy, are the great self-imposed tasks that the European people seem now to have assumed ; and God grant that they may complete their labors with the moderation and success with which they would appear to have commenced them !

As for Peter, with the curse of ignorance weighing on his mind, it is to be presumed that he fancied his own great task of destroying the whites was so much the lighter in consequence of the feeble defence of the Yankees at Detroit. The runner was now questioned by the different chiefs for details, which he furnished with sufficient intelligence and distinctness. The whole of that discreditable story is too prominent in history, and of too recent occurrence, to stand in need of repetition here. When the runner had told his tale, the chiefs broke the order of their circle, to converse the more easily concerning the great events which had just occurred. Some were not backward in letting their contempt for the "Yankees" be known. Here were three of their strong places taken, in quick succession, and almost without a blow. Detroit, the strongest of them all, and defended by an army, had fallen in a way to bring the blush to the American face, seemingly leaving the whole of the northwestern frontier of the country ravished from the redman exposed to his incursions and depredations.

"What does my father think of this?" asked Bear's Meat of Peter, as the two stood apart, in a cluster of some three or four of the principal personages present. "Does the news make his heart stronger?"

"It is always strong when this business is before it. The Manitou has long looked darkly upon the redmen, but now his face brightens. The cloud is passing from before his countenance, and we can begin again to see his smile. It will be with our sons as it was with our fathers. Our hunting-grounds will be our own, and the buffalo and deer will be plenty in our wigwams. The fire-water will flow after them that brought it into the country, and the redman will once more be happy, as in times past !"

The *ignis fatuus* of human happiness employs all minds, all faculties, all pens, and all theories, just at this particular moment. A thousand projects have been broached, will

continue to be broached, and will fail, each in its time, showing the mistakes of men, without remedying the evils of
which they complain. This is not because a beneficent
Providence has neglected to enlighten their minds, and to
show them the way to be happy here and hereafter, but because human conceit runs *pari passu* with human woes, and
we are too proud to look for our lessons of conduct in that
code in which they have been set before us by unerring wisdom and ceaseless love. If the political economists and
reformers and revolutionists of the age would turn from
their speculations to those familiar precepts which all are
taught and so few obey, they would find rules for every
emergency ; and, most of all, would they learn the great
secret which lies so profoundly hid from them and their
philosophy, in the contented mind. Nothing short of this
will ever bring the mighty reform that the world needs. The
press may be declared free, but a very brief experience will
teach those who fancy that this one conquest will secure the
victory, that they have only obtained King Stork in the lieu
of King Log ; a vulgar and most hideous tyrant for one of
royal birth and gentle manners. They may set up the rule
of patriots by profession, in place of the dominion of those
who have so long pretended that the art of governing de-
scends from male to male, according to the order of primo-
geniture, and live to wonder that love of country should
have so many weaknesses in common with love of self.
They may rely on written charters for their liberties, instead
of the divine right of kings, and come perchance to learn
that neither language nor covenants nor signatures nor
seals, avail much, as against the necessities of nations and
the policy of rulers. Do we then regard reform as impossible, and society to be doomed to struggle on in its old
sloughs of oppression and abuses? Far from it. We believe and hope that at each effort of a sage character something is gained, while much more than had been expected
is lost ; and such we think will continue to be the course of
events until men shall reach that period in their history
when, possibly to their wonder, they will find that a fault-
less code for the government of all their affairs has been

lying neglected, daily and hourly, in their very hands, for eighteen centuries and a half, without their perceiving the all-important truth. In due season this code will supersede all others, when the world will for the first time be happy and truly free.

There was a marked resemblance between the hopes and expectations of Peter, in reference to the overthrow of his pale-face enemies on the American continent, and those of the revolutionists of the Old World in reference to the overthrow of their strongly-entrenched foes on that of Europe. Each fancies success more easy of attainment than the end is likely to show; both overlook the terrible power of their adversaries, and both take the suggestions of a hope that is lively rather than enlightened, as the substitute for the lessons of wisdom.

It was some little time ere the council had so far regained its calm as to think of inviting the missionary to resume his discourse. The last had necessarily heard the news, and was so much troubled by it as to feel no great disposition to proceed; but Peter intimating that " the ears of his friends were open,'' he was of opinion it would be wisest to go on with his traditions.

"Thus it was, my children,'' Parson Amen continued, the circle being just as quiet and attentive as if no interruption had occurred, " the Great Spirit selected, from among the nations of the earth one to be his chosen people. I cannot stop now to tell you all he did for this nation, in the way of wonders and power ; but finally he placed them in a beautiful country, where milk and honey abounded, and made them its masters. From that people, in his earthly character, came the Christ whom we missionaries preach to you, and who is the great head of our church. Although the Jews, or Israelites, as we call that people, were thus honored and thus favored of the Manitou, they were but men, they had the weaknesses of men. On more than one occasion they displeased the Great Spirit, and that so seriously as to draw down condign punishment on themselves, and on their wives and children. In various ways were they visited for their backslidings and sins, each time repenting and receiving for-

17

giveness. At length the Great Spirit, tired of their forgetfulness and crimes, allowed an army to come into their land,
and to carry away as captives no less than ten of their twelve
tribes, putting their people in strange hunting-grounds. Now,
this happened many thousands of moons since, and no one can
say with certainty what has become of those captives, whom
Christians are accustomed to call 'the lost tribes of Israel.'"

Here the missionary paused to arrange his thoughts, and
a slight murmur was heard in the circle as the chiefs com-
muned together, in interested comments on what had just
been said. The pause, however, was short, and the speaker
again proceeded, safe from any ungracious interruption,
among auditors so trained in self-restraint.

"Children, I shall not now say anything touching the
birth of Christ, the redemption of the world, and the history
of the two tribes that remained in the land where God had
placed his people ; for that is a part of the subject that comes
properly within the scope of my ordinary teaching. At present I wish only to speak of yourselves ; of the redman of
America, of his probable origin and end, and of a great discovery that many of us think we have made on this most
interesting topic in the history of the good book. Does any
one present know aught of the ten lost tribes of whom I
have spoken?"

Eye met eye, and expectation was lively among those
primitive and untaught savages. At length Crowsfeather
arose to answer, the missionary standing the whole time
motionless, as if waiting for a reply.

"My brother has told us a tradition," said the Pottawattamie. "It is a good tradition. It is a strange tradition.
Redmen love to hear such traditions. It is wonderful that
so many as ten tribes should be *lost*, at the same time, and
no one know what has become of them ! My brother asks
us if *we* know what has become of these ten tribes. How
should poor redmen, who live on their hunting-grounds,
and who are busy when the grass grows in getting together
food for their squaws and pappooses, against a time when
the buffalo can find nothing to eat in this part of the world,
know anything of a people that they never saw? My

brother has asked a question that he only can answer. Let him tell us where these ten tribes are to be found, if he knows the place. We should like to go and look at them.''

"Here!" exclaimed the missionary, the instant Crows-feather ceased speaking, and even before he was seated. "Here—in this council—on these prairies—in these Openings—here, on the shores of the great lakes of sweet water, and throughout the land of America, are these tribes to be found. The redman is a Jew; a Jew is a redman. The Manitou has brought the scattered people of Israel to this part of the world, and I see his power in the wonderful fact. Nothing but a miracle could have done this!''

Great was the admiration of the Indians at this announcement! None of their own traditions gave this account of their origin; but there is reason to believe, on the other hand, that none of them contradict it. Nevertheless, here was a medicine-priest of the pale-faces boldly proclaiming the fact, and great was the wonder of all who heard, thereat! Having spoken, the missionary again paused, that his words might produce their effect. Bear's Meat now became his interrogator, rising respectfully, and standing during the colloquy that succeeded.

"My brother has spoken a great tradition," said the Menominee. "Did he first hear it from his fathers?''

"In part only. The history of the lost tribes has come down to us from our fathers; it is written in the good book of the pale-faces, the book that contains the word of the Great Spirit.''

"Does the good book of the pale-faces say that the redmen are the children of the people he has mentioned?''

"I cannot say that it does. While the good book tells us so much, it also leaves very much untold. It is best that we should look for ourselves, that we may find out some of its meanings. It is in thus looking that many Christians see the great truth which makes the Indians of America and the Jews beyond the great salt lake one and the same people.''

"If this be so, let my brother tell us how far it is from our hunting-grounds to that distant land across the great salt lake?''

" I cannot give you this distance in miles exactly ; but I suppose it may be eleven or twelve times the length of Michigan."

" Will my brother tell us how much of this long path is water, and how much of it is dry land ? "

" Perhaps one fourth is land, as the traveller may choose ; the rest must be water, if the journey be made from the rising towards the setting sun, which is the shortest path ; but, let the journey be made from the setting towards the rising sun, and there is little water to cross; rivers and lakes of no great width, as is seen here, but only a small breadth of salt lake."

" Are there, then, two roads to that far-off land where the redmen are thought to have once lived ? "

" Even so. The traveller may come to this spot from that land by way of the rising sun, or by way of the setting sun."

The general movement among the members of the council denoted the surprise with which this account was received. As the Indians, until they have had much intercourse with the whites, very generally believe the earth to be flat, it was not easy for them to comprehend how a given point could be reached by directly opposite routes. Such an apparent contradiction would be very likely to extort further questions.

" My brother is a medicine-man of the pale-faces ; his hairs are gray," observed Crowsfeather. "Some of your medicine-men are good, and some wicked. It is so with the medicine-men of the redskins. Good and bad are to be found in all nations. A medicine-man of your people cheated my young men by promising to show them where fire-water grows. He did not show them. He let them smell, but he did not let them drink. That was a wicked medicine-man. His scalp would not be safe did my young men see it again "— Here the bee-hunter, insensibly to himself, felt for his rifle, making sure that he had it between his legs ; the corporal being a little surprised at the sudden start he gave. " His hair does not grow on his head closer than the trees grow to the ground. Even a tree can be cut down. But all medicine-men are not alike. My brother is a *good* medicine-man. All he says may not be just as he thinks, but he *believes* what he says. It is wonderful how men can look two ways; but it is more wonderful that they should go to the same place by paths that lead before and behind. This we do not understand; my brother will tell us how it can be."

"I believe I understand what it is that my children would know. They think the earth is flat, but the pale-faces know that it is round. He who travels and travels towards the setting sun would come to this very spot, if he travelled long enough. The distance would be great, but the end of every straight path in this world is the place of starting."

"My brother says this. He says many curious things. I have heard a medicine-man of his people say that the pale-faces have seen their Great Spirit, talked with him, walked with him. It is not so with us Indians. Our Manitou speaks to us in thunder only. We are ignorant, and wish to learn more than we now know. Has my brother ever travelled on that path which ends where it begins? Once, on the prairies, I lost my way. There was snow, and glad was I to find tracks. I followed them tracks. But one traveller had passed. After walking an hour, two had passed. Another hour, and three had passed. Then I saw the tracks were my own, and that I had been walking, as the squaws reason, round and round, but not going ahead."

"I understand my friend, but he is wrong. It is no matter which path them lost tribes travelled to get here. The main question is whether they came at all. I see in the redmen, in their customs, their history, their looks, and even in their traditions, proofs that they are these Jews, once the favored people of the Great Spirit."

"If the Manitou so well loves the Indians, why has he permitted the pale-faces to take away their hunting-grounds? Why has he made the redman poor and the white man rich? Brother, I am afraid your tradition is a lying tradition, or these things would not be so."

" It is not given to men to understand the wisdom that cometh from above. That which seems so strange to us may be right. The lost tribes had offended God ; and their scattering and captivity and punishment are but so many proofs of his displeasure. But, if lost, we have reason to believe that one day they will be found. Yes, my children, it will be the pleasure of the Great Spirit, one day, to re-store you to the land of your fathers, and make you again, what you once were, a great and glorious people ! "

As the well-meaning but enthusiastic missionary spoke with great fervor, the announcement of such an event, coming as it did from one whom they respected, even while they could not understand him, did not fail to produce a deep sensation. If their fortunes were really the care of the Great Spirit, and justice was to be done to them by his love and wisdom, then would the projects of Peter and those who acted and felt with him be unnecessary, and might lead to evil instead of to good. That sagacious sav-age did not fail to discover this truth ; and he now believed it might be well for him to say a word, in order to lessen the influence Parson Amen might otherwise obtain among those whom it was his design to mould in a way entirely to meet his own wishes. So intense was the desire of this mysterious leader to execute vengeance on the pale-faces, that the redemption of the tribes from misery and poverty, unaccompanied by this part of his own project, would have given him pain in lieu of pleasure. His very soul had got to be absorbed in this one notion of retribution and of an-nihilation for the oppressors of his race ; and he regarded all things through a medium of revenge, thus created by his feelings, much as the missionary endeavored to bend every fact and circumstance connected with the Indians to the support of his theory touching their Jewish origin.

When Peter arose, therefore, fierce and malignant pas-sions were at work in his bosom, such as a merciful and a benignant deity never wishes to see in the breast of man, whether civilized or savage. The self-command of the Tribeless, however, was great, and he so far succeeded in suppressing the volcano that was raging within as to speak with his usual dignity and an entire calmness of exterior.

"My brothers have heard what the medicine-man had to say," Peter commenced. "He has told them that which was new to them. He has told them an Indian is not an Indian. That a redman is a pale-face, and that we are not what we thought we were. It is good to learn. It makes the difference between the wise and the foolish. The pale-faces learn more than the redskins. That is the way they have learned how to get our hunting-grounds. That is the way they have learned to build their villages on the spots where our fathers killed the deer. That is the way they have learned how to come and tell us that we are not Indians, but Jews. I wish to learn. Though old, my mind craves to know more. That I may know more, I will ask this medicine-man questions, and my brothers can open their ears, and learn a little, too, by what he answers. Perhaps we shall believe that we are not redskins, but pale-faces. Perhaps we shall believe that our true hunting-grounds are not near the great lakes of sweet water, but under the rising sun. Perhaps we shall wish to go home, and to leave these pleasant Openings for the pale-faces to put their cabins on them, as the small-pox that they have also given to us puts its sores on our bodies. Brother," turning towards the missionary, "listen. You say we are no longer Indians, but Jews; is this true of *all* redmen, or only of the tribes whose chiefs are *here*?"

"Of *all* redmen, as I most sincerely believe. You are now red, but once all of your people were fairer than the fairest of the pale-faces. It is climate and hardships and sufferings that have changed your color."

"If suffering can do *that*," returned Peter, with emphasis, "I wonder we are not *black*. When *all* our hunting-grounds are covered with the farms of your people, I think we shall be *black*."

Signs of powerful disgust were now visible among the listeners, an Indian having much of the contempt that seems to weigh so heavily on that unfortunate class, for all of the color mentioned. At the South, as is known, the redman has already made a slave of the descendants of the children of Africa, but no man has ever yet made a slave of a son of the American forests ! *That* is a result which no human power has yet been able to accomplish. Early in the settlement of the country, attempts were indeed *made*, by sending a few individuals to the islands ; but so unsuccessful did the experiment turn out to be that the design was soon abandoned. Whatever may be his degradation and poverty and ignorance and savage ferocity, it would seem to be the settled purpose of the American Indian of our own territories—unlike the aborigines who are to be found farther south—to live and die a free man.

"My children," answered the missionary, "I pretend not to say what will happen, except as it has been told to us in the word of God. You know that we pale-faces have a book in which the Great Spirit has told us his laws, and foretold to us many of the things that are to happen. Some of these things *have* happened, while some remain *to* happen. The loss of the ten tribes was foretold, and *has* happened ; but their being *found* again has not *yet* happened, unless indeed I am so blessed as to be one of those who have been permitted to meet them in these Openings. Here is the book—it goes where I go, and is my companion and friend, by day and by night, in good and evil, in season and out of season. To this book I cling as to my great anchor, that is to carry me through the storms in safety ! Every line in it is precious, every word true !"

Perhaps half the chiefs present had seen books before, while those who now laid eyes on one for the first time had heard of this art of the pale-faces, which enabled them to set down their traditions in a way peculiar to themselves. Even the Indians have their records, however, though resorting to the use of natural signs and a species of hieroglyphics, in lieu of the more artistical process of using words and letters in a systemized written language. The Bible, too, was a book of which all had heard more or less, though not one of those present had ever been the subject of its influence. A Christian Indian, indeed,— and a few of those were to be found even at that day,—

would hardly have attended a council convened for the objects which had caused this to be convened. Still, a strong but regulated curiosity existed to see and touch and examine the great medicine-book of the pale-faces. There was a good deal of superstition blended with the Indian manner of regarding the sacred volume, some present having their doubts about touching it, even while most excited by admiration and a desire to probe its secrets.

Peter took the little volume, which the missionary extended as if inviting any one who might so please to examine it also. It was the first time the wary chief had ever suffered that mysterious book to touch him. Among his other speculations on the subject of the manner in which the white men were encroaching, from year to year, on the lands of the natives, it had occurred to his mind that this extraordinary volume, which the pale-faces all *seemed* to reverence, even to the drunkards of the garrisons, might contain the great elements of their power. Perhaps he was not very much out of the way in this supposition, though they who use the volume habitually are not themselves aware, one half the time, why it is so.

On the present occasion, Peter saw the great importance of not betraying apprehension, and he turned over the pages awkwardly, as one would be apt to handle a book for the first time, but boldly and without hesitation. Encouraged by the impunity that accompanied this hardihood, Peter shook the leaves open, and held the volume on high, in a way that told his own people that he cared not for its charms or power. There was more of seeming than of truth, however, in this bravado; for never before had this extraordinary being made so heavy a draft on his courage and self-command as in the performance of this simple act. He did not, could not know what were the virtues of the book, and his imagination very readily suggested the worst. As the great medicine volume of the pale-faces, it was quite likely to contain that which was hostile to the redmen; and this fact, so probable in his eyes, rendered it likely that some serious evil to himself might follow from the contact. It did not, however; and a smile of grim

satisfaction lighted his swarthy countenance, as, turning to
the missionary, he said with point,—

"Let my brother open his eyes. I have looked into his
medicine-book, but do not see that the redman is anything
but a redman. The Great Spirit made him ; and what the
Great Spirit makes lasts. The pale-faces have made their
book, and it lies."

"No, no—Peter, Peter, thou utterest wicked words !
But the Lord will pardon thee, since thou knowest not
what thou sayest. Give me the sacred volume, that I may
place it next my heart, where I humbly trust so many of
its divine precepts are already entrenched."

This was said in English, under the impulse of feeling,
but, being understood by Peter, the latter quietly relinquished the Bible, preparing to follow up the advantage he
perceived he had gained, on the spot.

"My brother has his medicine-book again," said Peter,
"and the redmen live. This hand is not withered like
the dead branch of the hemlock, yet it has held his word
of the Great Spirit ! It may be that a redskin and a
pale-face book cannot do each other harm. I looked into
my brother's great charm, but did not see or hear a tradition that tells me we are Jews. There is a bee-hunter in
these Openings. I have talked with him. He has told
me who these Jews are. He says they are a people who
do not go with the pale-faces, but live apart from them,
like men with the small-pox. It is not right for my
brother to come among the redmen and tell them that
their fathers were not good enough to live and eat and go
on the same paths as his fathers."

"This is all a mistake, Peter,—a great and dangerous
mistake ! The bee-hunter has heard the Jews spoken of
by those who do not sufficiently read the good book. They
have been, and are still, the chosen people of the Great
Spirit, and will one day be received back to his favor.
Would that I were one of them, only enlightened by the
words of the New Testament ! No real Christian ever
can or does now despise a son of Israel, whatever has been

done in times past.   It is an honor, and not a disgrace, to
be what I have said my friends are.''

" If this be so, why do not the pale-faces let us keep our
hunting-grounds to ourselves?   We are content.   We do
not wish to be Jews.   Our canoes are too small to cross the
great salt lake.   They are hardly large enough to cross the
great lakes of sweet water.   We should be tired of paddling
so far.   My brother says there is a rich land under the
rising sun, which the Manitou gave to the redmen.   Is
this so?''

"Beyond all doubt.   It was given to the children of
Israel for a possession forever ; and though you have been
carried away from it for a time, there the land still is,
open to receive you, and waiting the return of its ancient masters.   In good season that return must come,
for we have the word of God for it, in our Christian
Bible.''

" Let my brother open his ears very wide, and hear
what I have to say.   We thank him for letting us know
that we are Jews.   We believe that he thinks what he
says.   Still, we think we are redmen, and Injins, and not
Jews.   We never saw the place where the sun rises.   We
do not wish to see it.   Our hunting-grounds are nearer to
the place where he sets.   If the pale-faces believe we
have a right to that distant land, which is so rich in good
things, we will give it to them, and keep these Openings
and prairies and woods.   We know the game of this
country, and have found out how to kill it.   We do not
know the game under the rising sun, which may kill us.
Go to your friends and say, ' The Injins will give you
that land near the rising sun, if you will let them alone
on their hunting-grounds, where they have so long been.
They say that your canoes are larger than their canoes,
and that one can carry a whole tribe.   They have seen
some of your big canoes on the great lakes, and have
measured them.   Fill all you have got with your squaws
and pappooses, put your property in them, and go back
by the long path through which you came.   Then will the

redman thank the pale-face and be his friend. The white man is welcome to that far-off land. Let him take it, and build his villages on it, and cut down its trees. This is all the Injins ask. If the pale-faces can take away with them the small-pox and the fire-water, it will be better still. They brought both into this country, it is right that they should take them away.' Will my brother tell this to his people?''

"It would do no good. They know that the land of Judea is reserved by God for his chosen people, and they are not Jews. None but the children of Israel can restore that land to its ancient fertility. It would be useless for any other to attempt it. Armies have been there, and it was once thought that a Christian kingdom was set up on the spot; but neither the time nor the people had come. Jews alone can make Judea what it was, and what it will be again. If my people owned that land, they could not use it. There are also too many of us, now, to go away in canoes."

"Did not the fathers of the pale-faces come in canoes?" demanded Peter, a little sternly.

"They did; but since that time their increase has been so great that canoes enough to hold them could not be found. No, the Great Spirit, for his own wise ends, has brought my people hither, and here must they remain to the end of time. It is not easy to make the pigeons fly south in the spring."

This declaration, quietly but distinctly made, as it was the habit of the missionary to speak, had its effect. It told Peter and those with him, as plainly as language could tell them, that there was no reason to expect the pale-faces would ever willingly abandon the country, and seemed the more distinctly, in all their uninstructed minds, to place the issue on the armed hand. It is not improbable that some manifestation of feeling would have escaped the circle, had not an interruption to the proceedings occurred, which put a stop to all other emotions but those peculiar to the lives of savages.

CHAPTER XVIII.

"Nearer the mount stood Moses; in his hand
The rod which blasted with strange plagues the realm
Of Mizraim, and from its time-worn channels
Upturned the Arabian Sea. Fair was his broad
High front, and forth from his soul-piercing eye
Did legislation look; which full he fix'd
Upon the blazing panoply undazzled."

HILLHOUSE.

IT often happens, in the recesses of the wilderness, that in the absence of men the animals hunt each other. The wolves, in particular, following their instincts, are often seen in packs, pressing upon the heels of the antelope, deer, and other creatures of that family, which depend for safety more on their speed than on their horns. On the present occasion, a fine buck, with a pack of fifty wolves close after it, came bounding through the narrow gorge that contained the rill, and entered the amphitheatre of the bottom-land. Its headlong career was first checked by the sight of the fire; then arose a dark circle of men, each armed and accustomed to the chase. In much less time than it has taken to record the fact, that little piece of bottom-land was crowded with wolves, deer, and men. The headlong impetuosity of the chase and flight had prevented the scent from acting, and all were huddled together, for a single instant, in a sort of inextricable confusion. Brief as was this *mêlée*, it sufficed to allow of a young hunter's driving his arrow through the heart of the buck, and enabled others among the Indians to kill several of the wolves; some with arrows, others with knives, etc. No rifle was used, probably from a wish not to give an alarm.

The wolves were quite as much astonished at this unexpected rencontre as the Indians. They were not a set of hungry and formidable beasts, that famine might urge to any pass of desperation, but a pack hunting, like gentlemen, for their own amusement. Their headlong speed was checked less by the crowd of men than by the sight of fire. In their impetuosity, it is probable that they would have gone clean through five hundred men, but no wild beast will willingly encounter fire. Three or four of the chiefs, aware of this dread, seized brands, and throwing themselves, without care, into the midst of the pack, the animals went howling off, scattering in all directions. Unfortunately for his own welfare, one went directly through the circle, plunged into the thicket beyond, and made its way quite up to the fallen tree on which the bee-hunter and the corporal had taken their stations. This was altogether too much for the training or for the philosophy of Hive. Perceiving a recognized enemy rushing towards him, that noble mastiff met him in a small cleared spot, open-mouthed, and for a few moments a fierce combat was the consequence. Dogs and wolves do not fight in silence, and loud were the growls and yells on this occasion. In vain did Le Bourdon endeavor to drag his mastiff off; the animal was on the high road to victory, when it is ever hard to arrest the steps of the combatant. Almost as a matter of course, some of the chiefs rushed towards the spot, when the presence of the two spectators first became known to them. At the next moment the wolf lay dead at the feet of Hive, and the parties stood gazing at each other, equally taken by surprise, and equally at a loss to know what to do next.

It was perhaps fortunate for the bee-hunter that neither Crowsfeather, nor any other of the Pottawattamies was present at this first rencontre, or he might have fallen on the spot, a victim to their disappointed hopes of drinking at a whiskey spring. The chiefs present were strangers to Le Bourdon, and they stared at him in a way to show that his person was equally unknown to them. But it was necessary, now, to follow the Indians back to their circle, where the whole party soon collected again, the wolves having gone off on their several routes, to put up some other animal and run him to death.

During the whole of that exciting and tumultuous scene, which would probably now be termed a "*stampede*," in the Mexican-Americo-English of the day, Peter had not stirred. Familiar with such occurrences, he felt the importance of manifesting an unmoved calm, as a quality most likely to impress the minds of his companions with a profound sense of his dignity and self-command. While all around him was in a tumult, he stood in his tracks, motionless as a statue. Even the fortitude of the worthy missionary was shaken by the wild tempest that momentarily prevailed ; and the good man forgot the Jews in his alarm at wolves, forgot the mighty past in his apprehensions for the uncomfortable and ill-boding present time. All this, however, was soon over, and order and quiet and a dignified calm once more reigned in the circle. Fagots were thrown on the fire, and the two captives, or spectators, stood as near it, the observed of all observers, as the heat rendered comfortable. It was just then that Crowsfeather and his companions first recognized the magician of the whiskey spring.

Peter saw the discovery of the two spectators with some uneasiness. The time had not come when he intended to strike his blow, and he had seen signs among those Pottawattamies, when at the mouth of the river, which had told him how little they were disposed to look with favor on one who had so grievously trifled with their hopes. His first care, therefore, was to interpose his authority and influence between Le Bourdon and any project of revenge which Crowsfeather's young men might be apt to devise, as soon as they too laid eyes on the offender. This was done in a characteristic and wily manner.

"Does my brother love honey ? " asked the tribeless chief of the leader of the Pottawattamies present, who sat near him, gazing on Le Bourdon much as the cat looks upon the mouse ere it makes it its prey. "Some Injins are fond of that sweet food ; if my brother is one of that sort, I can tell him how to fill his wigwam with honey with little trouble."

At this suggestion, coming from such a source, Crows-feather could not do less than express his thanks and his readiness to hear what further might be in reserve for him. Peter then alluded to Le Bourdon's art, describing him as being the most skilful bee-hunter of the West. So great was his art in that way, that no Indian had ever yet seen his equal. It was Peter's intention to make him exercise his craft soon, for the benefit of the chiefs and warriors present, who might then return to their villages, carrying with them stores of honey to gladden the hearts of their squaws and pappooses. This artifice succeeded; for the Indians are not expert in taking this article of food, which so much abounds in the forests, both on account of the difficulty they find in felling the trees, and on account of the "angle-ing" part of the process, which much exceeds their skill in mathematics. On the other hand, the last is just the sort of skill a common white American would be likely to manifest, his readiness and ingenuity in all such processes almost amounting to an instinct.

Having thus thrown his mantle around Le Bourdon for the moment, Peter then deemed it the better course to finish the historical investigation in which the council had been so much interested when the strange interruption by the wolves occurred. With this view, therefore, he rose himself, and recalled the minds of all present to this interesting subject by a short speech. This he did especially to prevent any premature attack on the person of Le Bourdon.

"Brothers," said this mysterious chief, "it is good for Injins to learn. When they learn a thing, they know it; then they may learn another. It is in this way that the pale-faces do; it makes them wise, and puts it in their power to take away our hunting-grounds. A man that knows nothing is only a child that has grown up too fast. He may be big—may take long steps—may be strong enough to carry burdens—may love venison and buffaloes' humps; but his size is only in the way; his steps he does not know where to direct; his burdens he does not know how to choose; and he has to beg food of the squaws, instead of carrying it himself to their wigwams. He has not learned how to take game. We must all learn. It is right. When we have learned how to take game, and how to strike the enemy, and how to keep the wigwam fitted, then we may learn traditions. Traditions tell us of our fathers. We have many traditions. Some are talked of even to the squaws. Some are told around the fires of the tribes. Some are known only to the aged chiefs. This is right too. Injins ought not to say too much, nor too little. They should say what is wise, what is best. But my brother, the medicine-man of the pale-faces, says that our traditions have not told us everything. Something has been kept back. If so, it is best to learn that too. If we are Jews, and not Injins, we ought to know it. If we are Injins, and not Jews, our brother ought to know it, and not call us by a wrong name. Let him speak. We listen.''

Here Peter slowly resumed his seat. As the missionary understood all that had been said, he next arose, and proceeded to make good, as far as he was able, and in such language as his knowledge of Indian habits suggested, his theory of the lost tribes.

'' I wish my children to understand,'' resumed the missionary, '' that it is an honor to be a Jew. I have not come here to lessen the redmen in their own eyes, but to do them honor. I see that Bear's Meat wishes to say something ; my ears are open and my tongue is still.''

'' I thank my brother for the opportunity to say what is on my mind,'' returned the chief mentioned. '' It is true, I have something to say ; it is this : I wish to ask the medicine-man if the pale-faces honor and show respect to Jews ? ''

This was rather an awkward question for the missionary, but he was much too honest to dissemble. With a reverence for truth that proceeded from his reverence for the Father of all that is true, he replied honestly, though not altogether without betraying how much he regretted the necessity of answering at all. Both remained standing while the dialogue proceeded ; or, in parliamentary language, each may be said to have had the floor at the same time.

'' My brother wishes to know if the pale-faces honor the

18

Jews," returned the missionary. "I wish I could answer 'yes'; but the truth forces me to say 'no.' The pale-faces have traditions that make against the Jews, and the judgments of God weigh heavy on the children of Israel. But all good Christians, now, look with friendly eyes on this dispersed and persecuted people, and wish them well. It will give the white men very great pleasure to learn that I have found the lost tribes of Israel in the redmen of America."

"Will my brother tell us *why* this will give his people pleasure? Is it because they will be glad to find old enemies poor, living on narrow hunting-grounds, off which the villages and farms of the pale-faces begin to push them still nearer to the setting sun ; and towards whom the small-pox has found a path to go, but none to come from?"

" Nay, nay, Bear's Meat, think not so unkindly of us of the white race ! In crossing the great salt lake, and in coming to this quarter of the world, our fathers were led by the finger of God. We do but obey the will of the Great Spirit, in pressing forward into this wilderness, directed by his wisdom how to spread the knowledge of his name among those who, as yet, have never heard of it ; or, having heard, have not regarded it. In all this, the wisest men are but babes, not being able to say whither they are to go, or what is to be done."

" This is strange," returned the unmoved Indian. " It is not so with the redmen. Our squaws and pappooses do know the hunting-ground of one tribe from the hunting-ground of another. When they put their feet on strange hunting-grounds, it is because they *intended* to go there, and to steal game. This is sometimes right. If it is right to take the scalp of an enemy, it is right to get his deer and his buffalo too. But we never do this without knowing it. If we did, we should be unfit to go at large, unfit to sit in council. This is the first time I have heard that the pale-faces are so weak, and they have such feeble minds, too, that they do not know where they go."

" My brother does not understand me. No man can see into the future—no man can say what will happen to-morrow. The Great Spirit only can tell. It is for him, then, to guide his children in their wanderings. When our fathers first came out of their canoes upon the land, on this side of the great salt lake, not one among them knew anything of this country between the great lakes of sweet water. They did not know that redmen lived here. The Great Spirit did know, and intended then that I should this night stand up in this council and speak of his power and of his name, and do him reverence. It was the Great Spirit that put it into my mind to come among the Indians; and it is the Great Spirit who has led me, step by step, as warriors move towards the graves of their fathers, to make the discovery that the Indians are in truth the children of Israel, a part of his own chosen and once much favored people. Let me ask my friends one or two questions. Do not your traditions say that your fathers once came from a far-off land ?''

Bear's Meat now took his seat, not choosing to answer a question of this nature in the presence of a chief so much respected as Peter. He preferred to let the last take up the dialogue where he now saw fit to abandon it. As the other very well understood the reason of this sudden movement, he quietly assumed the office of spokesman, the whole affair proceeding much as if there had been no change.

"Our traditions *do* tell us that our fathers came from a far-off land," answered Peter, without rising.

"I thought so ! I thought so !" exclaimed the simple-minded and confiding missionary. "How wonderful are the ways of God ! Yes, my brothers, Judea is a far-off land, and your traditions say that your fathers came from such a distance ! This, then, is something proved. Do not your traditions say that once your tribes were more in favor with the Great Spirit than they are now ?"

"Our traditions do say this : Once our tribes did not see the face of the Manitou looking dark upon them, as it now does. That was before the pale-faces came in their big canoes across the great salt lake, to drive the Indians from their hunting-grounds. It was when the small-pox had not found the path to their villages ; when fire-water was unknown to them, and no Indian had ever burned his throat with it."

" Oh, but I speak of a time much more distant than that ; of a time when your prophets stood face to face with God, and talked with the Creator. Since that day a great change has come over your people. Then your color was light, like that of the fairest and handsomest of the Circassian race ; now it has become red. When even the color is changed, it is not wonderful that men should no longer be the same in other particulars. Yes, once all the races of men were of the same color and origin."

" This is not what our traditions say. We have heard from our fathers that the Great Spirit made men of different colors ; some he made light, like the pale-faces ; some red, like the Injins ; some black, like the pale-faces' slaves. To some he gave high noses ; to some low noses ; to some flat noses. To the pale-faces he gave eyes of many colors. This is the reason why they see so many things, and in so many different ways. To the redmen he gave eyes of the same color, and they always see things of the same color. To a redman there is no change. Our fathers have always been red. This we know. If them Jews, of whom my brother speaks, were ever white, they have not been our fathers. We tell this to the medicine-man, that he may know it too. We do not wish to lead him on a crooked path, or to speak to him with a forked tongue. What we have said is so. Now the road is open to the wigwam of the pale-faces, and we wish them safe on their journey home. We Injins have a council to hold around this fire, and will stay longer."

At this plain intimation that their presence was no longer desirable, it became necessary for them to depart. The missionary, filled with zeal, was reluctant to go ; for, in his eyes, the present communications with the savages promised him not only the conversion of pagans, but the restoration of the Jews ! Nevertheless, he was compelled to comply ; and when Le Bourdon and the corporal took their departure, he turned and pronounced in a solemn tone the Christian benediction on the assembly. The meaning of this last impressive office was understood by most of the chiefs, and they rose as one man, in acknowledgment.

The three white men, on retiring from the circle, held their way towards Castle Meal. Hive followed his master, having come out of the combat but little injured. As they got to a point where a last look could be had of the bottom-land of the council, each turned to see what was now in the course of proceeding. The fire glimmered just enough to show the circle of dark faces, but not an Indian spoke or moved. There they all sat, patiently waiting for the moment when the "strangers" might "withdraw" to a sufficient distance to permit them to proceed with their own private affairs without fear of interruption.

"This has been to me a most trying scene," observed the missionary, as the three pursued their way towards the "garrison." "How hard it is to convince men against their wishes! Now, I am as certain as a man can be, that every one of these Injins is in fact a Jew; and yet, you have seen how small has been my success in persuading them to be of the right way of thinking on this subject."

"I have always noticed that men stick even to their defects, when they're nat'ral," returned the bee-hunter. "Even a nigger will stand up for his color, and why shouldn't an Injin. You began wrong, parson. Had you just told these chiefs that they were Jews, they might have stood *that*, poor creatures, for they hardly know how mankind looks upon a Jew; but you went to work to skin them, in a lump, making so many poor, wishy-washy palefaces of all the redskins, in a body. You and I may fancy a white face better than one of any other color, but nature colors the eye when it colors the body, and there's not a nigger in America who doesn't think black the pink of beauty."

"Perhaps it was proceeding too fast to say anything about the change of color, Bourdon. But what can a Christian minister do, unless he tell the truth? Adam could have been but of one color; and all the races on earth, one excepted, must have changed from that one color."

"Ay, and my life on it that all the races on 'arth believe

that one color to have been just that which has fallen to the luck of each partic'lar shade. Hang me if I should like to be persuaded out of my color, any more than these Injins! In America color goes for a great deal; and it may count for as much with an Injin as among us whites. No, no, parson; you should have begun with persuading these savages into the notion that they're Jews; if you could get along with *that*, the rest might be all the easier."

"You speak of the Jews, not as if you considered them a chosen people of the Lord, but as a despised and hateful race. This is not right, Bourdon. I know that Christians are thus apt to regard them, but it does not tell well for their charity or their knowledge."

"I know very little about them, Parson Amen; not being certain of ever having seen a Jew in my life. Still, I will own that I have a sort of grudge against them, though I can hardly tell you why. Of one thing I feel certain—no man breathing should ever persuade me into the notion that *I'm* a Jew, lost or found; ten tribes or twenty. What say you, corporal, to this idee?"

"Just as you say, Bourdon. Jews, Turks, and infidels I despise; so was I brought up, and so I shall remain."

"Can either of you tell me *why* you look in this uncharitable light on so many of your fellow-creatures? It cannot be Christianity, for such is not its teachings or feelings. Nor is either of you very remarkable for his observance of the laws of God, as they have been revealed to Christian people. *My* heart yearns towards these Injins, who are infidels, instead of entertaining any of the feelings that the corporal has just expressed."

"I wish there were fewer of them, and that them few were farther from Castle Meal," put in Le Bourdon, with point. "I have known all along that Peter meant to have a great council; but will own, now that I have seen something of it, I do not find it quite as much to my mind as I had expected it would be."

"There's a strong force on 'em," said the corporal, "and a hard set be they to look at. When a man's a young soldier, all this paint, and shaving of heads, and rings in noses

and ears, makes some impression ; but a campaign or two
ag'in the fellows soon brings all down to one color and one
uniform, if their naked hides can be so called. I told 'em
off, Bourdon, and reconn'itred 'em pretty well, while they
was a-making speeches ; and, in my judgment, we can hold
good the garrison ag'in 'em all, if so be we do not run short
of water. Provisions and water is what a body may call
fundamentals, in a siege.''

" I hope we shall have no need of force—nay, I feel persuaded there will not be,'' said Parson Amen. '' Peter is
our friend, and his command over these savages is wonderful !   Never before have I seen redmen so completely under
the control of a chief. Your men at Fort Dearborn, corporal, were scarcely more under the orders of their officers
than these redskins are under the orders of this chief !''

" I will not go to compare rig'lars with Injins, Mr. Parson,'' answered the corporal, a little stiffly. " They be not
of the same natur' at all, and ought not to be put on a footing, in any partic'lar. These savages may obey their orders,
after a fashion of their own ; but I should like to see them
manœuvre under fire. I 've fit Injins fourteen times, in my
day, and have never seen a decent line, or a good, honest,
manly, stand-up charge made by the best among 'em, in
any field, far or near. Trees and covers is necessary to their
constitutions, just as sartain as a deer chased will take to
water to throw off the scent. Put 'em up with the baggonet,
and they 'll not stand a minute.''

" How should they, corporal,'' interrupted Le Bourdon,
laughing, "when they 've no baggonets of their own to
make a stand with ? You put me in mind of what my father
used to say. He was a soldier in revolution times, and
sarved his seven years with Washington. The English used
to boast that the Americans would n't ' stand up to the rack,'
if the baggonet was set to work ; ' but this was before we
got our own tooth-picks,' said the old man. ' As soon as
they gave *us* baggonets, too, there was no want of standing
up to the work.' It seems to me, corporal, you overlook the
fact that Injins carry no baggonets.''

" Every army uses its own weapons. If an Injin prefers his knife and his tomahawk to a baggonet, it is no affair of mine. I speak of a charge as I see it ; and the soldier who relies on a tomahawk instead of a baggonet should stand in his tracks and give tomahawk play. No, no, Bourdon, seeing is believing. These redskins can do nothing with our people, when our people is properly regimented, well officered, and thoroughly drilled. They're skeary to new-beginners—*that* I must acknowledge ; but beyond that I set them down as nothing remarkable as military men."

"Good or bad, I wish there were fewer of them, and that they were farther off. This man Peter is a mystery to me ; sometimes he seems quite friendly ; then, ag'in, he appears just ready to take all our scalps. Do you know much of his past history, Mr. Amen?"

"Not as much as I wish I did," the missionary replied. "No one can tell me aught concerning Peter beyond the fact of his being a sort of a prophet, and a chief of commanding influence. Even his tribe is unknown ; a circumstance that points us to the ancient history of the Jews for the explanation. It is my own opinion that Peter is of the race of Aaron, and that he is designed by Divine Providence to play an important part in the great events on which we touch. All that is wanting is to persuade *him* into this belief, himself. Once persuade a man that he is intended to be something, and your work is half done to your hands. But the world is so full of ill-digested and random theories that truth has as much as it can do to obtain a sober and patient hearing!"

Thus is it with poor human nature. Let a man get a crotchet into his head, however improbable it may be, however little supported by reason or fact, however ridiculous, indeed, and he becomes indisposed to receive any evidence but that which favors his theory ; to see any truths but such as he fancies will harmonize with *his* truths ; or to allow of any disturbing causes in the great workings of his particular philosophy. This notion of Parson Amen's concerning the origin of the North American savage did not originate with that simple-minded enthusiast by any means. In this way are notions formed and nurtured. The missionary had read somewhat concerning the probability that the American Indians were the lost tribes of Israel, and, possessed with the idea, everything he saw was tortured into evidence in support of his theory. There is just as much reason for supposing that any and all of the heathen savages that are scattered up and down the earth have this origin, as to ascribe it to our immediate tribes; but to this truth the good parson was indifferent, simply because it did not come within the circle of his particular belief.

Thus, too, was it with the corporal. Unless courage and other military qualities were manifested precisely in the way in which *he* had been trained, they were not courage and military qualities at all. Every virtue has its especial and conventional accessories, according to this school of morals; nothing of the sort remaining as it came from above, in the simple abstract qualities of right and wrong. On such feelings and principles as these do men get to be dogmatical, narrow-minded, and conceited!

Our three white men pursued their way back to the "garrison," conversing as they went, much in the manner they did in the dialogue we have just recorded. Neither Parson Amen nor the corporal seemed to apprehend any thing, notwithstanding the extraordinary scene in which one had been an actor, and of which the other had been a witness. Their wonder and apprehensions, no doubt, were much mitigated by the fact that it was understood Peter was to meet a large collection of the chiefs in the Openings, and the minds of all were more or less prepared to see some such assemblage as had that night got together. The free manner in which the mysterious chief led the missionary to the circle was, of itself, some proof that *he* did not desire concealment; and even Le Bourdon admitted, when they came to discuss the details, that this was a circumstance that told materially in favor of the friendliness of his intentions. Still, the bee-hunter had his doubts; and most sincerely did he wish that all in Castle Meal, Blossom in particular, were safe within the limits of civilized settlements.

On reaching the "garrison," all was safe. Whiskey Centre watched the gate, a sober man now, perforce if not by inclination; for being in the Openings, in this respect, is like being at sea with an empty spirit-room. He was aware that several had passed out, but was surprised to learn that Peter was of the number. That gate Peter had not passed, of a certainty; and how else he could quit the palisades was not easily understood. It was possible to climb over them, it is true; but the feat would be attended with so great an exertion, and would be so likely to lead to a noise which would expose the effort, that all had great difficulty in believing a man so dignified and reserved in manner as this mysterious chief would be apt to resort to such means of quitting the place.

As for the Chippewa, Gershom reported his return a few minutes before, and the bee-hunter entered to look for that tried friend, as soon as he learned the fact. He found Pigeonswing laying aside his accoutrements, previously to lying down to take his rest.

"So, Chippewa, *you* have come back, have you!" exclaimed Le Bourdon. "So many of your redskin brethren are about, that I didn't expect to see you again for these two or three days."

"No want to eat den, eh? How you all eat, if hunter don't do he duty? S'pose squaw don't cook vittles, you no like it, eh? Juss so wid hunter—no *kill* vittles, don't like it nudder."

"This is true enough. Still, so many of your people are about, just now, that I thought it probable you might wish to remain outside with them for a day or two."

"How you know redman about, eh? You *see* him—you *count* him, eh?"

"I have seen something like fifty, and may say I counted that many. They were all chiefs, however, and I take it for granted a goodly number of common warriors are not far off. Am I right, Pigeonswing?"

"S'pose don't know—den can't tell. Only tell what he know."

"Sometimes an Injin *guesses*, and comes as near the

truth as a white man who has seen the thing with his own eyes.''

Pigeonswing made no answer, though Le Bourdon fancied, from his manner, that he had really something on his mind, and that, too, of importance, which he wished to communicate.

"I think you might tell me some news that I should like to hear, Chippewa, if you was so minded.''

"Why you stay here, eh?'' demanded the Indian, abruptly. "Got plenty honey—bess go home now. Always bess go home when hunt up. Home good place, when hunter well tired.''

"My home is here, in the Openings, Pigeonswing. When I go into the settlements, I do little but loaf about among the farm-houses on the Detroit River, having neither squaw nor wigwam of my own to go to. I like this place well enough, if your red brethren will let me keep it in peace.''

"Dis bad place for pale-face, juss now. Better go home dan stay in Openin'. If don't know short path to Detroit, I show you. Bess go soon as can ; and bess go *alone*. No good to be trouble wid squaw, when in hurry.''

The countenance of Le Bourdon changed at this last intimation, though the Indian might not have observed it in the darkness. After a brief pause, the first answered in a very determined way.

"I believe I understand you, Chippewa,'' he said. "I shall do nothing of the sort, however. If the squaws can't go, too, I shall not quit them. Would you desert *your* squaws because you thought them in trouble?''

"Ain't your squaw yet. Bess not have squaw at all, when Openin' so full of Injin. Where you t'ink is two buck I shoot dis mornin', eh? Skin 'em, cut 'em up, hang 'em on tree, where wolf can't get 'em. Well, go on arter anudder ; kill *him*, too. Dere he is, inside of palisade, but no tudder two. He bot' gone, when I get back to tree. Two good buck as ever see! How you like dat, eh?''

"I care very little about it, since we have food enough,

and are not likely to want. So the wolves got your venison from the trees, after all your care ; ha ! Pigeonswing ? "

" Wolf don't touch him—wolf *can't* touch him. Moccasin been under tree. See him mark. Bess do as I tell you ; go home, soon as ever can. Short path to Detroit ; ain't two hundred pale-face mile."

" I see how it is, Pigeonswing ; I see how it is, and thank you for this hint, while I honor your good faith to your own people. But I cannot go to Detroit, in the first place, for that town and fort have fallen into the hands of the British. It might be possible for a canoe to get past in the night, and to work its way through into Lake Erie, but I cannot quit my friends. If you can put us *all* in the way of getting away from this spot, I shall be ready to enter into the scheme. Why can't we all get into the canoe, and go down stream, as soon as another night sets in ? Before morning we could be twenty miles on our road."

" No do any good," returned Pigeonswing, coldly. " If can't go alone, can't go at all. Squaw no keep up, when so many be on trail. No good to try canoe. Catch you in two day—p'raps one. Well, I go to sleep—can't keep eye open all night."

Hereupon Pigeonswing coolly repaired to his skins, lay down, and was soon fast asleep. The bee-hunter was fain to do the same, the night being now far advanced ; but he lay awake a long time, thinking of the hint he had received, and pondering on the nature of the danger which menaced the security of the family. At length sleep asserted its power over even him, and the place lay in the deep stillness of night.

CHAPTER XIX.

" And stretching out on either hand,
    O'er all that wide and unshorn land,
    Till weary of its gorgeousness
    The aching and the dazzled eye
    Rests, gladden'd, on the calm, blue sky."

WHITTIER.

NO other disturbance occurred in the course of the night. With the dawn, Le Bourdon was again stirring; and as he left the palisades to repair to the run, in order to make his ablutions, he saw Peter returning to Castle Meal. The two met, but no allusion was made to the manner in which the night had passed. The chief paid his salutations courteously, and, instead of repairing to his skins, he joined Le Bourdon, seemingly as little inclined to seek for rest as if just arisen from his lair. When the bee-hunter left the spring, this mysterious Indian for the first time spoke of business.

" My brother wanted to-day to show Injin how to find honey," said Peter, as he and Bourdon walked towards the palisades, within which the whole family was now moving. " I nebber see honey find, myself, ole as I be."

" I shall be very willing to teach your chiefs my craft," answered the bee-hunter, " and this so much the more readily because I do not expect to prac*tyse* it much longer myself; not in this part of the country, at least."

" How dat happen? Expec' go away soon? " demanded Peter, whose keen, restless eye would at one instant seem to read his companion's soul, and then would glance off to some distant object, as if conscious of its own startling and

285

fiery expression. "Now Brish got Detroit, where my broder
go? Bess stay here, I t'ink."

"I shall not be in a hurry, Peter; but my season will
soon be up, and I must get ahead of the bad weather, you
know, or a bark canoe will have but a poor time of it on
Lake Huron. When am I to meet the chiefs, to give them
a lesson in finding bees?"

"Tell by-'em-by. No hurry for dat. Want to sleep
fuss. See so much better, when I open eye. So you t'ink
of makin' journey on long path. If can't go to Detroit,
where can go to?"

"My proper home is in Pennsylvany, on the other side
of Lake Erie. It is a long path, and I'm not certain of
getting safely over it in these troubled times. Perhaps it
would be best for me, however, to shape at once for Ohio;
if in that State I might find my way round the end of Erie,
and so go the whole distance by land."

The bee-hunter said this by way of throwing dust into
the Indian's eyes, for he had not the least intention of travelling in the direction named. It is true, it was *his* most
direct course, and the one that prudence would point out to
him, under all the circumstances, had he been alone. But
Le Bourdon was no longer alone, in heart and feelings at
least. Margery now mingled with all his views for the
future, and he could no more think of abandoning her in
her present situation, than he could of offering his own
person to the savages for a sacrifice. It was idle to think
of attempting such a journey in company with the females,
and most of all to attempt it in defiance of the ingenuity,
perseverance, and hostility of the Indians. The trail could
not be concealed; and, as for speed, a party of the young
men of the wilderness would certainly travel two miles to
Margery's one.

Le Bourdon, notwithstanding Pigeonswing's remonstrances, still had his eye on the Kalamazoo. He remembered the saying that "water leaves no trail," and was
not without hopes of reaching the lake again, where he
felt he should be in comparative security; his own canoe,
as well as that of Gershom, being large, well fitted, and

not altogether unsuited to those waters, in the summer
months. As it would be of the last importance, however,
to get several hours' start of the Indians, in the event of
his having recourse to such a mode of flight, it was of the
utmost importance also to conceal his intentions, and, if
possible, to induce Peter to imagine his eyes were turned
in another direction.

"Well, s'pose go dat way," answered the chief, quietly,
as if suspecting no artifice. "Set 'bout him by-'em-by.
To-day muss teach Injin how to find honey. Dat make
him good friend; and maybe he help my pale-face broders
back to deir country. Been better for ebberybody if none
come here at all."

Thus ended the discourse for that moment. Peter was
not fond of much talking, when he had not his great object
in view, but rather kept his mind occupied in observation.
For the next hour, every one in and about Castle Meal was
engaged in the usual morning avocations, that of breaking
their fasts included; and then it was understood that all
were to go forth to meet the chiefs, that Le Bourdon
might give a specimen of his craft.

One ignorant of the state of political affairs on the
American continent, and who was not aware of the vicinity
of savages, would have seen nothing that morning, as the
party proceeded on its little excursion in and around that
remote spot, but a picture of rural tranquillity and peace.
A brighter day never poured its glories on the face of
the earth; and the openings and the glades, and even the
dark and denser forests were all bathed in the sunlight, as
that orb is known to illuminate objects in the softer season
of the year, and in the forty-third degree of latitude.
Even the birds appeared to rejoice in the beauties of the
time, and sang and fluttered among the oaks in numbers
greater than common. Nature usually observes a stern
fitness in her adaptation of means to ends. Birds are to be
found in the forests, on the prairies, and in the still unten-
anted openings of the West, and often in countless numbers; more especially those birds which fly in flocks, and
love the security of unoccupied regions—unoccupied by

man is meant—wherein to build their nests, obey the laws of their instincts, and fulfil their destinies. Thus, myriads of pigeons and ducks and geese, etc., are to be found in the virgin woods, while the companionable and friendly robin, the little melodious wren, the thrush, the lark, the swallow, the marten, and all those pleasant little winged creatures that flit about our dwellings and grounds, and seem to be sent by Providence expressly to chant their morning and evening hymns to God in our ears, most frequent the peopled districts. It has been said by Europeans that the American birds are mute, in comparison with those of the Old World. This is true, to a certain extent, as respects those which are properly called forest birds, which do, in general, appear to partake of the sombre character that marks the solemn stillness of their native haunts. It is not true, however, with the birds which live in our fields and grounds and orchards, each of which sings its song of praise, and repeats its calls and its notes, as richly and as pleasantly to the ear as the birds of other lands. One large class, indeed, possesses a faculty that enables it to repeat every note it has ever heard, even to some of the sounds of quadrupeds. Nor is this done in the discordant tones of the parrot, but in octaves and trills, and in rich contraltos, and all the other pleasing intonations known to the most gifted of the feathered race. Thus it is that one American mocking-bird can outsing all the birds of Europe united.

It seemed that morning as if every bird that was accustomed to glean its food from the neighborhood of Castle Meal was on the wing, and ready to accompany the party that now sallied forth to catch the bee. This party consisted of Le Bourdon himself, as its chief and leader, of Peter, the missionary, and the corporal. Margery, too, went along; for as yet she had never seen an exhibition of Boden's peculiar skill. As for Gershom and his wife, they remained behind, to make ready the noontide meal; while the Chippewa took his accoutrements and again sallied out on a hunt. The whole time of this Indian appeared to be thus taken up; though, in truth, venison and bear's meat both abounded, and there was much less necessity for those constant efforts than he wished to make it appear. In good sooth, more than half his time was spent in making those observations which had led to the advice he had been urging on his friend, the bee-hunter, in order to induce him to fly. Had Pigeonswing better understood Peter, and had he possessed a clearer insight into the extent and magnitude of his plans of retributive vengeance, it is not probable his uneasiness, at the moment, would have been so great, or the urgency for an immediate decision on the part of Le Bourdon would have appeared as urgently pressing as it now seemed to be.

The bee-hunter took his way to a spot that was at some distance from his habitation, a small prairie of circular form, that is now generally known in that region of the country by the name of Prairie Round. Three hours were necessary to reach it, and this so much the more because Margery's shorter steps were to be considered. Margery, however, was no laggard on a path. Young, active, light of foot, and trained in exertions of this nature, her presence did not probably retard the arrival many minutes.

The extraordinary part of the proceedings was the circumstance that the bee-hunter did not tell any one whither he was going, and that Peter did not appear to care about putting the question to him. Notwithstanding this reserve on one side and seeming indifference on the other, when the party reached Prairie Round, every one of the chiefs who had been present at the council of the previous night was there before it. The Indians were straggling about, but remained sufficiently near the point where the bee-hunter and his followers reached the prairie, to assemble around the group in a very few minutes after it made its appearance. All this struck Le Bourdon as fearfully singular, since it proved how many secret means of communication existed between these savages. That the inmates of the habitations were closely observed, and all their proceedings noted, he could not but suspect, even before receiving this proof of Peter's power ; but he was not aware,

until now, how completely he and all with him were at the
mercy of these formidable foes. What hope could there be
for escape, when hundreds of eyes were thus watching their
movements, and every thicket had its vigilant and sagacious
sentinel? Yet must flight be attempted, in some way or
other, or Margery and her sister would be hopelessly lost, to
say nothing of himself and the three other men.

But the appearance of the remarkable little prairie that
he had just reached, and the collection of chiefs, now occupied all the present thoughts of Le Bourdon. As for
the first, it is held in repute, even at the present hour, as
a place that the traveller should see, though covered with
farms and the buildings that belong to husbandry. It is
still visited as a picture of ancient civilization, placed in the
setting of a new country. It is true that very little of this
part of Michigan wears much, if any, of that aspect of a
rough beginning, including stubs, stumps, and circled trees,
that it has so often fallen to our share to describe. There
are dense forests, and those of considerable extent; and
wherever the axe is put into *them*, the progress of improvement is marked by the same steps as elsewhere; but the
lovely Openings form so many exceptions as almost to com-
pose the rule.

On Prairie Round there was even a higher stamp of
seeming civilization—seeming, since it was nature, after all,
that had mainly drawn the picture. In the first place, the
spot had been burnt so recently as to leave the entire expanse covered with young grasses and flowers, the same as
if it were a well-kept park. This feature, at that advanced
period of the summer, was in some degree accidental, the
burning of the prairies depending more or less on contin-
gencies of that sort. We have now less to do with the
cause than with its consequences. These were most agreeable to the eye, as well as comfortable to the foot, the grass
nowhere being of a height to impede movement, or, what
was of still more importance to Le Bourdon's present pursuit, to overshadow the flowers. Aware of this fact, he had
led his companions all that distance, to reach this scene of
remarkable rural beauty, in order that he might make a

grand display of his art in the presence of the assembled chiefs of that region. The bee-hunter had pride in his craft, the same as any other skilful workman who had gained a reputation by his cunning, and he now trode the prairie with a firmer step and a more kindling eye than was his wont in the commoner haunts of his calling. Men were there whom it might be an honor to surprise, and pretty Margery was there also, she who had so long desired to see this very exhibition.

But, to revert once more to the prairie, ere we commence the narrative of what occurred on it. This well-known area is of no great extent, possessing a surface about equal to that of one of the larger parks of Europe. Its name was derived from its form, which, without being absolutely regular, had so near an approach to a circle as to justify the use of the appellation. The face of this charming field was neither waving, or what is called "rolling," nor a dead flat, as often occurs with river bottoms. It had just enough of undulation to prevent too much moisture, and to impart an agreeable variety to its plain. As a whole, it was clear of the forest; quite as much so as if the axe had done its work there a thousand years before, though wood was not wanting. On the contrary, enough of the last was to be seen, in addition to that which formed the frame of this charming landscape, to relieve the view from all appearance of monotony, and to break it up into copses, thickets, trees in small clusters, and in most of the varieties that embellish native scenery. One who had been unexpectedly transferred to the spot might well have imagined that he was looking on the site of some old and long-established settlement, from which every appliance of human industry had been suddenly and simultaneously abstracted. Of houses, out-buildings, fences, stacks, and husbandry, there were no signs; unless the even and verdant sward, that was spread like a vast carpet, sprinkled with flowers, could have been deemed a sign of the last. There were the glades, vistas, irregular lawns, and woods, shaped with the pleasing outlines of the free hand of nature, as if consummate art had been endeavoring to imitate our great mistress in one of her most graceful moods.

The Indians present served largely to embellish this scene. Of late years, horses have become so common among the western tribes, the vast natural meadows of those regions furnishing the means necessary to keep them, that one can now hardly form a picture of those savages without representing them mounted and wielding the spear ; but such was not the fact at the time of which we are writing, nor was it ever the general practice to go mounted among the Indians in the immediate vicinity of the great lakes. Not a hoof of any sort was now visible, with the exception of those which belonged to a herd of deer, that were grazing on a favorite spot less than a league distant from the place where Le Bourdon and his companions reached the prairie. All the chiefs were on foot, and very few were equipped with more than the knife and tomahawk, the side arms of a chief; the rifles having been secreted, as it might be, in deference to the festivities and peaceful character of the occasion. As Le Bourdon's party was duly provided with rifles, the missionary and Margery excepted, this was a sign that no violence was contemplated on that occasion at least. "Contemplated," however, is a word very expressive, when used in connection with the outbreakings of human passions, as they are wont to exhibit themselves among the ignorant and excited. It matters not whether the scene be the capital of some ancient European monarchy, or the wilds of America, the workings of such impulses are much the same. Now a throne is overturned, perhaps, before they who do it are yet fully aware of what they ought to set up in its place ; and now the deadly rifle or the murderous tomahawk is used, more in obedience to the incentives of demons than in furtherance of justly recognized rules of conduct. Le Bourdon was aware of all this, and did not so far confide in appearances as to overlook the watchfulness that he deemed indispensable.

The bee-hunter was not long in selecting a place to set up his apparatus. In this particular he was mainly governed by a lovely expanse of sweet-scented flowers, among which bees in thousands were humming, sipping of their precious gifts at will. Le Bourdon had a care, also, not to go far

from the forests which encircled the prairies, for among its
trees he knew he had to seek the habitations of the insects.
Instead of a stump, or a fallen tree, he had prepared a light
frame-work of lath, which the corporal bore to the field for
him, and on which he placed his different implements, as
soon as he had selected the scene of operations.

It will not be necessary for us to repeat the process, which
has already been described in our opening chapters ; but we
shall only touch such parts of it as have a direct connection
with the events of the legend. As Le Bourdon commenced
his preparations, however, the circle of chiefs closed around
him, in mute but close attention to everything that passed.
Although every one of them had heard of the bee-hunters
of the pale-faces, and most of them had heard of this particular individual of their number, not an Indian present
had ever seen one of these men practise his craft. This may
seem strange, as respects those who so much roamed the
woods ; but we have already remarked that it exceeded the
knowledge of the redman to make the calculations that are
necessary to take the bee by the process described. Usually, when he obtains honey, it is the result of some chance-
meeting in the forest, and not the fruits of that far-sighted and
persevering industry which enables the white man to lay in
a store large enough to supply a neighborhood, in the course
of a few weeks' hunting.

Never was a juggler watched with closer attention than
was Le Bourdon while setting up his stand and spreading his
implements. Every grave, dark countenance was turned
towards him, and each keen, glistening eye was riveted on
his movements. As the vessel with the comb was set down,
the chiefs nearest, recognizing the substance, murmured
their admiration ; for to them it seemed as if the operator
were about to make honey with honey. Then the glass was
a subject of surprise ; for half of those present had never
seen such an utensil before. Though many of the chiefs
present had visited the "garrisons" of the Northwest, both
American and English, many had not, and of those who
had, not one in ten had got any clear idea of the commonest
appliances of civilized life. Thus it was, then, that almost

every article used by the bee-hunter, though so simple and homely, was the subject of a secret but well-suppressed admiration.

It was not long ere Le Bourdon was ready to look for his bee. The insects were numerous on the flowers, particularly on the white clover, which is indigenous in America, springing up spontaneously wherever grasses are permitted to grow. The great abundance of the bees, however, had its usual effect, and our hero was a little difficult to please. At length a fine and already half-loaded little animal was covered by the glass, and captured. This was done so near the group of Indians that each and all noted the process. It was curious, and it was inexplicable! Could the pale-faces compel bees to reveal the secret of their hives, and was that encroaching race about to drive all the insects from the woods and seize their honey, as they drove the Indians before them and seized their lands? Such was the character of the thoughts that passed through the minds of more than one chief, that morning, though all looked on in profound stillness.

When the imprisoned bee was put over the comb, and Le Bourdon's cap was placed above all, these simple-minded children of the woods and the prairies gazed, as if expecting a hive to appear beneath the covering, whenever the latter should be removed. It was not long before the bee "settled," and not only the cap, but the tumbler, was taken away. For the first time since the exhibition commenced, Le Bourdon spoke, addressing himself to Peter.

"If the tribeless chief will look sharply," he said, "he will soon see the bee take flight. It is filling itself with honey, and the moment it is loaded—look—look—it is about to rise—there, it is up—see it circling around the stand, as if to take a look that it may know it again—there it goes!"

There it did go, of a truth, and in a regular bee-line, or as straight as an arrow. Of all that crowd, the bee-hunter and Margery alone saw the insect in its flight. Most of those present lost sight of it while circling around the stand; but the instant it darted away, to the remainder it seemed to vanish into air. Not so with Le Bourdon and Margery,

however. The former saw it from habit ; the latter from a
quick eye, intense attention, and the wish not to miss anything that Le Bourdon saw fit to do for her information or
amusement. The animal flew in an air line towards a point
of wood distant fully half a mile, and on the margin of the
prairie.

Many low exclamations arose among the savages. The
bee was gone, but whither they knew not, or on what errand.
Could it have been sent on a message by the pale-face, or
had it flown off to give the alarm to its companions, in order
to adopt the means of disappointing the bee-hunter? As
for the last, he went coolly to work to choose another insect ;
and he soon had three at work on the comb—all in company,
and all uncovered. Had the number anything to do with
the charm, or were these three to be sent to bring back the
one that had already gone away? Such was the sort of
reasoning, and such the queries put to themselves, by several
of the stern children of nature who were drawn up around
the stand.

In the meantime Le Bourdon proceeded with his operations in the utmost simplicity. He now called Peter and
Bear's Meat and Crowsfeather nearer to his person, where
they might share with Margery the advantage of more
closely seeing all that passed. As soon as these three chiefs
were near enough, Ben pointed to one bee in particular,
saying in the Indian dialect,—

"My brothers see that bee in the centre—he is about to
go away. If he go after the one that went before him I
shall soon know where to look for honey."

"How can my brother tell which bee will first fly away?"
demanded Bear's Meat.

The bee-hunter was able to foresee this, by knowing which
insect had been longest on the comb ; but so practised had
his eye become that he knew with tolerable accuracy, by the
movements of the creatures, those that had filled themselves
with honey from those that had not. As it did not suit his
purposes, however, to let all the minutiæ of his craft be
known, his answer was evasive. Just at that moment a
thought occurred to him, which it might be well to carry out

in full.   He had once saved his life by necromancy, or what
seemed to the simple children of the woods to be necromancy, and why might he not turn the cunning of his regular art to account, and render it the means of rescuing the
females, as well as himself, from the hands of their captors?
This sudden impulse from that moment controlled his conduct ; and his mind was constantly casting about for the
means of effecting what was now his one great purpose—
escape.   Instead of uttering, in reply to Bear's Meat's question, the simple truth, therefore, he rather sought for such
an answer as might make the process in which he was engaged appear imposing and mystical.

"How do the Injins know the path of the deer?" he
asked, by way of reply.   "They look at the deer, get to
know him, and understand his ways.   This middle bee will
soon fly."

"Which way will he go?" asked Peter.   "Can my
brother tell us *that?*"

"To his hive," returned Le Bourdon, carelessly, as if he
did not fully understand the question.   "All of them go to
their hives, unless I tell them to go in another direction.
See, the bee is up!"

The chiefs now looked with all their eyes.   They saw,
indeed, that the bee was making its circles above the stand.
Presently they lost sight of the insect, which to them seemed
to vanish ; though Le Bourdon distinctly traced its flight
for a hundred yards.   It took a direction at right angles to
that of the first bee, flying off into the prairie, and shaping
its course towards an island of wood, which might have been
of three or four acres in extent, and distant rather less than
a mile.

While Le Bourdon was noting this flight, another bee
arose.   This creature flew towards the point of forest already
mentioned as the destination of the insect that had first
risen.   No sooner was this third little animal out of sight,
than the fourth was up, humming around the stand.   Ben
pointed it out to the chiefs ; and this time they succeeded in
tracing the flight for perhaps a hundred feet from the spot
where they stood.   Instead of following either of its com-

panions, this fourth bee took a course which led it off the prairie altogether, and towards the habitations.

The suddenly-conceived purpose of Le Bourdon to attempt to mystify the savages, and thus get a hold upon their minds which he might turn to advantage, was much aided by the different directions taken by these several bees. Had they all gone the same way, the conclusion that all went home would be so very natural and obvious as to deprive the discovery of a hive of any supernatural merit, at least; and to establish this was just now the great object the bee-hunter had in view. As it was, the Indians were no wiser, now all the bees were gone, than they had been before one of them had flown. On the contrary, they could not understand how the flights of so many insects, in so many different directions, should tell the bee-hunter where honey was to be found. Le Bourdon saw that the prairie was covered with bees, and well knew that, such being the fact, the inmates of perhaps a hundred different hives must be present. All this, however, was too novel and too complicated for the calculations of savages; and not one of those who crowded near, as observers, could account for so many of the bees going different ways.

Le Bourdon now intimated a wish to change his ground. He had noted two of the bees, and the only question that remained to be decided, as *it* respected *them*, was whether they belonged to the precise points towards which they had flown, or to points beyond them. The reader will easily understand that this is the nature of the fact determined by taking an angle, the point of intersection between any two of the lines of flight being necessarily the spot where the hive is to be found. So far from explaining this to those around him, however, Boden kept it a secret in his own breast. Margery knew the whole process, for to *her* he had often gone over it in description, finding a pleasure in instructing one so apt, and whose tender, liquid blue eyes seemed to reflect every movement of his own soul and feelings. Margery he could have taught forever, or fancied for the moment he could; which is as near the truth as men under the influence of love often get. But as for the Indians, so

far from letting them into any of his secrets, his strong desire was now to throw dust into their eyes, in all possible
ways, and to make their well-established character for superstition subservient to his own projects.

Boden was far from being a scholar, even for one in his
class in life. Down to this hour, the neglect of the means
of public instruction is somewhat of a just ground of reproach against the venerable and respectable commonwealth
of which he was properly a member, though her people
have escaped a knowledge of a great deal of small philosophy and low intriguing which it is fair to presume that
evil spirits thrust in among the leaves of a more legitimate
information, when the book of knowledge is opened for the
instruction of those who, by circumstances, are prevented
from doing more than bestowing a few hurried glances at
its contents. Still, Ben had read everything about bees on
which he could lay his hands. He had studied their habits
personally, and he had pondered over the various accounts
of their communities,—a sort of limited monarchy in which
the prince is deposed occasionally, or when matters go very
wrong—some written by really very observant and intelligent persons, and others again not a little fanciful. Among
other books that had thus fallen in Le Bourdon's way was
one which somewhat minutely described the uses that were
made of the bees by the ancient soothsayers in their divina-
tions. Our hero had no notion of reviving those rites, or of
attempting to imitate the particular practices of which he
had read and heard ; but the recollection of them occurred
most opportunely to strengthen and encourage the design,
so suddenly entertained, of making his present operations
aid in opening the way to the one great thing of the hour—
an escape into Lake Michigan.

"A bee knows a great deal," said Le Bourdon to his
nearest companions, while the whole party was moving some
distance to take up new ground. "A bee often knows more
than a man."

"More than pale-face?" demanded Bear's Meat, a chief
who had attained his authority more by means of physical
than of intellectual qualities.

"Sometimes. Pale-faces have gone to bees to ask what

will happen. Let me ask our medicine-man this question. Parson Amen, have *you* any knowledge of the soothsayers of old using bees when they wished to know what was going to happen?"

Now the missionary was not a learned man any more than the bee-hunter; but many an unlearned man has heard of this, and he happened to be one of the number. Of Virgil, for instance, Parson Amen knew but little; though in the progress of a very loose but industrious course of reading, he had learned that the soothsayers put great faith in bees. His answer was given in conformity with this fact, and in the most perfect good faith, for he had not the smallest suspicion of what Boden wished to establish.

"Certainly, most certainly," answered the well-meaning missionary; "the fortune-tellers of old times often went to their bees when they wished to look into the future. It has been a subject much talked of among Christians, to account for the soothsaying and witchcraft and other supernatural dealings of those who lived in the times of the prophets; and most of them have held the opinion that evil spirits have been—nay, still are—permitted to work their will on certain men in the flesh. But bees were in much favor with the soothsayers of old."

This answer was given in English, and little of it was comprehended by Peter, and the others who had more or less knowledge of that language, beyond the part which asserted the agency of bees in witchcraft. Luckily, this was all Le Bourdon desired, and he was well satisfied at seeing that the idea passed from one chief to another; those who did not know the English at all being told by those who had some knowledge of the tongue, that "bees were thought to be ' medicine' among the pale-faces."

Le Bourdon gained a great deal of ground by this fortunate corroboration of his own still more fortunate thought. Matters were pretty nearly desperate with him, and with all his friends, should Peter really meditate evil; and as desperate diseases notoriously require remedies of the same character, he was ready to attempt anything that promised even the smallest chance of success.

"Yes, yes," the bee-hunter pursued the discourse by say-

ing, "bees know a great deal. I have sometimes thought
that bees know more than bears, and my brother must be
able to tell something of them?"

"Yes ; my name is Bear's Meat," answered that chief,
complacently. "Injins always give name that mean some-
t'ing. Kill so many bear one winter, got dat name."

"A good name it is ! To kill a bear is the most honorable thing a hunter can do, as we all know. If my brother
wishes to hear it, I will ask my bees when he is to kill another."

The savage to whom this was addressed fairly started
with delight. He was eagerly signifying his cheerful assent to the proposal, when Peter quietly interposed, and
changed the discourse to himself, in a way that he had,
and which would not easily admit of denial. It was apparent to Le Bourdon that this mysterious Indian was not
content that one so direct and impetuous in his feelings as
Bear's Meat, and who was at the same time so little qualified to manage his portion of an intellectual conversation,
should be foremost any longer. For that reason he brought
himself more into the foreground, leaving to his friend the
capacity of listener and observer, rather than that of a
speaker and actor. What took place under this new arrangement will appear as the narrative proceeds.

CHAPTER XX.

"Therefore, go with me ;
I 'll give thee fairies to attend on thee ;
And they shall fetch thee jewels from the deep,—
Peaseblossom ! Cobweb ! Moth ! and Mustardseed ! "
Midsummer-Night's Dream.

A S Le Bourdon kept moving across the prairie while the remarks were made that have been recorded in the preceeding chapter, he soon reached the new position where he intended to again set up his stand. Here he renewed his operations, Peter keeping nearest his person, in jealous watchfulness of the least movement he made. Bees were caught, and scarce a minute elapsed ere the bee-hunter had two of them on the piece of comb, uncovered and at liberty. The circumstance that the cap was momentarily placed over the insects struck the savages as a piece of necromancy, in particular. The reader will understand that this is done in order to darken the tumbler, and induce the bee to settle down on the honey so much the sooner. To one who understood the operation and its reason, the whole was simple enough ; but it was a very different matter with men as little accustomed to prying into the habits of creatures as insignificant as bees. Had deer, or bisons, or bears, or any of the quadrupeds of those regions been the subject of the experiment, it is highly probable that individuals could have been found in that attentive and wondering crowd who could have enlightened the ablest naturalists on the subject of the animals under examination ; but when the inquiry descended to the bee, it went below the wants and usages of savage life.

"Where you t'ink dis bee go?" demanded Peter, in English, as soon as Le Bourdon raised the tumbler.

"One will go in this direction, the other in that," answered the bee-hunter, pointing first towards the corner of the woods, then towards the island in the prairie, the two points towards which two of the other bees had flown.

The predictions might or might not prove true. If they did, the effect must be great; if they did not, the failure would soon be forgotten in matters of more interest. Our hero, therefore, risked but little, while he had the chance of gaining a very great advantage. By a fortunate coincidence, the result completely justified the prediction. A bee rose, made its circles around the stand, and away it went towards the island-like copse in the prairie; while its companion soon imitated its example, but taking the other prescribed direction. This time Peter watched the insects so closely that he was a witness of their movements, and with his own eyes he beheld the flight, as well as the direction taken by each.

"You tell bee do dis?" demanded Peter, with a surprise that was so sudden, as well as so great, that it overcame in some slight degree his habitual self-command.

"To be sure I did," replied Le Bourdon, carelessly. "If you wish to see another, you may."

Here the young man coolly took another bee, and put it on the comb. Indifferent as he appeared, however, he used what was perhaps the highest degree of his art in selecting this insect. It was taken from the bunch of flowers whence one of his former captives had been taken, and there was every chance of its belonging to the same hive as its companion. Which direction it might take, should it prove to be a bee from either of the two hives of which the positions were now known, it altogether exceeded Boden's art to tell, so he dexterously avoided committing himself. It was enough that Peter gazed attentively, and that he saw the insect dart away, disappearing in the direction of the island. By this time more of the savages were on the alert, and now knowing how and where to look for the bee, they also saw its course.

"You tell him ag'in go dere?" asked Peter, whose interest by this time was so manifest as to defy all attempts at concealment.

"To be sure I did. The bees obey *me*, as your young men obey *you*. I am their chief, and they *know* me. I will give you further proof of this. We will now go to that little bit of wood, when you shall all see what it contains. I have sent three of my bees there; and here one of them is already back, to let me know what he has seen."

Sure enough, a bee was buzzing around the head of Le Bourdon, probably attracted by some fragment of comb, and he cunningly converted it into a messenger from the copse! All this was wonderful to the crowd, and it even greatly troubled Peter. This man was much less liable to the influence of superstition than most of his people; but he was very far from being altogether above it. This is the fact with very few civilized men; perhaps with no man whatever, let his philosophy and knowledge be what they may; and least of all is it true with the ignorant. There is too much of the uncertain, of the conjectural, in our condition as human beings, to raise us altogether above the distrusts, doubts, wonder, and other weaknesses of our present condition. To these simple savages, the manner in which the bees flew, seemingly at Le Bourdon's bidding, to this or that thicket, was quite as much a matter of astonishment as any of our most elaborate deceptions are wonders to our own ignorant and vulgar. Ignorant! And where is the line to be drawn that is to place men beyond the pale of ignorance? Each of us fails in some one, if not in very many, of the important branches of the knowledge that is even reduced to rules among us. Here is seen the man of books, so ignorant of the application of his own beloved theories as to be a mere child in practice; and there again can be seen the expert in practice, who is totally unacquainted with a single principle of the many that lie at the root of his very handicraft. Let us not, then, deride these poor children of the forest, because that which was so entirely new to them should also appear inexplicable and supernatural.

As for Peter, he was more confounded than convinced. His mind was so much superior to those of the other chiefs as to render him far more difficult to mislead, though even he was not exempt from the great weaknesses of ignorance —superstition, and its concomitants, credulity and a love of the marvellous. His mind was troubled, as was quite apparent to Ben, who watched *him* quite as narrowly as he was observed himself, in all he did. Willing to deepen the impression, our artist now determined to exhibit some of the higher fruits of his skill. The production of a considerable quantity of honey would of itself be a sort of peace-offering, and he now prepared to turn the certainty of there being a hive in the little wood to account—certainty, because three bees had taken wing for it, and a very distinct angle had been made with two of them.

" Does my brother wish any honey? " asked Le Bourdon, carelessly ; " or shall I send a bee across Lake Michigan, to tell the Injins farther west that Detroit is taken? "

" Can Bourdon find honey now? " demanded Peter.

" Easily. Several hives are within a mile of us. The bees like this prairie, which is so well garnished with flowers, and I am never at a loss for work in this neighborhood. This is my favorite bee-ground ; and I have got all the little creatures so that they know me, and are ready to do everything that I tell them. As I see that the chiefs love honey, and wish to eat some, we will now go to one of my hives."

Thus saying, Le Bourdon prepared for another march. He moved with all his appliances, Margery keeping close at his side, carrying the honey-comb and honey. As the girl walked lightly, in advance of the Indians, some fifteen or twenty bees, attracted by the flavor of what she carried, kept circling around her head, and consequently around that of Boden ; and Peter did not fail to observe the circumstance. To him it appeared as if these bees were so many accompanying agents, who attended their master in order to do his bidding. In a word, Peter was fast getting into that frame of mind when all that is seen is pressed into the support of the theory we have adopted. The bee-hunter had some mysterious connection with and control over the bees, and this was one among the many other signs of the existence of his power. All this, however, Boden himself disregarded. His mind was bent on throwing dust into the eyes of the Indians ; and he was cogitating the means of so doing on a much larger scale than any yet attempted.

"Why dem bee fly 'round young squaw?" demanded Peter ; "and fly round you, too?"

"They know us, and go with us to their hive ; just as Injins would come out of their villages to meet and honor visitors."

This was a ready reply, but it scarcely satisfied the wily savage to whom it was given. Just then Crowsfeather led Peter a little aside, and began talking earnestly to that chief, both continuing on with the crowd. Le Bourdon felt persuaded that the subject of this private conference was some of his own former backslidings in the character of a conjurer, and that the Pottawattamie would not deal very tenderly with his character. Nevertheless, it was too late to retrace his steps, and he saw the necessity of going on.

"I wish you had not come out with us," the bee-hunter found an occasion to say to Margery. "I do not half like the state of things, and this conjuration about the bees may all fall through."

"It is better that I should be here, Bourdon," returned the spirited girl. "My being here may make them less unfriendly to you. When I am by, Peter always seems more human, and less of a savage, they all tell me, than when I am not by."

"No one can be more willing to own your power, Margery, than I ; but Injins hold the squaws too cheap to give you much influence over this old fellow."

"You do not know ; he may have had a daughter of about my age, or size, or appearance ; or with my laugh, or voice, or something else that reminds him of her, when he sees me. One thing I am sure of—Peter is no enemy of *mine*."

"I hope this may prove to be true! I do not see, after

all, why an Injin should not have the feelings you name. He is a man, and must feel for his wife and children, the same as other—"

"Bourdon, what ails the dog? Look at the manner in which Hive is behaving."

Sure enough, the appearance of Hive was sufficiently obvious to attract his master's attention. By this time the crowd had got within twenty rods of the little island-like copse of wood, the mastiff being nearly half that distance in advance. Instead of preceding the party, however, Hive had raised his form in a menacing manner, and moved cautiously from side to side, like one of his kind that scents a foe. There was no mistaking these movements, and all the principal chiefs soon had their attention also drawn to the behavior of the dog.

"Why he do so?" asked Peter. "He 'fraid of bee, eh?"

"He waits for me to come up," answered Le Bourdon. "Let my brother and two other chiefs come with me, and let the rest stay here. Bees do not like crowds. Corporal, I put Margery in your keeping, and Parson Amen will be near you. I now go to show these chiefs what a bee can tell a man."

Thus saying, Le Bourdon advanced, followed by Peter, Bear's Meat, and Crowsfeather. Our hero had made up his mind that something more than bees were to be found in the thicket; for, the place being a little marshy, bushes as well as trees were growing on it, and he fully expected a rencontre with bears, the creatures most disposed to prey upon the labors of the bee—man excepted. Being well armed, and accompanied by men accustomed to such struggles, he had no apprehensions, and led the way boldly, feeling the necessity of manifesting perfect confidence in all his own acts, in order to command the respect of the observers. As soon as the bee-hunter passed the dog, the latter growled, showed his teeth fiercely, and followed, keeping closely at his side. The confidence and alacrity with which Le Bourdon moved into the thicket compelled his companions to be on the alert; though the first broke through the belt of hazels which inclosed the more open area within, a few instants before the Indians reached the place. Then it was that there arose such a yell, such screechings and cries, as reached far over the prairie, and might have appalled the stoutest heart. The picture that was soon offered to the eye was not less terrific than the sounds which assailed the ear. Hundreds of savages, in their war-paint, armed, and in a crowded maze, arose as it might be by one effort, seemingly out of the earth, and began to leap and play their antics amid the trees. The sudden spectacle of a crowd of such beings, nearly naked, frightfully painted, and tossing their arms here and there, while each yelled like a demon, was enough to overcome the nerves of a very resolute man. But Le Bourdon was prepared for a conflict, and even felt relieved, rather than alarmed, when he saw the savages. His ready mind at once conceived the truth. This band belonged to the chiefs, and composed the whole or a principal part of the force which he knew they must have outlying somewhere on the prairies, or in the openings. He had sufficiently understood the hints of Pigeonswing to be prepared for such a meeting, and at no time, of late, had he approached a cover without remembering the possibility of its containing Indians.

Instead of betraying alarm, therefore, when this cloud of phantom-like beings rose before his eyes, Le Bourdon stood firm, merely turning towards the chiefs behind him, to ascertain if they were taken by surprise as well as himself. It was apparent that they were; for, understanding that a medicine ceremony was to take place on the prairie, these "young men" had preceded the party from the hut, and had, unknown to all their chiefs, got possession of this copse, as the best available cover whence to make their observations on what was going on.

"My brother sees his young men," said Le Bourdon, quietly, the instant a dead calm had succeeded to the outcries with which he had been greeted. "I thought he might wish to say something to them, and my bees told me where to find them. Does my brother wish to know anything else?"

Great was the wonder of the three chiefs at this exhibition of medicine power! So far from suspecting the truth, or of detecting the lucky coincidence by which Le Bourdon had been led to the cover of their warriors, it all appeared to them to be pure necromancy. Such an art must be of great service; and how useful it would be to the warrior on his path, to be accompanied by one who could thus command the vigilance of the bees!

"You find enemy all same as friend?" demanded Peter, letting out the thought that was uppermost, in the question.

"To be sure. It makes no difference with a bee; one can find an enemy as easily as he can find a friend."

"No whiskey spring dis time?" put in Crowsfeather, a little inopportunely, and with a distrust painted in his swarthy face that Le Bourdon did not like.

"Pottawattamie, you do not understand medicine-men. *Ought* I to have shown your young men where whiskey was to be had for nothing? Ask yourself that question. Did you wish to see your young men wallowing like hogs in such a spring? What would the great medicine-priest of the pale-faces, who is out yonder, have said to *that*?"

This was a *coupe de maître* on the part of the bee-hunter. Until that moment, the affair of the whiskey spring had weighed heavily in the balance against him; but now it was suddenly changed over in the scales, and told as strongly in his favor. Even a savage can understand the morality which teaches men to preserve their reason, and not to lower themselves to the level of brutes by swallowing "fire-water"; and Crowsfeather suddenly saw a motive for regarding our hero with the eyes of favor, instead of those of distrust and dislike.

"What the pale-face says is true," observed Peter to his companion. "Had he opened his spring, your warriors would have been weaker than women. He is a wonderful medicine-man, and we must not provoke him to anger. How *could* he know, but through his bees, that our young men were here?"

This question could not be answered; and when the chiefs, followed by the whole band of warriors, some three or four hundred in number, came out upon the open prairie, all that had passed was communicated to those who awaited their return, in a few brief but clear explanations. Le Bourdon found a moment to let Margery comprehend his position and views, while Parson Amen and the corporal were put sufficiently on their guard not to make any unfortunate blunder. The last was much more easily managed than the first. So exceedingly sensitive was the conscience of the priest, that had he clearly understood the game Le Bourdon was playing, he might have revolted at the idea of necromancy, as touching on the province of evil spirits ; but he was so well mystified as to suppose all that passed was regularly connected with the art of taking bees. In this respect he and the Indians equally resembled one of those familiar pictures in which we daily see men, in masses, contributing to their own deception and subjection, while they fondly but blindly imagine that they are not only inventors, but masters. This trade of mastery, after all, is the property of a very few minds ; and no precaution of the prudent, no forethought of the wary, nor any expedient of charters, constitutions, or restrictions, will prevent the few from placing their feet on the neck of the many. We may revive the fable of King Log and King Stork, as often and in as many forms as we will ; it will ever be the fable of King Log and King Stork. We are no admirers of political aristocracies, as a thousand paragraphs from our pen will prove ; and as for monarchs, we have long thought they best enact their parts when most responsible to opinion ; but we cannot deceive ourselves on the subject of the atrocities that are daily committed by those who are ever ready to assume the places of both, making their fellow-creatures in masses their dupes, and using those that they affect to serve.

Ben Boden was now a sort of "*gouvernement provisoire*" among the wondering savages who surrounded him. He had got them to believe in necromancy, a very considerable step toward the exercise of despotic power. It is true, he hardly knew himself what was to be done next ; but he saw quite distinctly that he was in a dilemma, and must manage to get out of it by some means or other.   If he could only succeed in this instance as well as he had succeeded in his former essay in the black art, all might be well, and Margery be carried in triumph into the settlements.   Margery, *pro hæc vice*, was his goddess of liberty, and he asked for no higher reward than to be permitted to live the remainder of his days in the sunshine of her smiles. Liberty ! a word that is, just now, in all men's mouths, but in how few hearts in its purity and truth !   What a melancholy mistake, moreover, to suppose that, could it be enjoyed in that perfection with which the imaginations of men love to cheat their judgments, it is the great good of life !   One hour spent in humble veneration of the Being that gave it, in common with all of earth, its vacillating and uncertain existence, is of more account than ages passed in its service ; and he who fancies that in worshipping liberty he answers the great end of his existence, hugs a delusion quite as weak, and infinitely more dangerous, than that which now came over the minds of Peter and his countrymen in reference to the intelligence of the bees. It is a good thing to possess the defective and qualified freedom which we term "liberty" ; but it is a grave error to set it up as an idol to be worshipped.

"What my brother do next?" demanded Bear's Meat, who, being a somewhat vulgar-minded savage, was all for striking and wonder-working exhibitions of necromancy. "P'raps he find some honey now?"

"If you wish it, chief.   What says Peter?   Shall I ask my bees to tell where there is a hive?"

As Peter very readily assented, Le Bourdon next set about achieving this new feat in his art.   The reader will recollect that the positions of two hives were already known to the bee-hunter, by means of that very simple and everyday process by which he earned his bread.   One of these hives was in the point of wood already mentioned, that lay along the margin of the prairie ; while the other was in this very copse where the savages had secreted themselves. Boden had now no thought of giving any further disturbance to this last-named colony of insects ; for an insight into their existence might disturb the influence obtained by the jugglery of the late discovery, and he at once turned his attention towards the other hive indicated by his bees.

Nor did Le Bourdon now deem it necessary to resort to his usual means of carrying on his trade. These were not necessary to one who knew already where the hive was to be found, while it opened the way to certain mummeries that might be made to tell well in support of his assumed character. Catching a bee, then, and keeping it confined within his tumbler, Ben held the last to his ear, as if listening to what the fluttering insect had to say. Having seemingly satisfied himself on this point, he desired the chiefs once more to follow him, having first let the bee go, with a good deal of ceremony. This set all in motion again, the party being now increased by the whole band of savages who had been "put up" from their cover.

By this time Margery began to tremble for the consequences. She had held several short conferences with Le Bourdon, as they walked together, and had penetrated far enough into his purposes to see that he was playing a ticklish game. It might succeed for a time, but she feared it must fail in the end; and there was always the risk of incurring the summary vengeance of savages. Perhaps she did not fully appreciate the power of superstition, and the sluggishness of the mind that once submits to its influence; while her woman's heart made her keenly alive to all those frightful consequences that must attend an exposure. Nevertheless, nothing could now be done to avert the consequences. It was too late to recede, and things must take their course, even at all the hazards of the case. That she might not be wholly useless, when her lover was risking so much for herself,—Margery well understanding that *her* escape was the only serious difficulty the bee-hunter apprehended,—the girl turned all her attention to Peter, in whose favor she felt she had been daily growing, and on whose pleasure so much must depend. Changing her position a little, she now came closer to the chief than she had hitherto done.

"Squaw like medicine-man?" asked Peter, with a significance of expression that raised a blush in Margery's cheek.

"You mean to ask me if I like to *see* medicine-men perform," answered Margery, with the readiness of her sex. "White women are always curious, they say; how is it with the women of the redmen?"

"Juss so—full of cur'osity. Squaw is squaw—no matter what color."

"I am sorry, Peter, you do not think better of squaws. Perhaps you never had a squaw—no wife, or daughter?"

A gleam of powerful feeling shot athwart the dark countenance of the Indian, resembling the glare of the electric fluid flashing on a cloud at midnight; but it passed away as quickly as it appeared, leaving in its stead the hard, condensed expression which the intensity of a purpose so long entertained and cultivated had imprinted there, as indelibly as if cut in stone.

"All chief have squaw—all chief have pappoose," was the answer that came at last. "What he good for, eh?"

"It is always good to have children, Peter; especially when the children themselves are good."

"Good for pale-face, maybe—no good for Injin. Pale-face glad when pappoose born—redskin sorry."

"I hope this is not so. Why should an Injin be sorry to see the laugh of his little son?"

"Laugh when he little—p'raps so; he little, and don't know what happen. But Injin don't laugh any more when he grow up. Game gone; land gone; corn-field gone. No more room for Injin—pale-face want all. Pale-face young man laugh—redskin young man cry. Dat how it is."

"Oh, I hope not, Peter! I should be sorry to think it was so. The redman has as good a right—nay, he has a *better* right to this country than the whites; and God forbid that he should not always have his full share of the land!"

Margery probably owed her life to that honest, natural burst of feeling, which was uttered with a warmth and sincerity that could leave no doubt that the sentiment expressed came from the heart. Thus singularly are we

constructed. A minute before, and no exemption was made in the mind of Peter, in behalf of this girl, in the plan he had formed for cutting off the whites; on the contrary, he had often bethought him of the number of young pale-faces that might be, as it were, strangled in their cradles, by including the bee-hunter and his intended squaw in the contemplated sacrifice. All this was changed, as in the twinkling of an eye, by Margery's honest and fervent expression of her sense of right, on the great subject that occupied all of Peter's thoughts. These sudden impulses in the direction of love for our species, the second of the high lessons left by the Redeemer to his disciples, are so many proofs of the creation of man in the image of his maker. They exert their power often when least expected, and are ever stamped by the same indelible impression of their divine origin. Without these occasional glimpses at those qualities which are so apt to lie dormant, we might indeed despair of the destinies of our race. We are, however, in safe and merciful hands; and all the wonderful events that are at this moment developing themselves around us are no other than the steps taken by Providence in the progress it is steadily making towards the great and glorious end! Some of the agencies will be corrupt; others deluded; and no one of them all, perhaps, will pursue with unerring wisdom the precise path that ought to be taken; but even the crimes, errors, and delusions will be made instrumental in achieving that which was designed before the foundations of this world were laid!

"Does my daughter wish this?" returned Peter, when Margery had thus frankly and sincerely given vent to her feelings. "Can a pale-face squaw wish to leave an Injin any of his hunting-grounds?"

"Thousands of us wish it, Peter, and I for one. Often and often have we talked of this around our family fire, and even Gershom, when his head has not been affected by fire-water, has thought as we all have thought. I know that Bourdon thinks so, too; and I have heard him say that he thought Congress ought to pass a law to prevent white men from getting any more of the Injin's lands."

The face of Peter would have been a remarkable study, during the few moments that his fierce will was in the process of being brought in subjugation to the influence of his better feelings. At first he appeared bewildered ; then compunction had its shade ; and human sympathy came last, asserting its long dormant but inextinguishable power. Margery saw some of this, though it far exceeded her penetration to read all the workings of that stern and savage mind ; yet she felt encouraged by what she did see and understand.

While an almighty and divine Providence was thus carrying out its own gracious designs in its own way, the bee-hunter continued bent on reaching a similar end by means of his own. Little did he imagine how much had been done for him within the last few moments, and how greatly all he had in view was jeoparded and put at risk by his own contrivances—contrivances which seemed to him so clever, but which were wanting in the unerring simplicity and truth that render those that come from above infallible. Still, the expedients of Le Bourdon may have had their agency in bringing about events, and may have been intended to be a part of that moral machinery which was now at work in the breast of Peter for good.

It will be remembered that the bee-hunter habitually carried a small spy-glass as a part of the implements of his calling. It enabled him to watch the bees as they went in and came out of the hives, on the highest trees, and often saved him hours of fruitless search. This glass was now in his hand ; for an object on a dead tree, that rose a little apart from those around it, and which stood quite near the extreme point in the forest towards which they were all proceeding, had caught his attention. The distance was still too great to ascertain by the naked eye what that object was ; but a single look with the glass showed that it was a bear. This was an old enemy of the bee-hunter, who often encountered the animal endeavoring to get at the honey, and he had on divers occasions been obliged to deal with these plunderers before he could succeed in his own plans of pilfering. The bear now seen continued in sight but an instant, the height to which he had clambered being so great, most probably, as to weary him with the effort, and to compel him to fall back again. All this was favorable to Le Bourdon's wishes, who immediately called a halt.

The first thing that Bourdon did, when all the dark eyes were gleaming on him in fierce curiosity, was to catch a bee and hold it to his ear, as it buzzed about in the tumbler.

"You t'ink dat bee talk?" Peter asked of Margery, in a tone of confidence, as if a newly awakened principle now existed between them.

"Bourdon must think so, Peter," the girl evasively answered, "or he would hardly listen to hear what it says."

"It strange, bee should talk! Almos' as strange as pale-face wish to leave Injin any land! Sartain bee talk, eh?"

"I have never heard one talk, Peter, unless it might be in its buzzing. That may be the tongue of a bee, for anything I know to the contrary."

By this time Le Bourdon seemed to be satisfied, and let the bee go; the savages murmuring their wonder and admiration.

"Do my brothers wish to hunt?" asked the bee-hunter in a voice so loud that all near might hear what he had to say.

This question produced a movement at once. Skill in hunting, next to success on the war-path, constitutes the great merit of an Indian; and it is ever his delight to show that he possesses it. No sooner did Le Bourdon throw out his feeler, therefore, than a general exclamation proclaimed the readiness of all the young men, in particular, to join in the chase.

"Let my brothers come closer," said Ben, in an authoritative manner; "I have something to put into their ears. They see that point of wood, where the dead bass-wood has fallen on the prairie. Near that bass-wood is honey, and near the honey are bears. This my bees have told me. Now let my brothers divide, and some go into the woods, and some stay on the prairie; then they will have plenty of sweet food."

As all this was very simple, and easily to be comprehended, not a moment was lost in the execution. With surprising order and aptitude the chiefs led off their parties, one line of dark warriors penetrating the forest on the eastern side of the bass-wood and another on its western, while a goodly number scattered themselves on the prairie itself, in its front. In less than a quarter of an hour, signals came from the forest that the *battue* was ready, and Peter gave the answering sign to proceed.

Down to this moment, doubts existed among the savages concerning the accuracy of Le Bourdon's statement. How was it possible that his bees should tell him where he could find bears? To be sure, bears were the great enemies of bees,—this every Indian knew,—but could the bees have a faculty of thus arming one enemy against another? These doubts, however, were soon allayed by the sudden appearance of a drove of bears, eight or ten in number, that came waddling out of the woods, driven before the circle of shouting hunters that had been formed within.

Now commenced a scene of wild tumult and of fierce delight. The warriors on the prairie retired before their enemies until all of their associates were clear of the forest, when the circle swiftly closed again, until it had brought the bears to something like close quarters. Bear's Meat, as became his appellation, led off the dance, letting fly an arrow at the nearest animal. Astounded by the great number of their enemies, and not a little appalled by their yells, the poor quadrupeds did not know which way to turn. Occasionally attempts were made to break through the circle, but the flight of arrows, aimed directly at their faces, invariably drove the creatures back. Fire-arms were not resorted to at all in this hunt, spears and arrows being the weapons depended on. Several ludicrous incidents occurred, but none that were tragical. One or two of the more reckless of the hunters, ambitious of shining before the representatives of so many tribes, ran rather greater risks than were required, but they escaped with a few smart scratches. In one instance, however, a young Indian had a still narrower *squeeze* for his life. Literally a *squeeze* it was;

for, suffering himself to get within the grasp of a bear, he came near being pressed to death, ere his companions could despatch the creature. As for the prisoner, the only means he had to prevent his being bitten was to thrust the head of his spear into the bear's mouth, where he succeeded in holding it, in spite of the animal's efforts to squeeze him into submission. By the time this combat was terminated, the field was strewed with the slain, every one of the bears having been killed by hunters so much practised in the art of destroying game.

CHAPTER XXI.

"She was an only child—her name Ginevra ;
   The joy, the pride of an indulgent father ;
   And in her fifteenth year became a bride,
   Marrying an only son, Francesco Doria,
   Her playmate from her birth, and her first love."
                          ROGERS.

DURING the hunt there was little leisure for reflection on the seemingly extraordinary manner in
which the bee-hunter had pointed out the spot
where the bears were to be found. No one of the
Indians had seen him apply the glass to his eye, for, leading
the party, he had been able to do this unobserved ; but,
had they witnessed such a procedure, it would have been as
inexplicable as all the rest. It is true, Crowsfeather and one
or two of his companions had taken a look through that
medicine-glass, but it rather contributed to increase the conjurer's renown, than served to explain any of the marvels
he performed.

Peter was most struck with all that had just occurred.
He had often heard of the skill of those who hunted bees,
and had several times met with individuals who practised
the art, but this was the first occasion on which he had ever
been a witness, in his own person, of the exercise of a craft
so wonderful ! Had the process been simply that of catching a bee, filling it with honey, letting it go, and then following it to its hive, it would have been so simple as to
require no explanation. But Peter was too intelligent, as
well as too observant, not to have seen that a great deal more
than this was necessary. On the supposition that the bee
flew *towards* the forest, as had been the fact with two of the

318

bees taken that morning, in what part of that forest was the hunter to look for the bee-tree? It was the angle that perplexed Peter, as it did all the Indians; for that angle, to be understood, required a degree of knowledge and calculation that entirely exceeded all he had ever acquired. Thus it is with us ever. The powers and faculties and principles that are necessary fully to comprehend all that we see, and all that surrounds us, exist and have been bestowed on man by his beneficent Creator. Still, it is only by slow degrees that he is to become their master, acquiring knowledge step by step, as he has need of its services, and learns how to use it. Such seems to be the design of Providence, which is gradually opening to our inquiries the arcana of nature, in order that we may convert their possession into such uses as will advance its own wise intentions. Happy are they who feel this truth in their character of individuals! Thrice happy the nations who can be made to understand that the surest progress is that which is made on the clearest principles, and with the greatest caution! The notion of setting up anything new in morals is as fallacious in theory as it will be found to be dangerous in practice.

It has been said that a sudden change had come over the fierce purposes of Peter. For some time, the nature, artlessness, truth, feminine playfulness, and kindness, not to say personal beauty, of Margery had been gradually softening the heart of this stern savage, as it respected the girl herself. Nothing of a weak nature was blended with this feeling, which was purely the growth of that divine principle that is implanted in us all. The quiet, earnest manner in which the girl had that day protested her desire to see the rights of the redman respected completed her conquest, and, so far as the great chief was concerned, secured her safety. It may seem singular, however, that Peter, with all his influence, was unable to say that even one that he was so much disposed to favor should be spared. By means of his own eloquence and perseverance and deep desire for vengeance, however, he had aroused a spirit among his followers that was not so easily quelled. On several occasions he had found it difficult to prevent the younger and more impetuous of the chiefs from proceeding at once to secure the scalps of those who were in their power ; and this he had done only by promising to increase the number of the victims.   How was he then to lessen that number ? and that, too, when circumstances did not seem likely to throw any more immediately into his power, as he had once hoped. This council must soon be over, and it would not be in his power to send the chiefs away without enumerating the scalps of the pale-faces present among those which were to make up the sum of their race.

Taking the perplexity produced by the bee-hunter's necromancy, and adding it to his concern for Margery, Peter found ample subject for all his reflections.   While the young men were dressing their bears, and making the preparations for a feast, he walked apart, like a man whose thoughts had little in common with the surrounding scene.   Even the further proceedings of Le Bourdon, who had discovered his bee-tree, had felled it, and was then distributing the honey among the Indians, could not draw him from his meditations.   The great council of all was to be held that very day, there, on Prairie Round, and it was imperative on Peter to settle the policy he intended to pursue, previously to the hour when the fire was to be lighted, and the chiefs met in final consultation.

In the meantime, Le Bourdon, by his distribution of the honey, no less than by the manner in which he had found it, was winning golden opinions of those who shared in his bounty.   One would think that the idea of property is implanted in us by nature, since men in all conditions appear to entertain strong and distinct notions of this right.   Natural it may not be, in the true signification of the term ; but it is a right so interwoven with those that are derived from nature, and more particularly with our wants, as almost to identify it with the individual being.   It is certain that all we have of civilization is dependent on a just protection of this right ; for, without the assurance of enjoying his earnings, who would produce beyond the supply necessary for his own immediate wants?   Among the American savages the rights of property are distinctly recognized, so far as their habits and resources extend. The hunting-ground belongs to the tribe, and occasionally the field ; but the wigwam and the arms and the skins, both for use and for market, and often the horses, and all other movables, belong to the individual. So sacred is this right held to be, that not one of those who stood by and saw Le Bourdon fell his tree, and who witnessed the operation of bringing to light its stores of honey, appeared to dream of meddling with the delicious store, until invited so to do by its lawful owner. It was this reserve, and this respect for a recognized principle, that enabled the bee-hunter to purchase a great deal of popularity by giving away liberally an article so much prized. None, indeed, was reserved, Boden seeing the impossibility of carrying it away. Happy would he have been, most happy, could he have felt the assurance of being able to get Margery off, without giving a second thought to any of his effects, whether present or absent.

As has been intimated, the bee-hunter was fast rising in the favor of the warriors, particularly of those who had a weakness on the score of the stomach. This is the first great avenue to the favor of man,—the belly ruling all the other members, the brains included. All this Peter noted, and was now glad to perceive ; for, in addition to the favor that Margery had found in his eyes, that wary chief had certain very serious misgivings on the subject of the prudence of attempting to deal harshly with a medicine-man of Boden's calibre. Touching the whiskey spring he had been doubtful from the first ; even Crowsfeather's account of the wonderful glass through which that chief had looked, and seen men reduced to children and then converted into giants, had failed to conquer his skepticism ; but he was not altogether proof against what he had that day beheld with his own eyes. These marvels shook his previous opinion touching the other matters ; and, altogether, the effect was to elevate the bee-hunter to a height that it really appeared dangerous to assail.

While Peter was thus shaken with doubts, and that too on a point on which he had hitherto stood as firm as a rock, there was another in the crowd who noted the growing favor

21

of Le Bourdon with deep disgust. This man could hardly
be termed a chief, though he possessed a malignant power
that was often wielded to the discomfiture of those who were.
He went by the significant appellation of "The Weasel," a
sobriquet that had been bestowed on him for some supposed
resemblance to the little pilfering, prowling quadruped after
which he was thus named. In person and in physical qualities generally this individual was mean and ill-favored ; and
squalid habits contributed to render him even less attractive
than he otherwise might have been. He was, moreover,
particularly addicted to intemperance ; lying, wallowing
like a hog, for days at a time, whenever his tribe received
any of the ample contribution of fire-water which it was
then more the custom than it is to-day to send among the
aborigines. A warrior of no renown, a hunter so indifferent
as to compel his squaw and pappooses often to beg for food
in strange lodges, of mean presence, and a drunkard, it may
seem extraordinary that The Weasel should possess any
influence amid so many chiefs renowned for courage, wisdom, deeds in arms, on the hunt, and for services around
the council fire. It was all due to his tongue. Ungque, or
The Weasel, was eloquent in a high degree, possessing that
variety of his art which most addresses itself to the passions ;
and, strange as it may seem, men are oftener and more easily
led by those who do little else than promise, than by those
who actually perform. A lying and fluent tongue becomes
a power of itself, with the masses, subverting reason, looking
down justice, browbeating truth, and otherwise placing the
wrong before the right. This quality The Weasel possessed
in a high degree, and was ever willing to use, on occasions
that seemed most likely to defeat the wishes of those he
hated. Among the last was Peter, whose known ascendency in his own particular tribe had been a source of great
envy and uneasiness to this Indian. He had struggled hard
to resist it, and had even dared to speak in favor of the pale-
faces, and in opposition to the plan of cutting them all off,
purely with a disposition to oppose this mysterious stranger.
It had been in vain, however, the current running the other
way, and the fiery eloquence of Peter proving too strong

even for him. Now, to his surprise, from a few words dropped casually, this man ascertained that their greatest leader was disposed so far to relent as not to destroy *all* the pale-faces in his power. Whom and how many he meant to spare, Ungque could not tell; but his quick, practised discernment detected the general disposition, and his ruthless tendency to oppose caused him to cast about for the means of resisting this sudden inclination to show mercy. With The Weasel, the moving principle was ever that of the demagogue; it was to flatter the mass that he might lead it; and he had an innate hostility to whatever was frank, manly, and noble.

The time had now come when the Indians wished to be alone. At this council it was their intention to come to an important decision; and even the "young men," unless chiefs, were to be merely distant spectators. Peter sent for Le Bourdon, accordingly, and communicated his wish that all the whites would return to the castle, whither he promised to join them about the setting of the sun, or early the succeeding day.

"One of you, you know—dat my wigwam," said the grim chief, smiling on Margery with a friendly eye, and shaking hands with the bee-hunter, who thought his manner less constrained than on former similar occasions. "Get good supper for ole Injin, young squaw—dat juss what squaw good for."

Margery laughingly promised to remember his injunction, and went her way, closely attended by her lover. The corporal followed, armed to the teeth, and keeping at just such a distance from the young people as might enable them to converse without being overheard. As for the missionary, he was detained a moment by Peter, the others moving slowly, in order to permit him to come up ere they had gone their first mile. Of course the mysterious chief had not detained Parson Amen without a motive.

"My brother has told me many curious things," said Peter, when alone with the missionary, and speaking now in the language of the Ojebways, "many very curious things. I like to listen to them. Once he told me how the pale-face young men take their squaws."

" I remember to have told you this. We ask the Great Spirit to bless our marriages, and the ceremony is commonly performed by a priest. This is our practice, Peter ; though not necessary, I think it good."

" Yes ; good alway for pale-face to do pale-face fashion, and for Injin to do Injin fashion. Don't want medicine-man to get redskin squaw. Open wigwam door, and she come in. Dat 'nough. If she don't wish to come in, can't make her. Squaw go to warrior she likes ; warrior ask squaw he likes. But it is best for pale-face to take his wife in pale-face fashion. Does not my brother see a young man of his people, and a young maiden, that he had better bring together and bless? "

" You must mean Bourdon and Margery," answered the missionary, in English, after a moment's reflection. " The idea is a new one to me ; for my mind has been much occupied of late, with other and more important matters ; though I now plainly see what you mean ! "

" That flower of the Openings would soon fade, if the young bee-hunter should leave it alone on the prairies. This is the will of the Great Spirit. He puts it into the minds of the young squaws to see all things well that the hunters of their fancy do. Why he has made the young with this kindness for each other, perhaps my brother knows. He is wise, and has books. The poor Injins have none. They can see only with the eyes they got from Injins like themselves. But one thing they know. What the Great Spirit has commanded is good. Injins can't make it any better. They can do it harm, but they can do it no good. Let my brother bless the couple that the Manitou has brought together."

" I believe I understand you, Peter, and will think of this. And now that I must leave you for a little while, let me beg you to think of this matter of the origin of your tribes candidly, and with care. Everything depends on your people's not mistaking the truth in this great matter. It is as necessary for a nation to know its duties, as for a single man. Promise me to think of this, Peter."

" My brother's words have come into my ears—they are

good," returned the Indian, courteously. "We will think of them at the council, if my brother will bless his young man and young maiden, according to the law of his people."

"I will promise to do this, Peter, or to urge Bourdon and Margery to do it, if you will promise to speak to-day, in council, of the history of your forefathers, and to take into consideration, once more, the great question of your being Hebrews."

"I will speak as my brother wishes—let him do as I wish. Let him tell me that I can say to the chiefs, before the sun has fallen the length of my arm, that the young pale-face bee-hunter has taken the young pale-face squaw into his wigwam."

"I do not understand your motive, Peter; but that which you ask is wise, and according to God's law, and it shall be done. Fare you well, then, for a season. When we meet again, Bourdon and Margery shall be one, if my persuasions can prevail, and you will have pressed this matter of the lost tribes again home to your people. Fare you well, Peter; fare you well."

They separated; the Indian with a cold smile of courtesy, but with his ruthless intentions as respected the missionary in no degree changed. Boden and Margery alone were exempt from vengeance, according to his present designs. An unaccountable gentleness of feeling governed him, as connected with the girl; while superstition, and the dread of an unknown power, had its full influence on his determination to spare her lover. There might be some faint ray of human feeling glimmering among the fierce fires that so steadily burned in the breast of this savage, but they were so much eclipsed by the brighter light that gleamed around them as to be barely perceptible, even to himself. The result of all these passions was a determination in Peter to spare those whom he had advised the missionary to unite, making that union a mysterious argument in favor of Margery, and to sacrifice all the rest. The red American is so much accustomed to this species of ruthless proceedings, that the anguish he might occasion the very beings to whom he now wished to be merciful gave the stern chief very little concern. Leaving the Indians in the exclusive possession of Prairie Round, we will return to the rest of the party.

The missionary hastened after his friends as fast as he could go. Boden and Margery had much to say to each other in that walk, which had a great deal about it to bring their thoughts within the circle of their own existence. As has been said, the fire had run through that region late, and the grasses were still young, offering but little impediment to their movements. As the day was now near its heat, Le Bourdon led his spirited but gentle companion through the groves, where they had the benefit of a most delicious shade, a relief that was now getting to be very grateful. Twice had they stopped to drink at cool, clear springs, in which the water seemed to vie with the air in transparency. As this is not the general character of the water of that region, though marked exceptions exist, Margery insisted that the water was eastern and not western water.

"Why do we always think the things we had in childhood better than those we enjoy afterwards?" asked Margery, after making one of these comparisons, somewhat to the disadvantage of the part of the country in which she then was. "I can scarce ever think of home—what I call home, and which was so long a home to me—without shedding tears. Nothing here seems as good of its kind as what I have left behind me. Do you have the same longings for Pennsylvania that I feel for the sea-coast and for the rocks about Quincy?"

"Sometimes. When I have been quite alone for two or three months, I have fancied that an apple, or a potato, or even a glass of the cider, that came from the spot where I was born, would be sweeter than all the honey bees ever gathered in Michigan."

"To me it has always seemed strange, Bourdon, that one of your kind feelings should ever wish to live alone at all; yet I have heard you say that a love of solitude first drew you to your trade."

"It is these strong cases which get a man under, as it might be, and almost alter his nature. One man will pass his days in hunting deer; another in catching fish: my taste has been for the bees, and for such chances with other creatures as may offer. What between hunting and hiving and getting the honey to market, I have very little time to long for company. But my taste is altering, Margery; *has* altered."

The girl blushed, but she also smiled, and, moreover, she looked pleased.

"I am afraid that you are not as much altered as you think," she answered, laughingly, however. "It may seem so *now*; but when you come to *live* in the settlements again you will get tired of crowds."

"Then I will come with you, Margery, into these Openings, and we can live *together* here, surely, as well, or far better, than I can live here *alone*. You and Gershom's wife have spoiled my housekeeping. I really did not know, until you came up here, how much a woman can do in a *chienté*!"

"Why, Bourdon, you have lived long enough in the settlements to know *that*!"

"That is true; but I look upon the settlements as one thing, and on the Openings as another. What will do there isn't needed here; and what will do here won't answer there. But these last few days have so changed Castle Meal that I hardly know it myself."

"Perhaps the change is for the worse, and you wish it undone, Bourdon," observed the girl, in the longing she had to hear an assurance to the contrary, at the very moment she felt certain that assurance would be given.

"No, no, Margery. Woman has taken possession of my cabin, and woman shall now always command there, unless you alter your mind and refuse to have me. I shall speak to the missionary to marry us, as soon as I can get him alone. His mind is running so much on the Jews that he has hardly a moment left for us Christians."

The color on Margery's cheek was not lessened by this declaration; though, to admit the truth, she looked none the less pleased. She was a warm-hearted and generous girl, and sometimes hesitated about separating herself and her fortunes from those of Gershom and Dorothy ; but the bee-hunter had persuaded her this would be unnecessary, though she did accept him for a husband. The point had been settled between them on previous occasions, and much conversation had already passed in that very walk, which was confined to that interesting subject. But Margery was not now disposed to say more, and she adroitly improved the hint thrown out by Boden, to change the discourse.

"It is the strangest notion I ever heard of," she cried, laughing, " to believe Injins to be Jews !"

" He tells me he is by no means the first who has fancied it. Many writers have said as much before him, and all he claims is to have been among them, and to have seen these Hebrews with his own eyes. But here he comes, and can answer for himself."

Just as this was said, Parson Amen joined the party, Corporal Flint closing to the front, as delicacy no longer required him to act as a rear-guard. The good missionary came up a little heated ; and, in order that he might have time to cool himself, the rate of movement was slightly reduced. In the meantime the conversation did not the less proceed.

" We were talking of the lost tribes," said Margery, half smiling as she spoke, "and of your idea, Mr. Amen, that these Injins are Jews. It seems strange to me that they should have lost so much of their ancient ways and notions and appearances, if they are really the people you think."

"Lost ! It is rather wonderful that, after the lapse of two thousand years and more, so much should remain. Whichever way I look, signs of these people's origin beset me. You have read your Bible, Margery—which I am sorry to say all on this frontier have not—but *you* have read your Bible, and one can make an allusion to *you* with some satisfaction. Now let me ask you if you remember such a thing as the scape-goat of the ancient Jews. It is to be found in Leviticus, and is one of those mysterious customs with which that extraordinary book is full."

"Leviticus is a book I never read but once, for we do not read it in our New England schools. But I do remember that the Jews were commanded to let one of two goats go, from which practice it has, I believe, been called a scape-goat."

"Well," said Le Bourdon, simply, "what a thing is l'arnin'! Now this is all news to me, though I have *heard* of 'scape-goats,' and *talked* of 'scape-goats' a thousand times! There's a meanin' to everything, I find; and I do not look upon this idee of the lost tribes as half as strange as I did before I l'arnt this!"

Margery had not fallen in love with the bee-hunter for his biblical knowledge, else might her greater information have received a rude shock by this mark of simplicity; but instead of dwelling on this proof of Le Bourdon's want of "schooling," her active mind was more disposed to push the allusion to scape-goats to some useful conclusion.

"And what of the goat, Mr. Amen?" she asked; "and how can it belong to anything here?"

"Why were all those goats turned into the woods and deserts, in the olden time, Margery? Doubtless to provide food for the ten tribes, when these should be driven forth by conquerors and hard task-masters. Time and climate and a difference of food have altered them, as they have changed the Jews themselves, though they still retain the cleft hoof, the horns, the habits, and the general characteristics of the goats of Arabia. Yes, naturalists will find in the end that the varieties of the deer of this continent, particularly the antelope, are nothing but the scape-goats of the ancient world, altered, and perhaps improved, by circumstances."

As this was much the highest flight the good missionary had ever yet taken, not trifling was the astonishment of his young friends thereat. Touching the Jews, Le Bourdon did not pretend to, or in fact did not possess much knowledge; but when the question was reduced down to one of venison or bears' meat or bisons' humps, with the exception of the professed hunters and trappers few knew more about them all than he did himself. That the deer or even

the antelopes of America ever had been goats, he did not
believe; nor was he at all backward in letting his dissent to
such a theory be known.

"I'm sorry, Parson Amen, you've brought in the deer,"
he cried. "Had you stuck to the Jews, I might have believed all that you fancy in this business; but the deer have
spoiled all. As for scape-goats, since Margery seems to
agree with you, I suppose you are right about *them*, though
my notion of such creatures has been to keep clear of them,
instead of following them up, as you seem to think these
Hebrews have done. But if you are no nearer right in your
doctrine about the Injins than you are about their game,
you'll have to change your religion."

"Do not think that my religion depends on any thread
so slight, Bourdon. A man may be mistaken in interpret-
ing prophecy, and still be a devout Christian. There are
more reasons than you may at first suppose for believing
in this theory of the gradual change of the goat into the
deer, and especially into the antelope. We do not any of
us believe that Noah had with him, in the ark, all the animals that are now to be found, but merely the parent-stems,
in each particular case, which would be reducing the number
many fold. If all men came from Adam, Bourdon, why
could not all deer come from goats?"

"Why, this matter about men has a good deal puzzled
me, Parson, and I hardly know what answer to give. Still,
men are men, wherever you find them. They may be
lighter or darker, taller or shorter, with hair or wool, and
yet you can see they are *men*. Perhaps food and climate
and manner of living may have made all the changes we
see in them; but Lord, Parson, a goat has a beard!"

"What has become of the thousands of scape-goats that
the ancient Hebrews must have turned loose in the wilderness? Answer me that, Bourdon!"

"You might as well ask me, sir, what has become of the
thousands of Hebrews who turned them loose. I suppose
all must be dead a thousand years ago. Scape-goats are
creatures that even Injins would not like."

"All this is a great mystery, Bourdon—a much greater

mystery than our friend Peter, whom you have so often said was a man so unaccountable. By the way, he has given me a charge to perform an office between you and Margery, that I had almost forgotten. From what he said to me, I rather think it may have some connection with our safety. We have enemies among these savages, I feel very certain ; though I believe we have also warm friends.''

"But what have you in charge that has anything to do with Bourdon and me ?" asked the wondering Margery, who was quick to observe the connection, though utterly at a loss to comprehend it.

The missionary now called a halt, and finding convenient seats, he gradually opened the subject with which he had been charged by Peter, to his companions. The reader is probably prepared to learn that there was no longer any reserve between Le Bourdon and Margery on the subject of their future marriage. The young man had already pressed an immediate union, as the wisest and safest course to be pursued. Although the savage American is little addicted to abusing his power over female captives, and seldom takes into his lodge an unwilling squaw, the bee-hunter had experienced a good deal of uneasiness on the score of what might befall his betrothed. Margery was sufficiently beautiful to attract attention even in a town ; and more than one fierce-looking warrior had betrayed his admiration that very day, though it was in a very Indian-like fashion. Rhapsody and gallant speeches and sonnets form no part of Indian courtship ; but the language of admiration is so very universal, through the eyes, that it is sufficiently easy of comprehension. It was possible that some chief, whose band was too formidable to be opposed, might take it into his head to wish to see a pale-face squaw in his wigwam ; and, while it was not usual to do much violence to a female's inclinations on such occasions, it was not common to offer much opposition to those of a powerful warrior. The marriage tie, if it could be said to exist at all, however, was much respected ; and it was far less likely that Margery, a wife, would thus be appropriated, than Margery, unmarried. It is true, cases of an unscrupulous exercise of power are to be found among Indians, as well as among civilized men, but they are rare, and usually are much condemned.

The bee-hunter, consequently, was well disposed to second Peter's project. As for Margery herself, she had half yielded all her objections to her lover's unaided arguments, and was partly conquered before this reinforcement was brought into the field against her. Peter's motive was much canvassed, no one of them all being able to penetrate it. Boden, however, had his private opinion on the subject, nor was it so very much out of the way. He fancied that the mysterious chief was well disposed to Margery, and wished to put her as far as possible beyond the chances of an Indian wigwam ; marriage being the step of all others most likely to afford her this protection. Now this was not exactly true, but it was right enough in the main. Peter's aim was to save the life of the girl, her gentle attractions and kind attentions to himself having wrought this much in her favor ; and he believed no means of doing so as certain as forming a close connection for her with the great medicine bee-hunter. Judging of them by himself, he did not think the Indians would dare to include so great a conjurer in their schemes of vengeance, and was willing himself that Le Bourdon should escape, provided Margery could go free and unharmed with him. As for the bee-hunter's powers, he had many misgivings ; they might be dangerous to the redmen, and they might not. On this subject he was in the painful doubts of ignorance, and had the wide area of conjecture open before his mind. He saw, but it was " as in a glass, darkly."

Margery was disposed to delay the ceremony, at least until her brother and sister might be present. But to this Le Bourdon himself was not much inclined. It had struck him that Gershom was opposed to an early marriage, most probably because he fancied himself more secure of the bee-hunter's ingenious and important aid in getting back to the settlements, so long as this strong inducement existed to cling to himself, than if he should release his own hold of Margery by giving her at once to her lover.

Right or wrong, such was the impression taken up by Le Bourdon, and he was glad when the missionary urged his request to be permitted to pronounce the nuptial benediction on the spot.

Little ceremony is generally used in an American marriage. In a vast many cases no clergyman is employed at all ; and where there is, most of the sects have no ring, no giving away, nor any of those observances which were practised in the churches of old. There existed no impediment, therefore ; and, after a decent interval spent in persuasions, Margery consented to plight her vows to the man of her heart before they left the spot. She would fain have had Dorothy present, for woman loves to lean on her own sex on such occasions, but submitted to the necessity of proceeding at once, as the bee-hunter and the missionary chose to term it.

A better altar could not have been selected in all that vast region. It was one of nature's own erecting ; and Le Bourdon and his pretty bride placed themselves before it with feelings suited to the solemnity of the occasion. The good missionary stood within the shade of a burr-oak, in the centre of those park-like Openings, every object looking fresh, and smiling, and beautiful. The sward was green, and short as that of a well-tended lawn ; the flowers were, like the bride herself, soft, modest, and sweet ; while charming rural vistas stretched through the trees, much as if art had been summoned in aid of the great mistress who had designed the landscape. When the parties knelt in prayer, which all present did, not excepting the worthy corporal, it was on the verdant ground, with first the branches of the trees, and then the deep, fathomless vault of heaven for a canopy. In this manner was the marriage benediction pronounced on the bee-hunter and Margery Waring, in the venerable Oak Openings. No Gothic structure, with its fretted aisles and clustered columns, could have been one half as appropriate for the union of such a couple.

CHAPTER XXII.

"No shrift the gloomy savage brooks,
 As scowling on the priest he looks ;
 Cowesass—cowesass—tawhich wessasseen ?
 Let my father look on Bornazeen—
 My father's heart is the heart of a squaw,
 But mine is so hard that it does not thaw."

WHITTIER.

LEAVING the newly-married couple to pursue their way homeward, it is now our province to return to Prairie Round. One accustomed to such scenes would easily have detected the signs of divided opinions and of agitating doubts among the chiefs, though nothing like contention or dispute had yet manifested itself. Peter's control was still in the ascendant, and he had neglected none of his usual means of securing influence. Perhaps he labored so much the harder, from the circumstance that he now found himself so situated as to be compelled to undo much that he had previously done.

On the other hand, Ungque appeared to have no particular cause of concern. His manner was as much unoccupied as usual ; and to his habit of referring all his influence to sudden and powerful bursts of eloquence, if design of any sort was entertained, he left his success.

We pass over the details of assembling the council. The spot was not exactly on the prairie, but in a bit of lovely "Opening" on its margin, where the eye could roam over a wide extent of that peculiar natural meadow, while the body enjoyed the shades of the wood. The chiefs alone were in the circle, while the "braves" and the "young men" generally formed a group on the outside ; near

enough to hear what passed, and to profit by it if so
disposed. The pipe was smoked, and all the ordinary customs observed, when Bear's Meat arose, the first speaker on
that momentous occasion.

"Brothers," he said, "this is the great council on Prairie
Round to which we have been called. We have met before,
but not here. This is our first meeting here. We have
travelled a long path to get here. Some of our brethren have
travelled farther. They are at Detroit. They went there to
meet our great Canada Father, and to take Yankee scalps.
How many scalps they have taken I do not know, or I
would tell you. It is pleasant to me to count Yankee scalps.
I would rather count them than count the scalps of redmen.
There are still a great many left. The Yankees are many,
and each Yankee has a scalp. There should not be so many.
When the buffaloes came in the largest droves, our fathers
used to go out to hunt them in the strongest parties. Their
sons should do the same. We are the sons of those fathers.
They say we look like them, talk like them, live like them
—we should *act* like them. Let another speak, for I have
done."

After this brief address, which bore some resemblance to
a chairman's calling a meeting of civilized men to order,
there was more smoking. It was fully expected that Peter
would next arise, but he did not. Perceiving this, and willing to allow time to that great chief to arrange his thoughts,
Crowsfeather assumed the office of filling the gap. He was
far more of a warrior than of an orator, and was listened to
respectfully, but less for what he said than for what he had
done. A good deal of Indian boasting, quite naturally,
was blended with *his* discourse.

"My brother has told you of the Yankee scalps," he
commenced. "He says they are many. He says there
ought to be fewer. He did not remember who sat so near
him. Perhaps he does not know that there are less now
than there were a moon since. Crowsfeather took three at
Chicago. Many scalps were taken there. The Yankees
must be plentier than the buffaloes on the great prairies, if
they can lose so many scalps often, and send forth their war-

riors. I am a Pottawattamie. My brothers know that tribe. It is not a tribe of Jews, but a tribe of Injins. It is a great tribe. It never was *lost*. It *cannot* be lost. No tribe better knows all the paths, and all the best routes to every point where it wishes to go. It is foolish to say you can lose a Pottawattamie. A duck would be as likely to lose itself as a Pottawattamie. I do not speak for the Ottawas : I speak for the Pottawattamies. We are not Jews. We do not wish to be Jews ; and what we do not wish to be we will not be. Our father who has come so far to tell us that we are not Injins, but Jews, is mistaken. I never heard of these Jews before. I do not wish to hear of them again. When a man has heard enough, he does not keep his ears open willingly. It is then best for the speaker to sit down. The Pottawattamies have shut their ears to the great medicine-priest of the pale-faces. What he says may be true of other tribes, but it is not true of the Pottawattamies. We are not lost ; we are not Jews. I have done.''

This speech was received with general favor. The notion that the Indians were not Indians, but Jews, was far from being agreeable to those who had heard what had been said on the subject ; and the opinions of Crowsfeather possessed the great advantage of reflecting the common sentiment on this interesting subject. When this is the case, a very little eloquence or logic goes a great way ; and, on the whole, the address of the last speaker was somewhat better received than that of the first.

It was now confidently believed that Peter would rise. But he did not. That mysterious chief was not yet prepared to speak, or he was judiciously exciting expectation by keeping back. There were at least ten minutes of silent smoking, ere a chief, whose name rendered into English was Bough of the Oak, arose, evidently with a desire to help the time along. Taking his cue from the success of Crowsfeather, he followed up the advantage obtained by that chief, assailing the theory of the missionary from another quarter.

''I am an Injin,'' said Bough of the Oak ; '' my father was an Injin, and my mother was the daughter of an Injin. All my fathers were redmen, and all their sons. Why should I wish to be anything else ?   I asked my brother, the medicine-priest, and he owned that Jews are pale-faces. This he should not have owned if he wished the Injins to be Jews. My skin is red. The Manitou of my fathers so painted it, and their child will not try to wash out the color. Were the color washed out of my face, I should be a pale-face ! There would not be paint enough to hide my shame. No ; I was born red, and will die a redman. It is not good to have two faces. An Injin is not a snake, to cast his skin. The skin in which he was born he keeps. He plays in it when a child ; he goes in it to his first hunt : the bears and the deer know him by it ; he carries it with him on the war-path, and his enemies tremble at the sight of it ; his squaw knows him by that skin when he comes back to his wig-wam ; and when he dies, he is put aside in the same skin in which he was born. There is but one skin, and it has but one color. At first, it is little. The pappoose that wears it is little. There is no need of a large skin. But it grows with the pappoose, and the biggest warrior finds his skin around him. This is because the Great Spirit fitted it to him. Whatever the Manitou does is good.

" My brothers have squaws—they have pappooses. When the pappoose is put into their arms do they get the paint-stones and paint it red ? They do not. It is not necessary. The Manitou painted it red before it was born. How this was done I do not know. I am nothing but a poor Injin, and only know what I see. I have seen that the pappooses are red when they are born, and that the warriors are red when they die. They are also red while living. It is enough. Their fathers could never have been pale-faces or we should find some white spots on their children. There are none.

" Crowsfeather has spoken of the Jews as lost. I am not surprised to hear it. It seems to me that all pale-faces get lost. They wander from their own hunting-grounds into those of other people. It is not so with Injins. The Pottawattamie does not kill the deer of the Iowa, nor the Ottawa the deer of the Menominees. Each tribe knows its own game. This is because they are not lost. My pale-face father appears to wish us well. He has come on a long

22

and weary path, to tell us about his Manitou. For this I thank him. I thank all who wish to do me good. Them that wish to do me harm I strike from behind. It is our Injin custom. I do not wish to hurt the medicine-priest, because I think he wishes to do me good and not to do me harm. He has a strange law. It is to do good to them that do harm to you. It is not the law of the redmen. It is not a good law. I do not wonder that the tribes which follow such a law get lost. They cannot tell their friends from their enemies. They can have no people to scalp. What is a warrior if he cannot find some one to scalp? No ; such a law would make women of the bravest braves in the openings or on the prairie. It may be a good law for Jews, who get lost ; but it is a bad law for Injins, who know the paths they travel. Let another speak.''

This brief profession of faith, on the subject that had been so recently broached in the council, seemed to give infinite satisfaction. All present evidently preferred being redmen who knew where they were, than to be pale-faces who had lost their road. Ignorance of his path is a species of disgrace to an American savage, and not a man there would have confessed that this particular division of the great human family was in that dilemma. The idea that the Yankees were ''lost,'' and had got materially astray, was very grateful to most who heard it ; and Bough of the Oak gained a considerable reputation as an orator in consequence of the lucky hits made on this occasion.

Another long, ruminating pause, and much passing of the pipe of peace succeeded. It was near half an hour after the last speaker had resumed his seat ere Peter stood erect. In the long interval expectation had time to increase, and curiosity to augment itself. Nothing but a very great event could cause this pondering, this deliberation, and this unwillingness to begin. When, however, the time did come for the mysterious chief to speak, the man of many scalps to open his mouth, profound was the attention that prevailed among all present. Even after he had arisen, the orator stood silently looking around him, as if

the throes of his thoughts had to be a little suppressed
before he could trust his tongue to give them utterance.

"What is the earth?" commenced Peter, in a deep,
guttural tone of voice, which the death-like stillness rendered audible even to the outermost boundaries of the circle of admiring and curious countenances. "It is one
plain adjoining another; river after river; lake after lake;
prairie touching prairie; and pleasant woods, that seem to
have no limits, all given to men to dwell in. It would
seem that the Great Spirit parcelled out this rich possession
into hunting-grounds for all. He colored men differently.
His dearest children he painted red, which is his own color.
Them that he loved less he colored less, and they have red
only in spots. Them he loved least he dipped in a dark
dye, and left them black. These are the colors of men.
If there are more, I have not seen them. Some say there
are. I shall think so, too, when I see them.

"Brothers, this talk about lost tribes is a foolish talk.
We are not lost. We know where we are, and we know
where the Yankees have come to seek us. My brother
has well spoken. If any are lost it is the Yankees. The
Yankees are Jews; they are lost. The time is near when
they will be found, and when they will again turn their
eyes towards the rising sun. They have looked so long
towards the setting sun that they cannot see clearly. It is
not good to look too long at the same object. The Yankees have looked at our hunting-grounds until their eyes
are dim. They see the hunting-grounds, but they do not
see all the warriors that are in them. In time they will
learn to count them.

"Brothers, when the Great Spirit made man he put
him to live on the earth. Our traditions do not agree in
saying of what he was made. Some say it was of clay,
and that when his spirit starts for the happy hunting-
grounds his body becomes clay again. I do not say that
this is so, for I do not know. It is not good to say that
which we do not know to be true. I wish to speak only
the truth. This we do know. If a warrior die, and we

put him in the earth, and come to look for him many years afterwards, nothing but bones are found. All else is gone. I have heard old men say that, in time, even these bones are not to be found. It is so with trees ; it may be so with men. But it is not so with hunting-grounds. They were made to last forever.

" Brothers, you know why we have come together on this prairie. It was to count the pale-faces, and to think of the way of making their number less. Now is a good time for such a thing. They have dug up the hatchet against each other ; and when we hear of scalps taken among them it is good for the redmen. I do not think our Canada Father is more our friend than the great Yankee, Uncle Sam. It is true he gives us more powder and blankets and tomahawks and rifles than the Yankee, but it is to get us to fight his battles. We will fight his battles. They are our battles, too. For this reason we will fight his enemies.

" Brothers, it is time to think of our children. A wise chief once told me how many winters it is since a pale-face was first seen among redmen. It was not a great while ago. Injins are living who have seen Injins whose own fathers saw them first pale-faces. They were few. They were like little children then ; but now they are grown to be men. Medicine-men are plenty among them, and tell them how to raise children. The Injins do not understand this. Small-pox, fire-water, bad hunting, and frosts, keep us poor, and keep our children from growing as fast as the children of the pale-faces.

" Brothers, all this has happened within the lives of three aged chiefs. One told to another, and he told it to a third. Three chiefs have kept that tradition. They have given it to me. I have cut notches on this stick " (holding up a piece of ash, neatly trimmed, as a record), " for the winters they told me, and every winter since I have cut one more. See ; there are not many notches. Some of our people say that the pale-faces are already plentier than leaves on the trees. I do not believe this. These notches tell us differently. It is true the pale-faces grow fast, and have many children, and small-pox does not kill many of them, and their wars are few; but look at this stick. Could a canoe-full of men become as many as they say in so few winters? No; it is not so. The stories we have heard are not true. A crooked tongue first told them. We are strong enough still to drive these strangers into the great salt lake, and get back all our hunting-grounds. That is what I wish to have done.

"Brothers, I have taken many scalps. This stick will tell the number." Here one of those terrible gleams of ferocity to which we have before alluded passed athwart the dark countenance of the speaker, causing all present to feel a deeper sympathy in the thoughts he would express. "There are many. Every one has come from the head of a pale-face. It is now twenty winters since I took the scalp off of a redman. I shall never take another. We want all of our own warriors to drive back the strangers.

"Brothers, some Injins tell us of different tribes. They talk about distant tribes as strangers. I tell you we are all children of the same father. All our skins are red. I see no difference between an Ojebway and a Sac or a Sioux. I love even a Cherokee." Here very decided signs of dissatisfaction were manifested by several of the listeners; parties of the tribes of the great lakes having actually marched as far as the Gulf of Mexico to make war on the Indians of that region, who were generally hated by them with the most intense hatred. "He has the blood of our fathers in him. We are brothers, and should live together as brothers. If we want scalps, the pale-faces have plenty. It is sweet to take the scalp of a pale-face. I know it. My hand has done it often, and will do it again. If every Injin had taken as many scalps as I have taken, few of these strangers would now remain.

"Brothers, one thing more I have to say. I wish to hear others, and will not tell all I know this time. One thing more I have to say, and I now say it. I have told you that we must take the scalps of all the pale-faces who are now near us. I thought there would have been more, but the rest do not come. Perhaps they are frightened. There are only

six. Six scalps are not many. I am sorry they are so few.
But we can go where there will be more. One of these six
is a medicine-man. I do not know what to think. It may
be good to take his scalp. It may be bad. Medicine-men
have great power. You have seen what this bee-hunter can
do. He knows how to talk with bees. Them little insects
can fly into small places, and see things that Injins cannot
see. The Great Spirit made them so. When we get back
all the land, we shall get the bees with it, and may then hold
a council to say what it is best to do with them. Until we
know more, I do not wish to touch the scalp of that bee-
hunter. It may do us great harm. I knew a medicine-man
of the pale-faces to lose his scalp, and small-pox took off
half the band that made him prisoner and killed him. It is
not good to meddle with medicine-men. A few days ago,
and I wanted this young man's scalp very much. Now I do
not want it. It may do us harm to touch it. I wish to let
him go and to take his squaw with him. The rest we can
scalp.''

Peter cunningly made no allusion to Margery until just
before he resumed his seat, though now deeply interested in
her safety. As for Le Bourdon, so profound was the impression he had made that morning, that few of the chiefs
were surprised at the exemption proposed in his favor. The
superstitious dread of witchcraft is very general among the
American savages; and it certainly did seem to be hazardous to plot the death of a man who had even the bees that
were humming on all sides of them under his control. He
might at that very moment be acquainted with all that was
passing; and several of the grim-looking and veteran warriors who sat in the circle, and who appeared to be men able
and willing to encounter aught human, did not fail to remember the probability of a medicine-man's knowing who were
his friends and who his enemies.

When Peter sat down, there was but one man in the circle
of chiefs who was resolved to oppose his design of placing
Boden and Margery without the pale of the condemned.
Several were undecided, scarce knowing what to think of
so sudden and strange a proposition, but could not be said

to have absolutely adhered to the original scheme of cutting off all. The exception was Ungque. This man—a chief by a sort of sufferance, rather than as a right—was deadly hostile to Peter's influence, as has been said, and was inclined to oppose all his plans, though compelled by policy to be exceedingly cautious how he did it. Here, however, was an excellent opportunity to strike a blow, and he was determined not to neglect it. Still, so wily was this Indian, so much accustomed to put a restraint on his passions and wishes, that he did not immediately arise, with the impetuous ardor of frank impulses, to make his reply, but awaited his time.

An Indian is but a man, after all, and is liable to his weaknesses, notwithstanding the self-command he obtains by severe drilling. Bough of the Oak was to supply a proof of this truth. He had been so unexpectedly successful in his late attempt at eloquence, that it was not easy to keep him off his feet, now that another good occasion to exhibit his powers offered. He was accordingly the next to speak.

"My brothers," said Bough of the Oak, "I am named after a tree. You all know that tree. It is not good for bows or arrows; it is not good for canoes; it does not make the best fire, though it will burn and is hot when well lighted. There are many things for which the tree after which I am named is not good. It is not good to eat. It has no sap that Injins can drink, like the maple. It does not make good brooms. But it has branches like other trees, and they are tough. Tough branches are good. The boughs of the oak will not bend like the boughs of the willow, or the boughs of the ash, or the boughs of the hickory.

"Brothers, I am a bough of the oak. I do not like to bend. When my mind is made up, I wish to keep it where it was first put. My mind has been made up to take the scalps of *all* the pale-faces who are now in the Openings. I do not want to change it. My mind can break, but it cannot bend. It is tough."

Having uttered this brief but sententious account of his view of the matter at issue, the chief resumed his seat, reasonably well satisfied with this his second attempt to be

eloquent that day. His success this time was not as un-
equivocal as on the former occasion, but it was respectable.
Several of the chiefs saw a reasonable, if not a very log-
ical analogy, between a man's name and his mind; and to
them it appeared a tolerably fair inference that a man
should act up to his name. If his name was tough he
ought to be tough, too. In this it does not strike us that
they argued very differently from civilized beings, who are
only too apt to do that which their better judgments really
condemn, because they think they are acting "in character," as it is termed.

Ungque was both surprised and delighted with this unexpected support from Bough of the Oak. He knew
enough of human nature to understand that a new-born
ambition, that of talking against the great mysterious
chief Peter, was at the bottom of this unexpected opposition; but with this he was pleased rather than otherwise.
An opposition that is founded in reason may always be
reasoned down if reasons exist therefor; but an opposition that has its rise in any of the passions is usually
somewhat stubborn. All this the mean-looking chief, or
The Weasel, understood perfectly and appreciated highly.
He thought the moment favorable, and was disposed to
"strike while the iron was hot." Rising after a decent
interval had elapsed, this wily Indian looked about him, as
if awed by the presence in which he stood, and doubtful
whether he could venture to utter his thoughts before so
many wise chiefs. Having made an impression by this air
of diffidence, he commenced his harangue.

"I am called The Weasel," he said modestly. "My
name is not taken from the mightiest tree of the forest,
like that of my brother; it is taken from a sort of rat—
an animal that lives by its wits. I am well named. When
my tribe gave me that name it was just. All Injins have
not names. My great brother, who told us once that we
ought to take the scalp of every white man, but who *now*
tells us that we ought not to take the scalp of every white
man, has no name. He is called Peter by the pale-faces.
It is a good name. But it is a pale-face name. I wish

we knew the real name of my brother. We do not know his nation or his tribe. Some say he is an Ottawa, some an Iowa, some even think him a Sioux. I have heard he was a Delaware, from towards the rising sun. Some, but they must be Injins with forked tongues, think and say he is a Cherokee! I do not believe this. It is a lie. It is said to do my brother harm. Wicked Injins will say such things. But we do not mind what *they* say. It is not necessary.

"My brothers, I wish we knew the tribe of this great chief, who tells us to take scalps and then tells us not to take scalps. Then we might understand why he has told us two stories. I believe all he says, but I should like to know *why* I believe it. It is good to know why we believe things. I have heard what my brother has said about letting this bee-hunter go to his own people, but I do not know why he believes this is best. It is because I am a poor Injin, perhaps; and because I am called The Weasel. I am an animal that creeps through small holes. That is my nature. The bison jumps through open prairies, and a horse is wanted to catch him. It is not so with the weasel; he creeps through small holes. But he always looks where he goes.

"The unknown chief, who belongs to no tribe, talks of this bee-hunter's squaw. He is afraid of so great a medicine-man, and wishes him to go, and take all in his wigwam with him. He has no squaw. There is a young squaw in his lodge, but she is not *his* squaw. There is no need of letting her go on his account. If we take her scalp, he cannot hurt us. In that my brother is wrong. The bees have buzzed too near his ears. Weasels can hear as well as other animals; and I have heard that this young squaw is not this bee-hunter's squaw.

"If Injins are to take the scalps of all the pale-faces, why should we not begin with these who are in our hands? When the knife is ready and the head is ready, nothing but the hand is wanting. Plenty of hands are ready too, and it does not seem good to the eyes of a poor, miserable weasel, who has to creep through very small holes to catch his game, to let that game go when it is taken. If my great brother, who has told us not to scalp this bee-hunter and her he calls his squaw, will tell us the name of his tribe, I shall be glad. I am an ignorant Injin, and like to learn all I can ; I wish to learn that. Perhaps it will help us to understand why he gave one counsel yesterday and another to-day. There is a reason for it. I wish to know what it is."

Ungque now slowly seated himself. He had spoken with great moderation as to manner, and with such an air of humility as one of our own demagogues is apt to assume when he tells the people of their virtues, and seems to lament the whole time that he himself was one of the meanest of the great human family. Peter saw at once that he had a cunning competitor, and had a little difficulty in suppressing all exhibition of the fiery indignation he actually felt at meeting opposition in such a quarter. Peter was artful, and practised in all the wiles of managing men, but he submitted to use his means to attain a great end. The virtual extinction of the white race was his object, and in order to effect it there was little he would have hesitated to do. Now, however, when for the first time in many years a glimmering of human feeling was shining on the darkness of his mind, he found himself unexpectedly opposed by one of those whom he had formerly found so difficult to persuade into his own dire plans ! Had that one been a chief of any renown, the circumstances would have been more tolerable ; but here was a man presuming to raise his voice against him, who, so far as he knew anything of his past career, had not a single claim to open his mouth in such a council. With the volcano raging within, that such a state of things would be likely to kindle in the breast of a savage who had been for years a successful and nearly unopposed leader, the mysterious chief rose to reply.

"My brother says he is a weasel," observed Peter, looking round at the circle of interested and grave countenances by which he was surrounded. "That is a very small animal. It creeps through very small holes, but not to do good.

It is good for nothing. When it goes through a small hole it is not to do the Injins a service, but for its own purposes. I do not like weasels."

"My brother is not afraid of a bee-hunter. Can *he* tell us what a bee whispers? If he can, I wish he would tell us. Let him show our young men where there is more honey—where they can find bear's meat for another feast —where they can find warriors hid in the woods.

"My brother says the bee-hunter has no squaw. How does he know this? Has he lived in the lodge with them —paddled in the same canoe—eat of the same venison? A weasel is very small. It might steal into the bee-hunter's lodge and see what is there, what is doing, what is eaten, who is his squaw, and who is not: has this weasel ever done so? I never saw him there.

"Brothers, the Great Spirit has his own way of doing things. He does not stop to listen to weasels. He knows there are such animals,—there are snakes and toads and skunks. The Great Spirit knows them all, but he does not mind them. He is wise, and hearkens only to his own mind. So should it be with a council of great chiefs. It should listen to its own mind. That is wisdom. To listen to the mind of a weasel is folly.

"Brothers, you have been told that this weasel does not know the tribe of which I am born. Why should you know it? Injins once were foolish. While the pale-faces were getting one hunting-ground after another from them, they dug up the hatchet against their own friends. They took each other's scalps. Injin hated Injin—tribe hated tribe. I am of no tribe, and no one can hate me for my people. You see my skin. It is red. That is enough. I scalp and smoke and talk, and go on weary paths for all Injins and not for any tribe. I am without a tribe. Some call me the Tribeless. It is better to bear that name than to be called a weasel. I have done."

Peter had so much success by this *argumentum ad hominem*, that most present fancied that the weasel would creep through some hole and disappear. Not so, however, with Ungque. He was a demagogue after an Indian fashion;

and this is a class of men that ever "make capital of abuses,"
as we Americans say, in our money-getting habits. Instead
of being frightened off the ground, he rose to answer as
promptly as if a practised debater, though with an air of
humility so profound that no one could take offence at his
presumption.

"The unknown chief has answered," he said. "I am
glad. I love to hear his words. My ears are always open
when he speaks, and my mind is stronger. I now see that
it is good he should not have a tribe. He may be a Cherokee, and then our warriors would wish him ill." This was
a home-thrust, most artfully concealed ; a Cherokee being
the Indian of all others the most hated by the chiefs present—the Carthaginians of those western Romans. "It is
better he should not have a tribe than be a Cherokee. He
might better be a weasel.

"Brothers, we have been told to kill *all* the pale-faces.
I like that advice. The land cannot have two owners. If
a pale-face owns it an Injin cannot. If an Injin owns it
a pale-face cannot. But the chief without a tribe tells us
not to kill all. He tells us to kill all but the bee-hunter
and his squaw. He thinks this bee-hunter is a medicine
bee-hunter, and may do us Injins great harm. He wishes
to let him go.

"Brothers, this is not my way of thinking. It is better
to kill the bee-hunter and his squaw while we can, that
there may be no more such medicine bee-hunters to frighten
us Injins. If one bee-hunter can do so much harm, what
would a tribe of bee-hunters do? I do not want to see any
more. It is a dangerous thing to know how to talk with
bees. It is best that no one should have that power. I
would rather never taste honey again than live among pale-
faces that can talk with bees.

"Brothers, it is not enough that the pale-faces know so
much more than the redmen, but they must get the bees
to tell them where to find honey, to find bears, to find warriors. No ; let us take the scalp of the bee-talker and of
his squaw, that there may never be such a medicine again.
I have spoken."

Peter did not rise again.   He felt that his dignity was
involved in maintaining silence.   Various chiefs now uttered their opinions in brief, sententious language.   For
the first time since he began to preach his crusade, the current was setting against the mysterious chief.   The Weasel
said no more, but the hints he had thrown out were improved
on by others.   It is with savages as with civilized men ; a
torrent must find vent.   Peter had the sagacity to see that
by attempting further to save Le Bourdon and Margery he
should only endanger his own ascendency without effecting
his purpose.   Here he completely overlaid the art of Ungque, turning his own defeat into an advantage.   After the
matter had been discussed for fully an hour, and this mysterious chief perceived that it was useless to adhere to his
new resolution, he gave it up with as much tact as the sagacious Wellington himself could manifest in yielding Catholic
emancipation or parliamentary reform ; or just in season to
preserve an appearance of floating in the current, and with a
grace that disarmed his opponents.

   " Brothers," said Peter, by way of closing the debate, " I
have not seen straight.   Fog sometimes gets before the eyes,
and we cannot see.   I have been in a fog.   The breath of
my brother has blown it away.   I now see clearly.   I see
that bee-hunters ought not to live.   Let this one die ; let his
squaw die, too ! "

   This terminated the discussion as a matter of course.
It was solemnly decided that all the pale-faces then in the
Openings should be cut off.   In acquiescing in this decision, Peter had no mental reservations.   He was quite
sincere.   When, after sitting two hours longer, in order to
arrange still more important points, the council arose, it
was with his entire assent to the decision.   The only power
he retained over the subject was that of directing the details of the contemplated massacre.

CHAPTER XXIII.

"Why is that graceful female here
With yon red hunter of the deer?
Of gentle mien and shape, she seems
For civil halls design'd ;
Yet with the stately savage walks,
As she were of his kind."

PINKNEY.

THE family at Castle Meal saw nothing of any Indian until the day that succeeded the council. Gershom and Dorothy received the tidings of their sister's marriage with very little emotion. It was an event they expected; and as for bride-cake and ceremonies, of one there was none at all, and of the other no more than has been mentioned. The relatives of Margery did not break their hearts on account of the neglect with which they had been treated, but received the young couple as if one had given her away, and the other " had pulled off her glove," as young ladies now express it, in deference to the act that generally gives the *coup de grace* to youthful female friendships. On the Openings neither time nor breath is wasted in useless compliments ; and all was held to be well done on this occasion because it was done legally. A question might have been raised, indeed, whether that marriage had taken place under the American or under the English flag ; for General Hull, in surrendering Detroit, had included the entire Territory of Michigan, as well as troops present, troops absent, and troops on the march to join him. Had he been in possession of Peter's ruthless secret, which we happen to know he was not, he could not have been more anxious to throw the mantle of

350

British authority around all of his race on that remote frontier than he proved himself to be. Still it is to be presumed that the marriage would have been regarded as legal,—conquered territories usually preserving their laws and usages for a time, at least. A little joking passed, as a matter of course ; for this is *de rigueur* in all marriages except in the cases of the most cultivated ; and certainly neither the corporal nor Gershom belonged to the *élite* of human society.

About the hour of breakfast Pigeonswing came in, as if returning from one of his ordinary hunts. He brought with him venison, as well as several wild ducks that he had killed in the Kalamazoo, and three or four prairie hens. The Chippewa never betrayed exultation at the success of his exertions, but on this occasion he actually appeared sad. Dorothy received his game, and as she took the ducks and other fowls she spoke to him.

"Thank you, Pigeonswing," said the young matron. "No pale-face could be a better provider, and many are not one half as good."

"What provider mean, eh ? " demanded the literal-minded savage. "Mean good, mean bad, eh ? "

"Oh, it means good, of course. I could say nothing against a hunter who takes so good care of us all."

"What he mean, den ? "

"It means a man who keeps his wife and children well supplied with food."

"You get 'nough, eh ? "

"I get enough, Pigeonswing, thanks to your industry, such as it is. Injin diet, however, is not always the best for Christian folk, though a body may live on it. I miss many things out here in the Openings, to which I have been used all the early part of my life."

"What squaw miss, eh ? P'raps Injin find him sometime."

"I thank you, Pigeonswing, with all my heart, and am just as grateful for your good intentions as I should be was you to do all you wish. It is the mind that makes the marcy, and not always the deed. But you can never find the food of a pale-face kitchen out here in the Openings of Michigan. When a body comes to reckon up all the good things of Ameriky, she don't know where to begin or where to stop. I miss tea as much as anything. And milk comes next. Then there's buckwheat and coffee—though things may be found in the woods to make coffee of, but tea has no substitute. Then, I like wheaten bread and butter and potatoes, and many other such articles that I was used to all my life until I came out here, close to sunset. As for pies and custards, I can't bear to think of 'em now !''

Pigeonswing looked intently at the woman, as she carefully enumerated her favorites among the dishes of her home-kitchen. When she had ended, he raised a finger, looked still more significantly at her, and said :

"Why don't go back, get all dem good t'ings? Better for pale-face to eat pale-face food, and leave Injin Injin food.''

"For my part, Pigeonswing, I wish such had ever been the law. Venison and prairie fowls and wild ducks and trout and bear's meat and wild pigeons, and the fish that are to be found in these western rivers, are all good for them that was brought up on 'em, but they tire an eastern palate dreadfully. Give me roast beef any day before buffalo's hump, and a good barn-yard fowl before all the game-birds that ever flew.''

"Yes ; dat the way pale-face squaw feel. Bess go back and get what she like. Bess go quick as she can—go to-day.''

"I'm in no such hurry, Pigeonswing, and I like these Openings well enough to stay a while longer, and see what all these Injins, that they tell me are about 'em, mean to do. Now we are fairly among your people, and on good terms with them, it is wisest to stay where we are. These are war-times, and travelling is dangerous, they tell me. When Gershom and Bourdon are ready to start, I shall be ready too.''

"Bess get ready now,'' rejoined Pigeonswing ; who, having given this advice with point as to manner, proceeded to the spring, where he knelt and slaked his thirst. The manner of the Chippewa was such as to attract the attention of the missionary, who, full of his theory, imagined that his desire to get rid of the whites was, in some way or other, connected with a reluctance in the Indians to confess themselves Jews. He had been quite as much surprised as he was disappointed with the backwardness of the chiefs in accepting this tradition, and was now in a state of mind that predisposed him to impute everything to this one cause.

"I hope, Pigeonswing," he said to the Chippewa, whom he had followed to the spring, "I hope, Pigeonswing, that no offence has been taken by the chiefs on account of what I told them yesterday concerning their being Jews. It is what I think, and it is an honor to belong to God's chosen people, and in no sense a disgrace. I hope no offence has been taken on account of my telling the chiefs they are Jews."

"Don't care anyt'ing 'bout it," answered the literal Indian, rising from his kneeling position, and wiping his mouth with the back of his hand. "Don't care wedder Jew or wedder Injin."

"For my own part, gladly would I have it to say that I am descended from Israel."

"Why don't say him if he make you grad? Good to be grad. All Injin love to be grad."

"Because I cannot say it with truth. No; I come of the Gentiles, and not of the Hebrews, else would I glory in saying I am a Jew, in the sense of extraction, though not now in the sense of faith. I trust the chiefs will not take offence at my telling them just what I think."

"Tell you he don't care," returned Pigeonswing, a little crustily. "Don't care if Jew—don't care if Injin. Know dat make no difference. Hunting-ground just same—game just same—scalps just same. Make no difference and don't care."

"I am glad of this; but why did you advise Dorothy to quit the Openings in the hasty manner you did, if all is right with the chiefs? It is not good to start on a journey without preparation and prayer. Why then did you give this advice to Dorothy to quit the Openings so soon?"

23

"Bess for squaw to go home when Injin dig up hatchet. Openin' full of warrior—prairie full of warrior—wood full of warrior. When dat so, bess for squaw to go home."

"This would be true, were the Indians our enemies. Heaven be praised, they are our friends, and will not harm us. Peter is a great chief, and can make his young men do what he tells them ; and Peter is our friend. With Peter to stand by us, and a merciful Providence to direct us where, when, and how to go, we can have nothing to fear. I trust in Divine Providence."

"Who he be?" asked Pigeonswing, innocently, for his knowledge of English did not extend far enough to comprehend a phrase so complicated, though so familiar to ourselves. "He know all paths, eh?"

"Yes ; and directs us on all paths—more especially such as are for our good."

"Bess get him to tell you path in to Detroit. Dat good path now for all pale-faces."

On uttering this advice, which he did also somewhat pointedly, the Chippewa left the spring, and walked towards the kennel of Hive, where the bee-hunter was busy feeding his old companion.

"You're welcome back, Pigeonswing," the last cordially remarked, without pausing in his occupation, however. "I saw that you came in loaded, as usual. Have you left any dead game in the Openings for me to go and back in with you?"

"You open ear, Bourdon—you know what Injin say," returned the Chippewa, earnestly. "When dog got 'nough, come wid me. Got somet'ing to tell. Bess hear it when he *can* hear it."

"You'll find me ready enough in a minute. There, Hive, my good fellow, that ought to satisfy any reasonable dog, and I've never found you unreasonable yet. Well, Chippewa, here I am, with my ears wide open : stop, I've a bit of news, first, for your ears. Do you know, Pigeonswing, my good fellow, that I'm married?"

"Marry, eh? Got squaw, eh? Where you get him?"

"Here, to be sure—where else should I get her? There

is but one girl in these Openings that I would ask to be my wife, and she has been asked, and answered yes. Parson Amen married us yesterday, on our way in from Prairie Round ; so that puts me on a footing with yourself. When you boast of your squaw that you've left in your wigwam, I can boast of mine that I have here. Margery is a girl to boast of too ! ''

"Yes ; good squaw dat. Like dat squaw pretty well. Nebber see better. Bess keep squaw alway in his own wigwam.''

"Well, mine is in my own wigwam. Castle Meal is my property, and she does it honor.''

"Dat an't what Injin mean. Mean dis. Bess have wig-wam at home dere where pale-face lives, and bess keep squaw in *dat* wigwam. Where my squaw, eh? She home, in my wigwam : take care of pappoose, hoe corn, and keep ground good. So bess wid white squaw—bess home, at work.''

"I believe I understand what you mean, Pigeon. Well, home we mean to go before the winter sets in, and when matters have a little settled down between the English and Yankees. It is n't safe travelling just now in Michigan : you must own that yourself, my good fellow.''

The Indian appeared at a loss, now, how to express him-self further. On one side was his faith to his color, and his dread of Peter and the great chiefs ; on the other, his strong regard for the bee-hunter. He pondered a moment, and then took his own manner of communicating that which he wished to say. The fact that his friend was married made no great difference in his advice, for the Indian was much too shrewd an observer not to have detected the bee-hunter's attachment. He had not supposed it possible to separate his friend from the family of Gershom, though he did suppose there would be less difficulty in getting him to go on a path different from that which the missionary and corporal might take. His own great purpose was to serve Le Bourdon, and how many or how few might incidentally profit by it he did not care. The truth compels us to own, that even Margery's charms and nature and warm-hearted interest in all around her had failed to make any impression on his marble-like feelings ; while the bee-hunter's habits, skill in his craft, and close connection with himself at the mouth of the river, and more especially in liberating him from his enemies, had united him in a comrade's friendship with her husband. It was a little singular that this Chippewa did not fall into Peter's superstitious dread of the bee-hunter's necromancy, though he was aware of all that had passed the previous day on the prairie. Either on account of his greater familiarity with Le Bourdon's habits, or because he was in the secret of the trick of the whiskey-spring, or from a closer knowledge of white men and their ways, this young Indian was freer from apprehensions of this nature, perhaps, than any one of the same color and origin within many miles of the spot. In a word, Pigeonswing regarded the bee-hunter as his friend, while he looked upon the other pale-faces as so many persons thrown by accident in his company. Now that Margery had actually become his friend's squaw, his interest in her was somewhat increased ; though she had never obtained that interest in his feelings that she had awakened in the breast of Peter, by her attentions to him, her gentleness, light-hearted gayety, and womanly care, and all without the least design on her own part.

" No," answered the Chippewa, after a moment's reflection, " no very safe for Yankee or Yankee Injin. Don't t'ink my scalp very safe if chief know'd I 'm Yankee runner. Bess alway to keep scalp safe. Dem Pottawattamie I take care not to see. Know all 'bout 'em too. Know what he *say*—know what he *do*—b'lieve I know what he *t'ink*."

" I did not see you, Pigeon, among the red young men, yesterday, out on Prairie Round."

" Know too much to go dere. Crowsfeader and Pottawattamie out dere. Bess not go near them when dey have eye open. Take 'em asleep. Dat bess way wid sich Injin. Catch 'em some time ! But your ear open, Bourdon ? "

" Wide open, my good friend : what have you to whisper in it ? "

" You look hard at Peter when he come in. If he t'ink

good deal, and don't say much, when he *do* speak, mind what he say. If he smile, and very much friend, must hab his scalp.''

"Chippewa, Peter is my friend, lives in my cabin, and eats of my bread ! The hand that touches him touches me."

"Which bess, eh—*his* scalp or your'n ? If he *very* much friend when he come in, his scalp muss come off or your'n. Yes, juss so. Dat de way. Know Injin better dan you know him, Bourdon. You good bee-hunter, but poor Injin. Ebberybody hab his way—Injin got his. Peter laugh and very much friend, when he come home, den he mean to hab *your* scalp. If don't smile, and don't seem very much friend, but look down, and t'ink, t'ink, t'ink, den he mean no hurt to you, but try to get you out of hand of chiefs. Dat all.''

As Pigeonswing concluded, he walked coolly away, leaving his friend to ruminate on the alternative of scalp or no scalp ! The bee-hunter now understood the Chippewa perfectly. He was aware that this man had means of his own to ascertain what was passing around him in the Openings, and he had the utmost confidence in his integrity and good wishes. If a redman is slow to forget an injury, he never forgets a favor. In this he was as unlike as possible to most of the pale-faces who were supplanting his race, for these last had, and have, as extraordinary a tenacity in losing sight of benefits as they have in remembering wrongs.

By some means or other it was now clear that Pigeonswing foresaw that a crisis was at hand. Had Le Bourdon been as disconnected and solitary as he was when he first met the Chippewa, it is not probable that either the words or the manner of his friend would have produced much impression on him, so little accustomed was he to dwell on the hazards of his frontier position. But the case was now altogether changed. Margery and her claims stood foremost in his mind ; and through Margery came Dolly and her husband. There was no mistaking Pigeonswing's intention. It was to give warning of some immediate danger, and a danger that, in some way, was connected with the deportment of Peter. It was easy enough to comprehend the allusions to the mysterious chief's smiles and melancholy; and the bee-hunter understood that he was to watch that Indian's manner, and take the alarm or bestow his confidence accordingly.

Le Bourdon was not left long in doubt. Peter arrived about half an hour after Pigeonswing had gone to seek his rest; and from the instant he came in sight our hero discerned the thoughtful eye and melancholy manner. These signs were still more obvious when the tribeless Indian came nearer; so obvious, indeed, as to strike more than one of those who were interested observers of all that this extraordinary being said and did. Among others, Margery was the first to see this change, and the first to let it influence her own manner. This she did notwithstanding Le Bourdon had said nothing to her on the subject, and in defiance of the bashful feelings of a bride; which, under circumstances less marked, might have induced her to keep more in the background. As Peter stopped at the spring to quench his thirst, Margery was, in truth, the first to approach and speak to him.

"You seem weary, Peter," said the young wife, somewhat timidly as to voice and air, but with a decided and honest manifestation of interest in what she was about. Nor had Margery gone empty-handed. She took with her a savory dish, one of these that the men of the woods love—meat cooked in its own juices, and garnished with several little additions that her skill in the arts of civilized life enabled her to supply.

"You seem tired, Peter, and if I did not fear to say it, I should tell you that you also seem sad," said Margery, as she placed her dish on a rude table that was kept at the spot for the convenience of those who seldom respected hours, or regularity of any sort in their meals. "Here is food that you like, which I have cooked with my own hands."

The Indian looked intently at the timid and charming young creature, who came forward thus to contribute to his comforts, and the saddened expression of his countenance deepened. He was fatigued and hungry, and he ate for some time without speaking, beyond uttering a brief expression of his thanks. When his appetite was appeased, however, and she who had so sedulously attended to his wants was about to remove the remains of the dish, he signed with his finger for her to draw nearer, intimating that he had something to say. Margery obeyed without hesitation, though the color flitted in her face like the changes in an evening sky. But so much good-will and confidence had been awakened between these two, that a daughter would not have drawn near to a father with more confidence than Margery stood before Peter.

"Medicine-man do what I tell him, young squaw, eh?" demanded Peter, smiling slightly, and for the first time since they had met.

"By medicine-man do you mean Mr. Amen or Bourdon?" the bride asked in her turn, her whole face reflecting the confusion she felt, scarcely knowing why.

"Bot'. One medicine-man say his prayer; t'odder medicine-man take young squaw's hand and lead her into his wigwam. Dat what I mean."

"I am married to Bourdon," returned Margery, dropping her eyes to the ground, "if that be what you wish to know. I hope you think I shall have a good husband, Peter?"

"Hope so, too—nebber know till time come. All good for little while—Injin good, squaw good. Juss like weadder. Sometime rain—sometime storm—sometime sunshine. Juss so wid Injin, juss so wid pale-face. No difference. All same. You see dat cloud?—he little now; but let wind blow, he grow big, and you see nuttin' but cloud. Let him have plenty of sunshine, and he go away; den all clear over head. Dat bess way to live wid husband."

"And that is the way which Bourdon and I *will* always live together. When we get back among our own people, Peter, and are living comfortably in a pale-face wigwam, with pale-face food and pale-face drinks, and all the other good things of pale-face housekeeping about us, then I hope you will come and see how happy we are, and pass some time with us. Every year I wish you to come and see us, and to bring us venison, and Bourdon will give you powder and lead and blankets, and all you may want, unless it be fire-water. Fire-water he has promised never again to give to an Injin."

"No find any more whiskey-spring, eh?" demanded Peter, greatly interested in the young woman's natural and warm-hearted manner of proposing her hospitalities. "So bess—so bess. Great curse for Injin. Plenty honey, no fire-water. All dat good. And I come, if—"

Here Peter stopped, nor could all Margery's questions induce him to complete the sentence. His gaze at the earnest countenance of the bride was such as to give her an indefinite sort of uneasiness, not to say a feeling of alarm. Still no explanation passed between them. Margery remained near Peter for some time, administering to his wants, and otherwise demeaning herself much as a daughter might have done. At length Le Bourdon joined them. The salutations were friendly, and the manner in which the mysterious chief regarded the equally mysterious bee-hunter was not altogether without a certain degree of awe. Bourdon perceived this, and was not slow to comprehend that he owed this accession of influence to the scene which had occurred on the prairie.

"Is the great council ended, Peter?" asked the bee-hunter, when the little interval of silence had been observed.

"Yes, it over. No more council, now, on Prairie Round."

"And the chiefs—have they all gone on their proper paths? What has become of my old acquaintance, Crows-feather?—and all the rest of them—Bear's Meat in particular?"

"All gone. No more council now. Agree what to do, and so go away."

"But are redmen always as good as their words?—do they *perform* always what they *promise*?"

"Sartain. Ebbery man ought do what he say. Dat Injin law—no pale-face law, eh?"

"It may be the *law*, Peter, and a very good law it is; but we white men do not always *mind* our own laws."

"Dat bad—Great Spirit don't like dat," returned Peter, looking grave, and slowly shaking his head. "Dat very bad. When Injin say he do it, den he do it if he can. If can't, no help for it. Send squaw away, now, Bourdon; bess not to let squaw hear what men say, or will always want to hear."

Le Bourdon laughed as he turned to Margery and repeated these words. The young wife colored, but she took it in good part, and ran up towards the palisaded lodge, like one who was glad to be rid of her companions. Peter waited a few moments, then turning his head slowly in all directions, to make sure of not being overheard, he began to lay open his mind.

"You been on Prairie Round, Bourdon—you see Injin dere—chief, warrior, young men, hunter, all dere."

"I saw them all, Peter, and a goodly sight it was— what between paint and medals, and bows and arrows and tomahawks, and all your bravery!"

"You like to see him, eh? Yes; he fine t'ing to look at. Well, dat council call togedder by *me*—you know dat, too, Bourdon?"

"I have heard you say that such was your intention, and I suppose you did it, chief. They tell me you have great power among your own people, and that they do very much as you tell them to do."

Peter looked graver than ever at this remark; and one of his startling gleams of ferocity passed over his dark countenance. Then he answered with his customary self-command.

"Sometime so," he said; "sometime not so. Yesterday, not so. Dere is chief dat want to put Peter under his foot! He try, but he no do it! I know Peter well, and know dat chief, too."

"This is news to me, Peter, and I am surprised to hear it. I did think that even the great Tecumthe was scarcely as big a chief as you are, yourself."

"Yes, pretty big chief; dat true. But, among Injin,

ebbery man can speak, and nebber know which way council
go. Sometime he go one way; sometime he go tudder.
You hear Bough of Oak speak, Bourdon, eh? Tell me
dat?"

"You will remember that I heard none of your speakers
on Prairie Round, Peter. I do not remember any such
orator as this Bough of Oak."

"He great rascal," said Peter, who had picked up some
of the garrison expressions among those from whom he acquired the knowledge of English he possessed, such as it
was. "Listen, Bourdon. Nebber bess stand too much in
Peter's way."

The bee-hunter laughed freely at this remark; for his
own success the previous day, and the impression he had
evidently made on that occasion, emboldened him to take
greater liberties with the mysterious chief than had been
his wont.

"I should think that, Peter," cried the young man, gayly;
"I should think all that. For one, I should choose to
get out of it. The path you travel is your own, and all
wise men will leave you to journey along it in your own
fashion."

"Yes; dat bess way," answered the great chief, with
admirable simplicity. "Don't like, when he say yes, to
hear anudder chief say no. Dat an't good way to do business." These were expressions caught from the trading
whites, and were often used by those who got their English
from them. "I tell you one t'ing, Bourdon—dat Bough of
Oak very foolish Injin if he put foot on my path."

"This is plain enough, Peter," rejoined Le Bourdon,
who was unconcernedly repairing some of the tools of his
ordinary craft. "By the way, I am greatly in your debt,
I learn, for one thing. They tell me I've got my squaw
in my wigwam a good deal sooner, by your advice, than I
might have otherwise done. Margery is now my wife, I
suppose you know; and I thank you heartily for helping
me to get married so much sooner than I expected to be."

Here Peter grasped Bourdon by the hand, and poured
out his whole soul, secret hopes, fears, and wishes. On

this occasion he spoke in the Indian dialect—one of those that he knew the bee-hunter understood. And we translate what he said freely into English, preserving as much of the original idiom as the change of language will permit.

"Listen, hunter of the bee, and great medicine of the pale-faces, and hear what a chief that knows the redmen is about to tell you. Let my words go into your ears; let them stay in your mind. They are words that will do you good. It is not wise to let such words come out again by the hole through which they have just entered.

"My young friend knows our traditions. They do not tell us that the Injins were Jews; they tell us that the Manitou created them redmen. They tell us that our fathers used these hunting-grounds ever since the earth was placed on the back of the big tortoise which upholds it. The pale-faces say the earth moves. If this be true, it moves as slowly as the tortoise walks. It cannot have gone far since the Great Spirit lifted his hand off it. If it move, the hunting-grounds move with it, and the tribes move with their own hunting-grounds. It may be that some of the pale-faces are lost, but no Injin is lost—the medicine-priest is mistaken. He has looked so often in his book, that he sees nothing but what is there. He does not see what is before his eyes, at his side, behind his back, all around him. I have known such Injins. They see but one thing; even the deer jump across their paths and are not seen.

"Such are our traditions. They tell us that this land was given to the redmen, and not to pale-faces. That none but redmen have any right to hunt here. The Great Spirit has laws. He has told us these laws. They teach us to love our friends and to hate our enemies. You don't believe this, Bourdon?" observing the bee-hunter to wince a little, as if he found the doctrine bad.

"This is not what our priests tell *us*," answered Le Bourdon. "They tell us that the white man's God commands us to love all alike—to do *good* to our enemies, to *love* them that wish us *harm*, and to treat all men as we would wish men to treat us."

Peter was a good deal surprised at this doctrine, and it was nearly a minute before he resumed the discourse. He had recently heard it several times, and it was slowly working its way into his mind.

"Such are our traditions, and such are our laws. Look at me. Fifty winters have tried to turn my hair white. Time can do that. The hair is the only part of an Injin that ever turns white; all the rest of him is red. That is his color. The game know an Injin by his color. The tribes know him. Everything knows him by his color. He knows the things which the Great Spirit has given him in the same way. He gets used to them, and they are his acquaintances. He does not like strange things. He does not like strangers. White men are strangers, and he does not like to see them on his hunting-ground. If they came singly to kill a few buffaloes, or to look for honey, or to catch beaver, the Injins would not complain. They love to give of their abundance. The pale-faces do not come in this fashion. They do not come as guests; they come as masters. They come and they stay. Each year of my fifty have I heard of new tribes that have been driven by them towards the setting sun.

"Bourdon, for many reasons I have thought of this. I have tried to find a way to stop them. There is but one. That way must the Injins try, or give up their hunting-grounds to the strangers. No nation likes to give up its hunting-grounds. They come from the Manitou, and one day he may ask to have them back again. What could the redmen say if they let the pale-faces take them away? No; this we cannot do. We will first try the one thing that is to be done."

"I believe I understand you, Peter," observed Le Bourdon, finding that his companion paused. "You mean war. War, in the Injin mode of redressing all wrongs; war against man, woman, and child!"

Peter nodded in acquiescence, fixing his glowing eyes on the bee-hunter's face as if to read his soul.

"Am I to understand, then, that you and your friends, the chiefs and their followers that I saw on Prairie Round, mean to begin with *us*, half-a-dozen whites, of whom two are women, who happen to be here in your power—that *our* scalps are to be the first taken?"

"First!—no, Bourdon. Peter's hand has taken a great many, years since. He has got a name for his deeds, and no longer dare go to the white men's forts. He does not look for Yankees, he looks for pale-faces. When he meets a pale-face on the prairies or in the woods, he tries to get his scalp. This has he done for years, and many has he taken."

"This is a bloody account you are giving of yourself, Peter, and I would rather you should not have told it. Some such account I have heard before; but living with you, and eating and drinking and sleeping and travelling in your company, I had not only hoped, but begun to think, it was not true."

"It is true. My wish is to cut off the pale-faces. This must be done, or the pale-faces will cut off the Injins. There is no choice. One nation or the other must be destroyed. I am a redman; my heart tells me that the pale-faces should die. They are on strange hunting-grounds, not the redmen. They are wrong, we are right. But, Bourdon, I have friends among the pale-faces, and it is not natural to scalp our friends. I do not understand a religion that tells us to love our enemies, and to do good to them that do harm to us: it is a strange religion. I am a poor Injin, and do not know what to think! I shall not believe that any do this till I see it. I understand that we ought to love our friends. Your squaw is my daughter. I have called her daughter: she knows it, and my tongue is not forked like a snake's. What it says I mean. Once I meant to scalp your young squaw, because she was a pale-face squaw, and might be the mother of more. Now I do not mean to scalp her; my hand shall never harm her. My wisdom shall tell her how to escape from the hands of redmen who seek her scalp. You, too; now you are her husband, and are a great medicine-man of the bees, my hand shall not hurt you either. Open your ears wide, for big truths must go into them."

Peter then related in full his attempt to procure a safe passage for Le Bourdon and Margery into the settlements, and its total failure.　He owned that by his previous combinations he had awakened a spirit among the Indians that his present efforts could not quell.　In a word, he told the whole story as it must have been made apparent to the reader, and he now came with his plans to defeat the very schemes that he had himself previously projected.　One thing, however, that he did not conceal, filled the mind of his listener with horror, and created so strong an aversion to acting in concert with one who could even allude to it so coolly, that there was danger of breaking off all communications between the parties, and placing the result purely on force; a course that must have proved totally destructive to all the whites.　The difficulty arose from a *naïve* confession of Peter's, that he did not even wish to save any but Le Bourdon and Margery, and that he still desired the deaths of all the others, himself!

CHAPTER XXIV.

" For Thou wert born of woman !   Thou didst come,
  O Holiest ! to this world of sin and gloom,
Not in thy dread omnipotent array ;
    And not by thunders strewed
    Was thy tempestuous road,
Nor indignation burnt before thee on thy way.
    But Thee, a soft and naked child,
      Thy mother undefiled,
    In the rude manger laid to rest
      From off her virgin breast."

THE blood of the bee-hunter curdled in his veins as
he listened to Peter's business-like and direct manner of treating this terrible subject.   Putting the
most favorable view on his situation, it was frightful to look on.   Admitting that this fanatical savage was
sincere in all his professions of a wish to save him and Margery, and Le Bourdon did not, nay, *could* not doubt this,
after his calm but ferocious revelations ; but, admitting all
this to be true, how was he to escape with his charming
bride, environed as they were by so large a band of hostile
Indians.   Then the thought of abandoning his other companions, and attempting, in cold selfishness, to escape with
Margery alone, was more than he could bear.   Never before,
in his adventurous and bold life, had Le Bourdon been so
profoundly impressed with a sense of his danger, or so much
overcome.

Still, our hero was not unmanned.   He saw all the hazards, as it were, at a glance, and felt how terrible might
be the result should they really fall into the hands of the
warriors, excited to exercise their ingenuity in devising the

means of torture ; and he gazed into the frightful perspective with a manly steadiness that did him credit, even while
he sickened at the prospect.

Peter had told his story in a way to add to its horrible
character.   There was a manner of truth, of directness, of
work, if one may use such an expression on such a subject,
that gave a graphic reality to all he said.   As if his task
was done, the mysterious chief now coolly arose, and
moved away to a little grove in which the missionary and
the corporal had thrown themselves on the grass, where
they lay speculating on the probable course that the bands
in their neighborhood would next pursue.   So thoroughly
possessed was the clergyman with his one idea, however,
that he was expressing regret at his failure in the attempt
to convince the savages that they were Jews, when Peter
joined them.

" You tired—you lie down in daytime, like sick squaw,
eh ? " asked the Indian, in a slightly satirical manner.
"Bess be up, sich fine day, and go wid me to see some
more chief."

" Most gladly, Peter," returned the missionary, springing to his feet with alacrity—" and I shall have one more
opportunity to show your friends the truth of what I have
told them."

" Yes, Injin love to hear trut'—hate to hear lie.   Can tell
'em all you want to say.   He go too, eh ? " pointing to the
corporal, who rather hung back, as if he saw that in the
invitation which was not agreeable to him.

" I will answer for my friend," returned the confiding
missionary, cheerfully.   " Lead on, Peter, and we will
follow."

Thus pledged, the corporal no longer hesitated ; but he
accompanied Parson Amen, as the latter fell into the tracks
of the chief, and proceeded rapidly in the direction of the
spring in the piece of bottom-land where the council first
described had been held.   This spot was about two miles
from the palisaded house, and quite out of view as well as
out of reach of sound.   As they walked side by side, taking
the footsteps of the great chief for their guide, the corporal,

however, expressed to his companion his dislike of the whole movement.

"We ought to stand by our garrison in times like these, Mr. Amen," said the well-meaning soldier. "A garrison is a garrison ; and Injins seldom do much on a well-built and boldly defended spot of that natur'. They want artillery, without which their assaults are never very formidable."

"Why talk you of warlike means, corporal, when we are in the midst of friends? Is not Peter our known and well-tried associate, one with whom you and I have travelled far ; and do we not know that we have friends among these chiefs whom we are now going to visit? The Lord has led me into these distant and savage regions to carry his word and to proclaim his name ; and a most unworthy and unprofitable servant should I prove were I to hesitate about approaching them I am appointed to teach. No, no ; fear nothing. I will not say that you carry Cæsar and his fortunes, as I have heard was once said of old, but I will say you follow one who is led of God, and who marches with the certainty of being divinely commanded."

The corporal was ashamed to oppose so confident an enthusiasm, and he offered no further resistance. Together the two followed their leader, who, turning neither to the right hand nor to the left, soon had them out of sight of the castle, and well on their way towards the spring. When about half the distance was made, the direction took the party through a little thicket, or rather along its margin, and the missionary, a good deal to his surprise, saw Pigeonswing within the cover, seemingly preparing for another hunt. This young warrior had so lately returned from one excursion of this nature, that he was not expected to go forth so soon on another. Nor was he accustomed to go out so early in the day. This was the hour in which he ordinarily slept ; but there he was, beyond a question, and apparently looking at the party as it passed. So cold was his manner, however, and so indifferent did he seem, that no one would have suspected that he knew aught of what was in contemplation. Having satisfied himself that his friend, the bee-hunter, was not one of those who followed

24.

Peter, the Chippewa turned coldly away, and began to examine the flint of his rifle. The corporal noted his manner, and it gave him additional confidence to proceed; for he could not imagine that any human being would manifest so much indifference when sinister designs existed.

Peter turned neither to the right hand nor to the left, until he had led the way down upon the little arena of bottom-land already described, and which was found well sprinkled with savages. A few stood, or sat about in groups, earnestly conversing; but most lay extended at length on the greensward, in the indolent repose that is so grateful to an Indian warrior in his hours of inaction. The arrival of Peter, however, instantly put a new face on the appearance of matters. Every man started to his feet, and additions were made to those who were found in the arena by those who came out of the adjacent thickets, until some two or three hundred of the redmen were assembled in a circle around the newly-arrived pale-faces.

"There," said Peter, sternly, fastening his eye with a hostile expression on Bough of the Oak and Ungque in particular,—"there are your captives. Do with them as you will. As for them that have dared to question my faith, let them own that they are liars!"

This was not a very amicable salutation, but savages are accustomed to plain language. Bough of the Oak appeared a little uneasy, and Ungque's countenance denoted dissatisfaction; but the last was too skilful an actor to allow many of the secrets of his plotting mind to shine through the windows of his face. As for the crowd at large, gleams of content passed over the bright red faces, illuminating them with looks of savage joy. Murmurs of approbation were heard, and Crowsfeather addressed the throng there, where it stood, encircling the two helpless and as yet but half-alarmed victims of so fell a plot.

"My brothers and my young men can now see," said this Pottawattamie, "that the tribeless chief has an Injin heart. His heart is *not* a pale-face heart; it is that of a redman. Some of our chiefs have thought that he had lived too much with the stranger, and that he had forgotten the traditions of our fathers, and was listening to the song of the medicine-priest. Some thought that he believed himself lost and a Jew, and not an Injin. This is not so. Peter knows the path he is on. He knows that he is a redskin, and he looks on the Yankees as enemies. The scalps he has taken are so numerous they cannot be counted. He is ready to take more. Here are two that he gives to us. When we have done with these two captives he will bring us more. He will continue to bring them until the pale-faces will be as few as the deer in their own clearings. Such is the will of the Manitou.''

The missionary understood all that was said, and he was not a little appalled at the aspect of things. For the first time he began to apprehend that he was in danger. So much was this devout and well-intentioned servant of his church accustomed to place his dependence on a superintending Providence, that apprehension of personal suffering seldom had any influence on his exertions. He believed himself to be an object of especial care; though he was ever ready to admit that the wisdom which human minds cannot compass might order events that, at first sight, would seem to be opposed to that which ought to be permitted to come to pass. In this particular Parson Amen was a model of submission, firmly believing all that happened was in furtherance of the great scheme of man's regeneration and eventual salvation.

With the corporal it was very different. Accustomed to war with redmen, and most acquainted with them in their worst character, he ever suspected treachery, and had followed Peter with a degree of reluctance he had not dared to express. He now thoroughly took the alarm, however, and stood on his guard. Although he did not comprehend more than half of that which Peter had said, he understood quite enough to see that he and the missionary were surrounded by enemies, if not by executioners.

"We have fallen into a sort of ambush here, Parson Amen," cried the corporal, rattling his arms as he looked to their condition, "and it 's high time we beat the general. If there were four on us, we might form a square; but

being only two, the best thing we can do will be to stand
back to back, and for one to keep an eye on the right
flank, while he nat'rally watches all in front, and for the
other to keep an eye on the left flank, while he sees to the
rear. Place your back close to mine, and take the left
flank into your part of the lookout. Closer, closer, my
good sir ; we must stand solid as rooted trees to make
anything of a stand.''

The missionary, in his surprise, permitted the corporal
to assume the position described, though conscious of its
uselessness in their actual condition. As for the Indians,
the corporal's manner, and the rattling of his arms, induced the circle to recede several paces ; though nothing
like alarm prevailed among them. The effect, nevertheless,
was to leave the two captives space for their evolutions,
and a sort of breathing time. This little change had the
appearance of something like success, and it greatly encouraged the corporal. He began to think it even possible to
make a retreat that would be as honorable as any victory.

''Steady—keep shoulder to shoulder, Parson Amen,
and take care of your flank. Our movement must be by
our left flank, and everything depends on keeping that
clear. I shall have to give you my baggonet, for you 're
entirely without arms, which leaves my rear altogether exposed.''

''Think nothing of your arms, Brother Flint ; they
would be useless in my hands, in any case ; and, were we
made of muskets, they could be of no use against these
odds. My means of defence come from on high ; my
armor is faith ; and my only weapon prayer. I shall not
hesitate to use the last on this, as on all other occasions.''

The missionary then called on the circle of curious savages by whom he was surrounded, and who certainly contemplated nothing less than his death, in common with
those of all his white companions, to unite with him in
addressing the Throne of Grace. Accustomed to preach
and pray to these people in their own dialect, the worthy
parson made a strong appeal to their charities, while sup-
plicating the favors of Divine Providence in behalf of him-

self and his brother captive. He asked for all the usual benedictions and blessings on his enemies, and made a very happy exposition of those sublime dogmas of Christianity, which teach us to "bless them that curse us," and to "pray for those who despitefully use us." Peter, for the first time in his life, was now struck with the moral beauty of such a sentiment, which seldom fails, when duly presented, of producing an effect on even the dullest minds. His curiosity was touched, and instead of turning coldly, as had been his intention, and leaving the captives in the hands of those to whom he had delivered them, he remained in the circle, and paid the closest attention to all of the proceedings. He had several times previously heard the missionary speak of his duty as a command of God's, but never before had he deemed it possible to realize such a thing in practice.

The Indians, if not absolutely awe-struck by the singular spectacle before them, seemed well disposed to let the missionary finish his appeal; some wondering, others doubting, and all more or less at a loss to know what to make of an exhibition so unusual. There stood the corporal, with his back pressed closely to that of his companion, his musket at "make ready," and his whole mien that of a man with every nerve screwed to the sticking point; while the missionary, the other side of the picture, with outstretched arms was lifting his voice in prayer to the throne of the Most High. As this extraordinary scene continued, the corporal grew excited; and ere long his voice was occasionally heard, blended with that of the clergyman, in terms of advice and encouragement.

"Blaze away, Mr. Amen," shouted the soldier. "Give 'em another volley; you're doing wonders, and their front has given ground! One more such volley as the last, and we'll make a forward movement ourselves—attention!—prepare to march by the left flank, as soon as there is a good opening!"

That good opening, however, was never made. The savages, though astonished, were by no means frightened, and had not the smallest idea of letting their captives escape. On the contrary, Bear's Meat, who acted as commander-in-chief on this occasion, was quite self-possessed, and so far from being impressed with the missionary's prayer, he listened to it only in the hope of hearing some admission of weakness escape. But the excitement of the corporal soon produced a crisis. His attempts to make a movement "by the left flank" caused his column of defence to be broken, and obtaining no assistance from Parson Amen, who was still pouring out his soul in prayer, while endeavoring to bring things back to their original state, he suddenly found himself surrounded and disarmed. From that instant the corporal changed his tactics. So long as he was armed, and comparatively free, he had bethought him only of the means of resistance; now that these were denied him, he submitted, and summoned all his resolution to bear the penalties of his captivity in a manner that might not do discredit to his regiment. This was the third time that Corporal Flint had been a prisoner among the Indians, and he was not now to learn the nature of their tender mercies. His forebodings were not of the most pleasant character; but that which could not be helped he was disposed to bear with manly fortitude. His greatest concern, at that fearful moment, was for the honor of his corps.

All this time Parson Amen continued his prayer. So completely was his spirit occupied with the duty of offering up his petition that he was utterly unconscious of what else had passed; nor had he heard one of the corporal's appeals for "attention," and to be "steady," and to march "by the left flank." In a word, the whole man was intent on prayer; and when thus employed, a six-pounder discharged in the circle would hardly have disconcerted him. He persevered, therefore, uninterrupted by his conquerors, until he concluded in his own way. Having thus fortified his soul, and asked for succor where he had now so long been accustomed to seek and to find it, the worthy missionary took his seat quietly on a log, on which the corporal had been previously placed by his captors.

The time had arrived for the chiefs to proceed in the execution of their purposes. Peter, profoundly struck with the prayers of the missionary in behalf of his enemies, had taken a station a little on one side, where he stood ruminating on what he had just heard. If ever precept bore the stamp of a divine origin it is this. The more we reflect on it, the clearer do our perceptions of this truth become. The whole scheme of Christ's redemption and future existence is founded in love, and such a system would be imperfect while any were excluded from its benefits. To love those who reciprocate our feelings is so very natural, that the sympathies which engender this feeling are soonest attracted by a knowledge of their existence ; love producing love as power increases power. But to love those who hate us, and to strive to do good to those who are plotting evil against ourselves, greatly exceeds the moral strength of man, unaided from above. This was the idea that puzzled Peter, and he now actually interrupted the proceedings, in order to satisfy his mind on a subject so totally new to him. Previously, however, to taking this step, he asked the permission of the principal chiefs, awakening in their bosoms, by means of his explanations, some of the interest in this subject that he felt himself.

" Brother medicine-man," said the mysterious chief, drawing nearer to the missionary, accompanied himself by Bear's Meat, Crowsfeather, and one or two more, " you have been talking to the Great Spirit of the pale-faces. We have heard your words, and think them well. They are good words for a man about to set out on the path that leads to the unknown lands. Thither we must all go some time, and it matters little when. We may not all travel the same path. I do not think the Manitou will crowd tribes of different colors together there, as they are getting to be crowded together here.

" Brother, you are about to learn how all these things really are. If redmen and pale-faces and black-men are to live in the same land after death, you will shortly know it. My brother is about to go there. He and his friend, this warrior of his people, will travel on that long path in company. I hope they will agree by the way, and not trouble each other. It will be convenient to my brother to have a hunter with him ; the path is so long, he will be hungry before he gets to the end. This warrior knows how to use a musket, and we shall put his arms with him in his grave.

"Brother, before you start on this journey, from which no traveller ever returns, let his color be what it may, we wish to hear you speak further about loving our enemies. This is not the Indian rule. The redmen hate their enemies and love their friends. When they ask the Manitou to do anything to their enemies, it is to do them harm. This is what our fathers taught us; it is what we teach our children. Why should we love them that hate us? Why should we do good to them that do us harm? Tell us now, or we may never hear the reason."

"Tell you I will, Peter, and the Lord so bless my words that they may soften your hearts and lead you all to the truth, and to dependence on the mediation of his blessed Son ! We should do good to them that do evil to us, because the Great Spirit has commanded us so to do. Ask your own heart if this is not right? If they sound like words that are spoken by any but those who have been taught by the Manitou himself? The devils tell us to revenge, but God commands us to forgive. It is easy to do good to them that do good to us ; but it tries the heart sorely to do good to them that do us evil. I have spoken to you of the Son of the Great Spirit. He came on earth, and told us with his own mouth all these great truths ; he said that next to the duty of loving the Manitou is the duty of loving our neighbors. No matter whether friend or enemy ; it is our duty to love them, and do them all the good we can. If there is no venison in their wigwams, we should take the deer from off our own poles and carry it and put it on theirs. Why have I come here to tell you this? When at home, I lived under a good roof, eat of abundance, and slept in a soft and warm bed. You know how it is here. We do not know to-day what we shall eat to-morrow. Our beds are hard and our roofs are of bark. I come because the Son of the Manitou, he who came and lived among men, told us to do all this. His commands to his medicine-men were to

go forth and tell all nations and tribes and colors the truth
—to tell them to ' love them that sought to do them harm,
and to do good for evil.' ''

Parson Amen pausing a moment to take breath, Ungque,
who detected the wavering of Peter's mind, and who acted
far more in opposition to the mysterious and tribeless
chief than from any other motive, profited by the occasion
thus afforded to speak. Without this pause, however, the
breeding of an Indian would have prevented any interruption.

"I open my mouth to speak," said The Weasel, in his
humblest manner. "What I say is not fit for the wise
chiefs to hear. It is foolish, but my mind tells me to say
it. Does the medicine-man of the pale-faces tell us that
the Son of the Great Spirit came upon earth and lived
among men?"

"I do; such is our belief; and the religion we believe and
teach cometh directly from his mouth."

"Let the medicine-man tell the chiefs how long the Son
of the Great Spirit stayed on earth, and which way he went
when he left it?"

Now, this question was put by Ungque through profound
dissimulation. He had heard of the death of Christ, and
had obtained some such idea of the great sacrifice as would
be apt to occur to the mind of a savage. He foresaw that
the effect of the answer would be very likely to destroy
most of the influence that the missionary had just been
building up by means of his doctrine and his prayers. Parson Amen was a man of singular simplicity of character, but
he had his misgivings touching the effect of this reply. Still,
he did not scruple about giving it, or attempt in any manner
to mystify or to deceive.

"It is a humiliating and sad story, my brethren, and one
that ought to cause all heads to be bowed to the earth in
shame," he answered. " The Son of the Great Spirit came
among men; he did nothing but good; told those who
heard him how to live and how to die. In return for all
this, wicked and unbelieving men put him to death. After
death, his body was taken up into heaven, the region of

departed spirits and the dwelling-place of his Father, where
he now is, waiting for the time when he is to return to the
earth, to reward the good and to punish the wicked. That
time will surely come ; nor do I believe the day to be very
distant.''

The chiefs listened to this account with grave attention.
Some of them had heard outlines of the same history before.
Accounts savoring of the Christian history had got blended
with some of their own traditions, most probably the fruits
of the teachings of the earlier missionaries, but were so
confused and altered as to be scarcely susceptible of being
recognized. To most of them, however, the history of the
incarnation of the Son of God was entirely new ; and it
struck *them* as a most extraordinary thing altogether that
any man should have injured such a being ! It was, perhaps, singular that no one of them all doubted the truth
of the tradition itself. This they supposed to have been
transmitted with the usual care, and they received it as
a fact not to be disputed. The construction that was put
on its circumstances will best appear in the remarks that
followed.

"If the pale-faces killed the Son of the Great Spirit,"
said Bough of the Oak, pointedly, "we can see why they
wish to drive the redmen from their lands. Evil spirits
dwell in such men, and they do nothing but what is bad.
I am glad that our great chief has told us to put the foot
on this worm and crush it while yet the Indian foot is
large enough to do it. In a few winters they would kill us,
as they killed the Spirit that did them nothing but good !"

"I am afraid that this mighty tradition hath a mystery
in it that your Indian minds will scarcely be willing to receive," resumed the missionary, earnestly. "I would not
for a thousand worlds, or to save ten thousand lives as
worthless as my own, place a straw in the way of the faith
of any ; yet must I tell the thing as it happened. This
Son of the Great Spirit was certainly killed by the Jews of
that day, so far as he *could* be killed. He possessed two
natures, as indeed do all men ; the body and soul. In his
body he was man, as we all are men ; in his soul he was a

part of the Great Spirit himself. This is the great mystery
of our religion. We cannot tell how it can happen, but we
believe it. We see around us a thousand things that we
cannot understand, and this is one of them."

Here Bear's Meat availed himself of another pause to
make a remark. This he did with the keenness of one accustomed to watch words and events closely, but with a simplicity that showed no vulgar disposition to skepticism.

"We do not expect that all the Great Spirit does can be
clear to us Injins," he said. "We know very little; he
knows everything. Why should we think to know all that
he knows. We do not. That part of the tradition gives
us no trouble. Indians can believe without seeing. They
are not squaws that wish to look behind every bush. But
my brother has told too much for his own good. If the
pale-faces killed their Great Spirit, they can have no Manitou, and must be in the hands of the Evil Spirit. This is
the reason they want our hunting-grounds. I will not let
them come any nearer to the setting sun. It is time to
begin to kill them as they killed their Great Spirit. The
Jews did this. My brother wishes us to think that redmen
are Jews! No; redmen never harmed the Son of the
Great Spirit. They would receive him as a friend, and
treat him as a chief. Accursed be the hand that should
be raised to harm him. This tradition is a wise tradition.
It tells us many things. It tells us that Injins are not Jews.
They never hurt the Son of the Great Spirit. It tells us
that the redmen have always lived on these hunting-grounds,
and did not come from towards the rising sun. It tells us
that pale-faces are not fit to live. They are too wicked.
Let them die."

"I would ask a question," put in Peter. "This tradition is not new. I have heard it before. It entered but
a little way into my ears. I did not think of it. It has
now entered deeper; and I wish to hear more. Why did
not the Son of the Great Spirit kill the Jews? Why did
he let the Jews kill him? Will my brother say?"

"He came on earth to die for man, whose wickedness was
so deep that the Great Spirit's justice could not be satisfied

with less. *Why* this is so, no one knows. It is enough that it should be so. Instead of thinking of doing harm to his tormentors and murderers, he died for them, and died asking for benefits on them, and on their wives and children, for all time to come. It was he who commanded us to do good to them that do harm to us.''

Peter gave the utmost attention to this answer, and when he had received it he walked apart, musing profoundly. It is worthy of being observed that not one of these savages raised any hollow objections to the incarnation of the Son of the Great Spirit, as would have been the case with so many civilized men. To them this appeared no more difficult and incomprehensible than most of that which they saw around them. It is when we begin to assume the airs of philosophy, and to fancy, because we know a little, that the whole book of knowledge is within our grasp, that men become skeptics. There is not a human being now in existence who does not daily, hourly see that which is just as much beyond his powers of comprehension, as this account of the incarnation of the Deity and the whole doctrine of the Trinity ; and yet he acquiesces in that which is before his eyes, because it is familiar and he sees it, while he cavils at all else, though the same unknown and inexplicable cause lies behind everything. The deepest philosophy is soon lost in this general mystery, and, to the eye of a meek reason, all around us is a species of miracle which must be referred to the power of the Deity.

While thus disposed to receive the pale-face traditions with respect, however, the redmen did not lose sight of their own policy and purposes. The principal chiefs now stepped aside, and held a brief council. Though invited to do so, Peter did not join them ; leaving to Bough of the Oak, Ungque, and Bear's Meat the control of the result. The question was, whether the original intention of including this medicine-priest to be cut off should or should not be adhered to. One or two of the chiefs had their doubts, but the opinion of the council was adverse.

" If the pale-faces killed the Son of their Great Spirit, why should we hesitate about killing them ?'' The Weasel asked,

with malicious point, for he saw that Peter was now sorely
troubled at the probability of his own design being fully
carried out. "There is no difference. This is a medicine-
priest; in the wigwam is a medicine bee-hunter, and that
warrior may be a medicine-warrior. We do not know. We
are poor Injins that know but little. It is not so with the
pale-faces; they talk with the conjurer's bees, and know
much. We shall not have ground enough to take even a
muskrat soon, unless we cut off the strangers. The Manitou has given us these; let us kill them."

As no one very strenuously opposed the scheme, the question was soon decided, and Ungque was commissioned to
communicate the result to the captives. One exception,
however, was to be made in favor of the missionary. His
object appeared to be peaceful, and it was determined that
he should be led a short distance into the surrounding
thicket and be there put to death, without any attempt to
torture, or aggravate his sufferings. As a mark of singular
respect, it was also decided not to scalp him.

As Ungque and those associated with him led the missionary to the place of execution, the former artfully invited
Peter to follow. This was done simply because The Weasel
saw that it would now be unpleasant to the man he hated—
hated, merely because he possessed an influence that he coveted for himself.

"My father will see a pleasant sight," said the wily
Weasel, as he walked at Peter's side towards the indicated
spot; "he will see a pale-face die, and know that his foot
has been put upon another worm."

No answer was made to this ironical remark, but Peter
walked in silence to the place where the missionary was stationed, surrounded by a guard. Ungque now advanced and
spoke.

"It is time for the medicine-priest of the pale-faces to
start after the spirits of his people who have gone before
him," he said. "The path is long, and unless he walks
fast and starts soon, he may not overtake them. I hope he
will see some of them that helped to kill the Son of his
Great Spirit, starving and footsore on the way."

"I understand you," returned the missionary, after a few moments passed in recovering from the shock of this communication. "My hour is come. I have held my life in my hand ever since I first put foot in this heathen region, and if it be the Creator's will that I am now to die, I bow to the decree. Grant me a few minutes for prayer to my God."

Ungque signed that the delay should be granted. The missionary uncovered his head, knelt, and again lifted up his voice in prayer. At first the tones were a little tremulous; but they grew firmer as he proceeded. Soon they became as serene as usual. He first asked mercy for himself, threw all his hopes on the great atonement, and confessed how far he was from that holiness which alone could fit him to see God. When this duty was performed, he prayed for his enemies. The language used was his mother tongue, but Peter comprehended most of that which was said. He heard his own people prayed for; he heard his own name mentioned, as the condemned man asked the mercy of the Manitou in his behalf. Never before was the soul of this extraordinary savage so shaken. The past seemed like a dream to him, while the future possessed a light that was still obscured by clouds. Here was an exemplification in practice of that divine spirit of love and benevolence which had struck him already as so very wonderful. There could be no mistake. There was the kneeling captive, and his words, clear, distinct, and imploring, ascended through the cover of the bushes to the throne of God.

As soon as the voice of the missionary was mute, the mysterious chief bowed his head and moved away. He was then powerless. No authority of his could save the captive, and the sight that so lately would have cheered his eyes was now too painful to bear. He heard the single blow of the tomahawk which brained the victim, and he shuddered from head to foot. It was the first time such a weakness had ever come over him. As for the missionary, in deference to his pursuits, his executioners dug him a grave, and buried him unmutilated on the spot where he had fallen.

CHAPTER XXV.

"Brutal alike in deed and word,
    With callous heart and hand of strife,
How like a fiend may man be made,
Plying the foul and monstrous trade
    Whose harvest-field is human life."

WHITTIER.

A VEIL, like that of oblivion, dropped before the form of the missionary. The pious persons who had sent him forth to preach to the heathen never knew his fate ; a disappearance that was so common to that class of devoted men as to produce regret rather than surprise. Even those who took his life felt a respect for him ; and, strange as it may seem, it was to the eloquence of the man who now would have died to save him that his death was alone to be attributed. Peter had awakened fires that he could not quench, and aroused a spirit that he could not quell. In this respect he resembled most of those who, under the guise of reform or revolution, in moments of doubt, set in motion a machine that is found impossible to control when it is deemed expedient to check exaggeration by reason. Such is often the case with even well-intentioned leaders, who constantly are made to feel how much easier it is to light a conflagration than to stay its flames when raging.

Corporal Flint was left seated on the log while the bloody scene of the missionary's death was occurring. He was fully alive to all the horrors of his own situation, and comprehended the nature of his companion's movements. The savages usually manifested so much respect for missionaries, that he was in no degree surprised. Parson Amen had been taken apart for his execution, and when those who had caused his removal returned, the corporal looked anxiously for the usual but revolting token of his late companion's death. As has been said, however, the missionary was suffered to lie in his wild grave without suffering a mutilation of his remains.

Notwithstanding this moderation, the Indians were getting to be incited by this taste of blood. The principal chiefs became sterner in their aspects, and the young men began to manifest some such impatience as that which the still untried pup betrays when he first scents his game. All these were ominous symptoms, and were well understood by the captive.

Perhaps it would not have been possible, in the whole range of human feelings, to find two men under influences more widely opposed to each other than were the missionary and the corporal, in this their last scene on earth. The manner of Parson Amen's death has been described. He died in humble imitation of his Divine Master, asking for blessings on those who were about to destroy him, with a heart softened by Christian graces, and a meekness that had its origin in the consciousness of his own demerits. On the other hand, the corporal thought only of vengeance. Escape he knew to be impossible, and he would fain take his departure like a soldier, or as he conceived a soldier should die, in the midst of fallen foes.

Corporal Flint had a salutary love of life, and would very gladly escape did the means offer ; but, failing of these, all his thoughts turned towards revenge. Some small impulses of ambition, or what it is usual to dignify with that term, showed themselves even at that serious moment. He had heard around the camp-fires and in the garrisons so many tales of heroism and of fortitude manifested by soldiers who had fallen into the hands of the Indians, that a faint desire to enroll his own name on the list of these worthies was beginning to arise in his breast. But truth compels us to add, that the predominant feeling was the wish to revenge his own fate, by immolating as many of his foes as possible. To this last purpose, therefore, his thoughts were mainly directed during that interval which his late companion had employed in prayers for those under whose blows he was about to fall. Such is the difference in man, with his heart touched or untouched by the power of the Holy Spirit.

It was, however, much easier for the corporal to entertain designs of the nature mentioned than to carry them out; unarmed, surrounded by watchful enemies, and totally without support of any sort, the chances of effecting his purpose were small indeed. Once, for a minute only, the veteran seriously turned his thoughts to escape. It occurred to him that he might possibly reach the castle, could he get a little start; and should the Indians compel him to run the gauntlet, as was often their practice, he determined to make an effort for life in that mode. Agreeable to the code of frontier warfare, a successful flight of this nature was scarcely less creditable than a victory in the field.

Half an hour passed after the execution of the missionary, before the chiefs commenced their proceedings with the corporal. The delay was owing to a consultation, in which The Weasel had proposed despatching a party to the castle to bring in the family, and thus make a common destruction of the remaining pale-faces known to be in that part of the Openings. Peter did not dare to oppose this scheme himself; but he so managed as to get Crowsfeather to do it, without bringing himself into the foreground. The influence of the Pottawattamie prevailed, and it was decided to torture this one captive and to secure his scalp, before they proceed to work their will on the others. Ungque, who had gained ground rapidly by his late success, was once more commissioned to state to the captive the intentions of his captors.

"Brother," commenced The Weasel, placing himself directly in front of the corporal, "I am about to speak to you. A wise warrior opens his ears when he hears the voice of his enemy. He may learn something it will be good for him to know. It will be good for you to know what I am about to say.

"Brother, you are a pale-face, and we are Injins. You
25

wish to get our hunting-grounds, and we wish to keep them. To keep them, it has become necessary to take your scalp. I hope you are ready to let us have it.''

The corporal had but an indifferent knowledge of the Indian language, but he comprehended all that was uttered on this occasion. Interest quickened his faculties, and no part of what was said was lost. The gentle, slow, deliberate manner in which The Weasel delivered himself contributed to his means of understanding. He was fortunately prepared for what he heard, and the announcement of his approaching fate did not disturb him to the degree of betraying weakness. This last was a triumph in which the Indians delighted, though they ever showed the most profound respect for such of their victims as manifested a manly fortitude. It was necessary to reply, which the corporal did in English, knowing that several present could interpret his words. With a view to render this the more easy, he spoke in fragments of sentences and with great deliberation.

''Injins,'' returned the corporal, ''you surrounded me, and I have been taken prisoner : had there been a platoon on us, you might n't have made out quite so well. It's no great victory for three hundred warriors to overcome a single man. I count Parson Amen as worse than nothing, for he looked to neither rear nor flank. If I could have half an hour's work upon you with only half of our late company, I think we should lower your conceit. But that is impossible, and so you may do just what you please with me. I ask no favors.''

Although this answer was very imperfectly translated it awakened a good deal of admiration. A man who could look death so closely in the face with so much steadiness became a sort of hero in Indian eyes ; and with the North American savage fortitude is a virtue not inferior to courage. Murmurs of approbation were heard, and Ungque was privately requested to urge the captive further, in order to see how far present appearances were likely to be maintained.

''Brother, I have said that we are Injins,'' resumed The Weasel, with an air so humble and a voice so meek that a stranger might have supposed he was consoling instead of endeavoring to intimidate the prisoner. "It is true. We are nothing but poor, ignorant Injins. We can only torment our prisoners after Injin fashion. If we were pale-faces we might do better. We did not torment the medicine-priest. We were afraid he would laugh at our mistakes. He knew a great deal. We know but little. We do as well as we know how.

"Brother, when Injins do as well as they know how, a warrior should forget their mistakes. We wish to torment you in a way to prove that you are all over man. We wish so to torment you, that you will stand up under the pain in such a way that it will make our young men think your mother was not a squaw,—that there is no woman in you. We do this for our own honor as well as for yours. It will be an honor to us to have such a captive ; it will be an honor to you to be such a captive. We shall do as well as we know how.

"Brother, it is most time to begin. The tormenting will last a long time. We must not let the medicine-priest get too great a start on the path to the happy hunting-grounds of your—"

Here a most unexpected interruption occurred that effectually put a stop to the eloquence of Ungque. In his desire to make an impression, the savage approached within reach of the captive's arm, while his own mind was intent on the words that he hoped would make the prisoner quail. The corporal kept his eye on that of the speaker, charming him as it were into a riveted gaze in return. Watching his opportunity, he caught the tomahawk from The Weasel's belt, and by a single blow felled him dead at his feet. Not content with this, the old soldier now bounded forward, striking right and left, inflicting six or eight wounds on others before he could be again arrested, disarmed, and bound. While the last was doing, Peter withdrew unobserved.

Many were the "hughs" and other exclamations of admiration that succeeded this display of desperate manhood. The body of The Weasel was removed and interred, while the wounded withdrew to attend to their hurts, leaving the arena to the rest assembled there. As for the corporal, he was pretty well blown, and, in addition to being now bound hand and foot, his recent exertions, which were terrific while they lasted, effectually incapacitated him from making any move so long as he was thus exhausted and confined.

A council was now held by the principal chiefs. Ungque had few friends. In this, he shared the fate of most demagogues, who are commonly despised even by those they lead and deceive. No one regretted him much, and some were actually glad of his fate. But the dignity of the conquerors must be vindicated. It would never do to allow a pale-face to obtain so great an advantage and not take a signal vengeance for his deeds. After a long consultation, it was determined to subject the captive to the trial by saplings, and thus see if he could bear the torture without complaining. As some of our readers may not understand what this fell mode of tormenting is, it may be necessary to explain.

There is scarcely a method of inflicting pain, that comes within the compass of their means, that the North American Indians have not essayed on their enemies. When the infernal ingenuity that is exercised on these occasions fails of its effect, the captives themselves have been heard to suggest other means of torturing that *they* have known practised successfully by their own people. There is often a strange strife between the tormentors and the tormented; the one to manifest skill in inflicting pain, and the other to manifest fortitude in enduring it. As has been said, quite as much renown is often acquired by the warrior in setting all the devices of his conquerors at defiance, while subject to their hellish attempts, as in deeds of arms. It might be more true to say that such *was* the practice among the Indians, than to say, at the present time, that such *is*; for it is certain that civilization in its approaches, while it has in many particulars even degraded the redman, has had a silent effect in changing and mitigating many of the fiercer customs,— this, perhaps, among the rest. It is probable that the more distant tribes still resort to all these ancient usages; but it is both hoped and believed that those nearer to the whites do not.

The " torture by saplings " is one of those modes of inflicting pain that would naturally suggest themselves to savages. Young trees that do not stand far apart are trimmed of their branches, and brought nearer to each other by bending their bodies; the victim is then attached to both trunks, sometimes by his extended arms, at others by his legs, or by whatever part of the frame cruelty can suggest, when the saplings are released, and permitted to resume their upright positions. Of course, the sufferer is lifted from the earth, and hangs suspended by his limbs, with a strain on them that soon produces the most intense anguish. The celebrated punishment of the "knout" partakes a good deal of this same character of suffering. Bough of the Oak now approached the corporal, to let him know how high an honor was in reserve for him.

" Brother," said this ambitious orator, " you are a brave warrior. You have done well. Not only have you killed one of our chiefs, but you have wounded several of our young men. No one but a brave could have done this. You have forced us to bind you, lest you might kill some more. It is not often that captives do this. Your courage has caused us to consult *how* we might best torture you, in a way most to manifest your manhood. After talking together, the chiefs have decided that a man of your firmness ought to be hung between two young trees. We have found the trees, and have cut off their branches. You can see them. If they were a little larger their force would be greater, and they would give you more pain, would be more worthy of you; but these are the largest saplings we could find. Had there been any larger, we would have let you have them. We wish to do you honor, for you are a bold warrior, and worthy to be well tormented.

" Brother, look at these saplings! They are tall and straight. When they are bent by many hands, they will come together. Take away the hands, and they will become straight again. Your arms must then keep them together. We wish we had some pappooses here, that they might shoot arrows into your flesh. That would help much to torment you. You cannot have this honor, for we have no pappooses. We are afraid to let our young men shoot arrows into your flesh. They are strong, and might kill you. We wish you to die between the saplings, as is your right, being so great a brave.

"Brother, we think much better of you since you killed The Weasel and hurt our young men. If all your warriors at Chicago had been as bold as you, Blackbird would not have taken that fort. You would have saved many scalps. This encourages us. It makes us think the Great Spirit means to help us, and that we shall kill all of the palefaces. When we get farther into your settlements, we do not expect to meet many such braves as you. They tell us we shall then find men who will run, and screech like women. It will not be a pleasure to torment such men. We had rather torment a bold warrior, like you, who makes us admire him for his manliness. We love our squaws, but not in the war-path. They are best in the lodges; here we want nothing but men. You are a man —a brave—we honor you. We think, notwithstanding, we shall yet make you weak. It will not be easy, but we hope to do it. We shall try. We may not think quite so well of you if we do it; but we shall always call you a brave. A man is not a stone. We can all feel, and when we have done all that is in our power no one can do more. It is so with Injins; we think it must be so with pale-faces. We mean to try and see how it is."

The corporal understood very little of this harangue though he perfectly comprehended the preparations of the saplings, and Bough of the Oak's allusions to *them*. He was in a cold sweat at the thought, for resolute as he was, he foresaw sufferings that human fortitude could hardly endure. In this state of the case, and in the frame of mind he was in, he had recourse to an expedient of which he had often heard, and which he now thought might be practised to some advantage. It was to open upon the savages with abuse, and to exasperate them by taunts and sarcasm to such a degree as might induce some of the weaker members of the tribe to despatch him on the spot. As the corporal, with the perspective of the saplings before his eyes, manifested a good deal of ingenuity on this occasion, we shall record some of his efforts.

"D' ye call yourselves chiefs and warriors?" he began, upon a pretty high key. "I call ye squaws! There is not a man among ye. Dogs would be the best name. You are poor Injins. A long time ago, the pale-faces came here in two or three little canoes. They were but a handful, and you were plentier than prairie wolves. Your bark could be heard throughout the land. Well, what did this handful of pale-faces? It drove your fathers before them, until they got all the best of the hunting-grounds. Not an Injin of you all, now, ever get down on the shores of the great salt-lake, unless to sell brooms and baskets, and then he goes sneaking like a wolf after a sheep. You have forgotten how clams and oysters taste. Your fathers had as many of them as they could eat; but not one of *you* ever tasted them. The pale-faces eat them all. If an Injin asked for one, they would throw the shell at his head and call him a dog.

"Do you think that my chiefs would hang one of you between two such miserable saplings as these? No! They would scorn to practise such pitiful torture. They would bring the tops of two tall pines together, trees a hundred and fifty feet high, and put their prisoner on the topmost boughs, for the crows and ravens to pick his eyes out. But you are miserable Injins! You know nothing. If you know'd any better, would you act such poor torment ag'in a great brave? I spit upon ye and call ye squaws. The pale-faces have made women of ye. They have taken out your hearts and put pieces of dog's flesh in their places."

Here the corporal, who delivered himself with an animation suited to his language, was obliged to pause, literally for want of breath. Singular as it may seem, this tirade excited great admiration among the savages. It is true, that very few understood what was said; perhaps no one understood *all*, but the manner was thought to be admirable. When some of the language was interpreted, a deep but smothered resentment was felt; more especially at the taunts touching the manner in which the whites had overcome the redmen. Truth is hard to be borne, and the individual or people who will treat a thousand injurious lies with contempt feel all their ire aroused at one reproach that has its foundation in fact. Nevertheless, the anger that the corporal's words did, in truth, awaken, was successfully repressed, and he had the disappointment of seeing that his life was spared for the torture.

"Brother," said Bough of the Oak, again placing himself before the captive, "you have a stout heart. It is made of stone and not of flesh. If our hearts be of dog's meat, yours is of stone. What you say is true. The pale-faces *did* come at first in two or three canoes, and there were but few of them. We are ashamed, for it is true. A few pale-faces drove towards the setting sun many Injins. But we cannot be driven any farther. We mean to stop here, and begin to take all the scalps we can. A great chief, who belongs to no one tribe but belongs to all tribes, who speaks all tongues, has been sent by the Great Spirit to arouse us. He has done it. You know him. He came from the head of the lake with you, and kept his eye on your scalp. He has meant to take it from the first. He waited only for an opportunity. That opportunity has come, and we now mean to do as he has told us we ought to do. This it right. Squaws are in a hurry; warriors know how to wait. We would kill you at once and hang your scalp on our pole, but it would not be right. We wish to do what is right. If we *are* poor Injins, and know but little, we know what is right. It is right to torment so great a brave, and we mean to do it. It is only just to you to do so. An old warrior who has seen so many enemies, and who has so big a heart, ought not to be knocked in the head like a pappoose or a squaw. It is his right to be tormented. We are getting ready, and shall soon begin. If my brother can tell us a new way of tormenting, we are willing to try it. Should we not make out as well as pale-faces, my brother will remember who we are. We mean to do our best, and we hope to make his heart soft. If we do this, great will be our honor. Should we not do it, we cannot help it. We shall try."

It was now the corporal's turn to put in a rebutter. This he did without any failure in will or performance. By this time he was so well warmed as to think or care very little about the saplings, and to overlook the pain they might occasion.

"Dogs can do little but bark, 'specially Injin dogs," he said. "Injins themselves are little better than their own dogs. They can bark, but they don't know how to bite. You have many great chiefs here. Some are panthers and some bears, and some buffaloes, but where are your weasels? I have fit you now these twenty years, and never have I known ye to stand up to the baggonet. It's not Injin natur' to do *that*."

Here the corporal, without knowing it, made some such reproach to the aboriginal warriors of America as the English used to throw into the teeth of ourselves, that of not standing up to a weapon which neither party possessed. It was matter of great triumph that the Americans would not stand the charge of the bayonet at the renowned fight on Breed's, for instance, when it is well known that not one man in five among the colonists had any such weapon at all to "stand up" with. A different story was told at Guildford, and Stony Point, and Eutaw, and Bennington, and Bemis's Heights, and fifty other places that might be named, after the troops were furnished with bayonets. *Then* it was found that the Americans could use them as well as others, and so might it have proved with the redmen, though their discipline, or mode of fighting, scarce admitted of such systematic charges. All this, however, the corporal overlooked, much as if he were a regular historian who was writing to make out a case.

"Harkee, brother, since you *will* call me brother; though, Heaven be praised, not a drop of nigger or Injin blood runs in *my* veins," resumed the corporal. "Harkee, friend redskin, answer me one thing. Did you never hear of such a man as Mad Anthony? He was the tickler for your infernal tribes. You pulled no saplings together for him. He put

you up with 'the long-knives and leather-stockings,' and
you outrun his fleetest horses. I was with him, and saw
more naked backs than naked faces among your people that
day. Your Great Bear got a rap on his nose that sent him
to his village yelping like a cur.''

Again was the corporal compelled to stop to take breath.
The allusion to Wayne, and his defeat of the Indians, excited so much ire that several hands grasped knives and
tomahawks, and one arrow was actually drawn nearly to
the head ; but the frown of Bear's Meat prevented any out-
break or actual violence. It was deemed prudent, however,
to put an end to this scene, lest the straightforward corporal,
who laid it on heavily, and who had so much to say about
Indian defeats, might actually succeed in touching some fes-
tering wound that would bring him to his death at once. It
was, accordingly, determined to proceed with the torture of
the saplings without further delay.

The corporal was removed accordingly, and placed between
the two bended trees, which were kept together by withes
around their tops. An arm of the captive was bound tightly
at the wrist to the top of each tree, so that his limbs were to
act as the only tie between the saplings, as soon as the withes
should be cut. The Indians now worked in silence, and the
matter was getting to be much too serious for the corporal to
indulge in any more words. The cold sweat returned, and
many an anxious glance was cast by the veteran on the fell
preparations. Still he maintained appearances, and when all
was ready not a man there was aware of the agony of dread
which prevailed in the breast of the victim. It was not
death that he feared as much as suffering. A few minutes,
the corporal well knew, would make the pain intolerable,
while he saw no hope of putting a speedy end to his existence. A man might live hours in such a situation. Then
it was that the teachings of childhood were revived in the
bosom of this hardened man, and he remembered the Being
that died for *him*, in common with the rest of the human
race, on the tree. The seeming similarity of his own execution struck his imagination, and brought a tardy but faint
recollection of those lessons that had lost most of their effi-

cacy in the wickedness and impiety of camps. His soul struggled for relief in that direction, but the present scene was too absorbing to admit of its lifting itself so far above his humanity.

"Warrior of the pale-faces," said Bough of the Oak, "we are going to cut the withes. You will then be where a brave man will want all his courage. If you are firm, we will do you honor; if you faint and screech, our young men will laugh at you. This is the way with Injins. They honor braves; they point the finger at cowards."

Here a sign was made by Bear's Meat, and a warrior raised the tomahawk that was to separate the fastenings. His hand was in the very act of descending when the crack of a rifle was heard, and a little smoke rose out of the thicket, near the spot where the bee-hunter and the corporal himself had remained so long hid, on the occasion of the council first held in that place. The tomahawk fell, however, the withes were parted, and up flew the saplings, with a violence that threatened to tear the arms of the victim out of their sockets.

The Indians listened, expecting the screeches and groans; they gazed, hoping to witness the writhings of their captive. But they were disappointed. There hung the body, its arms distended, still holding the tops of the saplings bowed, but not a sign of life was seen. A small line of blood trickled down the forehead, and above it was the nearly imperceptible hole made by the passage of a bullet. The head itself had fallen forward and a little on one shoulder. The corporal had escaped the torments reserved for him, by this friendly blow.

It was so much a matter of course for an Indian to revenge his own wounds,—to alleviate his smarts by retaliating on those who inflicted them,—that the chiefs expressed neither surprise nor resentment at the manner of the corporal's death. There was some disappointment, it is true; but no anger was manifested, since it was supposed that some one of those whom the prisoner had wounded had seen fit, in this mode, to revenge his own hurts. In this, however, the Indians deceived themselves. The well-intentioned and deadly shot, that saved the corporal from hours of agony, came from the friendly hand of Pigeonswing; who had no sooner discharged his rifle than he stole away through the thicket, and was never discovered. This he did, too, at the expense of Ungque's scalp, on which he had set his heart.

As for the Indians, perceiving that their hopes of forcing the captive to confess his weakness were frustrated, they conferred together on the course of future proceedings. There was an inquiry for Peter, but Peter was not to be found. Bough of the Oak suggested that the mysterious chief must have gone to the palisaded hut, in order to get the remaining scalps, his passion for this symbol of triumphs over pale-faces being well known. It was, therefore, incumbent on the whole band to follow, with the double view of sharing in the honor of the assault and of rendering assistance.

Abandoning the body of the corporal where it hung, away went these savages, by this time keenly alive to the scent of blood. Something like order was observed, however, each chief leading his own particular part of the band in his own way, but on a designated route. Bear's Meat acted as commander-in-chief, the subordinate leaders following his instructions with reasonable obedience. Some went in one direction, others in another, until the verdant bottom near the sweet spring was deserted.

In less than half an hour the whole band was collected around Castle Meal, distant, however, beyond the range of a rifle. The different parties, as they arrived, announced their presence by whoops, which were intended to answer the double purpose of signals, and of striking terror to the hearts of the besieged; the North American Indians making ample use of this great auxiliary in war.

All this time no one was seen in or about the fortified hut. The gate was closed, as were the doors and windows, manifesting preparations for defence ; but the garrison kept close. Nor was Peter to be seen. He might be a prisoner, or he might not have come in this direction. It was just possible that he might be stealing up to the building, to get a nearer view and a closer scout.

Indian warfare is always stealthy. It is seldom, indeed, that the aboriginal Americans venture on an open assault of any fortified place, however small and feeble it may be. Ignorant of the use of artillery, and totally without that all-important arm, their approaches to any cover, whence a bullet may be sent against them, are ever wary, slow, and well concerted. They have no idea of trenches, do not possess the means of making them, indeed ; but they have such substitutes of their own as usually meet all their wants, more particularly in portions of the country that are wooded. In cases like this before our present band, they had to exercise their wits to invent new modes of effecting their purposes.

Bear's Meat collected his principal chiefs, and, after a considerable amount of consultation, it was determined, in the present instance, to try the virtue of fire. The only sign of life they could detect about the hut was an occasional bark from Hive, who had been taken within the building, most probably to protect him from the bullets and arrows of the enemy. Even this animal did not howl, like a dog in distress ; but he barked, as if aware of the vicinity of strangers. The keenest scrutiny could not detect an outlet of any sort about the hut. Everything was tightly closed, and it was impossible to say when, or whence, a bullet might not be sent against the unwary.

The plan was soon formed, and was quite as rapidly executed. Bough of the Oak himself, supported by two or three other braves, undertook to set the building on fire. This was done by approaching the kitchen, dodging from tree to tree, making each movement with a rapidity that defeated aim, and an irregularity that defied calculation. In this way the kitchen was safely reached, where there was a log cover to conceal the party. Here also was fire, the food for dinner being left, just as it had been put over to boil, not long before. The Indians had prepared themselves with arrows and light wood, and soon they commenced sending their flaming missiles toward the roof of the hut. Arrow after arrow struck, and it was not long before the roof was on fire.

A yell now arose throughout the openings. Far and near the Indians exulted at their success. The wood was dry, and it was of a very inflammable nature. The wind blew, and in half an hour Castle Meal was in a bright blaze. Hive now began to howl, a sign that he knew his peril. Still, no human being appeared. Presently the flaming roof fell in, and the savages listened intently to hear the screeches of their victims. The howls of the dog increased, and he was soon seen, with his hair burned from his skin, leaping on the unroofed wall, and thence into the area within the palisades. A bullet terminated his sufferings as he alighted.

Bear's Meat now gave the signal, and a general rush was made. No rifle opposed them, and a hundred Indians were soon at the palisades. To the surprise of all, the gate was found unfastened. Rushing within, the door of the hut was forced, and a view obtained of the blazing furnace within. The party had arrived in sufficient season to perceive fragments of Le Bourdon's rude furniture and stores yet blazing, but nowhere was a human corpse visible. Poles were got, and the brands were removed, in the expectation of finding bones beneath them ; but without success. It was now certain that no pale-face had perished in that hut. Then the truth flashed on the minds of all the savages : Le Bourdon and his friends had taken the alarm in time, and had escaped !

CHAPTER XXVI.

"Behold, O Lord! the heathen tread
  The branches of thy fruitful vine,
That its luxurious tendrils spread
  O'er all the hills of Palestine.
And now the wild boar comes to waste
Even us, the greenest boughs and last,
That, drinking of its choicest dew,
On Zion's hill in beauty grew."

MILMAN.

THE change in Peter had been gradually making itself apparent ever since he joined the party of the bee-hunter. When he entered the Kalamazoo, in the company of the two men who had now fallen the victims of his own designs, his heart was full of the fell intention of cutting off the whole white race. Margery had first induced him to think of exceptions. He had early half-decided that she should be spared, to be carried to his own lodge, as an adopted daughter. When he became aware of the state of things between his favorite and her lover, there was a severe struggle in his breast on the subject of sparing the last. He saw how strongly the girl was attached to him, and something like human sentiments forced their way among his savage plans. The mysterious communication of Le Bourdon with the bees, however, had far more influence in determining him to spare so great a medicine-man than Margery's claims; and he had endeavored to avail himself of a marriage as a means of saving the bride instead of saving the bridegroom. All the Indians entertained a species of awe for Le Bourdon, and all hesitated about laying hands on one who appeared so gifted. It was therefore the expectation of this extraordinary being that the wife might be permitted to escape with the husband. The effect of The Weasel's cunning has been described. Such was the state of Peter's mind when he met the band in the scenes last described. There he had been all attention to the demeanor of the missionary. A hundred times had he seen warriors die uttering maledictions on their enemies; but this was the first occasion on which he had ever known a man to use his latest breath in asking for blessings on those "who persecuted him." At first Peter was astounded. Then the sublime principles had their effect, and his heart was deeply touched with what he heard. How far the Holy Spirit aided these better feelings it might be presumptuous, on the one hand, to say; while on the other, it will be equally presuming to think of denying the possibility—nay, the probability—that the great change which so suddenly came over the heart of Peter was produced by more than mere human agencies. We know that this blessed Spirit is often poured out, in especial cases, with affluent benevolence, and there can be no sufficient reason for supposing this savage might not have been thus signally favored, as soon as the avenues of his heart opened to the impulses of a generous humanity. The very qualities that would induce such a being to attempt the wild and visionary scheme of vengeance and retribution that had now occupied his sleeping and waking thoughts for years might, under a better direction, render him eminently fit to be the subject of divine grace. A latent sense of right lay behind all his seeming barbarity, and that which to us appears as a fell ferocity was, in his own eyes, no less than a severe justice.

The words, the principles, the prayers, and more than all the *example* of the missionary, wrought this great change, so far as human agencies were employed; but the power of God was necessary to carry out and complete this renewal of the inner man. We do not mean that a miracle was used in the sudden conversion of this Indian to better feelings, for that which is of hourly occurrence, and which may happen to all, comes within the ordinary

workings of a Divine Providence, and cannot thus be designated with propriety; but we do wish to be understood as saying that no purely human power could have
cleared the moral vision, changed all the views, and softened the heart of such a man, as was so promptly done in
the case of Peter. The way had been gradually preparing, perhaps, by the means already described; but the
great transformation came so suddenly and so powerfully
as to render him a different being, as it might almost be,
in the twinkling of an eye! Such changes often occur,
and though it may suit the self-sufficiency of the worldling
to deride them, he is the wisest who submits in the meek-
est spirit to powers that exceed his comprehension.

In this state of mind, then, Peter left the band as soon
as the fate of the missionary was decided. His immediate
object was to save the whites who remained, Gershom and
Dorothy now having a place in his good intentions as well
as Le Bourdon and Margery. Although he moved swiftly,
and nearly by an air-line, his thoughts scarce kept company
with his feet. During that rapid walk, he was haunted
with the image of a man dying while he pronounced benedictions on his enemies!

There was little in common between the natural objects
of that placid and rural scene and the fell passions that
were so actively at work among the savages. The whole
of the landscape was bathed in the light of a clear, warm,
summer's day. These are the times when the earth truly
seems a sanctuary, in spots remote from the haunts of man,
and least exposed to his abuses. The bees hum around the
flowers, the birds carol on the boughs and from amid their
leafy arbors, while even the leaping and shining waters
appear to be instinct with the life that extols the glory of
God.

As for the family near the palisaded hut, happiness had
not, for many a month, been so seated among them as on
this very occasion. Dorothy sympathized truly in the feelings of the youthful and charming bride, while Gershom
had many of the kind and affectionate wishes of a brother
in her behalf. The last was in his best attire, as indeed

26

were the females, who were neatly though modestly clad, and Gershom had that air of decent repose and of quiet enjoyment which is so common of a Sabbath with the men of his class among the people from whom he sprung. The fears lately excited were momentarily forgotten. Everything around them wore an air so placid; the vault above them was so profoundly tranquil; the light of day was so soft and yet so bright; the Openings seemed so rural and so much like pictures of civilization, that apprehension had been entirely forgotten in present enjoyment. Such was the moment when Peter suddenly stood before Le Bourdon and Margery, as the young couple sat beneath the shade of the oaks near the spring. One instant the Indian regarded this picture of young wedded life with a gleam of pleasure on his dark face; then he announced his presence by speaking.

"Can't sit here lookin' at young squaw," said this literal being. "Get up, and put thing in canoe. Time come to go on path dat lead to pale-face country."

"What has happened, Peter?" demanded the bee-hunter, springing to his feet. "You come like a runner rushing in with his bad tidings. Has anything happened to give an alarm?"

"Up, and off, tell you. No use talkin' now. Put all he can in canoe, and paddle away fast as can." There was no mistaking Peter's manner. The bee-hunter saw the uselessness of questioning such a man at a time like that, and he called to Gershom to join him.

"Here is the chief to warn us to move," said the bee-hunter, endeavoring to appear calm, in order that he might not needlessly alarm the females, "and what he advises we had better do. I know there is danger by what has fallen from Pigeonswing as well as from himself; so let us lose no time, but stow the canoes and do as he tells us."

As Gershom assented, it was not two minutes ere all were at work. For several days, each canoe had been furnished with provisions for a hasty flight. It remained only to add such of the effects as were too valuable and necessary to be abandoned, and which had not been previously exposed without the palisades. For half an hour Le Bourdon and Gershom worked as for life. No questions were asked, nor was a single moment lost in a desire to learn more. The manner in which Peter bore himself satisfied Boden that the emergency was pressing, and it is seldom that more was done by so few hands in so short a period. Fortunately, the previous preparations greatly aided the present object, and nearly everything of any value was placed in the canoes within the brief space mentioned. It then became necessary to decide concerning the condition in which Castle Meal was to be left. Peter advised closing every aperture, shutting the gate, and leaving the dog within. There is no doubt that these expedients prevented the party's falling early into the hands of their enemies; for the time lost by the savages in making their approach to the hut was very precious to the fugitives.

Just as the canoes were loaded Pigeonswing came in. He announced that the whole band was in motion, and might be expected to reach the grove in ten minutes. Placing an arm around the slender waist of Margery, Le Bourdon almost carried her to his own canoe. Gershom soon had Dorothy in his little bark, while Peter entered that to the ownership of which he may be said to have justly succeeded, by the deaths of the corporal and the missionary. Pigeonswing remained behind, in order to act as a scout, having first communicated to Peter the course the last ought to steer. Before the Chippewa plunged into the cover in which it was his intention to conceal himself, he made a sign that the band was already in sight.

The heart of Le Bourdon sunk within him when he learned how near were the enemy. To him escape seemed impossible; and he now regretted having abandoned the defence of his late residence. The river was sluggish for more than a mile at that spot, and then occurred a rift, which could not be passed without partly unloading the canoes, and where there must necessarily be a detention of more than an hour. Thus, it was scarcely possible for canoes descending that stream to escape from so large a band of pursuers. The sinuosities, themselves, would enable the last to gain fifty points ahead of them, where ambushes, or even open resistance, must place them together at the mercy of the savages.

Peter knew all this as well as the bee-hunter, and he had no intention of trusting his new friends in a flight down the river. Pigeonswing, with the sententious brevity of an Indian, had made an important communication to him while they were moving for the last time towards the canoes, and he now determined to profit by it. Taking the lead, therefore, with his own canoe, Peter paddled *up*, instead of *down* the stream, going in a direction opposite to that which it would naturally be supposed the fugitives had taken. In doing this, also, he kept close under the bank which would most conceal the canoes from those who approached it on its southern side.

It will be remembered that the trees for the palisades had been cut from a swamp, a short distance above the bee-hunter's residence. They had grown on the margin of the river, which had been found serviceable in floating the logs to their point of destination. The tops of many of these trees, resinous and suited by their nature to preserve their leaves for a considerable time, lay partly in the stream, and partly on its banks; and Pigeonswing, foreseeing the necessity of having a place of refuge, had made so artful a disposition of several of them, that, while they preserved all the appearance of still lying where they had fallen, it was possible to haul canoes up beneath them, between the branches and the bank, in a way to form a place of perfect concealment. No Indian would have trusted to such a hiding-place, had it not been matter of notoriety that the trees had been felled for a particular purpose, or had their accidental disposition along the bank been discernibly deranged. But such was not the case; the hand of Pigeonswing having been so skilfully employed that what he had done could not be detected. He might be said to have assisted nature instead of disturbing her.

The canoes were actually paddling close under the bank, in the Castle Meal reach of the river, when the band arrived at the grove and commenced what might be called the investment of the place. Had not all the attention of the savages been drawn towards the hut, it is probable that some wandering eye might have caught a glimpse of some one of them, as inequalities in the bank momentarily exposed each, in succession, to view. This danger, however, passed away, and by turning a point the fugitives were effectually concealed from all who did not actually approach the river at that particular point. Here it was, however, that the swamp commenced, and the ground being wet and difficult, no one would be likely to do this. The stream flowed through this swamp, having a dense wood on each side, though one of no great extent. The reach, moreover, was short, making a completely sheltered haven of the Kalamazoo, within its limits.

Once in this wooded reach, Peter tossed an arm and assumed an air of greater security. He felt infinitely relieved, and knew that they were safe for a time, unless some wanderer should have taken to the swamp, a most improbable thing of itself. When high enough, he led the way across the stream, and entering below, he soon had all the canoes in their place of concealment.

"Dis good place," observed the great chief, as soon as all were fast; "bess take care, dough. Bess not make track too much on land; Injin got sharp eye, and see ebberyt'ing. Now I go and talk wid chief. Come back by-'em-by. You stay here. Good-by."

"Stop, Peter; one word before we part. If you see Parson Amen or the corporal, it might be well to tell *them* where we are to be found. They would be glad to know."

Peter looked grave—even sad. He did not answer for fully a minute. When he did, it was in a low, suppressed voice, such as one is apt to use when there is a weight felt on his mind.

"Nebber know anyt'ing ag'in," returned the chief. "Both dem pale-face dead."

"Dead!" echoed all within hearing.

"Juss so; Injin kill him. Mean to kill you, too—dat why I run away. Saw medicine-priest die. What you t'ink, Blossom? What you t'ink, Bourdon? Dat man die asking Great Spirit to do good to Injin!"

"I can believe it, Peter, for he was a good man, and such are our Christian laws, though few of us obey them. I can easily believe that Parson Amen was an exception, however."

"Yes, Peter, such are our Christian laws," put in Margery, earnestly. "When Christ, the Son of God, came on earth to redeem lost men, he commanded his followers to do good to them that did evil to us, and pray for them that tried to harm us. We have his very words written in our Bibles."

"You got him?" said Peter, with interest. "See you read him of'en. Got dat book here?"

"To be sure I have; it is the last thing I should have forgotten. Dolly has one, and I have another; we read in them every day, and we hope that, before long, brother and Bourdon will read in them too."

"Why, I'm no great scholar, Margery," returned her husband, scratching his full, curling head of hair, out of pure awkwardness; "to please *you*, however, I'd undertake even a harder job. It was so with the bees, when I began; I thought I should never succeed in lining the first bee to his hive; but since that time, I do think I've lined a thousand!"

"It's easy, it's easy, dear Benjamin, if you will only make a beginning," returned the much interested young wife. "When we get to a place of safety, if it be God's will that we ever shall, I hope to have you join me in reading the good book daily. See, Peter, I keep it in this little bag, where it is safe and always at hand."

"You read dem word for me, Blossom; I want to hear him, out of dis book, himself."

Margery did as desired. She was very familiar with the New Testament, and turning to the well-known and God-like passage, she read several verses in a steady, earnest voice. Perhaps the danger they were in, and the recent communication of the death of their late companions, increased her earnestness and solemnity of manner; for the effect produced on Peter was scarcely less than that he had felt when he witnessed a practical obedience to these sublime principles in the death of the missionary. Tears actually started to this stern savage's eyes, and he looked back on his late projects and endeavors to immolate a whole race with a shudder.   Taking Margery's hand, he courteously thanked her, and prepared to quit the place.   Previously to leaving his friends, however, Peter gave a brief account of the manner of the missionary's death, and of the state in which he had left the corporal.   Pigeonswing had told him of the fate of the last, as well as of the eagerness with which the band had set out in quest of more white scalps.

"Peter, we can count on you for a friend, I hope," said the bee-hunter, as the two were about to part, on the bank of the river.   "I fear you were once our enemy !"

"Bourdon," said Peter, with dignity, and speaking in the language of his own people, "listen.   There are Good Spirits, and there are Bad Spirits.   Our traditions tell us this.   Our own minds tell us this too.   For twenty winters a Bad Spirit has been whispering in my ear.   I listened to him, and did what he told me to do.   I believed what he said. His words were, 'Kill your enemies ; scalp all the pale-faces ; do not leave a squaw or a pappoose.   Make all their hearts heavy.   This is what an Injin should do.'   So has the Bad Spirit been whispering to me for twenty winters.   I listened to him.   What he said, I did.   It was pleasant to me to take the scalps of the pale-faces.   It was pleasant to think that no more scalps would be left among them to take.   I was Scalping Peter.

"Bourdon, the Good Spirit has at last made himself heard. His whisper is so low that at first my ears did not hear him. They hear him now.   When he spoke loudest, it was with the tongue of the medicine-priest of your people.   He was about to die.   When we are about to die, our voices become strong and clear.   So do our eyes.   We see what is before, and we see what is behind.   We feel joy for what is before, we feel sorrow for what is behind.   Your medicine-priest spoke well.   It sounded in my ears as if the Great Spirit himself was talking.   They say it was his Son.   I believe them.   Blossom has read to me out of the good book of your people, and I find it is so.   I feel like a child, and could sit down in my wigwam and weep.

" Bourdon, you are a pale-face and I am an Injin. You are strong and I am weak. This is because the Son of the Great Spirit has talked with your people, and has not talked with mine. I now see why the pale-faces overrun the earth and take the hunting-grounds. They know most, and have been told to come here, and to tell what they know to the poor ignorant Injins. I hope my people will listen. What the Son of the Great Spirit says must be true. He does not know how to do wrong.

" Bourdon, once it seemed sweet to me to take the scalps of my enemies. When an Injin did me harm, I took his scalp. This was my way. I could not help it then. The Wicked Spirit told me to do this. The Son of the Manitou has now told me better. I have lived under a cloud. The breath of the dying medicine-priest of your people has blown away that cloud. I see clearer. I hear him telling the Manitou to do me good, though I wanted his scalp. He was answered in my heart. Then my ears opened wider, and I heard what the Good Spirit whispered. The ear in which the Bad Spirit had been talking for twenty winters shut, and was deaf. I hear him no more. I do not want to hear him again. The whisper of the Son of the Manitou is very pleasant to me. It sounds like the wren singing his sweetest song. I hope he will always whisper so. My ear shall never again be shut to his words.

" Bourdon, it is pleasant to me to look forward. It is not pleasant to me to look back. I see how many things I have done in one way that ought to have been done in another way. I feel sorry, and wish it had not been so. Then I hear the Son of the Manitou asking his Father, who liveth above the clouds, to do good to the Jews who took his life. I do not think Injins are Jews. In this my brother was wrong. It was his own notion, and it is easy for a man to think wrong. It is not so with the Son of the Manitou. He thinketh always as his Father thinketh, which is right.

" Bourdon, I am no longer Peter—I must be another Injin. I do not feel the same. A scalp is a terrible thing in my eyes. I wish never to take another, never to see another ; a scalp is a bad thing. I now *love* the Yankees. I wish to do them good, and not to do them harm. I love most the Great Spirit, that let his own Son die for all men. The medicine-priest said He died for Injins as well as for palefaces. This we did not know, or we should have talked of him more in our traditions. We love to talk of good acts. But we are such ignorant Injins ! The Son of the Manitou will have pity on us, and tell us oftener what we ought to do. In time, we shall learn. Now, I feel like a child ; I hope I shall one day be a man.''

Having made this " confession of faith,'' one that would have done credit to a Christian church, Peter shook the bee-hunter kindly by the hand, and took his departure. He did not walk into the swamp, though it was practicable with sufficient care, but he stepped into the river and followed its margin, knowing that " water leaves no trail ! '' Nor did Peter follow the direct route towards the now blazing hut, the smoke from which was rising high above the trees, but he ascended the stream until, reaching a favorable spot, he threw aside all of his light dress, made it into a bundle, and swam across the Kalamazoo, holding his clothes above the element with one hand. On reaching the opposite shore, he moved on to the upper margin of the swamp, where he resumed his clothes. Then he issued into the Openings, carrying neither rifle, bow, tomahawk, nor knife. All his weapons he had left in his canoe, fearful that they might tempt him to do evil instead of good to his enemies. Neither Bear's Meat nor Bough of the Oak was yet regarded by Peter with the eye of love. He tried not to hate them, and this he found sufficiently difficult ; conscious of this difficulty, he had laid aside his arms accordingly. This mighty change had been gradually in progress ever since the chief's close communication with Margery, but it had received its consumation in the last acts and last words of the missionary.

Having got out into the Openings, it was not difficult for Peter to join his late companions without attracting observation from whence he came. He kept as much under cover as was convenient, and reached the kitchen just as the band broke into the defences and burst open the door of the blazing and already roofless hut. Here Peter paused, unwilling to seem inactive in such a scene, yet averse to doing anything that a sensitively tender conscience might tell him was wrong. He knew there was no human being there to save, and cared little for the few effects that might be destroyed. He did not join the crowd, therefore, until it was ascertained that the bee-hunter and his companions had escaped.

"The pale-faces have fled," said Bear's Meat to the great chief, when the last did approach him. "We have looked for their bones among the ashes, but there are none. That medicine-bee-hunter has told them that their scalps were wanted, and they have gone off!"

"Have any of the young men been down to the river to look for their canoes?" quietly demanded Peter. "If the canoes are gone, too, they have taken the route towards the Great Lake."

This was so obvious and probable that a search was immediately set on foot. The report was soon made, and great was the eagerness to pursue. The Kalamazoo was so crooked that no one there doubted of overtaking the fugitives, and parties were immediately organized for the chase. This was done with the customary intelligence and shrewdness of Indians. The canoes that belonged to Crows-feather and his band had been brought up the river, and they lay concealed in rushes not a mile from the hut. A party of warriors brought them to the landing, and they carried one division of the party to the opposite shore, it being the plan to follow each bank of the river, keeping close to the stream, even to its mouth, should it prove necessary. Two other parties were sent in direct lines, one on each side of the river also, to lay in ambush at such distant points ahead as would be almost certain to anticipate the arrival of the fugitives. The canoes were sent down the stream, to close the net against return, while Bear's Meat, Bough of the Oak, Crowsfeather, and several others of the leading chiefs remained near the still burning hut, with a strong party, to examine the surrounding Openings for foot-prints and trails. It was possible that the canoes had been sent adrift, in order to mislead them, while the pale-faces had fled by land.

It has been stated that the Openings had a beautiful sward near Castle Meal. This was true of that particular spot, and was the reason why Le Bourdon had selected it for his principal place of residence. The abundance of flowers drew the bees there, a reason of itself why he should like the vicinity. Lest the reader should be mis-led, however, it may be well to explain that an absence of sward is characteristic of these Openings, rather than the reverse, it being to a certain degree a cause of complaint, now that the country is settled, that the lands of the Oak Openings are apt to be so light that the grasses do not readily form as firm a turf as is desirable for meadows and pastures. We apprehend this is true, however, less as a rule than as exceptions; there being variety in the soils of these Openings as well as in other quarters.

Nevertheless, the savages were aware that the country around the burned hut, for a considerable extent, differed, in this particular, from most of that which lay farther east, or more inland. On the last, a trail would be much more easily detected than on the first, and a party, under the di-rection of a particularly experienced leader, was despatched several miles to the eastward, to look for the usual signs of the passage of any towards Detroit, taking that route. This last expedient troubled Peter exceedingly, since it placed a body of enemies in the rear of the fugitives, thereby rendering their position doubly perilous. There was no help for the difficulty, however, and the great chief saw the party depart without venturing on remonstrance, advice, or any other expedient to arrest the movement. Bear's Meat now called the head chiefs, who remained, into a circle, and asked for opinions concerning the course that ought next to be taken.

"What does my brother, the tribeless chief, say?" he asked, looking at Peter in a way to denote the expectation which all felt, that he ought to be able to give useful coun-sel in such a strait. "We have got but two scalps from six heads; and one of *them* is buried with the medicine-priest."

"Scalps cannot be taken from them that get off," re-

turned Peter, evasively. "We must first catch these pale-
faces. When they are found, it will be easy to scalp them.
If the canoes are gone, I think the medicine-bee-hunter and
his squaws have gone in them. We may find the whole
down the river."

To this opinion most of the chiefs assented, though the
course of examining for a trail farther east was still approved. The band was so strong, while the pale-faces were
so few, that a distribution of their own force was of no
consequence, and it was clearly the most prudent to send
out young men in all directions. Every one, however, expected that the fugitives would be overtaken on or near the
river, and Bear's Meat suggested the propriety of their moving down stream, themselves, very shortly.

"When did my brother last see the pale-faces?" asked
Crowsfeather. "This bee-hunter knows the river well,
and may have started yesterday ; or even after he came
from the Great Council of the Prairie."

This was a new idea, but one that seemed probable
enough. All eyes turned towards Peter, who saw at once
that such a notion must greatly favor the security of the
fugitives, and felt a strong desire to encourage it. He
found evasion difficult, however, and well knew the danger
of committing himself. Instead of giving a straightforward
answer, therefore, he had recourse to circumlocution and
subterfuge.

"My brother is right," he answered. "The pale-faces
have had time to get far down the stream. As my brothers
know, I slept among them at the Round Prairie. To-day,
they know I was with them at the council of the spring of
gushing waters."

All this was true, as far as it went, although the omis-
sions were very material. No one seemed to suspect the
great chief, whose fidelity to his own principles was believed to be of a character amounting to enthusiasm. Little
did any there know of the power of the unseen Spirit of
God to alter the heart, producing what religionists term the
new birth. We do not wish, however, to be understood
that Peter had, as yet, fully experienced this vast change.

It is not often the work of a moment, though well-authenticated modern instances do exist, in which we have every reason to believe that men have been made to see and feel the truth almost as miraculously as was St. Paul himself. As for this extraordinary savage, he had entered into the strait and narrow way, though he was not far advanced on its difficult path.

When men tell us of the great progress that the race is making towards perfection, and point to the acts which denote its wisdom, its power to control its own affairs, its tendencies towards good when most left to its own self-control, our minds are filled with skepticism. The everyday experience of a life now fast verging towards three-score contradicts the theory and the facts. We believe not in the possibility of man's becoming even a strictly rational being, unaided by a power from on high ; and all that we have seen and read goes to convince us that *he* is most of a philosopher, the most accurate judge of his real state, the most truly learned, who most vividly sees the necessity of falling back on the precepts of revelation for all his higher principles and practice. We conceive that this mighty truth furnishes unanswerable proof of the unceasing agency of a Providence, and when we once admit this, we concede that our own powers are insufficient for our own wants.

That the world as a whole is advancing towards a better state of things, we as firmly believe as we do that it is by ways that have not been foreseen by man ; and that whenever the last has been made the agent of producing portions of this improvement, it has oftener been without design or calculation than with it. Who, for instance, supposes that the institutions of this country, of which we boast so much, could have stood as long as they have without the conservative principles that are to be found in the *Union* ; and who is there so vain as to ascribe the overshadowing influence of this last great power to any wisdom in man? We all know that perfectly fortuitous circumstances, or what appear to us to be such, produced the Federal Government, and that its strongest and least exceptionable features are precisely those which could not be withstood, much less invented, as parts of the theory of a polity.

A great and spasmodic political movement is at this moment convulsing Christendom. That good will come of it, we think is beyond a question ; but we greatly doubt whether it will come in the particular form or by the specified agencies that human calculations would lead us to expect. It must be admitted that the previous preparation which has induced the present efforts are rather in opposition to, than the consequences of, calculated agencies ; overturning in their progress the very safeguards which the sagacity of man had interposed to the advance of those very opinions that have been silently, and by means that would perhaps baffle inquiry, preparing the way for the results that have been so suddenly and unexpectedly obtained. If the course is onward, it is more as the will of God than from any calculations of man ; and it is when the last are the most active, that there is the greatest reason to apprehend the consequences.

Of such a dispensation of the Providence of Almighty God do we believe Peter to have been the subject. Among the thousand ways that are employed to touch the heart, he had been most affected by the sight of a dying man's asking benedictions on his enemies ! It was assailing his besetting sin ; attacking the very citadel of his savage character, and throwing open at once an approach into the deepest recesses of his habits and dispositions. It was like placing a master-key in the hands of him who would go through the whole tenement for the purpose of purifying it.

CHAPTER XXVII.

"Thou to whom every faun and satyr flies
    For willing service; whether to surprise
    The squatted hare, while in half-sleeping fits,
    Or upward ragged precipices flit
    To save poor lambkins from the eagle's maw;
    Or by mysterious enticement draw
    Bewildered shepherds to their path again."

KEATS.

IT can easily be understood that the party with the canoes were left by Peter in a state of great anxiety. The distance between the site of the hut and their place of concealment was but little more than a quarter of a mile, and the yell of the savages had often reached their ears, notwithstanding the cover of the woods. This proximity of itself was fearful; but the uncertainty that Le Bourdon felt on the subject of Peter's real intentions added greatly to his causes of concern. Of course he knew but little of the sudden change that had come over this mysterious chief's feelings; nor is it very likely that he would have been able to appreciate it, even had the fact been more fully stated. Our hero had very little acquaintance with the dogmas of Christianity, and would have most probably deemed it impossible that so great a revolution of purpose could have been so suddenly wrought in the mind of man, had the true state of the case been communicated to him. He would have been ready enough to allow that with God nothing is impossible, but might have been disposed to deny the influence of his Holy Spirit as exhibited in this particular form, for a reason no better than the circumstance that he himself had never been the subject of such a power.

All that Peter had said, therefore, served rather to mystify him than to explain, in its true colors, what had actually occurred. With Margery it was different. Her schooling had been far better than that of any other of the party, and, while she admired the manly appearance, and loved the free, generous character of her husband, she had more than once felt pained at the passing thoughts of his great indifference to sacred things. This feeling in Le Bourdon, however, was passive rather than active, and gave her a kind interest in his future welfare, rather than any present pain through acts and words.

But as respects their confidence in Peter, this young couple were much farther apart than in their religious notions. The bee-hunter had never been without distrust, though his apprehensions had been occasionally so far quieted as to leave him nearly free of them altogether ; while his wife had felt the utmost confidence in the chief, from the very commencement of their acquaintance. It would be useless, perhaps, to attempt to speculate on the causes ; but it is certain that there are secret sources of sympathy that draw particular individuals towards each other, and antipathies that keep them widely separated. Men shall meet for the first time, and feel themselves attracted towards each other, like two drops of water, or repelled, like the corks of an electric machine.

The former had been the case with Peter and Margery. They liked each other from the first, and kind offices had soon come to increase this feeling. The girl had now seen so much of the Indians as to regard them much as she did others, or with the discriminations and tastes or distastes with which we all regard our fellow-creatures ; feeling no particular cause of estrangement. It is true that Margery would not have been very likely to fall in love with a young Indian, had one come in her way of a suitable age and character ; for her American notions on the subject of color might have interposed difficulties ; but apart from the tender sentiments, she could see good and bad qualities in one of the aborigines as well as in a white man. As a consequence of this sympathy between Peter and Margery, the last had ever

felt the utmost confidence in the protection and friendship of
the first. This she did even while the struggle was going
on in his breast on the subject of including her in his fell
designs, or of making an exception in her favor. It shows
the waywardness of our feelings, that Margery had never
reposed confidence in Pigeonswing, who was devotedly the
friend of Le Bourdon, and who remained with them for no
other reason than a general wish to be of use. Something
brusque in his manner, which was much less courteous and
polished than that of Peter, had early rendered her dissatis-
fied with him, and, once estranged, she had never felt disposed to be on terms of intimacy sufficient to ascertain his
good or bad qualities.

The great change of feeling in Peter was not very clearly
understood by Margery any more than it was by her husband ; though, had her attention been drawn more strictly to
it, she would have best known how to appreciate it. But this
knowledge was not wanting to put *her* perfectly at peace,
so far as apprehensions of his doing her harm were concerned. This sense of security she now manifested in a
conversation with Le Bourdon, that took place soon after
Peter had left them.

" I wish we were n't in the hands of this redskin, Margery," said her husband, a little more off his guard than
was his wont.

" Of Peter ! You surprise me, Benjamin. I think we
could not be in better hands, since we have got this risk to
run with the savages. If it was Pigeonswing that you
feared, I could understand it."

" I will answer for Pigeonswing with my life."

" I am glad to hear you say so, for *I* do not half like *him*.
Perhaps I am prejudiced against him. The scalp he took
down at the mouth of the river set me against him from the
first."

" Do you not know, Margery, that your great friend goes
by the name of ' Scalping Peter ' ? "

" Yes, I know it very well ; but I do not believe he ever
took a scalp in his life."

" Did he ever tell you as much as that ? "
27

"I can't say that he did ; but he has never paraded anything of the sort before my eyes, like Pigeonswing. I do not half like that Chippewa, dear Bourdon."

"No fear of him, Margery ; nor, when I come to think it all over, do I see why Peter should have brought us here if he means anything wrong. The man is so mysterious that I cannot line him down to his hole."

"My word for it, Bourdon, that when you *do*, it will take you to a friendly hive. I have put almost as much faith in Peter as in you or Gershom. You heard what he said about Parson Amen and the corporal."

"And how coolly he took it all," answered her husband, shaking his head. "It has been a sudden departure for them, and one would think even an Injin might have felt it more."

Margery's cheek grew pale, and her limbs trembled a little. It was a minute ere she could pursue the discourse.

"This is terrible, but I will not, cannot believe it," she said. "I'm sure, Bourdon, we ought to be very thankful to Peter for having brought us here. Remember how earnestly he listened to the words of the Saviour."

"If he has brought us here with a good intention, I thank him for it. But I scarce know what to think. Pigeonswing has given me many a hint, which I have understood to mean that we ought not to trust this unknown Injin too much."

"So has he given me some of his hints, though I would sooner trust Peter than trust him, any time."

"Our lives are in the care of Providence, I see. If we can really rely on these two Injins, all may be well, for Peter has brought us to an admirable cover, and he says that the Chippewa prepared it."

The young husband and his wife now landed, and began to examine more particularly into the state of the swamp, near their place of concealment. Just at that spot the bank of the river was higher than in most of the low land, and was dry, with a soil that approached sand. This was the place where the few young pines had grown. The dry ground might have covered four or five acres, and so many

trees having been felled, light and air were admitted in a
way to render the place comparatively cheerful. The
branches of the felled trees made a sufficient cover in all
directions, though the swamp itself was more than that,
almost a defence, towards the Openings. The bee-hunter
found it was possible, though it was exceedingly difficult,
to make his way through it. He ascertained the fact, however, since it might be important to their future movements
to know it.

In a word, Le Bourdon made a complete reconnoissance
of his position. He cleared a spot for the females, and made
a sort of hut, that would serve as a protection against rain,
and in which they all might sleep at night. There was little doubt that this place must be occupied for some days, if
Peter was acting in good faith, since an early movement
would infallibly lead to detection. Time must be given to
the Indians to precede them, or the great numbers of the savages would scarce leave a hope of escape. A greater sense
of security succeeded this examination and these arrangements. The danger was almost entirely to be apprehended
on the side of the river. A canoe passing up-stream might,
indeed, discover their place of concealment, but it was
scarcely to be apprehended that one would wade through
the mud and water of the swamp to approach them in any
other direction.

Under these circumstances, Le Bourdon began to feel
more security in their position. Could he now be certain of
Peter, his mind would be comparatively at ease, and he
might turn his attention altogether to making the party
comfortable. Margery, who seldom quitted his side, reasoned with him on the subject of the mysterious chief's good
faith ; and by means of her own deep reliance on him she
came at last to the point of instilling some of her own confidence into the mind of her husband. From that time he
worked at the shelter for the females, and the other little
arrangements their situation rendered necessary, with greater
zest and with far more attention to the details. So long as
we are in doubt of accomplishing good, we hesitate about
employing our energies ; but once let hope revive within us,

in the shape of favorable results, and we become new men, bracing every nerve to the task, and working with redoubled spirit ; even should it be at the pump of the sinking ship, which we believe ranks the highest among the toils that are inflicted on the unfortunate.

For three days and nights did Le Bourdon and his friends remain on that dry land of the swamp, without hearing or seeing anything of either Peter or Pigeonswing. The time was growing long, and the party anxious, though the sense of security was much increased by this apparent exemption from danger. Still, uncertainty and the wish to ascertain the precise state of things in the Openings were gradually getting to be painful, and it was with great satisfaction that the bee-hunter met his young wife as she came running towards him, on the morning of the fourth day, to announce that an Indian was approaching, by wading in the margin of the river, keeping always in the water, so as to leave no trail. Hurrying to a point whence their visitor might be seen, Le Bourdon soon perceived it was no other than Pigeonswing. In a few minutes this Indian arrived, and was gladly received by all four of the fugitives, who gathered around him, eager to hear the news.

"You are welcome, Chippewa," cried Le Bourdon, shaking his friend cordially by the hand. "We were half afraid we might never see you again. Do you bring us good or evil tidings?"

"Must n't be squaw, and ask too much question, Bourdon," returned the redskin, carefully examining the priming of his rifle, in order to make sure it was not wet. "Got plenty venison, eh?"

"Not much venison is left, but we have caught a good many fish, which have helped us along. I have killed a dozen large squirrels, too, with your bow and arrows, which I find you left in your canoe. But—"

"Yes, he good bow, dat—might kill hummin'-bird wid dat bow. Fish good here, eh?"

"They are eatable, when a body can get no better. But *now*, I should think, Pigeonswing, you might give us some of the news."

"Must n't be squaw, Bourdon—bad for warrior be squaw. Alway bess be man, and be patient, like man. What you t'ink, Bourdon? Got him at last!"

"Got *what*, my good fellow? I see nothing about you but your arms and ammunition."

"Got scalp of dat Weasel! Was n't dat well done? Nebber no young warrior take more scalp home dan Pigeons-wing carry dis time! Got t'ree; all hid, where Bear's Meat nebber know. Take 'em away when he get ready to march."

"Well, well, Chippewa, I suppose it will not be easy to reason you out of this feelin'—but what has become of the redskins who burned my cabin, and who killed the missionary and the corporal?"

"All about—dough most go down river. Look here, Bourdon, some of dem chief fool enough to t'ink bee carry you off on his wing!"

Here the Chippewa looked his contempt for the credulity and ignorance of the others, though he did not express it after the boisterous manner in which a white man of his class might have indulged. To him Le Bourdon was a good fellow, but no conjurer, and he understood the taking of the bee too well to have any doubts as to the character of that process. His friend had let him amuse himself by the hour in looking through his spy-glass, so that the mind of this one savage was particularly well fortified against the inroads of the weaknesses that had invaded those of most of the members of the Great Council. Consequently he was amused with the notion taken up by some of the others, that Le Bourdon had been carried off by bees, though he manifested his amusement in a very Indian-like fashion.

"So much the better," answered Le Bourdon; "and I hope they have followed, to line me down to my hive in the settlements."

"Most on 'em go: yes, dat true. But some don't go. Plenty of Injins still about dis part of Opening."

"What are we then to do? We shall soon be in want of food. The fish do not bite as they did, and I have killed all the squirrels I can find. You know I dare not use a rifle."

"Don't be squaw, Bourdon. When Injin get marry he grows good deal like squaw at fuss ; but dat soon go away. I s'pose its juss so wid pale-face. Must n't be squaw, Bourdon. Dat bad for warrior. What you do for eat? Why, see dere," pointing to an object that was floating slowly down the river, the current of which was very sluggish just in that reach. "Dere as fat buck as ever did see, eh?"

Sure enough, the Indian had killed a deer, of which the Openings were full, and having brought it to the river he had constructed a raft of logs, and placing the carcass on it he had set his game adrift, taking care to so far precede it as to be in readiness to tow it into port. When this last operation was performed, it was found that the Chippewa did not heedlessly vaunt the quality of his prize. What was more, so accurately had he calculated the time, and the means of subsistence in the possession of the fugitives, that his supply came in just as it was most needed. In all this he manifested no more than the care of an experienced and faithful hunter. Next to the war-path, the hunting-ground is the great field for an Indian's glory ; deeds and facts so far eclipsing purely intellectual qualifications with savages as to throw oratory, though much esteemed by them, and wisdom at the council fires, quite into the shade. In all this we find the same propensity among ourselves. The common mind, ever subject to these impulses, looks rather to such exploits as address themselves to the senses and the imagination, than to those qualities which the reason alone can best appreciate ; and in this, ignorance asserts its negative power over all conditions of life.

Pigeonswing now condescended to enter on such explanations as the state of the case rendered necessary. His account was sufficiently clear, and it manifested throughout the sagacity and shrewdness of a practised hunter and scout. We shall not attempt to give his words, which would require too much space, but the substance of his story was briefly this.

As has been alluded to already, the principal chiefs, on

a suggestion of Bear's Meat, had followed the young men down the Kalamazoo, dividing themselves by a part of their body's crossing the stream at the first favorable spot. In this way the Indians proceeded, sweeping the river before them, and examining every place that seemed capable of concealing a canoe. Runners were kept in constant motion between the several parties, in order to let the state of the search be known to all ; and, feigning to be one of these very men, Pigeonswing had held communication with several whom he purposely met, and to whom he imparted such invented information as contributed essentially to send the young men forward on a false scent. In this way the main body of the savages descended the river some sixty miles, following its windings, in the first day and a half. Here Pigeonswing left them, turning his own face up stream, in order to rejoin his friends. Of Peter he had no knowledge, neither knowing, nor otherwise learning, what had become of the great chief. On his way up stream, Pigeonswing met several more Indians, runners like himself, or as he seemed to be ; or scouts kept on the lookout for the fugitives. He had no difficulty in deceiving these men. None of them had been of Crowsfeather's party, and he was a stranger to them all. Ignorant of his real character, they received his information without distrust, and the orders he pretended to convey were obeyed by them without the smallest hesitation. In this way, then, Pigeonswing contrived to send all the scouts he met away from the river, by telling them that there was reason to think the pale-faces had abandoned the stream, and that it was the wish of Bear's Meat that their trail should be looked for in the interior. This was the false direction that he gave to all, thereby succeeding better even than he had hoped in clearing the banks of the Kalamazoo of observers and foes. Nevertheless, many of those whom he knew to be out, some quite in the rear of the party and others in its front, and at no great distance from them, he did not meet; of course he could not get his false directions to their ears. There were, in fact, so many of the Indians and so few of the whites that it was an easy matter to cover the path with young warriors, any one party of whom would be strong enough to capture two men and as many women.

Having told the tale of his own doings Pigeonswing next came to his proposition for the mode of future proceeding. He proposed that the family should get into the canoes that very night, and commence its flight by going down the stream directly towards its foes ! This sounded strangely, but there did not seem to be any alternative. A march across the peninsula would be too much for the females, and there was the certainty that their trail would be found. It may seem strange to those who are unacquainted with the American Indian and his habits to imagine that, in so large an expanse, the signs of the passage of so small a party might not escape detection ; but such was the case. To one unaccustomed to the vigilance and intelligence of these savages it must appear just as probable that the vessel could be followed through the wastes of the ocean, by means of its wake, as that the footprints should be so indelible as to furnish signs that can be traced for days. Such, however, is the fact, and no one understood it better than the Chippewa. He was also aware that the country towards Ohio, whither the fugitives would naturally direct their course, now that the English were in possession of Detroit, must soon be a sort of battle-ground, to which most of the warriors of that region would eagerly repair. Under all the circumstances, therefore, he advised the flight by means of the river. Le Bourdon reasoned on all he heard, and, still entertaining some of his latent distrust of Peter, and willing to get beyond his reach, he soon acquiesced in the proposition, and came fully into the plan.

It was now necessary to reload the canoes. This was done in the course of the day, and every arrangement was made so as to be ready for a start as soon as the darkness set in. Everybody was glad to move, though all were aware of the extent of the hazard they ran. The females, in particular, felt their hearts beat, as each, in her husband's canoe, issued out of the cover into the open river. Pigeonswing took the lead, paddling with a slow but steady sweep of his arm, and keeping as close as was convenient to one bank. By adopting this precaution, he effectually concealed the canoes from the eyes of all on that side of the river, unless they stood directly on its margin, and had the aid of the shadows to help conceal them from any who might happen to be on the other. In this way, then, the party proceeded, passing the site of the hut, and the grove of the Openings around it, undetected. As the river necessarily flowed through the lowest land, its banks were wooded much of the way, which afforded great protection to the fugitives ; and this so much the more because these woods often grew in swamps, where the scouts would not be likely to resort.

About midnight the canoes reached the first rift. An hour was lost in unloading and in reloading the canoes, and in passing the difficulties at that point. As soon as this was done, the party re-embarked, and resorted once more to the use of the paddle, in order to gain a particular sheltered reach of the river previously to the return of light. This was effected successfully, and the party landed.

It now appeared that Pigeonswing had chosen another swamp as a place of concealment for the fugitives to use during the day. These swamps, through which the river wound its way in short reaches, were admirably adapted to such purposes. Dark, sombre, and hardly penetrable on the side of the land, they were little likely to be entered after a first examination. Nor was it at all probable that females, in particular, would seek a refuge in such a place. But the Chippewa had found the means to obviate the natural obstacles of the low land. There were several spots where the water from the river set back into the swamp, forming so many little creeks ; and into the largest of one of these he pushed his canoe, the others following where he led. By resorting to such means the shelter now obtained was more complete, perhaps, than that previously left.

Pigeonswing forced his light boat up the shallow inlet, until he reached a bit of dry land, where he brought up, announcing *that* as the abiding-place during the day. Glad enough was every one to get on shore, in a spot that promised security, after eight hours of unremitted paddling and of painful excitement. Notwithstanding the rifts and carrying-places they had met, and been obliged to overcome, Le Bourdon calculated that they had made as many as thirty miles in the course of that one night. This was a great movement, and to all appearances it had been made without detection. As for the Chippewa, he was quite content, and no sooner was his canoe secured than he lighted his pipe and sat down to its enjoyment with an air of composure and satisfaction.

"And here, you think, Pigeonswing, that we shall be safe during the day?" demanded Le Bourdon, approaching the fallen tree on which the Indian had taken his seat.

"Sartain—no Pottawattamie come here. Too wet. Don't like wet. Ain't duck, or goose—like dry land, juss like squaw. Dis good 'baccy, Bourdon: hope you got more for friend."

"I have enough for us all, Pigeonswing, and you shall have a full share. Now, tell me; what will be your next move, and where do you intend us to pass the morrow?"

"Juss like diss. Plenty of swamp, Bourdon, on Kekal-amazoo.[1] Run canoe in swamp; den safe 'nough. Injins won't look 'ere, 'cause he don't know whereabout look. Don't like swamp. Great danger down at mouth of river."

"So it has seemed to me, Chippewa. The Injins must be there in a strong force, and we shall find it no easy matter to get through them. How do you propose to do it?"

"Go by in night. No udder way. When can't see, can't see. Dere plenty of rush dere; dat good t'ing, and p'raps dat help us. Rush good cover for canoe. Expec', when we get down 'ere, to get some scalp too. Plenty of Pottawattamie about dat lodge, sartain; and it very hard if don't get some on him scalp. You mean stop, and dig up *cache*, eh, Bourdon?"

The cool, quiet manner in which Pigeonswing revealed his own plans, and inquired into those of his friend, had at least the effect to revive the confidence of Le Bourdon. He could not think the danger very great so long as one

---

[1] This is the true Indian word, though the whites have seen fit to omit the first syllable.

so experienced as the Chippewa felt so much confidence in his own future proceedings ; and, after talking a short time longer with this man, the bee-hunter went to seek Margery, in order to impart to her a due portion of his own hopes.

The sisters were preparing the breakfast. This was done without the use of fire, it being too hazardous to permit smoke to rise above the tops of the trees. Many is the camp that has been discovered by the smoke, which can be seen at a great distance, and is a certain sign of the presence of man, when it ascends in threads or such small columns as denote a domestic fire beneath. This is very different from the clouds that float above the burning prairies, and which all at once impute to their true origin. The danger of using fire had been so much guarded against by our fugitives, that the cooking of the party had been done at night, the utmost caution having been used to prevent the fire itself from being seen, and care taken to extinguish it long before the return of day. A supply of cold meat was always on hand, and had it not been, the fugitives would have known how to live on berries, or, at need, to fast ; anything was preferable to being exposed to certain capture.

As soon as the party had broken their fast, arrangements were made for recruiting nature by sleep. As for Pigeonswing, Indian-like, he had eaten enormously, no reasonable quantity of venison sufficing to appease his appetite ; and when he had eaten, he lay down in the bottom of his canoe and slept. Similar dispositions were made of their persons by the rest, and half an hour after the meal was ended, all there were in a profound sleep. No watch was considered necessary, and none was kept.

The rest of the weary is sweet. Long hours passed ere any one there awoke ; but no sooner did the Chippewa move than all the rest were afoot. It was now late in the day, and it was time to think of taking the meal that was to sustain them through the toil and fatigues of another arduous night. This was done, the necessary preparations being made for a start ere the sun had set. The canoes were then shoved as near the mouth of the inlet as it was safe to go while the light remained. Here they stopped, and a consultation took place as to the manner of proceeding.

No sooner did the shades of evening close around the place, than the fugitives again put forth. The night was clouded and dark, and so much of the way now lay through forests that there was little reason to apprehend detection. The chief causes of delay were the rifts and the portages, as had been the case the night before. Luckily Le Bourdon had been up and down the stream so often, as to be a very tolerable pilot in its windings. He assumed the control, and by midnight the greatest obstacle to that evening's progress was overcome. At the approach of day, Pigeonswing pointed out another creek in another swamp, where the party found a refuge for the succeeding day. In this manner four nights were passed on the river, and as many days in swamps, without discovery. The Chippewa had nicely calculated his time and his distances, and not the smallest mistake was made. Each morning a place of shelter was reached in sufficient season ; and each night the fugitives were ready for the start as the day shut in. In this manner most of the river was descended, until a distance that could be easily overcome in a couple of hours of paddling alone remained between the party and the mouth of the stream. Extreme caution was now necessary, for signs of Indians in the neighborhood had been detected at several points, in the course of the last night's work. On one occasion, indeed, the escape was so narrow as to be worth recording.

It was at a spot where the stream flowed through a forest denser than common that Pigeonswing heard voices on the river, ahead of him. One Indian was calling to another, asking to be set across the stream in a canoe. It was too late to retreat, and so much uncertainty existed as to the nearness or distance of the danger, that the Chippewa deemed it safest to bring all three of his canoes together, and to let them float past the point suspected, or rather *known* to be occupied by enemies. This was done with the utmost care. The plan succeeded, though not without running a very great risk. The canoes did float past unseen, though there was a minute of time when Le Bourdon fancied by the sounds that savages were talking to each other, within a hundred feet of his ears. Additional security, however, was felt in consequence of the circumstance, since the pursuers must imagine the river below them to be free from the pursued.

The halt that morning was made earlier than had been the practice previously. This was done because the remaining distance was so small, that in continuing to advance the party would have incurred the risk of reaching the mouth of the river by daylight. This was to be avoided on every account, but principally because it was of great importance to conceal from the savages the direction taken. Were the chiefs certain that their intended victims were on Lake Michigan, it would be possible for them to send parties across the isthmus, that should reach points on Lake Huron days in advance of the arrival of the bee-hunter and his friends in the vicinity of Saginaw, or *Pointe aux Barques*, for instance, and where the canoes would be almost certain to pass near the shore, laying their ambushes to accomplish these ends. It was thought very material, therefore, to conceal the movements, even after the lake might be reached, though Le Bourdon had not a doubt of his canoes much out-sailing those of the savages. The Indians are not very skilful in the use of sails, while the bee-hunter knew how to manage a bark canoe in rough water with unusual skill. In the common acceptation, he was no sailor; but, in his own peculiar craft, there was not a man living who could excel him in dexterity or judgment.

The halting-place that morning was not in a swamp, for none offered at a suitable distance from the mouth of the river. On the contrary, it was in a piece of Opening that was tolerably well garnished with trees, however, and through which ran a small brook that poured its tribute into the Kalamazoo. The Chippewa had taken notice of this brook, which was large enough to receive the canoes, where they might be concealed in the rushes. A favorable copse, surrounded with elders, afforded a covered space on

shore, and these advantages were improved for an encampment.

Instead of seeking his rest as usual, on reaching this
cover, Pigeonswing left the party on a scout. He walked
up the brook some distance, in order to conceal his trail,
and then struck across the Opening, taking the direction
westward, or towards the river's mouth. As for Le Bourdon and his friends, they ate and slept as usual, undisturbed ; but arose some hours before the close of day.

Thus far a great work had been accomplished. The
canoes had descended the stream with a success that was
only equalled by the hardihood of the measure, conducted
by an intelligence that really seemed to amount to an instinct. Pigeonswing carried a map of the Kalamazoo in his
head, and seemed never at a loss to know where to find the
particular place he sought. It is true he had roamed through
those Openings ever since he was a child ; and an Indian
never passes a place susceptible of being made of use to his
habits that he does not take such heed of its peculiarities
as to render him the master of all its facilities.

Margery was now full of hope, while the bee-hunter was
filled with apprehensions. She saw all things *couleur de
rose*, for she was young, happy, and innocent ; but he better
understood that they were just approaching the most serious
moment of their flight. He knew the vigilance of the
American savage, and could not deceive himself on the subject of the danger they must run. The mouth of the river
was just the place that, of all others, would be the closest
watched, and to pass it would require not only all their skill
and courage, but somewhat of the fostering care of Providence. It might be done with success, though the chances
were much against it.

CHAPTER XXVIII.

" Yes ! we have need to bid our hopes repose
    On some protecting influence ; here confined,
Life hath no healing balm for mental woes ;
    Earth is too narrow for the immortal mind.
Our spirits burn to mingle with the day,
    As exiles panting for their native coast ;
Yet lured by every wild-flower from their way,
    And shrinking from the gulf that must be crossed :
Death hovers round us—in the zephyr's sigh
As in the storm he comes—and lo ! Eternity ! "
MRS. HEMANS.

IT was probably that inherent disposition to pry into unknown things which is said to mark her sex, and which was the weakness assailed by the serpent when he deluded Eve into disobedience, that now tempted Margery to go beyond the limits which Pigeonswing had set for her, with a view to explore and ascertain what might be found without. In doing this, however, she did not neglect a certain degree of caution, and avoided exposing her person as much as possible.

Margery had got to the very verge of prudence, so far as the cover was concerned, when her steps were suddenly arrested by a most unexpected and disagreeable sight. An Indian was seated on a rock within twenty feet of the place where she stood. His back was towards her, but she was certain it could not be Pigeonswing, who had gone in a contrary direction, while the frame of this savage was much larger and heavier than that of the Chippewa. His rifle leaned against the rock, near his arm, and the tomahawk and knife were in his belt ; still Margery thought, so far as she could ascertain, that he was not in his war-paint, as she

431

knew was the fact with those whom she had seen at Prairie Round. The attitude and whole deportment of this stranger, too, struck her as remarkable. Although our heroine stood watching him for several minutes, almost breathless with terror and anxiety to learn his object, he never stirred even a limb in all that time. There he sate, motionless as the rock on which he had placed himself; a picture of solitude and reflection !

It was evident, moreover, that this stranger also sought a species of concealment as well as the fugitives. It is true he had not buried himself in a cover of bushes; but his seat was in a hollow of the ground where no one could have seen him, from the rear or on either side, at a distance a very little greater than that at which Margery stood, while his front was guarded from view by a line of bushes that fringed the margin of the stream. Marius pondering on the mutations of fortune, amid the ruins of Carthage, could scarcely have presented a more striking object than the immovable form of this stranger. At length the Indian slightly turned his head, when his observer, to her great surprise, saw the hard, red, but noble and expressive profile of the well-known features of Peter.

In an instant all Margery's apprehensions vanished, and her hand was soon lightly laid on the shoulder of her friend. Notwithstanding the suddenness of this touch, the great chief manifested no alarm. He turned his head slowly, and when he saw the bright countenance of the charming bride, his smile met hers in pleased recognition. There was no start, no exclamation, no appearance of surprise; on the contrary, Peter seemed to meet his pretty young friend much as a matter of course, and obviously with great satisfaction.

" How lucky this is, Peter ! " exclaimed the breathless Margery. " Bourdon's mind will now be at rest, for he was afraid you had gone to join our enemies—Bear's Meat and his party."

"Yes; go and stay wid 'em. So bess. Now dey t'ink Peter all on deir side. But nebber forget you, young Blossom."

"I believe you, Peter; for I *feel* as if you are a true friend. How lucky that we should meet here!"

"No luck at all. Come a purpose. Pigeonswing tell me where you be, so come here. Juss so."

"Then you expected to find us in this cover! and what have you to tell us of our enemies?"

"Plenty of *dem*. All about mout' of river. All about woods and openin's here. More dan you count. T'ink of nuttin' but get your scalp."

"Ah! Peter, why is it that you redmen wish so much to take our lives? and why have you destroyed the missionary, a pious Christian, who wished for nothing but your good?"

Peter bent his eyes to the earth, and for more than a minute he made no reply. He was much moved, however, as was visible in his countenance, which plainly denoted that strong emotions were at work within.

"Blossom, listen to my words," he at length answered. "They are such as a fader would speak to his da'ghter. You my da'ghter. Tell you so, once; and what Injin say once, he say alway. Poor, and don't know much, but know how to do as he say he do. Yes, you my da'ghter! Bear's Meat can't touch *you* widout he touch *me*. Bourdon your husband; you his squaw. Husband and squaw go togedder on same path. Dat right. But, Blossom, listen. Dere is Great Spirit. Injin believe dat as well as pale-face. See dat is so. Dere is Great *Wicked* Spirit, too. Feel dat, too; can't help it. For twenty winter dat Great Wicked Spirit stay close to my side. He put his hand before one of my ear, and he put his mout' to tudder. Keep whisper, whisper, whisper, day and night, nebber stop whisper. Tell me to kill pale-face wherever I find him. Bess to kill him. If did n't kill pale-face, pale-face kill Injin. No help for it. Kill ole man, kill young man; kill squaws, pappoose and all. Smash eggs and break up 'e nest. Dat what he whisper, day and night, for twenty winter. Whisper so much, was force to b'lieve him. Bad to have too much whisper of same t'ing in ear. Den, I want scalp. Could n't have too much scalp. Took much scalp. All pale-face scalp. Heart grow hard. Great pleasure was to kill pale-

face. Dat feeling last, Blossom, till I see you. Feel like
fader to you, and don't want your scalp. Won'er great deal
why I feel so, but do feel so. Dat my natur'. Still want
all udder pale-face scalp. Want Bourdon scalp much as
any."

A slight exclamation from his companion, which could
scarcely be called a scream, caused the Indian to cease
speaking when the two looked towards each other and their
eyes met. Margery, however, saw none of those passing
gleams of ferocity, which had so often troubled her in the
first few weeks of their acquaintance ; in their stead, an expression of subdued anxiety, and an earnestness of inquiry
that seemed to say how much the chief's heart yearned to
know more on that mighty subject towards which his
thoughts had lately been turned. The mutual glance sufficed to renew the confidence our heroine was very reluctant to relinquish, while it awakened afresh all of Peter's
parental concern in the welfare of the interesting young
woman at his side.

"But this feeling has left you, Peter, and you no longer
wish Bourdon's scalp," said Margery, hastily. "Now he
is my husband, he is your son."

"Dat good, p'raps," answered the Injin ; "but dat not
a reason, nudder, Blossom. You right, too. Don't want
Bourdon scalp any longer. Dat true. But don't want *any*
scalp any more. Heart grow soft—an't hard, now."

"I wish I could let you understand, Peter, how much I
rejoice to hear this ! I have never felt afraid of you on my
own account, though I will own that I have sometimes feared
that the dreadful cruel stories which are told of your enmity
to my color are not altogether without truth. Now, you tell
me you are the white man's friend, and that you no longer
wish to injure him. These are blessed words, Peter ; and
humbly do I thank God, through his blessed Son, that I
have lived to hear them ! "

"Dat Son make me feel so," returned the Indian, earnestly. "Yes, juss so. My heart was hard till medicine-
priest tell dat tradition of Son of Great Spirit—how He die
for all tribes and nations, and ask his fader to do good to

dem dat take his life—dat won'erful tradition, Blossom! Sound like song of wren in my ear: sweeter dan mocking-bird when he do his bess. Yes, dat won'erful. He true, too; for medicine-priest ask his Manitou to bless Injin, just as Injin lift tomahawk to take his life. I see'd and heard dat myself. All, won'erful, won'erful!''

"It was the Spirit of God that enabled poor Mr. Amen to do that, Peter; and it is the Spirit of God that teaches you to see and feel the beauty of such an act. Without the aid of that Spirit we are helpless as children; with it, strong as giants. I do not wonder at all that the good missionary was able to pray for his enemies with his dying breath. God gave him strength to do so.''

Margery spoke as she felt, earnestly and with emphasis. Her cheeks flushed with the strength of her feelings, and Peter gazed on her with a species of reverence and wonder. The beauty of this charming young woman was pleasing rather than brilliant, depending much on expression for its power. A heightened color greatly increased it, and when, as in this instance, the eyes reflected the tints of the cheeks, one might have journeyed days in older regions without finding her equal in personal attractions. Much as he admired her, however, Peter had now that on his mind which rendered her beauty but a secondary object with him. His soul had been touched by the unseen, but omnipresent power of the Holy Spirit, and his companion's language and fervor contributed largely in keeping alive his interest in what he felt.

"Nebber know Injin do dat,"—said Peter, in a slow, deliberative sort of way; "no, nebber know Injin do so. Alway curse and hate his enemy, and moss when about to lose his scalp. Den, feelin' 's hottest. Den, most want to use tomahawk on his enemy. Den, most feel dat he hate him. But not so wid medicine-priest. Pray for Injin; ask Great Spirit to do him all 'e good he can; juss as Injin was goin' to strike. Won'erful, won'erful—most won'erful *dat*, in my eyes. Blossom, you know Peter. He your fader. He take you, and make you his da'ghter. His heart is soft to you, Blossom. But he nuttin' but poor Injin, dough a

great chief.   What he know?   Pale-face pappoose know
more than Injin chief.   Dat come from Great Spirit, too.
He wanted it so, and it is so.   Our chiefs say dat Great
Spirit love Injin.   May be so.   T'ink He love ebbery body ;
but He can't love Injin as much as He love pale-face, or He
would n't let redman know so little.   Don't count wigwams
and towns and canoes and powder and lead as proof of
Great Spirit's love.   Pale-face got more of dese dan Injin.
Dat I see and know, and dat I feel.   But it no matter.
Injin used to be poor, and don't care.   When used to be
poor, den used to it.   When used to be rich, den it hard not
to be rich.   All use.   Injin don't care.   But it bad not to
know.   I 'm warrior—I 'm hunter—I 'm great chief.   You
squaw — you young — you know so much as squaw of
chief.   But you know most.   I feel ashamed to know so
little.   Want to know more.   Want to know most how 'e
Son of Great Spirit die for all tribe, and pray to his fader
to bless 'em dat kill Him.   Dat what Peter now want moss
to know ! ''

"I wish I was better able to teach you, Peter, from the
bottom of my heart ; but the little I do know you shall hear.
I would not deny you for a thousand worlds, for I believe
the Holy Spirit has touched your heart, and that you will
become a new man.   Christians believe that all must become
new men, who are to live in the other world, in the presence
of God.''

"How can dat be?   Peter soon be ole—how can ole man
grow young ag'in ? ''

"The meaning of this is that we must so change in feelings as no longer to be the same persons.   The things that
we loved we must hate, and the things that we hated, or
at least neglected, we must love.   When we feel this
change in our hearts, then may we hope that we love and
reverence the Great Spirit, and are living under His holy
care.''

Peter listened with the attention of an obedient and respectful child.   If meekness, humility, a wish to learn the
truth, and a devout sentiment towards the Creator, are so
many indications of the " new birth,'' then might this sav-

age be said to have been truly "born again." Certainly, he was no longer the same man in a moral point of view, and of this he was himself entirely conscious. To him the wonder was what had produced so great and so sudden a change! But the reply he made to Margery will, of itself, sufficiently express his views of his own case.

"An Injin like a child," he said meekly, "nebber know. Even pale-face squaw know more dan great chief. Nebber feel as do now. Heart soft as young squaw's. Don't hate anybody no more. Wish well to all tribe and color and nation. Don't hate Bri'sh, don't hate Yankee; don't hate Cherokee even. Wish 'em all well. Don't know that heart is strong enough to ask Great Spirit to do 'em all good if dey want my scalp; p'raps dat too much for poor Injin; but don't wan't nobody's scalp myself. Dat som'-tin', I hope, for me."

"It is, indeed, Peter; and if you will get down on your knees, and humble your thoughts, and pray to God to strengthen you in these good feelings, He will be sure to do it, and make you altogether a new man."

Peter looked wistfully at Margery, and then turned his eyes towards the earth. After sitting in a thoughtful mood for some time he again regarded his companion, saying, with the simplicity of a child,—

"Don't know how to do dat, Blossom. Hear medicine-priest of pale-faces pray some time, but poor Injin don't know enough to speak to Great Spirit. You speak to Great Spirit for him. He know your voice, Blossom, and listen to what you say; but He won't hear Peter, who has so long hated his enemy. P'raps He angry if He hear Peter speak."

"In that you are mistaken, Peter. The ears of the Lord are ever open to our prayers, when put up in sincerity, as I feel certain that yours will now be. But after I have told you the meaning of what I am about to say, I will pray with you and for you. It is best that you should begin to do this as soon as you can."

Margery then slowly repeated to Peter the words of the Lord's Prayer. She gave him its history, and explained

the meaning of several of its words that might otherwise
have been unintelligible to him, notwithstanding his tolerable proficiency in English,—a proficiency that had greatly
increased in the last few weeks, in consequence of his constant communications with those who spoke it habitually.
The word "trespasses" in particular was somewhat difficult for the Indian to comprehend, but Margery persevered
until she succeeded in giving her scholar tolerably accurate
ideas of the meaning of each term. Then she told the Indian to kneel with her, and, for the first time in his life,
that man of the Openings and Prairies lifted his voice in
prayer to the one God. It is true that Peter had often
before mentally asked favors of his Manitou ; but the re-
quests were altogether of a wordly character, and the being
addressed was invested with attributes very different from
those which he now understood to belong to the Lord of
Heaven and Earth. Nor was the spirit in asking at all
the same. We do not wish to be understood as saying
that this Indian was already a full convert to Christianity,
which contains many doctrines of which he had not the
most distant idea ; but his heart had undergone the first
step in the great change of conversion, and he was now as
humble as he had once been proud ; as meek as he had
formerly been fierce ; and he felt that certain proof of an
incipient love of the Creator in a similar feeling towards
all the works of his hands.

When Peter arose from his knees after repeating the
prayer to Margery's slow leading, it was with the dependence of a child on the teaching of its mother. Physically,
he was the man he ever had been. He was able to endure
fatigue, as sinewy in his frame, and as capable of fasting
and of sustaining fatigue, as in his most warlike days ; but
morally the change was great indeed. Instead of the ob-
stinate confidence in himself and his traditions which had
once so much distinguished this chief, there was substituted
an humble distrust of his own judgment that rendered him
singularly indisposed to rely on his personal views in any
matter of conscience, and he was truly become a child in
all that pertained to his religious belief. In good hands,

and under more advantageous circumstances, the moral improvement of Peter would have been great; but, situated as he was, it could not be said to amount to much more than a very excellent commencement.

All this time both Peter and Margery had been too intent on their feelings and employment to take much heed to the precautions necessary to their concealment. The sun was setting ere they arose, and then it was that Peter made the important discovery that they were observed by two of the young men of the Pottawattamies; scouts kept out by Bear's Meat to look for the fugitives.

The time was when Peter would not have hesitated to use his rifle on these unwelcome intruders; but the better spirit that had come over him now led him to adopt a very different course. Motioning to the young men, he ordered them to retire, while he led Margery within the cover of the bushes. Formerly, Peter would not have scrupled to resort to deception, in order to throw these two young men on a wrong scent and get rid of them in that mode; but now he had a reluctance to deceive, and, no sooner did they fall back at his beckoning than he followed Margery to the camp. The latter was giving her husband a hurried account of what had just happened as Peter joined them.

"Our camp is known!" exclaimed the bee-hunter, the instant he beheld the Indian.

"Juss so. Pottawattamie see squaw, and go and tell his chief. Dat sartain," answered Peter.

"What is there to be done? Fight for our lives, or fly?"

"Get in canoe quick as can. It take them young men half hour to reach place where chief be. In dat half hour we muss go as far as we can. No good to stay here. Injin come in about one hour."

Le Bourdon knew his position well enough to understand this. Nevertheless there were several serious objections to an immediate flight. Pigeonswing was absent, and the bee-hunter did not like the notion of leaving him behind, for various reasons. Then it was not yet dark; and to descend down the river by daylight appeared like advancing into the jaws of the lion designedly. Nor was Le Bourdon at his ease on the subject of Peter. His sudden appearance, the insufficient and far from clear account of Margery, and the extraordinary course advised, served to renew ancient distrusts, and to render him reluctant to move. But of one thing there could be no doubt. Their present position must be known, for Margery had seen the two strange Indians with her own eyes, and a search might soon be expected. Under all the circumstances, therefore, our hero reluctantly complied with Margery's reiterated solicitations, and they all got into the canoes.

"I do not half like this movement, Peter," said Le Bourdon, as he shoved his own light craft down the brook, previously to entering the river. "I hope it may turn out to be better than it looks, and that you can keep us out of the hands of our enemies. Remember, it is broad daylight, and that redmen are plenty two or three miles below us."

"Yes, know dat. But muss go. Injin too plenty here soon. Yes, muss go. Bourdon, why you can't ask bee, now, what bess t'ing for you to do, eh? Good time, now, ask bee to tell what he know."

The bee-hunter made no reply, but his pretty wife raised her hand involuntarily, as if to implore the Indian to forbear. Peter was a little bewildered; for as yet he did not understand that a belief in necromancy was not exactly compatible with the notions of the Christian's Providence. In his ignorance, how much was he worse off than the wisest of our race? Will any discreet man who has ever paid close attention to the power of the somnambule deny that there is a mystery about such a person that exceeds all our means of explanation? That there are degrees in the extent of this power; that there are false as well as true somnambules, all who have attended to the subject must allow; but a deriding disbeliever in our own person once, we have since seen that which no laws, known to us, can explain, and which we are certain is not the subject of collusion, as we must have been a party to the fraud ourselves were any such practised. To deny the evidence of our senses is an act of greater weakness than to believe that there are mysteries connected with our moral and physical being that human sagacity has not yet been able to penetrate ; and we repudiate the want of manliness that shrinks from giving its testimony when once convinced, through an apprehension of being derided, as weaker than those who withhold their belief. We *know* that our own thoughts have been explained and rendered by a somnambule, under circumstances that will not admit of any information by means known to us by other principles ; and whatever others may think on the subject, we are perfectly conscious that no collusion did or could exist. Why, then, are we to despise the poor Indian because he still fancied Le Bourdon could hold communication with his bees? We happen to be better informed, and there may be beings who are aware of the as yet hidden laws of animal magnetism, —hidden as respects ourselves though known to them,— and who fully comprehend various mistakes and misapprehensions connected with our impressions on this subject, that escape our means of detection. It is not surprising, therefore, that Peter, in his emergency, turned to those bees, in the hope that they might prove of assistance, or that Margery silently rebuked him for the weakness in the manner mentioned.

Although it was still light, the sun was near setting when the canoes glided into the river. Fortunately for the fugitives the banks were densely wooded and the stream of great width, a little lake in fact, and there was not much danger of their being seen until they got near the mouth ; nor then, even, should they once get within the cover of the wild rice and of the rushes. There was no retreat, however ; and after paddling some distance in order to get beyond the observation of any scout who might approach the place where they had last been seen, the canoes were brought close together, and suffered to float before a smart breeze, so as not to reach the mouth of the stream before the night closed around them. Everything appeared so tranquil, the solitude was so profound, and their progress so smooth and uninterrupted, that a certain amount of confidence revived in the breasts of all, and even the bee-hunter had hopes of eventual escape.

A conversation now occurred in which Peter was questioned concerning the manner in which he had been occupied during his absence,—an absence that had given Le Bourdon so much concern. Had the chief been perfectly explicit he would have confessed that fully one half of his waking thoughts had been occupied in thinking of the death of the Son of God, of the missionary's prayer for his enemies, and of the sublime mortality connected with such a religion. It is true Peter did not, could not indeed, enter very profoundly into the consideration of these subjects ; nor were his notions either very clear or orthodox ; but they were sincere, and the feelings to which they gave birth were devout. Peter did not touch on these circumstances, however, confining his explanations to the purely material part of his proceedings. He had remained with Bear's Meat, Crowsfeather, and the other leading chiefs, in order to be at the fountain-head of information, and to interpose his influence should the pale-faces unhappily fall into the hands of those who were so industriously looking for them. Nothing had occurred to call his authority out, but a strange uncertainty seemed to reign among the warriors concerning the manner in which their intended victims eluded their endeavors to overtake them. No trail had been discovered, scout after scout coming in to report a total want of success in their investigations inland. This turned the attention of the Indians still more keenly on the river's mouth, it being certain that the canoes could not have passed out into the lake previously to the arrival of the two or three first parties of their young men, who had been sent so early to watch that particular outlet.

Peter informed Le Bourdon that his *câche* had been discovered, opened, and rifled of its stores. This was a severe loss to our hero, and one that would have been keenly felt at any other time ; but, just then, he had interests so much more important to protect, that he thought and said little about this mishap. The circumstance which gave him the most concern was this. Peter stated that Bear's Meat had directed about a dozen of his young men to keep watch day and night in canoes, near the mouth of the river, lying in wait among the wild rice like so many snakes in the grass.

The party was so much interested in this conversation that, almost insensibly to themselves, they had dropped down to the beginning of the rushes and rice, and had got rather dangerously near to the critical point of their passage. As it was still daylight, Peter now proposed pushing the canoes in among the plants, and their remaining until it might be safer to move. This was done, accordingly, and in a minute or two all three of the little barks were concealed within the cover.

The question was now whether the fugitives had been observed, but suffered to advance, as every foot they descended the stream was taking them nearer to their foes. Peter did not conceal his apprehension on this point, since he deemed it improbable that any reach near the mouth of the Kalamazoo was without its lookouts at a moment so interesting. Such was, indeed, the fact, as it was afterwards ascertained ; but the young men who had seen Peter and Margery had given the alarm, passing the word where the fugitives were to be found, and the sentinels along this portion of the stream had deserted their stations in order to be in at the capture. By such delicate and unforeseen means does Providence often protect those who are the subjects of its especial care, baffling the calculations of art by its own quiet control of events.

The bee-hunter had a feverish desire to be moving. After remaining in the cover about half an hour, he proposed that they should get the canoes into one of the open passages, of which there were many among the plants, and proceed. Peter had more of the patience of an Indian, and deemed the hour too early. But Le Bourdon was not yet entirely free from distrust of his companion, and telling Gershom to follow, he began paddling down one of the passages mentioned. This decisive step compelled the rest to follow, or to separate from their companions. They chose to do the first.

Had Le Bourdon possessed more self-command and re-

mained stationary a little longer, he would, in all probability, have escaped altogether from a very serious danger that
he was now compelled to run. Although there were many
of the open places among the plants, they did not always
communicate with each other, and it became necessary to
force the canoes through little thickets, in order to get out
of one into another, keeping the general direction of descending the river. It was while effecting the first of these
changes that the agitation of the tops of the plants caught
the eye of a lookout on the shore. By signals, understood
among themselves, this man communicated his discovery to
a canoe that was acting as one of the guard-boats, thus giving a general alarm along the whole line of sentinels, as well
as to the chiefs down at the hut or at the mouth of the river.
The fierce delight with which this news was received, after
so long a delay, became ungovernable, and presently yells
and cries filled the air, proceeding from both sides of the
stream, as well as from the river itself.

There was not a white person in those canoes who did
not conceive that their party was lost when this clamor
was heard. With Peter it was different. Instead of admitting of alarm, he turned all his faculties to use. While
Le Bourdon himself was nearly in despair, Peter was listening with his nice ears to catch the points on the river
whence the yells arose. For the banks he cared nothing.
The danger was from the canoes. By the keenness of his
faculties the chief ascertained that there were four canoes
out, and that they would have to run the gauntlet between
them or escape would be hopeless. By the sound he also
became certain that these four canoes were in the rice, two
on each side of the river, and there they would probably
remain, in expectation that the fugitives would be most
likely to come down in the cover.

The decision of Peter was made in a moment. It was
now quite dark, and those who were in canoes within the
rice could not well see the middle of the stream, even by
daylight. He determined, therefore, to take the very centre of the river, giving his directions to that effect with
precision and clearness. The females he ordered to lie down,

each in her own canoe, while their husbands alone were to remain visible. Peter hoped that, in the darkness, Le Bourdon and Gershom might pass for Indians on the look-out, and under his own immediate command.

One very important fact was ascertained by Le Bourdon as soon as these arrangements were explained and completed. The wind on the lake was blowing from the south, and of course was favorable to those who desired to proceed in the opposite direction. This he communicated to Margery in a low tone, endeavoring to encourage her by all the means in his power. In return, the young wife muttered a few encouraging words to her husband. Every measure was understood between the parties. In the event of a discovery, the canoes were to bury themselves in the rice, taking different directions, each man acting for himself. A place of rendezvous was appointed outside, at a headland known to Gershom and Le Bourdon, and signals were agreed on by which the latest arrivals might know that all was safe there. These points were settled as the canoes floated slowly down the stream.

Peter took and kept the lead. The night was star-lit and clear, but there was no moon. On the water, this made but little difference, objects not being visible at any material distance. The chief governed the speed, which was moderate but regular. At the rate he was now going it would require about an hour to carry the canoes into the lake. But nearly all of that hour must pass in the midst of enemies!

Half of the period just mentioned elapsed, positively without an alarm of any sort. By this time the party was abreast of the spot where Gershom and Le Bourdon had secreted the canoes in the former adventure at the mouth of the river. On the shores, however, a very different scene now offered. Then the fire burned brightly in the hut, and the savages could be seen by its light. Now all was not only dark but still as death. There was no longer any cry, sound, alarm, or foot-fall, audible. The very air seemed charged with uncertainty, and its offspring, apprehension.

As they approached nearer and nearer to what was conceived to be the most critical point in the passage, the canoes got closer together ; so close, indeed, that Le Bourden and Gershom might communicate in very guarded tones. The utmost care was taken to avoid making any noise, since a light and careless blow from a paddle on the side of a canoe, would be almost certain now to betray them. Margery and Dorothy could no longer control their feelings, and each rose in her seat, raising her body so as to bring her head above the gunwale of the canoe, if a bark canoe can be said to have a gunwale at all. They even whispered to each other endeavoring to glean encouragement by sympathy. At this instant, occurred the crisis in their attempt to escape.

CHAPTER XXIX.

"For an Indian isle she shapes her way
With constant mind both night and day;
She seems to hold her home in view;
And sails as if the path she knew,
So calm and stately in her motion
Across the unfathomed, trackless ocean."

WILSON.

IT has been said that Peter was in advance. When his canoe was nearly abreast of the usual landing at the hut, he saw two canoes coming out from among the rice, and distant from him not more than a hundred yards. At a greater distance, indeed, it would not have been easy to distinguish such an object on the water at all. Instead of attempting to avoid these two canoes, the chief instantly called to them, drawing the attention of those in them to himself, speaking so loud as to be easily overheard by those who followed.

"My young men are too late," he said. "The pale-faces have been seen in the openings above by our warriors, and must soon be here. Let us land, and be ready to meet them at the wigwam."

Peter's voice was immediately recognized. The confident, quiet, natural manner in which he spoke served to mislead those in the canoes; and when he joined them, and entered the passage among the rice that led to the landing, preceding the others, the last followed him as regularly as the colt follows its dam. Le Bourdon heard the conversation and understood the movement, though he could not see the canoes. Peter continued talking aloud, as he went up the passage, receiving answers to all he said from his

447

new companions, his voice serving to let the fugitives know precisely where they were. All this was understood and improved by the last, who lost no time in turning the adventure to account.

The first impulse of Le Bourdon had been to turn and fly up stream. But ascertaining that these dangerous enemies were so fully occupied by Peter as not to see the canoes behind, he merely inclined a little towards the other side of the channel, and slackened his rate of movement, in order not to come too near. The instant he was satisfied that all three of the canoes in advance had entered the passage mentioned, and were moving towards the landing, he let out, and glided down stream like an arrow. It required but half a minute to cross the opening of the passage, but Peter's conversation kept his followers looking ahead, which greatly lessened the risk. Le Bourdon's heart was in his mouth, several times, while thus running the gauntlet, as it might be; but fortune favored them, or, as Margery more piously understood the circumstances, a Divine Providence led them in safety past the danger.

At the mouth of the river both Le Bourdon and Gershom thought it highly probable that they should fall in with more lookouts, and each prepared his arms for a fight. But no canoe was there, and the fugitives were soon in the lake. Michigan is a large body of water, and a bark canoe is but a frail craft to put to sea in, when there is any wind, or commotion. On the present occasion there was a good deal of both; so much as greatly to terrify the females. Of all the craft known, however, one of these egg-shells is really the safest, if properly managed, among breakers, or amid the combing of seas. We have ourselves ridden in them safely through a surf that would have swamped the best man-of-war cutter that ever floated; and done it, too, without taking on board as much water as would serve to wash one's hands. The light vessel floats on so little of the element, indeed, that the foam of a large sea has scarce a chance of getting above it, or aboard it, the great point in the handling being to prevent the canoe from falling broadside to. By keeping it end-on to the sea, in our opinion, a smart gale might be weathered in one of these craft, provided the endurance of a man could bear up against the unceasing watchfulness, and incessant labor of sweeping with the paddle, in order to prevent broaching to.

Le Bourdon, it has been said, was very skilful in the management of his craft; and Gershom, now perforce a sober and useful man, was not much behind him in this particular. The former had foreseen this very difficulty, and made all his arrangements to counteract it. No sooner, therefore, did he find the canoes in rough water than he brought them together, side by side, and lashed them there. This greatly lessened the danger of capsizing, though it increased the labor of managing the craft when disposed to turn broadside to. It only remained to get sail on the catamaran, for some such thing was it now, in order to keep ahead of the sea as much as possible. Light cotton lugs were soon spread, one in each canoe, and away they went, as sailors term it, wing-and-wing.

It was now much easier steering, though untiring vigilance was still necessary. A boat may appear to fly, and yet the "send of the sea" shall glance ahead of it with the velocity of a bird. Nothing that goes through, or *on*, the water, and the last is the phrase best suited to the floating of a bark canoe, can ever be made to keep company with that feathery foam, which under the several names of "white-caps,"—an in-shore and lubber's term,—"combs," "breaking of the seas," the "wash," etc., etc., etc., glances by a vessel in a blow, or comes on board her even when she is running before it. We have often watched these clouds of water, as they have shot ahead of us, when ploughing our own ten or eleven knot through the brine, and they have ever appeared to us as so many useful admonishers of what the power of God is as compared to the power of man. The last shall construct his ship, fit her with all the appliances of his utmost art, sail her with the seaman's skill, and force her through her element with something like railroad speed; yet will the seas "send" their feathery crests past her like so many dolphins, or porpoises, sporting under her fore-foot. It is this following

29

sea which becomes so very dangerous in heavy gales, and which compels the largest ships frequently to heave-to, in order that they may present their bows to its almost resistless power.

But our adventures had no such gales as those we mean, or any such seas to withstand. The wind blew fresh from the south, and Michigan can get up a very respectable swell at need. Like the seas in all the Great Lakes, it was short, and all the worse for that. The larger the expanse of water over which the wind passes, the longer is the sea, and the easier is it for the ship to ride on it. Those of Lake Michigan, however, were quite long enough for a bark canoe, and glad enough were both Margery and Dorothy when they found their two little vessels lashed together, and wearing an air of more stability than was common to them. Le Bourdon's sail was first spread, and it produced an immediate relief from the washing of the waves. The drift of a bark canoe in a smart blow is considerable, it having no hold on the water to resist it; but our adventurers fairly flew as soon as the cotton cloth was opened. The wind being exactly south, by steering due north, or dead before it, it was found possible to carry the sail in the other canoe, borne out on the opposite side ; and from the moment that was opened, all the difficulty was reduced to steering so "small," as seamen term it, as to prevent one or the other of the luggs from jibing. Had this occurred, however, no very serious consequences would have followed, the precaution taken of lashing the craft together rendering capsizing next to impossible.

The Kalamazoo and its mouth were soon far behind, and Le Bourdon no longer felt the least apprehension of the savages left in it. The Indians are not bold navigators, and he felt certain that the lake was too rough for the savages to venture out, while his own course gradually carried him off the land, and out of the track of anything that kept near the shore. A short time produced a sense of security, and the wind appearing to fall, instead of increasing in violence, it was soon arranged that one of the men should sleep while the other looked to the safety of the canoes.

It was about nine o'clock when the fugitives made sail, off the mouth of the Kalamazoo; and at the return of light, seven hours later, they were more than forty miles from the place of starting. The wind still stood, with symptoms of growing fresher again as the sun rose, and the land could just be seen in the eastern board, the coast in that direction having made a considerable curvature inland. This had brought the canoes farther from the land than Le Bourdon wished to be, but he could not materially change his course without taking in one of his sails. As much variation was made, however, as was prudent, and by nine o'clock, or twelve hours after entering the lake, the canoes again drew near to the shore, which met them ahead. By the bee-hunter's calculations, they were now about seventy miles from the mouth of the Kalamazoo, having passed the outlets of two or three of the largest streams of those regions.

The fugitives selected a favorable spot, and landed behind a headland that gave them a sufficient lee for the canoes. They had now reached a point where the coast trends a little to the eastward, which brought the wind in a slight degree off the land. This change produced no very great effect on the seas, but it enabled the canoes to keep close to the shore, making something of a lee for them. This they did about noon, after having lighted a fire, caught some fish in a small stream, killed a deer and dressed it, and cooked enough provisions to last for two or three days. The canoes were now separated again; it being easier to manage them in that state than when lashed together, besides enabling them to carry both sails. The farther north they got the more of a lee was found, though it was in no place sufficient to bring smooth water.

In this manner several more hours were passed, and six times as many more miles were made in distance. When Le Bourdon again landed, which he did shortly before the sun set, he calculated his distance from the mouth of the Kalamazoo to be rather more than a hundred miles. His principal object was to ascend a bluff and to take a look at the coast, in order to examine it for canoes. This his glass enabled him to do with some accuracy, and when he rejoined the party, he was rejoiced to have it in his power to report that the coast was clear. After refreshing themselves, the canoes were again brought together in order to divide the watches, and a new start was made for the night. In this manner did our adventurers make their way to the northward for two nights and days, landing often to fish, hunt, rest, and cook, as well as to examine the coast. At the end of the time mentioned, the celebrated straits of the Michillimackinac, or Mackinaw, as they are almost universally termed, came in sight. The course had been gradually changing towards the eastward, and luckily for the progress of the fugitives, the wind with it, leaving them always a favorable breeze. But it was felt to be no longer safe to use a sail, and recourse was had to the paddles until the straits and island were passed. This caused some delay, and added a good deal to the labor; but it was deemed so dangerous to display their white cotton sails, objects that might be seen for a considerable distance, that it was thought preferable to adopt this caution. Nor was it useless. In consequence of this foresight a fleet of canoes was passed in safety, which were crossing from the post at Mackinaw towards the main-land of Michigan. The number of the canoes in this fleet could not have been less than fifty, but getting a timely view of them, Le Bourdon hid his own craft in a cove, and remained there until the danger was over.

The course now changed still more, while the wind got quite round to the westward. This made a fair wind at first, and gave the canoes a good lee as they advanced. Lake Huron, which was the water the fugitives were now on, lies nearly parallel to Michigan, and the course was southeasterly. As Le Bourdon had often passed both ways on these waters, he had his favorite harbors, and knew those signs which teach navigators how to make their prognostics of the weather. On the whole, the fugitives did very well, though they lost two days between Mackinaw and Saginaw Bay; one on account of the strength of the wind, and one on account of rain. During the last, they remained in a hut that Le Bourdon had himself constructed in one of his many voyages, and which he had left standing. These empty cabins or *chientés* are of frequent occurrence in new countries, being used, like the refuges in the Alps, by every traveler as he has need of them.

The sight of the fleet of canoes in the straits of Michillimackinac caused the fugitives the only real trouble they had felt, between the time when they left the mouth of the Kalamazoo and the ten days that succeeded. By the end of that period the party had crossed Saginaw, and was fast coming up with Pointe au Barques, a landmark for all who navigate the waters of Huron, when a canoe was seen coming out from under the land, steering as if to intercept them. This sight gave both concern and pleasure: concern, as it might lead to a hostile encounter ; and pleasure, because the bee-hunter hoped for information that might be useful in governing his future course. Here his glass came in play with good effect. By means of that instrument it was soon ascertained that the strange canoe contained but two men, both Indians, and as that was just their own force, no great danger was apprehended from the meeting. The craft, therefore, continued to approach each other, Le Bourdon keeping his glass levelled on the strangers much of the time.

"As I live, yonder are Peter and Pigeonswing," suddenly exclaimed our hero. "They have crossed the peninsula, and have come out from the point in that canoe to meet us."

"With important news then, depend on it, Benjamin," answered the wife. "Tell this to brother, that he and Dolly may not feel more alarm than is necessary."

The bee-hunter called out to his friends in the other canoe and communicated the discovery just made, the two craft keeping always within hailing distance of each other.

"Them Injins are not here for nothing," answered Dorothy. "You will find they have something serious to say."

"We shall soon know," called out Le Bourdon. "Ten minutes will bring us alongside of them."

The ten minutes did that much, and before the expiration of the short space the three canoes were fastened together, that of Peter being in the centre. The bee-hunter saw at a glance that the expedition of the Indians had been hurried ; for their canoe, besides being of very indifferent qualities, was not provided with the implements and conveniences usual to a voyage of any length. Still, he would not ask a question, but lighting his pipe, after a few puffs he passed it courteously over to Peter. The great chief smoked awhile, and gave it to Pigeonswing, in his turn, who appeared to enjoy it quite as much as any of the party.

"My father does not believe he is a Jew?" said Le Bourdon, smiling ; willing to commence a discourse, though still determined not to betray a womanish curiosity.

"We are poor Injins, Bourdon ; just as the Great Spirit made us. Dat bess. Can't help what Manitou do. If he don't make us Jew, can't be Jew. If he make us Injin, muss be Injin. For my part, b'lieve I'm Injin, and don't want to be pale-face. Can love pale-face now juss as well as love Injin."

"Oh, I hope this is true, Peter," exclaimed Margery, her handsome face flushing with delight at hearing these words. "So long as your heart tells you this, be certain that the Spirit of God is in you."

Peter made no answer, but he looked profoundly impressed with the novel feeling that had taken possession of his soul. As for the bee-hunter, he did not meddle with Margery's convictions or emotions on such subjects, resembling in this particular most men, who, however indifferent to religion in their own persons, are never sorry to find that their wives profoundly submit to its influence. After a short pause, a species of homage involuntarily paid to the subject, he thought he might now inquire into the circumstances that brought the Indians on their route, without incurring the imputation of a weak and impatient curiosity. In reply Peter's story was soon told. He had rejoined the chiefs without exciting distrust, and all had waited for the young men to come in with the captives. As soon as it was ascertained that the intended victims had escaped, and by water, parties proceeded to different points in order to intercept them. Some followed in canoes, but being less bold in their navigation than the bee-hunter, they did not make the straits until some time after the fugitives had passed. Peter himself had joined Bear's Meat and some twenty warriors who had crossed the peninsula, procured canoes at the head of Saginaw Bay, and had come out at Pointe au Barques, the very spot our party was now approaching, three days before its arrival.

Tired with waiting, and uncertain whether his enemies had not got the start of him, Bear's Meat had gone into the river below, intending to keep his watch there, leaving Peter at the Pointe, with three young men and one canoe, to have a lookout. These young men the great chief had found an excuse for sending to the head of the bay in quest of another canoe, which left him, of course, quite alone on the Pointe. Scarce had the young men got out of sight ere Pigeonswing joined his confederate, for it seems that this faithful friend had kept on the skirts of the enemy the whole time, travelling hundreds of miles and enduring hunger and fatigue, besides risking his life at nearly every step, in order to be of use to those whom he considered himself pledged to serve.

Of course Peter and Pigeonswing understood each other. One hour after they joined company, the canoes of the fugitives came in sight, and were immediately recognized by their sails. They were met as has been mentioned, and the explanations that we have given were made before the party landed at the Pointe.

It was something to know where the risk was to be apprehended; but Le Bourdon foresaw great danger. He had brought his canoes already quite five hundred miles along a hazardous coast, though a little craft like one of those he navigated ran less risk perhaps than a larger vessel, since a shelter might at any time be found within a reasonable distance for it. From Pointe au Barques to the outlet of the lake was less than a hundred miles more. This outlet was a river, as it is called, a strait in fact, which communicates with the small, shallow lake of St. Clair, by a passage of some thirty miles in length. Then the lake St. Clair was to be crossed, about an equal distance, when the canoes would come out in what is called the Detroit River, a strait again, as its name indicates. Some six or eight miles down this passage, and on its western side, stands the city of Detroit, then a village of no great extent, with a fort better situated to repel an attack of the savages than to withstand a siege of white men. This place was now in the possession of the British, and, according to Le Bourdon's notions, it was scarcely less dangerous to him than the hostility of Bear's Meat and his companions.

Delay, however, was quite as dangerous as anything else. After cooking and eating, therefore, the canoes continued their course, Peter and Pigeonswing accompanying them, though they abandoned their own craft. Peter went with the bee-hunter and Margery, while the Chippewa took a seat and a paddle in the canoe of Gershom. This change was made in order to put a double power in each canoe, since it was possible that downright speed might become the only means of safety.

The wind still stood at the westward, and the rate of sailing was rapid. About the close of the day the party drew near to the outlet, when Peter directed the sails to be taken in. This was done to prevent their being seen, a precaution that was now aided by keeping as near to the shore as possible, where objects so small and low would be very apt to be confounded with others on the land.

It was quite dark when the canoes entered the St. Clair River. Favored by the current and the wind their progress was rapid, and ere the day returned, changing his direction from the course ordinarily taken, Peter entered the lake by a circuitous passage,—one of the many that lead from the river to the lake, among aquatic plants that form a perfect shelter. This detour saved the fugitives from falling into the hands of one party of their enemies, as was afterwards ascertained by the Indians. Bear's Meat had left two canoes, each manned by five warriors, to watch the principal passages into Lake St. Clair, not anticipating that any particular caution would be used by the bee-hunter and his friends at this great distance from the place where they had escaped from their foes. But the arrival of Peter, his sagacity and knowledge of Indian habits, prevented the result that was expected. The canoes got into the lake unseen, and crossed it a little diagonally, so as to reach the Canada shore in the middle of the afternoon of the succeeding day, using their sails only when far from the land, and not exposed to watchful eyes.

The bee-hunter and his friends landed that afternoon at the cabin of a Canadian Frenchman, on the shore of the lake, and at a safe distance from the outlet, which led still farther south. Here the females were hospitably received, and treated with that kindness which marks the character of the Canadian French. It mattered little to these simple people whether the travellers were of the hostile nation or not. It is true they did not like the "Yankees," as all Americans are termed by them, but they were not particularly in love with their English masters. It was well enough to be repossessed of both banks of the Detroit, for both banks were then peopled principally by their own race, the descendants of Frenchmen of the time of Louis XIV., and who still preserved much of the language and many of the usages of the French of that period. They spoke then, as now, only the language of their fathers.

The bee-hunter left the cottage of these simple and hospitable people as soon as the night was fairly set in ; or, rather, as soon as a young moon had gone down. Peter now took the command, steering the canoe of Le Bourdon, while Gershom followed so close as to keep the bow of his little craft within reach of the Indian's arm. In less than an hour the fugitives reached the opening of the river, which is here divided into two channels by a large island. On that very island, and at that precise moment, was Bear's Meat lying in wait for their appearance, provided with three canoes, each having a crew of six men. It would have been easy for this chief to go to Detroit and give the alarm to the savages, who were then collected there in a large force, and to have made such a disposition of the canoes as would have rendered escape by water impossible ; but this would have been robbing himself and his friends of all the credit of taking the scalps, and throwing away what is termed "honor," among others as well as among savages. He chose, therefore, to trust to his own ability to succeed; and supposing the fugitives would not be particularly on their guard at this point, had little doubt of intercepting them there, should they succeed in eluding those he had left above.

The bee-hunter distrusted that island, and used extra caution in passing it. In the first place, the two canoes were brought together, so as to give them, in the dark, the appearance of only one; while the four men added so much to the crew as to aid the deception. In the end it proved that one of Bear's Meat's canoes, that was paddling about in the middle of the river, had actually seen them, but mistook the party for a canoe of their own, which ought to have been near that spot, with precisely six persons in it, just at that time. These six warriors had landed, and gone up among the cottages of the French to obtain some fruit, of which they were very fond, and of which they got but little in their own villages. Owing to this lucky coincidence, which the pretty Margery ever regarded as another special interposition of Providence in their favor, the fugitives passed the island without molestation, and actually got below the last lookout of Bear's Meat, though without their knowledge.

It was by no means a difficult thing to go down the river, now that so many canoes were in motion on it at all hours. The bee-hunter knew what points were to be avoided, and took good care not to approach a sentinel. The river, or strait, is less than a mile wide, and, by keeping in the centre of the passage, the canoes, favored by both wind and current, drove by the town, then an inconsiderable village, without detection. As soon as far enough below, the canoes were again cast loose from each other, and sail was made on each. The water was smooth, and some time before the return of light the fugitives were abreast of Malden, but in the American channel. Had it been otherwise, the danger could not have been great. So completely were the Americans subdued by Hull's capitulation, and so numerous were the Indian allies of the British, that the passage of a bark canoe, more or less, would hardly have attracted attention. At that time Michigan was a province of but little more than a name. The territory was wide, to be sure, but the entire population was not larger than that of a moderately-sized English market town, and Detroit was then regarded as a distant and isolated post. It is true that Mackinac and Chicago were both more remote, and both more isolated ; but an English force in possession of Detroit could be approached by the Americans on the side of the land only by overcoming the obstacles of a broad belt of difficult wilderness. This was done the succeeding year, it is true ; but time is always necessary to bring out Jonathan's latent military energies. When aroused, they are not trifling, as all his enemies have been made to feel ; but a good deal of miscalculation, pretending ignorance, and useless talking must be expended, before the really efficient are allowed to set about serving the country in their own way.

In this respect, thanks to West Point, a well-organized staff, and well-educated officers, matters are a little improving. Congress has not been able to destroy the army in the present war, though it did its best to attain that end ; and all because the nucleus was too powerful to be totally eclipsed by the gas of the usual legislative tail of the Great National Comet, of which neither the materials nor the orbit can any man say he knows. One day it declares war with a hurrah ; the next it denies the legislation necessary to carry it on, as if it distrusted its own acts and already repented of its patriotism. And this is the body, soulless, the very school of faction, as a whole of very questionable quality in the outset, that, according to certain expounders of the Constitution, is to perform all the functions of a government ; which is not only to pass laws, but is to interpret them ; which is to command the army, ay, even to wheeling its platoons ; which reads the Constitution as an abbé mumbles his *aves* and *paters*, or looking at everything but his texts ; and which is never to have its acts vetoed, unless in cases where the Supreme Court would spare the Executive that trouble ! We never yet could see either the elements or the fruits of this great sanctity in the National Council. In our eyes it is scarcely ever in its proper place on the railway of the Union ; has degenerated into a mere electioneering machine, performing the little it really does convulsively, by sudden impulses, equally without deliberation or a sense of responsibility. In a word, we deem it the power of all others in the state that needs the closest watching ; and were we what is termed in this country " politicians," we should go for the Executive who is the most ready to apply the curb to these vagaries of factious and interested partisans. Vetoes ! Would to Heaven we could see the days of Good Queen Bess revived for one session of Congress at least, and find that more laws were sent back for the second thoughts of their framers than were approved ! Then, indeed, might the country be brought back to a knowledge of the very material constitutional facts, that the legislature is not commander-in-chief, does not negotiate or make treaties, and has no right to do that it has done so often, appoint to office by act of Congress !

As a consequence of the little apprehension entertained by the English of being soon disturbed in their new conquests, Le Bourdon and his friends got out of the Detroit River, and into Lake Erie, without discovery or molestation. There still remained a long journey before them. In that day the American side of the shores of all the Great Lakes was little more than a wilderness. There were exceptions at particular points, but these were few and far asunder. The whole coast of Ohio—for Ohio has its coast as well as Bohemia [1]—was mostly in a state of nature, as was much of those of Pennsylvania and New York, on the side of the fresh water. The port which the bee-hunter had in view was Presque Isle, now known as Erie, a harbor in Pennsylvania that has since become somewhat celebrated in consequence of its being the port out of which the American vessels sailed about a year later than the period of which we are writing, to fight the battle that gave them the mastery of the lake. This was a little voyage of itself, of near two hundred miles, following the islands and the coast, but

[1] See Shakespeare—*The Winter's Tale.*

it was safely made in the course of the succeeding week. Once in Lake Erie, and on the American side, our adventurers felt reasonably safe against all dangers but those of the elements. It is true that a renowned annalist, whose information is sustained by the collected wisdom of a State Historical Society, does tell us that the enemy possessed both shores of Lake Erie in 1814 ; but this was so small a mistake, compared with some others that this Nestor in history had made, that we shall not stop to explain it. Le Bourdon and his party found all the south shore of Lake Erie in possession of the Americans, so far as it was in the possession of any one, and consequently ran no risks from this blunder of the historian and his highly intelligent associates !

Peter and Pigeonswing left their friends before they reached Presque Isle. The bee-hunter gave them his own canoe, and the parting was not only friendly but touching. In the course of their journey, and during their many stops, Margery had frequently prayed with the great chief. His constant and burning desire now was to learn to read, that he might peruse the word of the Great Spirit, and regulate his future life by its wisdom and tenets. Margery promised, should they ever meet again, and under circumstances favorable to such a design, to help him attain his wishes.

Pigeonswing parted from his friend with the same light-hearted vivacity as he had manifested in all their intercourse. Le Bourdon gave him his own rifle, plenty of ammunition, and various other small articles that were of value to an Indian, accepting the Chippewa's arms in return. The exchange, however, was greatly to the advantage of the savage. As for Peter he declined all presents. He carried weapons now, indeed, merely for the purpose of hunting ; but the dignity of his character and station would have placed him above such compensations had the fact been otherwise.

CHAPTER XXX.

"Come to the land of peace!
Come where the tempest hath no longer sway,
The shadow passes from the soul away—
The sounds of weeping cease.

"Fear hath no dwelling there!
Come to the mingling of repose and love,
Breathed by the silent spirit of the dove,
Through the celestial air."

MRS. HEMANS.

IT is now more than thirty-three years since the last war with the English terminated, and about thirty-six to the summer in which the events recorded in this legend occurred. This third of a century has been a period of mighty changes in America. Ages have not often brought about as many in other portions of the earth, as this short period of time has given birth to among ourselves. We had written thus far on the evidence of documents sent to us, when an occasion offered to verify the truth of some of our pictures, at least, by means of personal observation.

Quitting our own quiet and secluded abode in the mountains in the pleasant month of June, and in this current year of 1848, we descended into the valley of the Mohawk, got into the cars, and went flying by rails towards the setting sun. Well could we remember the time when an entire day was required to pass between that point on the Mohawk, where we got on the rails and the little village of Utica. On the present occasion, we flew over the space in less than three hours, and dined in a town of some fifteen thousand souls.

We reached Buffalo, at the foot of Lake Erie, in about twenty hours after we had entered the cars. This journey would have been the labor of more than a week at the time in which the scene of this tale occurred. Now, the whole of the beautiful region, teeming with its towns and villages, and rich with the fruits of a bountiful season, was almost brought into a single landscape by the rapidity of our passage.

At Buffalo we turned aside to visit the cataract. Thither, too, we went on rails. Thirty-eight years had passed away since we had laid eyes on this wonderful fall of water. In the intervening time we had travelled much, and had visited many of the renowned falls of the Old World, to say nothing of the great number which are to be found in other parts of our own land. Did this visit, then, produce disappointment? Did time and advancing years, and feelings that had become deadened by experience, contribute to render the view less striking, less grand, in any way less pleasing than we had hoped to find it? So far from this, all our expectations were much more than realized. In one particular, touching which we do not remember ever to have seen anything said, we were actually astonished at the surpassing glory of Niagara. It was the character of sweetness, if we can so express it, that glowed over the entire aspect of the scene. We were less struck with the grandeur of this cataract than with its sublime softness and gentleness. To water in agitation use had so long accustomed us, perhaps, as in some slight degree to lessen the feeling of awe that is apt to come over the novice in such scenes ; but we at once felt ourselves attracted by the surpassing loveliness of Niagara. The gulf below was more imposing than we had expected to see it, but it was Italian in hue and softness, amid its wildness and grandeur. Not a drop of the water that fell down that precipice inspired terror ; for everything appeared to us to be filled with attraction and love. Like Italy itself, notwithstanding so much that is grand and imposing, the character of softness and the witchery of the gentler properties is the power we should ascribe to Niagara, in preference to that of its majesty. We think this feeling, too, is more general than is commonly supposed ; for we find those who dwell near the cataract playing around it, even to the very verge of its greatest fall, with a species of affection, as if they had the fullest confidence in its rolling waters. Thus is it that we see the little steamer, the *Maid of the Mists*, paddling up quite near to the green sheet of the Horse-Shoe itself, and gliding down in the current of the vortex, as it is compelled to quit the eddies, and come more in line with the main course of the stream. Wires, too, are suspended across the gulf below, and men pass it in baskets. It is said that one of these inventions is to carry human beings over the main fall, so that the adventurer may hang suspended in the air, directly above the vortex. In this way do men, and even women, prove their love for the place, all of which we impute to its pervading character of sweetness and attraction.

At Buffalo we embarked in a boat under the English flag, which is called the *Canada*. This shortened our passage to Detroit, by avoiding all the stops at lateral ports, and we had every reason to be satisfied with our selection. Boat, commander, and the attendance were such as would have done credit to any portion of the civilized world. There were many passengers, a motley collection, as usual, from all parts of the country.

Our attention was early drawn to one party by the singular beauty of its females. They seemed to us to be a grandmother, in a well-preserved, green old age ; a daughter, but a matron of a little less than forty ; and two exceedingly pretty girls of about eighteen and sixteen, whom we took to be children of the last. The strong family likeness between these persons led us early to make this classification, which we afterwards found was correct.

By occasional remarks, I gathered that the girls had been to an "eastern" boarding-school, that particular feature in civilization not yet flourishing in the Northwestern States. It seemed to us that we could trace in the dialect of the several members of this family the gradations and peculiarities that denote the origin and habits of individuals. Thus, the grandmother was not quite as western in her forms of speech as her matronly daughter, while the grand-children evidently spoke under the influence of boarding-school correction, or, like girls who had been often lectured on the subject. "First rate," and "Yes, *sir*," and "That's a *fact*," were often in the mouth of the pleasing mother, and even the grandmother used them all, though not as often as her daughter; while the young people looked a little concerned and surprised whenever they came out of the mouth of their frank-speaking mother. That these persons were not of a very high social class was evident enough, even in their language. There was much occasion to mention New York, we found, and they uniformly called it "the city." By no accident did either of them ever happen to use the expression that she had been "in town," as one of us would be apt to say. "He's gone to the *city*, or "she's in the *city*," are awkward phrases, and *tant soit peu* vulgar; but even our pretty young boarding-school *elevès* would use them. We have a horrror of the expression "city," and are a little fastidious, perhaps, touching its use.

But these little peculiarities were spots on the sun. The entire family, taken as a whole, was really charming; and long before the hour for retiring came we had become much interested in them all. We found there was a fifth person belonging to this party who did not make his appearance that night. From the discourse of these females, however, it was easy to glean the following leading facts. This fifth person was a male; he was indisposed, and kept his berth; and he was quite aged. Several nice little dishes were carried from the table into his state-room that evening by one or the other of the young sisters, and each of the party appeared anxious to contribute to the invalid's comfort. All this sympathy excited our interest, and we had some curiosity to see this old man long ere it was time to retire. As for the females, no name was mentioned among them but that of a Mrs. Osborne, who was once or twice alluded to in full. It was "grandma" and "ma" and "Dolly" and "sis." We should have liked it better had it been "mother" and "grandmother"; and that the

30

"sis" had been called Betsey or Molly; but we do not wish to be understood as exhibiting these amiable and good-looking strangers as models of refinement. "Ma" and "sis" did well enough, all things considered, though "mamma" would have been better if they were not sufficiently polished to say "mother."

We had a pleasant night of it, and all the passengers appeared next morning with smiling faces. It often blows heavily on that lake, but light airs off the land were all the breezes we encountered. We were among the first to turn out, and on the upper deck forward, a place where the passengers are fond of collecting, as it enables them to look ahead, we found a single individual who immediately drew all of our attention to himself. It was an aged man, with hair already as white as snow. Still there was that in his gait, attitudes, all his movements which indicated physical vigor, not to say the remains, at least, of great elasticity and sinewy activity. Aged as he was, and he must have long since passed his fourscore years, his form was erect as that of a youth. In stature he was of rather more than middle height, and in movements deliberate and dignified. His dress was quite plain, being black and according to the customs of the day. The color of his face and hands, however, as well as the bold outlines of his countenance, and the still keen, restless, black eye, indicated the Indian.

Here, then, was a civilized red man, and it struck us, at once, that he was an ancient child of the forest, who had been made to feel the truths of the gospel. One seldom hesitates about addressing an Indian, and we commenced a discourse with our venerable fellow-passenger, with very little circumlocution or ceremony.

"Good morning, sir," we observed; "a charming time we have of it on the lake."

"Yes—good time"—returned my red neighbor, speaking short and clipped, like an Indian, but pronouncing his words as if long accustomed to the language.

"These steamboats are great inventions for the western lakes, as are the railroads for this vast inland region. I dare say *you* can remember Lake Erie when it was an unusual thing to see a sail of any sort on it; and now I should think we might count fifty.''

" Yes—great change—great change, friend !—all change from ole time.''

" The traditions of your people, no doubt, give you reason to see and feel all this?''

The predominant expression of this red man's countenance was that of love. On everything, on every human being towards whom he turned his still expressive eyes, the looks he gave them would seem to indicate interest and affection. This expression was so decided and peculiar that we early remarked it, and it drew us closer and closer to the old chief the longer we remained in his company. That expression, however, slightly changed when we made this allusion to the traditions of his people, and a cloud passed before his countenance. This change, nevertheless, was as transient as it was sudden, the benevolent and gentle look returning almost as soon as it had disappeared. He seemed anxious to atone for this involuntary expression of regrets for the past by making his communications to me as free as they could be.

" My tradition say a great deal,'' was the answer. " It say some good, some bad.''

" May I ask of what tribe you are?''

The redman turned his eyes on us kindly, as if to lessen anything ungracious there might be in his refusal to answer, and with an expression of benevolence that we scarcely remember ever to have seen equalled. Indeed, we might say with truth that the love which shone out of this old man's countenance habitually surpassed that which we can recall as belonging to any other human face. He seemed to be at peace with himself, and with all the other children of Adam.

" 'Tribe make no difference,'' he answered. " All children of same Great Spirit.''

" Redmen and pale-faces?'' I asked, not a little surprised with his reply.

" Redman and pale-face. Christ die for all, and his Fadder make all. No difference, excep' in color. Color only skin deep.''

"Do you then look on us, pale-faces, as having a right here? Do you not regard us as invaders, as enemies who have come to take away your lands?"

"Injin don't own 'arth. 'Arth belong to God, and He send whom He like to live on it. One time He send Injin; now He send pale-face. *His* 'arth, and He do what He please wid it. Nobody any right to complain. Bad to find fault wid Great Spirit. All He do right; nebber do any-t'ing bad. His blessed Son die for all color, and all color muss bow down to His holy name. Dat what dis good book say," showing a small pocket Bible, "and what dis good book say come from Great Spirit Himself."

"You read the Holy Scriptures, then—you are an educated Indian?"

"No; can't read at all. Don't know how. Try hard, but too ole to begin. Got young eyes, however, to help me," he added, with one of the fondest smiles I ever saw light a human face, as he turned to meet the pretty Dolly's "good morning, Peter," and to shake the hand of the elder sister. "She read good book for ole Injin when he want her; and when she off at school, in ' city,' den her mudder or her gran'mudder read for him. Fuss begin wid gran'-mudder; now got down to gran'da'ghter. But good book all de same, let who will read it."

This, then, was "Scalping Peter," the very man I was travelling into Michigan to see, but how wonderfully changed! The Spirit of the Most High God had been shed freely upon his moral being, and in lieu of the revenge-ful and vindictive savage, he now lived a subdued, benevo-lent Christian! In every human being he beheld a brother, and no longer thought of destroying races in order to secure to his own people the quiet possession of their hunting-grounds. His very soul was love; and no doubt he felt himself strong enough to "bless those who cursed him," and to give up his spirit, like the good missionary whose death had first turned him toward the worship of the one true God, praying for those who took his life.

The ways of Divine Providence are past the investigations of human reason. How often, in turning over the pages of history, do we find civilization, the arts, moral improvement, nay, Christianity itself, following the bloody train left by the conqueror's car, and good pouring in upon a nation by avenues that at first were teeming only with the approaches of seeming evils! In this way there is now reason to hope that America is about to pay the debt she owes to Africa; and in this way will the invasion of the forests and prairies and "openings" of the redmen be made to atone for itself by carrying with it the blessings of the gospel, and a juster view of the relations which man bears to his Creator. Possibly Mexico may derive lasting benefit from the hard lesson that she has so recently been made to endure.

This, then, was Peter, changed into a civilized man and a Christian! I have found, subsequently, that glimmerings of the former being existed in his character; but they showed themselves only at long intervals, and under very peculiar circumstances. The study of these traits became a subject of great interest with us, for we now travelled in company the rest of our journey. The elder lady, or "grandma," was the Margery of our tale; still handsome, spirited, and kind. The younger matron was her daughter and only child, and "Sis," another Margery, and Dorothy, were her grandchildren. There was also a son, or a grandson rather, Ben, who was on Prairie Round "with the general." The "general" was our old friend, Le Bourdon, who was still as often called "General Bourdon" as "General Boden." This matter of "generals" at the West is a little overdone, as all ranks and titles are somewhat apt to be in new countries. It causes one often to smile at the East; and no wonder that an eastern habit should go down in all its glory beneath the "setting sun." In after days, generals will not be quite as "plenty as blackberries."

No sooner did Mrs. Boden, or Margery, to use her familiar name, learn that we were the very individual to whom the "general" had sent the notes relative to his early adventures, which had been prepared by the "Rev. Mr. Varse," of Kalamazoo, than she became as friendly and communicative as we could possibly desire.

Her own life had been prosperous, and her marriage

happy. Her brother, however, had fallen back into his old habits, and died ere the War of 1812 was ended. Dorothy had returned to her friends in Massachusetts, and was still living, in a comfortable condition, owing to a legacy from an uncle. The bee-hunter had taken the field in that war, and had seen some sharp fighting on the banks of the Niagara. No sooner was peace made, however, than he returned to his beloved Openings, where he had remained, "growing with the country," as it is termed, until he was now what is deemed a rich man in Michigan. He has a plenty of land, and that which is good, a respectable dwelling, and is out of debt. He meets his obligations to an eastern man just as promptly as he meets those contracted at home, and regards the United States, and not Michigan, as his country. All these were good traits, and we were glad to learn that they existed in one who already possessed so much of our esteem. At Detroit we found a fine flourishing town, of a healthful and natural growth, and with a population that was fast approaching twenty thousand. The shores of the beautiful strait on which it stands, and which, by a strange blending of significations and languages, popularly called the Detroit "River," were alive with men and their appliances, and we scarce know where to turn to find a more agreeable landscape than that which was presented to us after passing the island of "Bobolo" (Bois Blanc), near Malden. Altogether it resembled a miniature picture of Constantinople, without its Eastern peculiarities. At Detroit commenced our surprise at the rapid progress of western civilization. It will be remembered that at the period of our tale, the environs of Detroit excepted, the whole peninsula of Michigan lay in a state of nature. Nor did the process of settlement commence actively until about twenty years since; but, owing to the character of the country, it already possesses many of the better features of a long inhabited region. There are stumps, of course, for new fields are constantly coming into civilization; but on the whole, the appearance is that of a middle-aged rather than that of a new region.

We left Detroit on a railroad, rattling away towards the setting sun at a good speed even for that mode of conveyance. It seemed to us that our route was well garnished with large villages, of which we must have passed through a dozen in the course of a few hours "railing." These are places varying in size from one to three thousand inhabitants. The vegetation certainly surpassed that of even Western New York, the trees alone excepted. The whole country was a wheat-field, and we now began to understand how America could feed the world. Our road lay among the "Openings" much of the way, and we found them undergoing the changes which are incident to the passage of civilized men. As the periodical fires had now ceased for many years, underbrush was growing in lieu of the natural grass, and in so much those groves are less attractive than formerly; but one easily comprehends the reason, and can picture to himself the aspect that these pleasant woods must have worn in times of old.

We left the railroad at Kalamazoo, an unusually pretty village, on the banks of the stream of that name. Those who laid out this place, some fifteen years since, had the taste to preserve most of its trees; and the houses and grounds that stand a little apart from the busiest streets, and they are numerous for a place of rather more than two thousand souls, are particularly pleasant to the eye, on account of the shade and the rural pictures they present. Here Mrs. Boden told us we were within a mile or two of the very spot where once had stood Castle Meal (*Château au Miel*), though the "General" had finally established himself at Schoolcraft, on Prairie Ronde.

The first prairie we had ever seen was on the road between Detroit and Kalamazoo,—distant from the latter place only some eight or nine miles. The axe had laid the country open in its neighborhood; but the spot was easily to be recognized by the air of cultivation and age that pervaded it. There was not a stump on it, and the fields were as smooth as any on the plains of Lombardy, and far more fertile, rich as the last are known to be. In a word, the beautiful perfection of that little natural meadow became apparent at once, though seated amid a landscape that was by no means wanting in interest of its own.

We passed the night at the village of Kalamazoo; but

the party of females, with old Peter, proceeded on to Prairie
Round, as that particular part of the country is called in the
dialect of Michigan, it being a corruption of the old French
name of *la prairie ronde*. The Round Meadow does not
sound as well as Prairie Round, and the last being quite as
clear a term as the other, though a mixture of the two languages, we prefer to use it. Indeed, the word " Prairie "
may now be said to be adopted into the English,—meaning
merely a natural, instead of an artificial meadow, though
one of peculiar and local characteristics. We wrote a note
to General Boden, as I found our old acquaintance Ben
Boden was universally termed, letting him know I should
visit Schoolcraft next day; not wishing to intrude at the
moment when that charming family was just reunited after
so long a separation.

The next day, accordingly, we got into a "buggy" and
went our way. The road was slightly sandy a good part
of the twelve miles we had to travel, though it became less
so as we drew near to the celebrated prairie. And celebrated, and that by an abler pen than ours, does this remarkable place deserve to be ! We found all our expectations
concerning it fully realized, and drove through the scene of
abundance it presented with an admiration that was not
entirely free from awe.

To get an idea of the Prairie Round, the reader must
imagine an oval plain of some five and twenty or thirty
thousand acres in extent, of the most surpassing fertility,
without an eminence of any sort ; almost without an in-
equality. There are a few small cavities, however, in
which there are springs that form large pools of water
that the cattle will drink. This plain, so far as we saw it,
is now entirely fenced and cultivated. The fields are large,
many containing eighty acres, and some one hundred and
sixty ; most of them being in wheat. We saw several of
this size in that grain. Farm-houses dotted the surface,
with barns and the other accessories of rural life. In the
centre of the prairie is an "island" of forest, containing
some five or six hundred acres of the noblest native trees
we remember ever to have seen. In the centre of this wood

is a little lake, circular in shape, and exceeding a quarter of a mile in diameter. The walk in this wood, which is not an Opening, but an old-fashioned virgin forest, we found delightful of a warm summer's day. One thing that we saw in it was characteristic of the country. Some of the nearest farmers had drawn their manure into it, where it lay in large piles, in order to get it out of the way of doing any mischief. Its effect on the land, it was thought, would be to bring too much straw !

On one side of this island of wood lies the little village, or large hamlet, of Schoolcraft. Here we were most cordially welcomed by General Boden, and all of his fine descendants. The head of this family is approaching seventy, but is still hale and hearty. His head is as white as snow, and his face as red as a cherry. A finer old man one seldom sees. Temperance, activity, the open air, and a good conscience have left him a noble ruin,—if ruin he can yet be called. He owes the last blessing, as he told us himself, to the fact that he kept clear of the whirlwind of speculation that passed over this region some ten or fifteen years since. His means are ample, and the harvest being about to commence, he invited me to the field.

The peculiar ingenuity of the American has supplied the want of laborers in a country where agriculture is carried on by wholesale, especially in the cereals, by an instrument of the most singular and elaborate construction. This machine is drawn by sixteen or eighteen horses, attached to it laterally so as to work clear of the standing grain, and who move the whole fabric on a moderate but steady walk. A path is first cut with a cradle on one side of the field, when the machine is dragged into the open place. Here it enters the standing grain, cutting off its heads with the utmost accuracy as it moves. Forks beneath prepare the way, and a rapid vibratory motion of a great number of two-edged knives, effect the object. The stalks of the grain can be cut as low, or as high as one pleases, but it is usually thought best to take only the heads. Afterwards the standing straw is burned, or fed off, upright.

The impelling power which causes the great fabric to

advance, also sets in motion the machinery within it. As soon as the heads of the grain are severed from the stalks, they pass into a receptacle where, by a very quick and simple process, the kernels are separated from the husks. Thence all goes into a fanning machine, where the chaff is blown away. The clean grain falls into a small bin, whence it is raised by a screw elevator to a height that enables it to pass out at an opening to which a bag is attached. Wagons follow the slow march of the machine, and the proper number of men are in attendance. Bag after bag is renewed until a wagon is loaded, when it at once proceeds to the mill where the grain is soon converted into flour. Generally the husbandman sells to the miller; but occasionally he pays for making the flour, and sends the latter off, by railroad, to Detroit, whence it finds its way to Europe, possibly to help feed the millions of the old world. Such, at least, was the course of trade the past season. As respects this ingenious machine, it remains only to say that it harvests, cleans, and *bags* from twenty to thirty acres of heavy wheat in the course of a single summer's day! Altogether it is a gigantic invention, well adapted to meet the necessities of a gigantic country.

Old Peter went afield with us that day. There he stood, like a striking monument of a past that was still so recent and wonderful. On that very prairie, which was now teeming with the appliances of civilization, he had hunted and held his savage councils. On that prairie had he meditated, or consented, to the deaths of the young couple, whose descendants were now dwelling there amid abundance, and happy. Nothing but the prayers of the dying missionary in behalf of his destroyers had prevented the dire consummation.

We were still in the field when General Boden's attention was drawn towards the person of another guest. This, too, was an Indian, old like himself, but not clad like Peter in the vestment of the whites. The attire of this sinewy old man was a mixture of that of the two races. He wore a hunting-shirt, moccasins, and a belt; but he also wore trousers, and otherwise had brought himself within the

habits of conventional decency. It was Pigeonswing, the
Chippewa, come to pay his annual visit to his friend, the
bee-hunter. The meeting was cordial, and we afterwards
ascertained that when the old man departed, he went away
loaded with gifts that would render him comfortable for
a twelvemonth.

But Peter, after all, was the great centre of interest with
us. We could admire the General's bee-hives, which were
numerous and ingenious ; could admire his still handsome
Margery, and all their blooming descendants ; and were
glad when we discovered that our old friend—made so by
means of a knowledge of his character, if not by actual acquaintance—was much improved in mind, was a sincere
Christian, and had been a senator of his own State,—respected and esteemed by all who knew him. Such a career,
however, has nothing peculiar in America ; it is one of
every-day occurrence, and shows the power of man when
left free to make his own exertions ; while that of the
Scalping Peter indicated the power of God. There he was,
living in the midst of the hated race, loving and beloved ;
wishing naught but blessings on all colors alike ; looking
back upon his traditions and superstitions with a sort of
melancholy interest, as we all portray in our memories the
scenes, legends, and feelings of an erring childhood.

We were walking in the garden after dinner, and looking
at the hives. There were the General, Margery, Peter, and
ourselves. The first was loud in praise of his buzzing
friends, for whom it was plain he still entertained a lively
regard. The old Indian at first was sad. Then he smiled,
and, turning to us, he spoke earnestly and with some of
his ancient fire and eloquence.

" Tell me you make a book," he said. " In dat book tell
trut'. You see me—poor ole Injin. My fadder was chief—
I was great chief, but we was children. Knowed nuttin'.
Like little child, dough great chief. Believe tradition.
T'ink dis 'arth flat—t'ink Injin could scalp all pale-face—
t'ink tomahawk and war-path and rifle bess t'ings in whole
world. In dat day my heart was stone. Afraid of Great
Spirit, but did n't love Him. In dat time I t'ink General

could talk wid bee. Yes; was very foolish den. Now all dem cloud blow away, and I see my Fadder dat is in heaven. His face shine on me day and night, and I never get tired of looking at it. I see Him smile, I see Him lookin' at poor ole Injin, as if he want him to come nearer; sometime I see Him frown and dat scare me. Den I pray, and his frown go away.

"Stranger, love God. B'lieve his Blessed Son, who pray for dem dat kill Him. Injin don't do dat. Injin not strong enough to do such a t'ing. It want de Holy Spirit to strengthen de heart afore man can do so great t'ing. When he got de force of de Holy Spirit, de heart of stone is changed to de heart of woman, and we all be ready to bless our enemy and die. I have spoken. Let dem dat read your book understand."

THE END.